GORDO

Other Books by Jasper Cooper:

GORDO

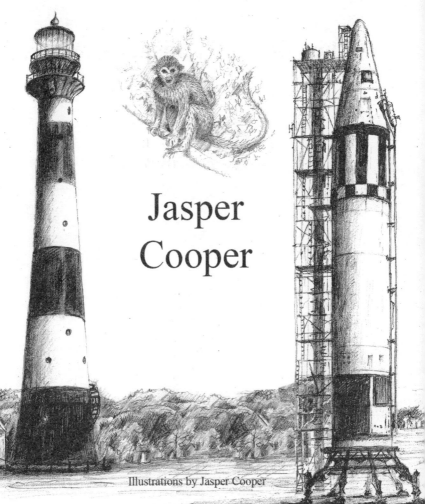

Jasper
Cooper

Illustrations by Jasper Cooper

SILVERWELL PUBLISHING

For more information on Jasper and his books, visit:
www.GordoMonkey.com
www.TheKingdomOfGems.com
www.JasperCooper.com

Published in 2014 by SilverWell Publishing
12, Mount Road, Canterbury, Kent CT1 1YD   UK

This book is based on a true event but has been fictionalised and all persons appearing in this work are fictitious. Any resemblance to real people, living or dead, is entirely coincidental.

First Edition

ISBN
978-0-9551653-3-7

Printed and bound by
CPI Group (UK) Ltd, Croydon, CR0 4YY

To get updates of Jasper's new books and other exciting news, make sure you sign up for his updates and newsletter here:

www.GordoMonkey.com/updates

"Really enjoyable book - loved every second of it! Couldn't take my eyes off it!"
Freya King, aged 11

"I found this book a brilliant read. It contained a great deal of vivid images which made me feel like I was there in the story, watching it happen. Jasper Cooper really brings the main character, Gordo, to life.

When I started reading it, the pages kept turning. I was unable to put it down. I thoroughly enjoyed this book and would recommend it to children of all ages."
Matthew Walkington, aged 10

"Gordo is a funny, gripping and exciting book which was so good I could not stop reading it! Gordo the monkey is portrayed brilliantly; who can resist the clever and witty monkey who has such an important role in the story.

I would definitely recommend Gordo to my friends."
Sophie Clare, aged 11

Contents

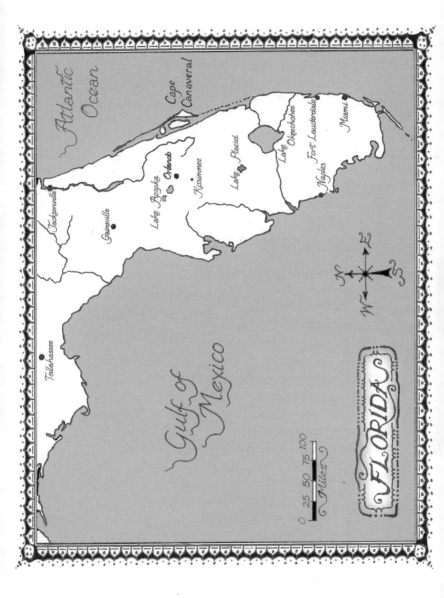

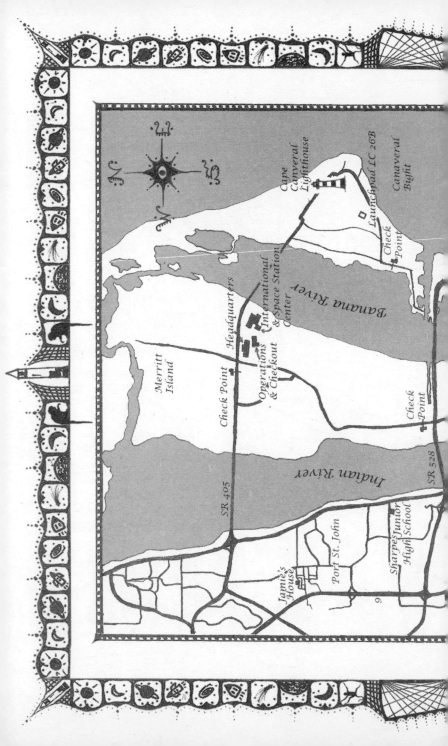

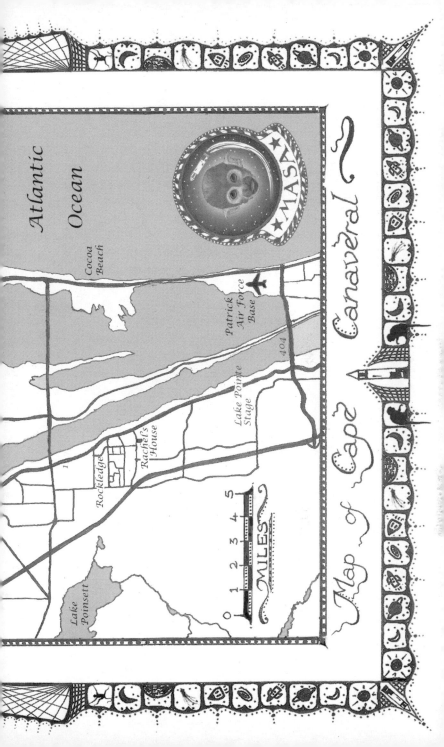

Atlantic Ocean

Cocoa Beach

Patrick Air Force Base

404

Lake Pointe Stage

Rockledge

Rachel's House

Lake Poinsett

MILES
0 1 2 3 4 5

Map of Cape Canaveral

This book is dedicated to Poll Scott, my wonderful aunt.

Also to the memory of my uncle Robin Scott, her husband. In 1994 he gave me a word processor, without which I would probably not have started writing and therefore none of these books would ever have been written.

PRELUDE

Tuesday 12th June 1951   11.47 p.m.

The six year old boy closed his eyes tightly in fear. He was sitting on the ground, huddled against a tree with his arms wrapped around his bent legs and his sandalled feet tucked up. Strange jungle sounds echoed in the warm, night air and pressed hard upon him. A full moon sent occasional beams of blue light through the gaps in the canopy, invading the deep darkness. A distant roar seemed loud, grating the boy's nerves as if it were next to him, and he shuddered.

He would stay here without moving, with the darkness as his only defence. He felt weak and feeble, so he would wait, unmoving, until daylight dispelled his fear.

Time passed slowly, each weary minute dragging on forever.

Then a movement close by made his shoulders jerk in shock. The foliage rustled and his face tensed in terror because he knew what it was. He was too afraid to open his eyes and look, feeling that even the flicker of his eyelids might give him away.

It touched his foot and slid across his skin. Cold scales.

15

He opened his eyes wide but in the deep darkness he could only see shadowy outlines. He kicked his leg forwards in panic and felt the snake. A sharp pain stabbed into his leg and he cried out, falling backwards, then scrabbling to his feet and trying to run. He crashed into a bush and fell, disappearing under its large spreading leaves. He lay there for a few minutes, completely still again.

Slowly, he reached out a hand to his leg and was shocked to feel the swelling. Numbness tingled as the venom spread like ink on blotting paper. A nauseating dizziness swept through his aching body and he felt he had to move. He stood up and blinked several times, finding it hard to focus; the snakebite was already affecting his sight. He looked around into the pitch black, softened here and there by pools of moonlight. He heard the snake move. Impulsively, driven by fear, he broke into a run.

His sudden movement did not go unnoticed. The jungle hunters heard the pounding of his small feet. They were ravenous for meat, their night-eyes glowing with primal instinct and their acute sense of smell alert with information. They instantly knew that this was prey.

The boy was already exhausted, physically and emotionally. After a short run, he slowed and then collapsed, one leg crumpling under him and the other burning with fatigue. His chest heaved for air. He stared up into the darkness, dimly seeing the canopy of leaves above against the black, starry sky. His vision moved in and out of focus.

The closest predator was a black jaguar, sleek and powerful, and almost invisible in the shadows of the night. Her great paws padded the jungle floor as she moved swiftly towards her prey. She followed the scent, slipping skilfully through the jungle undergrowth until she heard the boy's breathing. When she saw him, she stopped, one paw raised, now completely still, a black statue in the night. Her eyes fixed intently on the boy and hunger grumbling in her throat.

He heard her deep growl and he lifted his head. Their

eyes met, the hunter and the hunted. His heart thumped with fear. Cold sweat broke on his brow as his nausea intensified. Both legs and his side were paralysed now by the snake bite as the venom fed around his body. His head fell back in despair and he saw the stars fade into black as he passed out.

How the small boy survived was a mystery. No trace of his parents was ever found and the boy was flown back to Florida to be adopted by his grandmother.

His memories of what happened in the jungle were few and the doctors said it was the shock of nearly dying from the snake bite.

He did have a few memories but they were vague. He could recall the feeling of being carried through the tree tops and being terrified of falling. In one memory, he was lying in a mass of leaves and looking up through gaps in the branches above, and glimpsing the night sky with more stars than he had ever seen before. He could recollect eating some small, sweet berries.

Finally, there was the clearest memory. It was the sound of monkeys chattering all around him. And that was all.

7 years later...

CHAPTER 1

Monday 6th January 1958 Naples, Florida   8.15 a.m.

George paused momentarily beside the trees and gazed upwards. His hands were anchored in his coat pockets and his collar was up around his neck. He squinted through his glasses into the falling rain. His wife, Jo, linked arms with him.

"Come on, George," she said impatiently, "We won't get healthy this way."

George was still gazing up.

"Look!" he said, "Monkeys in the tops of the trees."

Jo looked up.

"Oh yes," she exclaimed, "I read about those in the paper. They're sweet little things aren't they? Look at their yellow arms and legs. Oh… that one's looking down at us. It's got a golden patch on its head! There!"

She pointed up at the monkey's wide-eyed face.

"Oh yeah," he nodded and smiled, and then said thoughtfully, "It's unusual though, to live here in Florida." He wiped his glasses with a finger. "Surely they should be in a rainforest somewhere."

"And we should be getting fitter," Jo said, patting George's tubby stomach, "A round of golf should start to get some of this weight off you. Come on. We'll have some breakfast first and see if the rain eases."

"OK," said George.

They turned together and hurried along a path lined with two rows of palm trees whose tall trunks were crowned by fans of bladed leaves. Beyond the group of trees, the beach sloped down to the lapping waters of the Gulf of Mexico. They walked quickly to the main door of the Larshley Beach Hotel & Golf Club where they were members, and went in.

High above, the group of twenty-three Squirrel Monkeys sat in a copse of palm trees. They were the size of squirrels, and fast, swinging through the branches with extraordinary skill. Curious tourists and passers-by threw food to them and took photographs. Local animal lovers had made efforts to have a law passed to protect them and now it was a crime to harm them in any way.

The monkeys watched George and Jo disappear into the building.

"They're gone," said one in their language. To humans their speech sounded like a meaningless row of random chirrups. "Let's go down."

She started descending through the branches and a few daring monkeys followed her, keen for a good breakfast. In a moment they were dropping down onto the ground to search for insects and low-growing fruits. This involved a risk; there were dangers of other creatures like cunning wildcats and alligators which sometimes wandered into the city and could attack and eat a small monkey.

Gogo was the monkey with the unique patch of golden fur on the top of his head. He always fed in the trees but in the winter there was barely enough for the healthy appetite of a young monkey. He was hungry and temptation arose in him to join the older monkeys who were foraging around on the ground. In a carefree moment his hunger and greed got the better of him and he swung down through the branches and jumped onto the grass below. He looked all around for food whilst keeping alert for predators. Following the others, he moved through the trees until he saw them stop in a small clearing. They had found something of interest.

"Look!" squealed one of them, pointing into a hole in the ground and then putting his hand in it, "There's food inside - a banana!"

The others had noticed more holes, and in a second they were all reaching into a hole and gripping a banana. Gogo wanted one as well. Bananas were rare delicacies which did not come their way very often. He ran over and looked into one of the holes. The hole was the mouth of a pot buried under the ground and inside the pot was a banana.

He hesitated and looked around. All was clear. The smell of banana filled his nostrils and his hunger took over as he reached into the pot for the delicious fruit. He closed his fingers around it.

There were now six monkeys with their hands in the pots, trying to get the bananas out but this was not as easy as it looked. As soon as they gripped the banana and pulled, their fist and the banana jammed in the mouth of the pot. Only one monkey managed to pull the banana out and rushed up a tree, proudly grasping his squashed trophy, while the other five struggled and pulled in vain.

All of a sudden the air was filled with piercing screeches. This was the monkey's alarm, their warning of danger. They were panicking.

"Look out," shouted one, "It's a trap!"

"Humans!" squealed another, "Run!"

The monkeys dropped the bananas, their hands slipped out of the pots and they scampered away from the clearing and back into the trees, swinging skilfully up to freedom. But one monkey was not scampering with them; one monkey was still gripping his banana. It was Gogo, reluctant to let go of such a wonderful treat. He was pulling at it until it began to squash and ease up through the hole. He knew the danger but he was so close. The banana moved a little more. One more pull and he would have it.

"Let go!" screeched a monkey from the trees, "Let go! Let go now, Gogo!"

Gogo gave a hard pull and the banana squashed through the hole. At the same time two massive hands closed around his arms, pinning them to his sides. He squealed as loudly as he could and struggled with all his might.

"Is it suitable?" asked a human voice.

"Yeah, looks perfect," came the reply, "Young and strong… just what they want."

"Excellent," said the first voice, "Pop him in the sack and let's go before anyone hears."

Gogo was terrified. He summoned all his strength to wriggle free and managed to pull an arm out which he flailed around wildly, clutching the banana. His arm whacked into the man's face, splatting squashed banana on his forehead and scratching his cheek.

"Ahhh!" the man yelled.

Gogo almost escaped but the man gripped tightly onto one of his legs, pulled him back and held him again. The squashed banana fell onto the grass. Gogo managed to pull an arm out once more, the other one this time, and swung it around.

"Can't you hold it properly," said the other man who was watching from beneath a cowboy hat.

"I'm trying! Help me!"

"Don't be silly, Jeff! If you can't catch a little monkey by yourself…"

Jeff glared back crossly. "You try then, Frank," he gasped, as he fought with the frantically wriggling animal, "You try!"

"I can't!" Frank replied, "I'm holding the sack. Come on! Put him in here. Quick! Before someone comes!"

He held the mouth of the sack open and waited. After a struggle Gogo's free arm was gripped again and he was held so tightly that he could hardly move. He was still screeching. The rain suddenly became heavier.

"Stop it making all that noise, can't you! Someone will hear," snapped Frank, glancing around.

Jeff put his hand around Gogo's mouth and the screeching became muffled but Gogo slipped his arm free again. Jeff jerked his hand away and scowled.

"Ahhh! It bit me!" he cried.

Gogo's squealing was now louder than ever.

"Get control!" shouted Frank, "It's only a little monkey! Come on!"

Frank held the sack closer with the open top near Gogo. Jeff managed to bundle Gogo in, and the opening was closed and tied. Just at that moment George and Jo came running out of the golf club.

"Hey!" shouted George, "What are you doing?"

Frank slung the sack over his shoulder with Gogo shrieking inside and the two men sprinted away across the grass and through the pouring rain. Frank's cowboy hat slipped off his head and onto his back, held on by the string around his neck. He was well over six foot and heavily built, whereas Jeff was shorter, slimmer and the faster runner. They dodged between palm trees, with Jeff leading, and then ran onto the wet driveway. In a moment they were out through the open gates at the entrance to the grounds. George and Jo ran after them.

"Stop!" shouted Jo, as she passed through the open gates first.

Frank and Jeff raced along Russell Boulevard to where a battered old Divco truck was parked. Jeff reached it first and grabbed a door handle, jerking the unusual folding door open and back. Frank reached the driver's door, opened it and threw the sack in. Then he turned to face their pursuers who were closing fast.

Jo called out, "Let that monkey go!"

Frank reached back into the truck and grabbed a baseball bat. He faced George and Jo again and shook the bat at them. They skidded to a halt on the damp pavement.

"This is none of your business!" shouted Frank, his voice harsh and threatening. He slapped the bat into his other hand several times to show he was ready to use it. "Go back in there!" He pointed at gates. "Go now, and forget all about it!"

"OK, OK," said George holding his hands up, "No problem."

Frank slapped his hand with the bat again.

"We're going," said Jo backing off and turning, "We're going. We'll forget all about it. Definitely."

Frank watched them until they had walked back through the gates. He heaved his heavy frame into the truck and placed his hat on the floor near his feet. There was only one chair for the driver, so Jeff was sitting on a wooden box with a cushion on it. Frank closed the door and dropped the bat onto the floor as well. The first two attempts to start the engine failed but then it spluttered into life. A plume of dark smoke blew out of the exhaust and the truck pulled away.

George and Jo heard the engine start and moved cautiously back to the gates. They peeped out warily, just in time to catch a glimpse of the truck turning the corner at the end of the road and then it was gone. They stood and watched the smoke disperse into the air. George leant against the gate post, breathing heavily and with drops of rain running down his face. He shook his head.

"They've got away with it," he sighed, "That wreck they were driving was a Divco truck... if only we had the plate number."

"17D – 264," said Jo calmly.

George looked at her and smiled with an expression of surprise and admiration. "Well done!"

8.37 a.m.

George leant against the reception desk inside the Larshley Beach Hotel and Golf Club. It had the air of an expensive hotel, with a thick green carpet in the spacious hallway. The receptionist was a young lady of nineteen with platinum blond hair and large round silver earrings. She was speaking on the phone and answering questions for a prospective new member.

She put a hand over the mouthpiece and mouthed to

George, "One moment… I'll be with you, sir."

Jo was beside George and jotting down the plate number on a piece of paper. She finished and looked up at him.

"If we phone now they might catch them," she said.

"Well, maybe," George lifted his eyebrows, "But they've got a bit of a start. And would the cops be bothered about the theft of a little monkey?"

"Well, it's a crime…" said Jo.

The receptionist put the phone down and looked up, "Morning, Mr. Pinter?"

"Good morning, Lizzie," he replied.

"You're not playing golf in this weather are you?" she queried.

"No, at least not yet…" he began, looking out of the window, "Maybe it will clear later."

"Locker keys and towels then, is it sir?"

"Yes, please," George nodded, "But first, if we could make a phone call. It's rather urgent."

"Of course, Mr. Pinter."

Lizzie picked up the phone and lifted it onto the top of the desk whilst looking at George with a quizzical expression. She wanted to know what this was about.

"What number for the local police?" George asked.

"Police?" Lizzie looked surprised. Now she was unable to curtail her curiosity, "The cops? What's happened, sir?"

"Two men caught one of the monkeys out there and drove off with it."

Lizzie's expression changed to one of concern. "No! A monkey! How odd. A little monkey!" she exclaimed, "What for?"

George shrugged, "I don't know."

Lizzie opened a drawer in her desk and pulled out a card. "I've got the number here…" she said.

He dialled as she read the number out.

"7…4…4…6…3…2…1"

George explained what had happened and gave all the

details he could remember. After answering a few questions he put the phone down.

"Well?" asked Jo, "What did they say?"

"They said they'd find out if the Divco truck was stolen and send a description to all their squad cars. He was very pleased with the plate number."

"Good," Jo nodded, "We've done all we can then. Let's just hope they catch them."

"Yeah," agreed Lizzie, "That poor little monkey. Now… locker keys and towels, wasn't it?"

She produced two white towels from under her desk and then reached over to the wall for the keys where a row of them hung on hooks. She passed them across to George and Jo.

"Thanks, Lizzie," he said cheerfully.

"Thank you, sir. Have a good day and I hope the weather clears for you."

George and Jo linked arms and walked down the hallway.

8.44 a.m.

Frank had been driving for ten minutes. They had captured the monkey in Naples on the east coast of Florida and were heading out of the town. The houses lining the shiny, wet streets were thinning as they approached the open countryside.

They were driving in an old snub-nosed Divco delivery truck. The two front doors were built with a hinge running down the middle so that they would fold back; it was a special design so that delivery men could leave the doors open and jump in and out easily. There were no windows in the sides or the back.

Some years before, the truck had looked smart with shining white paint, a red stripe down each side, blue wheel arches and red wheel hubs. Time had certainly taken its toll and now it was a battered, old Divco truck at the very end of its life. Rust had established itself in many places, staining the paintwork with brown smudges and creating some holes in the wheel arches.

It was a noisy old wreck. The engine roared loudly as if it was about to seize up and a variety of rattles could be heard as it swayed and bumped along. It had a split pane front windscreen with a vertical metal bar dividing the two sides.

The wipers, one for each side, beat back and forth but were labouring to clear the steady downpour of rain, one moment managing well but then the next slowing down to a laborious judder.

Franklin J. Leemas was forty-two. His face was round with small, brown eyes and a crooked nose, the legacy of a promising boxing career which ended in his early twenties when he turned to crime. His black hair was very short, in the crew-cut fashion of the day, and he wore a dirty, white t-shirt exposing his tattooed arms. His great interest, apart from crime, was watching western movies. He loved the rough character of the outlaw and adopted that attitude himself, always wearing his cowboy hat as part of his tough identity. He thought of himself as a hard-hitting guy who could get the better of anyone.

Jeffrey Marks was thirty-one, average height and as lean as a greyhound. His mouth was thin-lipped and mean but his blue eyes had a gentle look which bordered on sadness. He did not conform to the popular hairstyle fashion of the crew-cut; his hair fell untidily past his ears and down his neck. He had tried several times to give up his life of crime but had always failed when Frank, who was the boss of their partnership, had enticed him back with a new plan. It was laziness that had turned him to crime and laziness that had kept him there.

He was sitting on the box and leaning back against a wooden partition that separated the passenger area from the rest of the truck. He was uncomfortable but did not complain because he was the one who stole the truck.

Frank was leaning forwards slightly to peer out through the rain. Jeff had a plaster on his cheek where Gogo had scratched him and there was a smudge of blood on his chin. He gripped a handkerchief around his hand where the monkey's sharp, little teeth had bitten him.

"Well," Frank said, chewing on some gum, "We've got it! It's amazing how they fall for that old trick. I knew it would work! I knew there'd be at least one greedy one. At least it's stopped that terrible noise."

"And trying to escape," added Jeff, who had the sack on the floor by his feet, "but this little rascal fought so hard!"

"Shows it's healthy."

"Yeah, but it's not moving now," said Jeff, looking down at the sack on the floor and sounding concerned, "Do you think it's alright?"

"It's tired," said Frank.

"Perhaps it can't breathe in there, Frank."

"Sacks have holes in... remember, stupid?" snapped Frank, "Stop fussing."

Jeff gave the sack a push with one of his feet. "It's not responding, Frank. I hope it's OK."

"It'd better be," said Frank, "Remember what happened last time? And we've driven 500 miles to get this one. I don't want another wasted journey. Is it breathing?"

"I can't tell with this truck shaking. If you stop, Frank, I'll check it out and give it a banana."

Frank looked thoughtful.

"OK," he decided, "But we mustn't stop for long. We've got to deliver it before five. They want to start the tests tomorrow."

Frank turned down a small country road.

"Here," suggested Jeff, "On this grass."

Frank turned the wheel and, with a multitude of rattles, the truck bumped up onto the grass verge. He pulled up under some trees and stopped but kept the engine ticking over.

"I'm not stopping the engine," he said, "By the sounds of it this thing might not start again. Where did you get this old pile of rust?"

"I borrowed it."

"Who from?"

"A friend."

"Some friend to lend you this heap of nuts and bolts!" exclaimed Frank, "They either gave it to you to get rid of it, or… or…" he narrowed his eyes and pushed his lower jaw forwards slightly as he glared at Jeff suspiciously, "or, more like, you stole it. Stole it knowing you, Jeff. You stole it, didn't you?"

"Yep," admitted Jeff.

Frank shook his head with disapproval.

"Next time you steal something make sure it works properly. This old thing is only fit for the scrap heap."

"Yeah," Jeff sighed, "But the old ones are easy to get into and steal. And no one thinks anyone would steal it anyway… and when you have stolen it no one really cares… so it's easy."

"I see what you mean," Frank replied, "It's an interesting theory. But I'd still prefer something that doesn't shake my bones to pieces."

"It'll do the job," commented Jeff defensively.

"Let's hope so," sulked Frank, "If it doesn't get us there then you're in trouble. These doors are weird…" he continued, folding it back to open it, "And why's it only got one seat? That's weird as well."

"It's for delivering stuff… milk I think," said Jeff, and then cheerfully, "And we're delivering a monkey."

Frank suddenly remembered something.

"We'll have to put on the false plates… you had them made didn't you?"

"Yeah, but let's check the monkey first."

Jeff lifted up the sack and put it on his lap. The rain dripped off the trees in large drops, rattling onto the roof of the truck.

"It doesn't feel very alive, Frank," he said.

"OK," said Frank, "Let's have a look at it then."

Jeff untied the sack, opened it and looked in. Gogo leapt out, hitting Frank in the face and knocking him back towards the open door. Gogo fell to the floor.

"Close the door!" shouted Jeff.

Frank started frantically pulling at the folding door which

rattled but would not move. Gogo was quick. He climbed up Frank's leg and jumped for the open door. He flashed past Frank's face who grabbed at him with both hands, but missed. Gogo passed through the door and out. He was free.

Then he felt a jerk and a sharp pain. Frank had caught him by the very end of his tail, gripping as tightly as he could and swinging him back so that he bumped against the truck door and his cowboy hat fell off.

"Pull it back in!" shouted Jeff.

He pulled Gogo through the door, who fought and wriggled with all his might. The two men forced him back into the sack.

"I think it's alive, don't you?" Frank sneered sarcastically, "Satisfied?"

"Let's put it in the cage," said Jeff, "That'll cool it down."

"I need a drink first."

Frank took two bottles of Coca Cola from under his seat and handed one to Jeff.

8.55 a.m.

Jamie felt happy. He was cycling fast, with the wind in his hair and the warm morning sun on his back. He was just thirteen and on his way to school on the first day back after the Christmas holidays. School was a chore for him with long tedious lessons that did not agree with the young blood flowing though his veins; it was something that he had to do but would rather not. Surely life should be more exciting and fun. But this was a problem he had solved.

One day, nine months ago, his school life had been transformed. He had been talking with his best friend Doug about his science teacher, and how boring he was. Then a ridiculous idea came into his mind; what would happen if they put an explosive cap, which they used in their toy guns, into Mr. Tront's pipe?

The prank went ahead. It took three weeks of careful watching until Mr. Tront, who they nicknamed Trout because he looked vaguely like one, left his pipe lying invitingly on his desk during break. The two secret agents went to work. The cap was placed under the tobacco with the care of a surgeon performing the most delicate of operations. Then, as a clever afterthought, a sprinkling of sawdust was added for good luck before the pipe was replaced in exactly the same position. Jamie and Doug retreated hastily.

It was during a pause in one of Trout's most tedious monotone explanations that he decided to light his pipe, and puff on it to get it going. Jamie and Doug stared in expectation. For a moment nothing happened.

Then, the most memorable moment of all their school years took place. The sharp crack of the little explosion made Trout jump and fling the pipe away in shock, as if getting rid of a dangerous snake. The whole class was riveted and most leapt to their feet with a mixture of astonishment and amusement. Trout had never had such an attentive audience; this was the most interesting and dramatic experiment ever.

The explosion had cracked the bowl of the pipe and a tell-tale scatter of burnt sawdust and cinders lay on the floor beside it.

After this great success, Jamie and Doug planned many more daring and creative pranks. Part of their enjoyment was the planning itself which they constructed in fine detail. The two boys loved to watch these practical jokes unfolding before their eyes but they made sure they kept calm-looking faces, even though inside they were bubbling with excitement. As soon as they were on their own, they would explode with pent up laughter as they recalled every detail of the prank. Now Jamie felt more like a spy than a schoolboy; the enemy were the teachers and the mission was to outwit them.

Jamie turned a corner and into the school road. As he passed the children walking to school, he looked out for Doug; he was keen to share his latest idea.

9.00 a.m.

"OK," said Frank, reaching out for his cowboy hat, "Come on."

They got out, Frank put his hat on, and their shoes squelched into the sodden muddy grass. Rain was pouring through the trees. They both strode to the back of the truck, one either side, with Jeff clutching the sack.

Frank opened the back doors. Dark fumes were pumping out of the exhaust and clouding up around them. Frank coughed.

"This smoke!" he grumbled.

Inside the back was a cage and a few other things; a box, a rope, a few planks of wood and a hammer. It was completely partitioned off from the front seats except for a small opening with a shutter across it. They both climbed inside and Frank opened the cage door.

"Open the sack here and put it in, Jeff. But be careful."

Jeff held the mouth of the sack by the open cage door and loosened it cautiously. He felt Gogo begin to struggle.

"It's kicking about!" he shouted, panicking as the sack slipped from his hands, "Help me!"

Frank grabbed the sack, bundled it into the cage and slammed the door closed. Gogo's head popped out of the sack, then his whole body emerged and finally his long tail. He cowered timidly and stared at the two men with round frightened eyes.

"Look at that," remarked Jeff, "It's perfect. Look - it's got golden fur on its head. It's a sweet little animal."

"Don't be soppy!" said Frank, "It's a little beauty alright but only because it's worth beautiful money!" He dropped his head close to the bars. "You know what you're worth? $1,800 that's what." He turned back to Jeff. "Not bad for a day's work. Eh Jeff?"

"Not bad at all," replied Jeff. Then he smiled. "And they think we've gone all the way to South America to catch it. Shall we give it a banana?"

"Yeah, why not?"

Frank reached into the box for a banana, peeled it and took a bite. Then he broke a piece off and pushed it through the cage bars.

"Let's go," he said.

The two men climbed out of the back of the truck and into the rain. Their shoes sank into the muddy grass again as they walked to the front. Frank jumped in first and tried to close his door but it would not move. He thumped it with his fist, shook his head and then scowled at Jeff through the other door.

"This old junk-heap had better make it," he shouted with rain dripping off his hat, "Come on, let's go."

Jeff growled in frustration as he climbed in and sat on the box. Frank pulled again at the door and this time it suddenly jerked free and slammed closed. The truck rattled as it bumped down off the grass and chugged away. By the time they pulled back onto the main road Frank was whistling the theme tune from his favourite western movie, High Noon. He was thinking of the money.

In the back, Gogo was leaning against the bars of the cage, hanging his head in despair. He had been trying to work out a plan of escape but it seemed impossible.

There was just one thing that might help him and this was something that was totally unknown to the two criminals; Gogo could understand everything they said.

9.21 a.m.

The capture of Gogo had shocked the colony of monkeys. They were high up in the trees and chattering in their own language about what had happened. The falling rain created a fresh, earthy smell and splattered onto the large palm leaves around them. The air was warm. For a moment the low hazy sun tried to break through the clouds and then disappeared again.

Two old monkeys were sitting together, just above the chattering group. Jabe was nearly twenty-two, a good age for a squirrel monkey. He was increasingly grumpy, his hair was becoming grey on his cheeks and his movements were slow. His partner, Yulla, was nineteen. She was a grumbler too, and so they complained together on most issues which united them in glum agreement.

They were looking down and listening to the conversation between the younger monkeys. Jabe growled and then spoke gruffly.

"He's always been headstrong, that one," he said, shaking his head in disapproval, "and greedy. Serves him right."

"Yeah," Yulla agreed, "I know what you mean. Greedy little fella... he deserved what he got!"

"Young and stupid!" announced Jabe loudly, "That's what he is. He never listened to my advice did he? Young and stupid! He should never have gone down at all. I've told him that many times."

"It's too late now..." Yulla sighed, "he should have listened to us, but he didn't, so that's that. I just hope we see him again."

"No chance. Once humans get you... that's it. We'll never see him again. Never!"

Yulla sighed again. "I know. But surely there's a chance?"

Jabe growled, shook his head and then called down to the others. "Forget him. He's gone. And that's a lesson for you all. Don't be greedy and don't go down to the ground. Understand?"

A few of the monkeys called out, "Yes," and "OK," while most of them ignored him and carried on chattering and swinging around in the trees.

10.07 a.m.

The two thieves drove for over an hour without speaking. Jeff had fallen asleep with his head leaning against the window and his mouth open. The truck kept moving at a steady pace despite the knocking sounds of the engine and a chorus of rattles. They were well out of Naples now and on the journey which they intended would take them right across Florida.

The region they were passing through was fairly flat with fields stretching away into the distance. The rain had died out. Dark clouds still hung heavily above but ahead the weather looked brighter.

"Jeff!" exclaimed Frank, "Jeff! Wake up! Stop catching flies. I've just remembered something."

Jeff stirred and opened his eyes. He closed his mouth and swallowed, and then used his sleeve to wipe away some saliva that had trickled from the corner of his mouth.

"What is it?" he said sleepily.

"The number plates!" Frank barked, "We didn't change them."

"Oh yes," said Jeff casually, "We'd better do it..." he said.

"Jeff... this is important," snapped Frank, "Those two at the club... well, they could have seen the plates, couldn't they. Do you follow? They could have the number. Have you got those other plates you had made?"

"Yep," said Jeff, reaching down under Frank's seat and pulling them out.

"Good," Frank nodded.

He turned off the main road and in a couple of minutes he had parked under some overhanging trees by a lake. Once again he kept the engine running. They got out and walked to the front of the truck. Jeff held the new plate against the existing one and moved it around, trying to get it to fit.

"What is that thing?" exclaimed Frank as he snatched it from Jeff, "Who made this?" He tipped his hat back a little and held the number plate in front of Jeff. It was made of cardboard and obviously hand written. "I told you to get old Twister to make them. This isn't one of his!"

"He was too busy, Frank, so I made them."

Frank shook his head. "It doesn't even fit," he

complained. He glanced around and lowered his voice. "A child could've done better. They look terrible. For one thing - a shower of rain and the ink will be washed away."

"They'll do the job," said Jeff, using a screwdriver to remove the rusty screws holding the original plate on, "It's stopped raining now anyway."

After a while Jeff managed to get the metal plate off and replace it with his cardboard one, although it seemed fairly loose and slightly crooked. They moved around to the back where they were surrounded by dark exhaust fumes puffing out around them. They both coughed and spluttered until the plate was replaced. It took ten minutes in all to finish the job and afterwards they took a few steps away from the truck to look at their handiwork from a distance.

"Looks OK," said Jeff.

"From here… yes, I suppose. If you don't look too closely." Frank screwed up his eyes. "Oh well… it'll have to do. Let's go."

Frank picked up the old plates and climbed back into the driver's seat.

"I'm just gonna check the monkey, OK?" Jeff called out as he opened the back doors.

"Be quick then," shouted Frank.

Jeff climbed into the back.

"Hello, little fella," said Jeff.

Jeff knew that the monkey could not understand, but he hoped it would be comforted by the talking. He wanted to make sure that it was still alive on delivery and he was growing fonder of it each time he saw it.

However, Gogo understood everything that Jeff was saying, every word. He could not speak English but he could understand human speech. It was the same for most monkeys but they were very careful to keep it secret. They knew that if humans found out, it would be the end of their free life in the trees because the humans would capture them to study. So it was a rule that all monkeys were taught when they were very young – never let the humans know.

"You've had quite a shock!" continued Jeff, "You shouldn't have been so greedy!" he laughed, "You'll be alright, little fella. Here… have a banana."

Jeff picked one up, peeled it, and dropped about one third through the bars of Gogo's cage. Jeff took a large bite himself and then threw what was left out through the open doors.

"Bring us a banana!" shouted Frank from the front.

Jeff grabbed a bunch of bananas from the box and then jumped out, slamming the doors behind him. When he was in the front again, he sat down on the box and handed Frank a banana.

"Thanks," he said, spitting his chewing gum onto the floor, peeling the banana and taking a large bite.

"That monkey, Frank," began Jeff, "It's quite a nice little

creature…"

Frank looked astonished.

"What?!" he said, with his mouth full of banana.

"Do you think we should do this?" Jeff said, "I mean… that poor little monkey…"

"Money!" stated Frank sharply, glaring crossly, "That monkey is money. That's all… money in our pockets. OK?"

Jeff nodded reluctantly.

Frank crunched the truck into gear and pulled off the grass with a shuddering jerk. They joined the main road again. Frank felt the job was going well so he started whistling his favourite tune again.

In the back of the truck it was dark. Occasionally the truck took a sharp bend and the cage would slide across the floor and crash into the side. Gogo shuffled over to his piece of banana and tried to eat but his appetite had gone. He dropped the banana and began to shiver. It was not cold but fear; the fear that hit him when he heard, "They want to start the tests tomorrow." The words kept echoing over and over in his mind. "They want to start the tests tomorrow." They were going to deliver him somewhere for some sort of tests. What tests? He shuddered and huddled up in the corner of the cage feeling miserable and frightened.

He realised that his greed had blinded him to danger and now these men had caught him and he was imprisoned in this tiny cage. There was nothing he could do. He had to just wait to see what would happen next.

11.18 a.m. Naples Police Station

The officer on duty at the front desk of Naples Police Station was working through a pile of papers dealing with each one in turn. He studied the next sheet carefully.

Behind him and at a desk facing the back of the room, sat a young man who was in his first year of training to become a policeman. The officer lifted up the sheet.

"This is one for you," he announced.

"Yes, sir," said the young man perkily.

"You could handle this one," said the officer, still reading the sheet, "Looks like basic police work. A minor theft…" Then he laughed, "Ha! A monkey! And they've got a law there to protect the monkeys."

"What?" queried the young man.

The officer laughed again. "That's what it says here… a monkey… stolen. They got away in a Divco truck… and that vehicle may be stolen too. And… surprise, surprise… the witness had the wherewithal to note down the plate number! That's nice because we can trace this truck. Now, listen to me…"

He turned on his swivel chair to the young man and stretched out to hand him the piece of paper.

"Here you are. A little research for you to do before lunch. When you find out who owns the vehicle and where it's registered then circulate the info to the squad cars. OK?"

The young man nodded. He got up from his chair, stepped towards the officer and took the paper. He started reading it as he returned back to his own desk.

12.55 p.m.

Frank stopped whistling when the truck came to a steep hill. It crawled up, gradually losing speed as Frank moved down the gears. Just before it stopped completely, he crunched into first gear. The truck struggled up the last few metres, picking up as it levelled off on the crown of the hill and then gathering speed when it started rolling down the other side. Frank began whistling again.

They were making reasonable progress and it seemed certain that they would make the deadline of five o'clock. The roads were dry now and Frank was again thinking about the money. His finances really needed a boost and if this went well they could do it again. He felt he had something to whistle about.

"What's that?" asked Jeff.

"What?"

"That sound. Can't you hear it? Listen."

He tried to listen above the unhealthy sound of the engine.

"Holy Moly!" exclaimed Frank, realizing that it was a police siren, "It's the cops!"

He glanced at his wing mirror, but it was pointing to the ground.

"That's all we need. The cops. They're chasing us."

"We should've changed the plates earlier," said Jeff, looking terrified, "Those people who saw us with the monkey... I bet they told the cops the number and we've been seen before we replaced them... "

"You were in charge of the plates," Frank took his eyes off the road to glare at Jeff, "So if we get done it's your fault."

"But... but..." stammered Jeff, "we've changed them now... they won't know it's us, will they?"

"Your plates wouldn't fool my blind granny! And they'll recognize the truck..."

The police siren grew louder.

Jeff opened his door just enough to put his head out and look back behind them.

"They've just come over the hill, Frank," he grumbled, "What shall we do?"

"We'd better pull over," said Frank, "We'll have to talk our way out of it. We'll say we're just coming back from a holiday on the coast..."

"Yes, sure," Jeff sighed, "With no bags and a stolen monkey in the back. They'd believe that!"

"Look," Frank snapped crossly, "If you'd stolen a proper vehicle instead of this old wreck we might have a chance of getting away."

Frank pulled over to the side of the road.

The siren grew louder as the police car bore down on them like a tiger on its prey.

"What shall we say, then?" asked Jeff.

"I'll think of something," answered Frank shaking his head in annoyance, "We're workmen... builders or something... I don't know..."

Jeff laughed nervously. "With a monkey in the back and not a sign of a brick?"

"OK... OK..." Frank said, screwing up his face to think, "We left all the bricks at the site... and the monkey... it's a present for..."

"My wife," added Jeff quickly.

"Yes, why not?" Frank agreed, "But let me do the talking, OK?"

"OK."

The police car was just behind them now.

"The plates!" exclaimed Frank, reaching across and under Jeff's seat for them. "Where are they? Get them and throw them into the bushes! Quick!"

The police car flashed by. For a moment they both stared in disbelief as it sped away, then they relaxed and smiled.

"That," laughed Frank, "is a beautiful sight!"

Jeff nodded.

"Yeah," he agreed, "That's beautiful." He let out a long sigh. "Wow... that's one big relief!"

"Never in doubt," remarked Frank and he resumed his whistling.

As they pulled away the front number plate fell off under the truck, rose in the slipstream and then fluttered on the breeze. It landed on the side of the road face upwards.

3.24 p.m. Sharpes Junior High School, Florida

History was Jamie's least favourite lesson. He used to dislike it less, but since this school year began and he had a new teacher, he had almost lost interest completely and he had stopped trying. He wondered how it was possible for Egg to make it so tedious.

Egg was the school nickname for the bespectacled Mr. Cook, due to his almost complete lack of hair and shiny head. The children also connected the name Cook with 'cooking' the egg and they made sure that the nickname was in active use on a daily basis. They would hide behind walls as he was walking through the school and cry out, "Scramble, Egg is coming!"

Apart from this, Egg was of no entertainment value at all and Jamie found that the last lesson on Mondays, which was History, would creep more slowly than a lazy sloth.

Jamie was sitting at the front and by the window. This was the best place to hide from Egg who habitually addressed the central area of the class but rarely looked at those sitting on the edges. With his black hair flopping across his face, Jamie felt anonymous and virtually invisible. Sitting next to him was his friend Doug who discreetly pushed a sheet of paper to him. They were playing Carport and it was his turn. Jamie picked up his pencil, made his move and then jotted a note on the back of the paper which was already covered with scribbled writing and diagrams; they were working on their next prank.

He slid the paper to his friend. Doug made his move and then read Jamie's note. He smiled at Jamie's idea, which involved exchanging one of Egg's lenses from his glasses with the lens from another teacher's; he ticked it to show his approval before passing the paper back.

Egg was standing behind them and they both jumped when he reached between them and grabbed the paper.

"What's this?" he said sternly as he studied it, looking first at the game and then turning it over, "Is this your version of the Boston Tea Party of 1773?! No – just the useless, illegible scribbles of boys who do not work as they should and are heading for a life of failure!"

He stepped in front of them and glared down with anger etched into his face, keeping his eyes fixed on them as he screwed up the paper and threw it towards the bin.

"Lunchtime detention," he said, "Both of you... Thursday. Forty minutes writing practice."

Jamie sighed. As soon as Egg started talking again he retrieved the ball of paper with a leg and a ruler. When it was safely back in his possession, he looked out of the window and drifted on a daydream while Egg's voice droned in the background about the Boston Tea Party, and how it was the action of colonists protesting against taxes levied by the British government... and what then happened in the following two years... Ten minutes passed, then nearly twenty, until Jamie was shaken out of his mental wanderings when Egg raised his voice to get the attention of his unreceptive class.

"Look this way!" exclaimed Egg, glaring around the class until they fell silent, "All of you... and listen. The homework must be in by Thursday. Now... pack up."

Movement and chatter erupted throughout the classroom, until Egg's sharp voice once again established his position of complete control.

"In silence!" he ordered.

Every child knew they would not be released until there was complete silence in the room, so they all obeyed. Jamie felt happy because this meant they would leave on time. In a few minutes he would be on his bike and speeding away with freedom in his heart.

"Stand up and push your chairs in," Egg ordered.

Chair legs scraped on the floor followed by silence, and then the school bell rang. The children filed out. Once outside, Jamie and Doug ran between the tall school buildings and disappeared into the bike shed. A few seconds later they emerged and pushed their bikes down the path amongst the flood of children. As soon as they were outside the school gate, they were on their bikes and cycling as fast as the wind.

4.47 p.m.

The Divco truck stopped several times and on each occasion Jeff tried to give Gogo some banana to eat. Gogo had lost his appetite and could not stop his mind thinking back to his free life, living in the trees. How he wished he was still there now and he knew that had he not been so greedy then he would be climbing and swinging through the branches in freedom. He remembered the moment, holding on to the banana, the smell of it in his nostrils and the temptation. He could have let go and escaped. He had been stupid.

Now there were several pieces of banana in his cage, but he was not hungry. He leant against the side of the cage and hung his head. No amount of wishing would turn the clock back.

The truck bumped across a bridge and then along a straight road. About two hundred metres ahead, a checkpoint, with the barrier down, barred the way. Frank pulled up at the side of the road.

"Jeff," he said, "He'll want to see the delivery note. Have you got it?"

"Sure," replied Jeff slipping his hand into his pocket.

"Hmm," Jeff shook his head, "I was sure I put it in there this morning."

Frank sighed impatiently and shook his head. Jeff dug into his the other pocket.

"Jeff, if you've lost it…"

"It's here," he said pulling out two folded pieces of paper.

Jeff unfolded them and handed one to Frank.

"Why two?" Frank asked.

"One for the guard and one for when we deliver the monkey. They're very careful… all the paperwork has to be spot on."

Frank looked at the delivery note.

"Why's it all spattered with ink?"

"That was my cat," replied Geoff defensively, "stupid thing. It was perfect before *it* jumped on the table."

Frank shook his head and started reading it.

"Delivery Note No: 4731. James Jellyrock and Sons…" he read, "Jellyrock?!" he glanced at Jeff with a disapproving frown and shook his head.

"Go on," urged Jeff proudly, "Read the rest."

"Importers and exporters of living creatures… family business… established 1904… … one squirrel monkey captured in Brazil, South America. Delivery date Jan 14th 1958. Packaging… one cage. Payment… $1,800 cash on delivery."

"What do you think?" Jeff enquired.

"It's OK, I suppose," Frank nodded, "apart from all the ink blobs, not *too* bad. It's the right type of paper, although a bit crumpled up."

"That's normal for a delivery note," answered Jeff, "I got new pens and everything for that. I spent a long time on this one... making sure it looked authentic so that they fell for it... and they have."

"How do you know?"

Jeff looked smug. "They've sent letters and I've spoken to them too."

"Just checking," Frank said, "I'm still not sure about 'Jellyrock'."

"I explained that to you before, Frank... because it's unusual no one would be suspicious... get it? Who'd be foolish enough to make up such a name?"

"You!" snapped Frank.

"It'll work," said Jeff, "It *has* worked."

"Yeah..." Frank was still studying the note, "but what's this about... 'packaging... one cage'?"

"They always put 'packaging' on delivery notes," stated Jeff, "At least it was on the one I copied."

"And this address?" Frank queried pointing with his finger, "25, East Laker Avenue, Kissimmee, Orlando, USA? Sounds good... that's the people who are away, right?"

"Yeah," Jeff nodded and again looked very pleased with himself, "They're away in Australia for 3 months. I told you... I received the letters from the space people to confirm the deal. Relax, Frank... they've fallen for it. Hook, line and sinker."

"Well, let's hope it works now, Jeff," commented Frank, glancing up from the note to look at Jeff, "The logo's a bit strange." Frank looked back at the note again and smiled, "But this is the bit I really like... $1,800 cash on delivery!"

DELIVERY NOTE No: 4731.

Another on-time delevery from:

JAMES JELLYROCK AD SONS,,
25, East Laker Avenue,
Kissimmee,
Orlando,
USA

+ Importers and exporters of living creetures.

+ Family business - established 1904,

ITEM: One Sqirrel monky, captured in Brzil, South America.
PACAGING: One caGe.

TERMS OF PAYMENTS: $1,800 cash on dilivery,

DELIVERY TO:

Cape Canaveral Air Force Stasion,
Cape Canaveral,
Florida,
USA

DELEVERY DATE.- Jan 14th 1958.

Jeff pulled the note out of Frank's hands and put it under the windscreen. He put the other one back in his pocket.

"Let's do it then."

Frank pulled away. A guard saw them approaching and came out of his hut with a clip-board in his hand. The sun flashed on the metal badge on his cap.

Frank slowed the truck and stopped beside him.

The guard greeted them with a friendly, "Afternoon!"

Frank pulled open his folding door.

"Afternoon," said Frank and then announced, holding out the note, "Delivery."

The guard took it and scanned it with his eyes, frowning first and then smiling.

"A monkey!" he said, "Just the one, is it?"

"Yup," Frank confirmed.

"All the way from South America?" he asked.

"That's right," confirmed Frank, "Brazil."

The guard looked at his clip-board. He checked that 'Jellyrock and Sons, Delivery Note No: 4731' was on the list, ticked it and then jotted down the time.

"OK, fine," he said.

Then he looked at the smoke coming out of the back of the truck, chuckled and shook his head.

"You haven't come from Brazil in this thing have you?" he joked.

Frank laughed. "This is our reserve of reserves... when our other new vehicles are in the garage we have to use this old heap. Bit of an emergency. But at least it gets us down the road and back."

"By the looks of it," the guard remarked, still smiling, "You need downhill roads all the way! What's it run on... gas, diesel or luck?"

Frank laughed loudly. "Luck..." he said, "High octane luck!"

The guard turned to go into his hut, still laughing and shaking his head in disbelief at the state of the truck. "I'll let you in," he called.

"Thanks," said Frank.

The barrier lifted and the truck accelerated slowly and noisily. In the back Gogo had listened to the conversation. He realized that the journey would soon end and this filled him with fear. He put his head in his hands in despair and soon the truck jolted to a halt once again. He heard the noise of the little window in the partition sliding open. A shaft of bright light came through catching the swirling dust in the back of the truck. Gogo looked up to see Jeff's face peeping through.

"He's fine, Frank," he said. Then his voice softened with kindness. "Aww... look at his big round eyes looking at us! Little fella... he looks so human."

"Listen, Jeff...it's just a monkey. It does look a bit like a person, but it's not. It's just an animal."

"I know that!" exclaimed Jeff, "But I've been thinking. My wife would love him as a pet. Her birthday is only a few months away; it could be an early present. I'd really like to give her something special this time. Imagine her face if..."

"Don't get soppy," said Frank scornfully, "This is a job of work - one monkey for $1,800. Think of that. If we deliver this time they'll use us again."

"But, Frank, as I said, I've been thinking," Jeff continued, "These poor little creatures. It's not natural in there. You know... what they do is not natural."

"Listen..." Frank's brow furrowed with anger as he looked down at Jeff sitting on the box beside him. "I'll take it in. You don't even have to see."

"No!" shouted Jeff, suddenly raising his voice, "I've had enough of this. I won't let you do it!"

Jeff rattled his folding door open and Frank responded, opening his door quickly. They both raced along the sides of the truck. Jeff was far more agile than Frank and reached the back doors first. He pulled the handle down and both doors swung open.

"Stop!" shouted Frank, as he reached in and grabbed Jeff's ankle.

Jeff fell headlong, bumping into the cage with a crash and then onto the floor, where his head hit with a solid thump. The cage door sprang open and Gogo leapt for freedom. Frank was just climbing in and Gogo ran straight into him.

"No you don't!" exclaimed Frank.

Gogo screeched as he was grasped in Frank's powerful grip and thrown violently back into the cage. Frank closed the cage door and fixed it.

Jeff was lying on his back and completely still with blood trickling from a wound on his head. Frank looked down at him for a moment.

"Jeff?" he enquired with concern, "Jeff... you OK?"

Frank tapped him with his foot and Jeff's arm dropped off his chest and loosely to the floor. Frank froze with fear. He tapped him again with his foot. The body felt heavy and lifeless. Panic rose in him, rising from the pit of his stomach like a wave. Beads of cold sweat broke out on his forehead.

"Jeff... Jeff..." Frank said quickly, kneeling down beside him and shaking him.

The body was limp, like a rag doll. Was he dead? He had never killed anyone before. His mind began to spin with plans of how to get rid of the body. He would have to bury it, or throw it into a river somewhere. He had just driven across Indian River so that would be perfect. He would carry on as normal. First he would deliver the monkey and collect the money and then he would dispose of the body.

He lowered his head to listen for breathing and jerked back when Jeff groaned.

In a moment of relief, Frank adjusted all his thinking. He picked up the cage by the handle on the top and jumped out.

"Frank?" asked Jeff drowsily, "What's happening?"

Frank was still clutching the cage with Gogo cowering inside, as he closed the doors and then rushed to the front of the truck to get the keys. Then he hurried back.

"Frank!" called Jeff, "What are you doing?"

"Making money," Frank replied, "Without you to spoil it!"

Frank locked the back doors. He walked quickly to the front again to get the delivery note which he slipped into his pocket. A path led towards a building, so he took it, striding decisively and trying to ignore the banging sounds coming from the truck. He paused, then turned and rushed to the back of the truck.

"Be quiet, Jeff!"

The banging stopped.

"Someone will hear an' then we'll both be in trouble. Listen… I'll be back in a minute, then we'll dump this truck and I'll let you out and give you your money. OK?"

There was no answer. Jeff was seething with anger but he knew that Frank was right.

"Let me out now then," pleaded Jeff.

There was no answer because Frank was already striding up the path again. He entered the building with Gogo staring out through the bars of the cage, wide-eyed and frightened.

8.17 p.m.

On Highway US27 in central Florida, a police car was cruising northwards on regular duty, its headlights cutting through the dark and lighting up the road ahead. A railway line ran beside the road on the west side and beyond that lay the still waters of Lake Placid. Two officers were in the car.

"Quiet tonight, Lenny," said Marlon, who was driving.

"Yeah. Still… enjoy it whilst it lasts, eh?"

"Yup, you're right," replied Marlon, "It probably means it'll get busy later on."

Lenny pointed to something by the side of the road, picked out by the headlights.

"Hey, Marlon, what's that?"

Marlon laughed. "Just 'cos its quiet wc don't have to investigate everything we see lying in the road as if it's important evidence of some crime!"

"Pull up. It looks like a number plate. I'll take a look."

Marlon slowed to a halt and Lenny got out and slowly strode back along the road. He pulled a torch from its holster on his belt and clicked it on. The yellow beam appeared in front of him.

Inside the car the intercom hissed into life.

"Orlando police to all counties. We have more info on the stolen Divco truck... the one found in Hensen Street, Orlando. Add this to your notes. Plates 17D – 264 removed and found inside. False number plate only on the back ... 32F – 932... very poor job... not professional, kids maybe. As we said, the truck's a wreck... must've been idiots to steal it! There's a box of bananas in the back, but more importantly, the forensic guys found a patch of blood – human blood. Could be nothing, or could even be a homicide. That's why we're interested in this one. We're either looking for a banana thief or a murderer! Any further info let us know, guys. Out."

Marlon had his notebook out and had just jotted down the details when Lenny returned.

He got in and held up Jeff's makeshift number plate.

"It's nothing," he said, "This is made by kids – young kids I should think... just playing."

Marlon looked at it and then back at his notes.

"Ah haa," he said, "32F – 932. Whilst you were out there picking that up, Orlando police were messaging us."

"What did they say?" quizzed Lenny.

"They said that *that*," Marlon pointed, "fell off that stolen Divco truck they told us about... but... it's not just

any stolen Divco truck… it's a stolen Divco truck with blood in the back!"

"Sounds like I was right," Lenny said smugly, "This is evidence. We'd better let them know."

He reached out for the intercom and pressed the button.

CHAPTER 3

Tuesday 7th January   7.05 a.m.

Gogo awoke the next morning as it was dawning. He had slept right in the centre of a small laburnum tree where the main trunk divided into three branches. Someone had used some canvas to create a comfortable shape like a nest and even padded it with a soft blanket to make it cosy. Another piece of waterproof canvas was stretched between the branches above to make a roof. He had slept well.

He blinked a few times and then scanned his surroundings. There was a brick wall behind him and a small garden in front which rose with a gentle slope to a large building. The garden had been designed carefully with a variety of shrubs and bushes around the sides and a selection of plants in the flower beds. A pathway ran down the centre, bordered by grass and leading to a side entrance to the building. Half way down, the path was split by a small, round pond with water lillies and some fish.

Gogo's first impression of these new surroundings was good except for one thing which made his heart sink; he was locked in a cage. It was a very large cage which was high enough to enclose the small laburnum tree and long enough to include a row of bushes. It backed onto the wall and then rose above it so that he could see some trees through the mesh. The wall extended further to the corner of the garden where a small wooden shed stood.

Gogo thought back to the night before. He was carried from the truck and into a building, handed over to some people in long white jackets and then carried by them straight out here. They let him out of the small cage into this much larger one. He was the centre of attention with everyone showing great interest in him and staring intently. In spite of being treated with such care, Gogo felt frightened and now he waited with dread. What are these tests that will begin today?

Before he had settled down to sleep the night before, he had searched, without success, for a way to escape. Now he decided to check again. He climbed up the tree to the top where the leafless, winter branches had grown through the wire mesh. Then he swung skilfully around the top of the cage, using his hands and feet to climb and his long tail to balance. He worked his way methodically up and down all sides of the cage but this thorough inspection revealed nothing; the cage was secure. So he climbed up the tree again and into his nest in order to think about his situation.

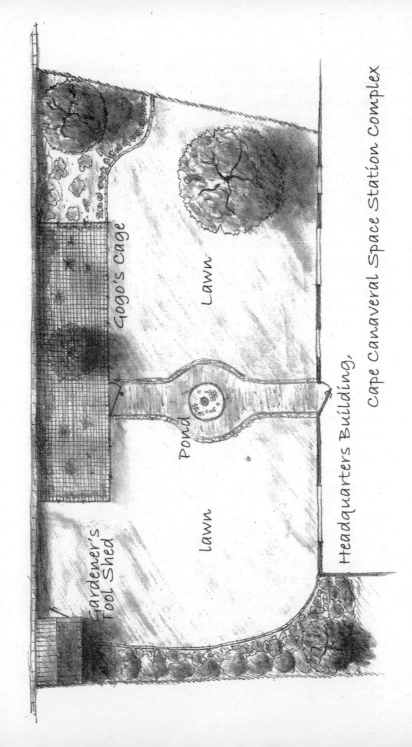

Gardener's Tool Shed

Gogo's Cage

Lawn

Pond

Lawn

Headquarters Building,
Cape Canaveral Space Station Complex

Maybe he could make a sudden dash as soon as the cage door was opened, leaping from his nest as fast as he could and scampering out. This gave him hope but really he knew that his chances of escape were slim. He had been told by other monkeys how careful humans were, especially when they caught monkeys.

After a while, two men in white jackets came for him and he tried his plan. After a struggle they managed to catch him in a net. They talked to him kindly and Gogo decided that the best approach was to try to befriend them.

They took him into the building for the tests. He was checked for illnesses and diseases. This involved taking a blood sample, a skin sample and some hairs from his fur. They peered into his eyes with a bright light and then into his ears. They checked his teeth and took some saliva for testing. Then they checked his breathing and his heart by connecting various wires to him. After this it was his blood pressure and so it went on through the day.

In the evening a woman and a man, both in their twenties, carried him in a small cage and released him into the large enclosure in the garden. Gogo scampered on all fours to the tree, leapt up the trunk and smoothly climbed through the branches. After a few swings around the higher branches, he dropped down into his nest, disappearing from sight. This made the two young people smile. They walked out through the gate and then locked it behind them. When they turned and looked in, Gogo's head popped up.

"He's perfect," said the young lady, looking at Gogo and laughing, "All the tests showed that he's in excellent health."

Her bright face shone with youthful enthusiasm and her auburn hair hung down past her shoulders, catching the evening light. He was dark-haired and bearded, and turned to the young woman with a nod.

"Yeah, it's looking good," he agreed, "I think he's the best we've ever had, Rachel."

Rachel glanced at him and then back at Gogo. "Everyone wants to start tomorrow, Ray… but do you think we should… or should we give him a day or two to settle in?"

"Hmm…" began Ray, scratching his beard thoughtfully,

"I know what you mean. We don't want him getting stressed at this stage, but he seems so calm and good natured. I think we should give him a day to settle in and then go ahead the next morning and see how it goes… but it's your decision, Rachel."

Rachel pondered on it for a moment as they both gazed in at Gogo.

"OK, I agree. But if it proves too much too soon, we stop and give Gordo more time, agreed?

"Yes, why not? Better to be safe than sorry," said Ray, and then smiling as he questioned, "Is he called Gordo?"

"Well, that's what some people started calling him! It's after Gordo… you know, that character in the cartoon. Perhaps it's because this one's certainly a little character! Anyway, he's got to have a name hasn't he… the cute little thing? You'll get used to it."

She turned and walked briskly up the path, around the pond and into the building. Gogo immediately liked the name 'Gordo'. It was surprisingly like Gogo.

Ray stood for a moment looking into the cage and trying to see Gogo who was now hiding in his nest in the tree.

"Gordo! Gordo!" he called.

Gogo popped his head up and looked at Ray. The light was fading now but the setting sun lit up Gogo's face and glinted in his eyes.

"Gordo it is!" Ray said as he turned and walked up the path.

Wednesday 8th January   6.55 a.m.

Gordo slept well in the soft blanket in his nest. He woke with the morning light and began to forage for food but there was very little to eat for a young squirrel monkey with a good appetite. He leapt from the tree onto the side of the cage and then swung downwards until he jumped onto the ground. He searched for food but was disappointed.

However, since he had been in this place he had been fed with his favourite foods so he hoped someone might arrive soon with his breakfast. He was being treated extremely well and this surprised him because human beings did not have a good reputation among monkeys. He was pleased that Rachel seemed to have been put in charge of him and she was looking after him with great care but he still had a terrible fear of what was to happen to him. He was completely in their control.

After a while he heard someone coming out of the building and down the sloping path. He scampered across the ground and up the side of the cage, and then along the top, clinging on with just his feet and hanging upside-down. After a moment he dropped down into the tree, his weight bending a slim branch. The branch sprang back as he jumped masterfully into his nest and peeped over the rim.

Rachel entered the cage carrying a bag, her attractive face radiant with a kind smile.

"Good morning Gordo," she said brightly, "And how are you today?"

Rachel was so friendly and talked to him as if he would understand. Without thinking, he found himself replying.

"I'm fine, but I'm worried!" Gordo said.

This would sound like a row of cheeps to Rachel - just the meaningless chatter of a little monkey.

Rachel dipped her hand into the bag and sprayed a handful of berries onto the ground. Then she held one up for Gordo.

"Here you are, Gordo," she said kindly, "You'll like these."

Gordo was cautious. Taking food from the hand of a human was something he had never done before. But he was hungry and Rachel seemed kind, so he tentatively lifted his body out of his nest and looked down.

"Come on, Gordo!" Rachel encouraged.

He was wary as he climbed out of the nest. With one movement he was hanging on by his arm and reaching down for the berry at full stretch. He grabbed it and then retreated up the tree and into the nest again. He popped it into his mouth, bit on it and enjoyed the delicious flavour.

"Thank you," he said.

"Would you like another one, Gordo?" Rachel asked, holding up another, "Here you are."

Gordo was more relaxed this time. He moved down and grasped the berry.

"Thank you," he said, "Do you like berries?"

It felt so natural to talk to her that he almost expected her to reply. He realized that this could be frustrating. Here was a human who he could understand, who he thought he liked and might hope to befriend, but she could not understand a word he was saying.

She smiled back and held up another berry.

"Here you are."

Gordo took it and ate it quickly.

"There are plenty more down here," she said, waving with her hand.

She gave him a friendly look as she went out through the gate, snapping the padlock closed and then walking up the path to the building. Gordo swung down the tree and enjoyed an excellent breakfast.

5.10 p.m.

Gordo was sitting in the highest branches of his tree when he heard the building door open. It was Rachel with a boy of about thirteen walking beside her. He was far from smart with a patch on each knee of his jeans and a hole in the sleeve of his floppy jumper. It was Jamie.

His black hair fell down over his ears, with strands over his eyes as well, and he looked untidy after his ten mile bike ride from school. He was strong and if he kept a steady pace he could do the journey in about forty minutes. He brushed his hair back with his hand.

"How's Bertha?" asked Rachel.

"Not good," replied Jamie bluntly, "She worries about lots of things… and takes it out on me." He frowned and dropped his eyes to the ground. "I think she hates me."

Rachel nodded sympathetically. "I don't think she hates you," she said, "She's just caught up in her own life… she's always been like that. I've been meaning to visit her… maybe next week."

Jamie shook his head. "You shouldn't…" he stated, "She grumbles about you behind your back and then puts on being all friendly when you come. But it does make her slightly nicer to me… until you've gone."

"In that case, I'll come next week. Will you tell her?"

Jamie nodded.

"And tell her I'll bring a cake… make it myself if I have time."

Jamie smiled. "Great! Chocolate?"

"Chocolate it is," she confirmed.

They reached the gate of the cage. Rachel unlocked the padlock and they went in, watched by Gordo who looked down from the top of the tree.

"There he is, Jamie," Rachel said, pointing, "He's wonderful! I've always liked monkeys... but this little fella! Well, he's beautiful. He's got a nice character too."

Jamie loved animals. He had a grey cat called Zorro who he looked after with great care, feeding him every morning and night. Zorro was a wonderful pet to have. Jamie lived with his grandmother, Bertha, whose bossy attitude towards him made his life a misery. He found that Zorro was a faithful companion who would run to him when he came home, sit on his lap and sleep on his bed, and this made his life much better.

Jamie looked up at Gordo and smiled. "Will he come down?"

"He's a bit timid still," Rachel commented, "Call him down and give him a berry. His name's Gordo. He'll come down if you call him."

"Gordo, like in the cartoon?" asked Jamie, picking up a berry.

"Yes, that's right... call him."

"Gordo!" called Jamie.

Gordo gazed down, wide-eyed.

"I've got lots to do," said Rachel, "Are you coming with me or staying here to get to know Gordo...?"

"I'd like to stay here, Rach..."

"Fine. See if you can entice him down." She turned to go. "I won't be long but if you get fed up I'll be in my office."

"OK."

"Don't forget to lock up," she said, "Just close the padlock, OK?"

"Sure," he replied.

As Rachel Chandler left the cage and walked up the path, she glanced back at her cousin. Jamie was like a younger brother to her. They were both only children who lived just a few miles from each other and were great friends. At the end of a school day, he often cycled over to meet Rachel at her work, sometimes doing odd jobs for some pocket money. Jamie watched her go and then turned his attention back to Gordo.

"Gordo!" he called, "Gordo… here's a berry for you."

Gordo had been listening to Jamie's conversation with Rachel but he was still very cautious. After a couple of wary excursions down the tree to get berries he became more confident. He jumped up to the cage roof, clinging onto the metal mesh with his hands and feet, swung across and then down the side. He scampered over the ground on all fours, up the tree and sat on a branch next to Jamie who held out the berry.

"Thank you," chirruped Gordo, taking it.

"That's OK…" Jamie began, and then he stopped abruptly.

He gazed at Gordo with an expression of astonishment. He had understood Gordo, but not only that, he had spoken in Gordo's monkey language. Gordo stared back, so stunned that he could hardly believe it. For a moment, both were speechless with the surprise of what had just happened.

"But… but…" stammered Jamie, in English, and then changing to the monkey language, "You can speak… and I can speak to you…" He smiled in excitement. "This is amazing!"

"How can you do it?" asked Gordo, "Where did you learn?"

"I don't know! I don't know how, or when… or anything! I can just speak. I know how to speak your language!"

Gordo fidgeted and stared, unblinking, at Jamie. "But… you must know how you learnt." He spread his hands in a gesture of amazement. "Humans can't speak our language!"

Jamie leant against the side of the cage and then slipped down until he was sitting on the ground. His legs felt weak.

"I don't know… er… I don't know," he stammered, and then shook his head, "This is impossible!"

Gordo swung down to a lower branch.

"Well, don't just sit there… give me another berry… and then tell me why I'm here."

Jamie reached out, picked up several berries and handed one to Gordo. He felt in a daze, as if he was dreaming. This was too incredible to be true.

"Gordo," he began slowly, thinking it through, "I can speak your language… but can you speak English?"

"No… but I can understand it… pretty well, anyway." He held out his hand. "Another berry, please."

Jamie was still in a daze as he handed the berry over. "This is great! Can other monkeys speak?"

"All the ones I know can. And I've been told that all others around the world can as well… except Howler Monkeys. They just look stupid and make a load of noise."

Jamie was trying to get used to this.

"And different monkeys speak different languages?"

"I think so," Gordo nodded. He swung around in a complete circle, falling underneath the branch and up the other side. "Another berry, please."

Jamie handed him the berry and then started laughing. This was so incredible but it was enjoyable too. He felt he was making a new friend. He held out another berry for him.

"No thanks," said the little monkey, holding up his hand and turning his head away, "Enough's enough."

Gordo suddenly climbed the tree and dropped into his nest.

"Are you alright in this cage?" called up Jamie.

"No," Gordo replied, sounding anxious, "I need to get out of here. Where am I? What is this place?"

"I'm not surprised you're worried," Jamie said kindly, "But I can tell you why you are here… and you are going to need all the help you can get… but I'll help you."

"Thanks. But why will I need help?" Gordo asked, raising his shoulders up over the edge of his nest, "Can't you just set me free? What is this place? What are they going to do to me?"

"I'll explain…" Jamie was looking up at him and into his round eyes. "This is Cape Canaveral Air Force Station where rockets are launched into space. You have been chosen to be a monkeynaut - to go into space!"

Gordo looked puzzled. "What's space?"

"Space is…" Jamie began, "up there." He pointed up and Gordo looked at the top of the cage. "No, no," Jamie added, "It's way up there… very high."

"Above the trees?" asked Gordo.

"Yes, that's right."

"Ahhhh," Gordo nodded, "Where the birds fly?"

"No… even higher than that. Higher than any bird can fly. Much higher. And you'll go up in a rocket."

Gordo looked very puzzled now.

"A rocket?"

Jamie smiled. This was hard to explain.

"A rocket goes up into space. Right up into the sky. And you will ride in a rocket."

Gordo blinked and tried to understand. Then he said slowly, "I will ride… in a rocket… above the birds?"

He was stunned. He felt weak and dipped down into his nest as his legs gave way under him.

"Gordo!" exclaimed Jamie.

He popped up again and stared at Jamie.

"Me?" he asked, "Going up above the birds… into this space place?"

"Yes, Gordo, that's right. It's like going in a car…" Jamie began, but realised that Gordo may not know what a car is either. "How did you get here?"

"In a human travel machine."

Jamie smiled. "OK… OK… well, we call that a car. A rocket is bigger, much bigger, and goes shooting up, very, very fast into space."

"Above the clouds?" asked Gordo.

"Yes... and much higher than that!"

Gordo dropped down to hang on the branch by one arm.

Then he swung up again.

"Sounds exciting!" he exclaimed.

"Very," agreed Jamie, "But it's also dangerous. Rockets have gone wrong and crashed sometimes, so you need to decide whether you want to do it."

"But… but do I have a choice?"

"Yes, of course you do," Jamie said earnestly, "Well… officially no, but unofficially, yes. And that's what counts. I am giving you the choice. If you don't want to do it… then I'll set you free. I don't know how yet, but somehow, I will. It shouldn't be too difficult."

There was a pause in the conversation.

Gordo's mind was swimming with thoughts. He was tempted to ask Jamie to set him free. That would be the simplest thing but he was also drawn by the excitement of going into space. Also, this young boy already felt like a friend, and Rachel had treated him with such respect. He found that he was enjoying their company.

"Anyway," Jamie said, "I'm Jamie."

He pulled himself up the tree by a branch until he could reach his hand towards Gordo. The little monkey stroked the back of his hand in greeting. Jamie dropped down again.

"My name's actually 'Gogo'," he said, "But I don't mind 'Gordo'. It seems to have caught on."

Jamie looked at him kindly. "Rachel's my cousin, you know." He looked down at the ground and shook his head. His black hair flopped around his face. "I don't like the way people catch monkeys just to sell them and make money." He lifted his head again and Gordo saw the concern in his eyes. "How did they catch you?"

"They tricked me," said Gordo, "But it was sort of my own fault. I was greedy. Tempted by a banana!"

"And you'd like to go back to the jungle?" Jamie asked, his voice soft with kindness.

"I'd love to live in the jungle!" said Gordo, "But I don't come from the jungle… I live in Suptim…"

"Where's that?"

"It's…" began Gordo, "it's… it takes a day to get from there to here. I was brought here in a human travel machine. Suptim's by the sea – it's not a jungle. I think it's in this country somewhere…"

"What!?" Jamie exclaimed, "But Rachel said that you came from a jungle in Brazil! What happened?"

"Two humans called Frank and Jeff. They caught me and put me in the machine and brought me here. I heard them talking… they're criminals."

Jamie was thinking this through.

"So these criminals, called Frank and… who was it?"

"Jeff," replied Gordo.

"And Jeff… they trapped you to sell. It seems like they've fooled the people here, told them they caught you in Brazil, and made some money. Would you recognize the two men?" he asked.

"Yes," Gordo replied, "I'd never forget their faces."

"Well, that's something," he said thoughtfully, "Unfortunately I wasn't here when you were delivered but I'll try to find out more about them."

Gordo looked at Jamie from his nest while Jamie looked up at him with his face bright and happy in the growing light. There was a sparkle in his blue eyes.

"Do you agree to do it…?" he asked, "Will you go up into space? I hope you do because then we can have lots of time together. But it's up to you."

"How dangerous is it?" asked Gordo.

Gordo gripped a branch with one hand and swung out of his nest. In a moment he was down the tree and settling back on the branch at Jamie's level so they were face to face. Jamie stroked him on the head and continued.

"There is danger, but not so much now. I know all about it… from Rachel, and books. The fact is that animals have been sent into space; mice, dogs, and some monkeys. Some have made it back, but quite a few have died. But your trip, if you agree that is, will be higher into space than any monkeynaut has been before… into real space. So it is risky. But a lot of progress has been made recently. Rockets are much better now. They are ready to do this... I think they can do it."

Gordo nodded slowly and then smiled. "It's a bit different than leaping from branch to branch…"

"Listen, Gordo," Jamie said kindly, "I'll leave you to think about it. I'll walk around this garden and you call me when you're ready. OK?"

"OK," said Gordo.

5.37 p.m.

"Jamie!" called Gordo from high up in the tree near the roof of the cage.

Jamie entered the cage and looked up.

"Well?" Jamie asked, "What do you think? Do you want to go into space?"

Gordo swung down expertly through the branches until he was hanging upside-down with his face close to his new human friend.

Jamie waited hopefully for the little monkey's reply.

CHAPTER 4

5.38 p.m.

1958 — Wednesday 8 January

"OK!"

THE SHORTEST CHAPTER EVER

CHAPTER 5

9.21 a.m.

Gordo nodded and then swung down and sat on a branch beside Jamie. The golden fur on the top of his head glinted in the sun.

"OK..." he repeated, "I'll go up into space, as long as I can live in the jungle, a proper jungle, when I get back. I want to be free again... really free."

Jamie laughed.

"Great!" he exclaimed, scratching his little friend on his head with affection. "You brave little monkey! It's a deal."

He held out his hand and Gordo stroked the back of it again with his small fingers.

"So after the trip into space you want to live in the jungle? I've heard that South America is the place. I've heard there are wonderful jungles there... you know, huge rain forests... and lots of monkeys like you."

Gordo smiled with a distant look of longing in his eyes.

"Yes, South America," nodded Jamie, "That's the place for you… yes, that would be great. I'll have to see what I can do," he said thoughtfully, and then added with confidence, "I have no idea how I'll get you there, but I will… somehow I will."

Gordo felt happy. There was something in Jamie's voice, a feeling of great kindness towards him that made him have complete faith in him. Gordo launched into an extraordinary swinging journey up the tree, around the roof of the cage and then down the side. In a moment he had scampered across the ground and was in the tree again and looking up at Jamie.

Jamie laughed. "That's amazing!"

"So when do I go up?" asked Gordo.

"You'll go up in December, a couple of weeks before Christmas."

"How long is that?"

"Well…" Jamie said thoughtfully, "We're in January now, so it's almost a year."

"And how long is that? How many days?"

"A year is 365, so almost that. Over 300 days…"

"What?!" exclaimed Gordo in surprise, "But that's ages and ages away."

"Tomorrow they begin training you," said Jamie, "You need to be a very fit and well-prepared monkey for something like this. It will take months and months to get you ready."

He moved closer to Gordo and looked into his brown eyes.

"I've got to go," he said, "My grandmother will worry if I'm not back soon… and then I'd be in big trouble! She's an old bat!"

"A bat?!" exclaimed Gordo.

"That's just something we say. She's not actually a bat, silly. It means she's an old dragon…"

Gordo looked equally puzzled, "A dragon?!"

Jamie tried to find the right words. "She's difficult… very, very difficult. She orders me around all the time and is always grumpy and cross."

Gordo nodded. "Why don't you just leave and live somewhere else?"

"It's not that easy," said Jamie sadly, "I wish it was."

Gordo turned his head on one side quizzically.

"You could just climb into another tree…" he said.

Jamie laughed.

"For us it's different," he replied, "Anyway… I must go. See you tomorrow."

"Just one thing before you go," said Gordo, "Don't tell anyone about our language. Because if humans find out we can speak it could be bad for monkeys… they'd be catching us, and studying us… it would be terrible. So it's really important. You must promise… promise to tell no one at all."

Jamie nodded solemnly. "I promise."

"Good," said Gordo, "Thank you. It's our secret then?"

"Yes… our secret."

Jamie gave Gordo a final rub on the head and passed out the through the cage gate. He pushed the padlock to with a click and walked up the path, smiling to himself as he thought of his new friend.

Thursday 9th January   2.24 a.m.

Jamie was asleep in his bed, dreaming that he was an astronaut in a rocket travelling to the Moon. He was enjoying floating weightlessly from one room to another when he noticed that there was someone else there, also wearing a space suit. He was surprised to see that it was a monkey who turned to him, smiled and started talking about the view from the window. They were looking back at Earth and chatting, when Jamie awoke.

As the dream faded he felt disappointed that the talking monkey was not real. Then he suddenly remembered what had happened the day before. He sat up and for a moment tried to work out whether his conversation with Gordo had been a dream as well.

Zorro was curled up on his bed and Jamie reached out and stroked him, following the lie of his thick fur in a circular motion.

"Yesterday, Zorro," he said, "I spoke to a monkey!"

He shook his head in disbelief, but he knew it was true. He chuckled again and a thrill ran through him leaving an excited smile on his face.

"It's amazing, Zorro!" he said, "Maybe I'll be talking to you next."

Zorro just purred.

9.01 a.m.

"Come on, Gordo," said Rachel, "Come with me."

Gordo was more relaxed now because he knew the reason why he was here. Rachel had given him some food and spent twenty minutes with him, stroking him and talking to him. She had no idea he could understand. Already he was beginning to grow fond of her.

She scooped him up in her arms and he climbed onto her shoulder and sat there with his long tail around the back of her neck. He looked perfectly at home. Someone came down the path humming happily. Rachel looked up to see Ray walking around the pond and towards the cage.

He called out to her. "So what's the big decision then? Do we start today or not?"

"We start," she replied, "He's fine...seems fit and well."

"Excellent!" said Ray.

A few more steps and he was next to the enclosure and looking in though the wire mesh of the door.

"You're sure he's ready? We don't want to rush him."

"He's ready," she said, stroking Gordo on the head, "Absolutely ready. Look at him. He's beautiful."

Rachel stepped out of the cage.

"Well, he obviously likes you, Rachel," Ray commented, reaching his hand out towards Gordo. Gordo grabbed his finger.

"Well, how do you do, Gordo?" said Ray, smiling and giving his hand a little shake. Gordo replied with a few little cheeps.

Ray laughed.

Together they walked up the path and towards the building.

At the door Rachel paused. "It's a shame we can't just tell him what he's here for..." she commented, smiling at Ray.

Ray chuckled. "That would be good!"

He opened the door for Rachel and they both passed inside.

9.06 a.m.

At this moment, Max McMurphy, dressed in a smart black suit and brightly polished shoes, entered another building in the Cape Canaveral Air Force Station Complex. He was dressed impeccably with a white shirt and deep red tie. He was a tall man of fifty-five years, standing at six feet three and with a wiry build and sharp features. His full head of white hair was silky smooth and always tidy. Black-rimmed, bifocal glasses sat on his slim nose, although they often slipped down a little, and a white moustache drooped above his small mouth.

He had worked all his life in offices, paving his way industriously up the ladder of prestige and fortune. Through the years, his driving force had been his desire to accumulate as much money as he could and to achieve this aim he had been ruthless; he had been prepared to lie, cheat and break the law for his own benefit. He had set his mind to the task with vigour. He had always wanted to be rich and now that he was, he craved for more.

He walked down the corridor and halted by the door to his office, pausing to admire the shiny brass sign that announced the position to which he was newly appointed:

MR. MAX J. P. MCMURPHY,
B.A. ASTRO PHYSICS, MSC, DIP.S.S, PMP.

DIRECTOR OF SPACE TRAVEL

This was his first day. He smiled with contentment. He felt proud that he had achieved what he had wanted for years

- a high position with authority and a large-scale salary. No one could take this away from him now. He pulled his jacket sleeve down over his hand, glanced around to check that no one was watching and rubbed the sign vigorously in an effort to make it shine more brightly. Then he turned the handle to go in, only to find that it was locked. Irritation spread across his face.

"Can somebody open my door!" he boomed down the corridor.

As he shouted his glasses slipped slightly down his nose so he touched them back with his index finger. A woman with brown wavy hair and in her mid-forties, appeared almost immediately carrying a bunch of keys and walking quickly towards him. It was his secretary Jean Smith.

"Terribly sorry, sir. It won't happen again," she stated calmly, as she searched for the right key on the bunch she was holding.

"I trust not," grumbled McMurphy, "I don't want mistakes happening in my department."

"Of course not, sir," Jean said, "It's just that you're earlier than expected because I was told…"

"Just open the door," he snapped, "And get it right next time."

Jean felt snubbed, and opened her mouth to finish her explanation, but decided not to. There seemed no point. She unlocked the door.

"Would you like tea or coffee, sir?"

"Coffee."

"Milk, sir?"

"No," he replied. His anger had subsided now, but his stern voice showed a complete lack of friendliness towards his new secretary. "Black with two sugars. And I'll need to speak to you at ten."

"Yes, sir," she said, retaining her poise in spite of his rudeness, "I have some papers that need looking at as soon as possible. Now, if that's alright sir."

"They'll have to wait," he said gruffly, "I said ten, Mrs. Smith."

She could tell there was no point arguing with him so she opened the door, stepped back and walked away down the corridor.

McMurphy stepped into his luxury office, walked across the deep pile carpet and sat down proudly behind the large mahogany desk. He settled into his comfortable swivel chair and thought about how he had worked for so many years for this moment - all those years of toil so that his ambitious plans could be put into action. Yes, he had been dishonest often and in many different ways but he felt that was a necessary element if you want to get on in life.

He sat in his leather chair and surveyed his office. He was thinking smugly about all he had achieved so far and he realized he still wanted more. He was not, as he thought he would be, completely content. There were things he still wanted to get. He lived in a huge house with a swimming pool and a five acre garden but he would like another large house abroad somewhere, maybe in Paris, where he could go from time to time. It would have an indoor swimming pool and a tennis court, or maybe two, in beautiful gardens. He would add another car to the four he had already. Yes, a Rolls Royce would suit him well. For these things he would need more money and if there was one thing Max McMurphy was good at, it was getting money. A flow of ideas passed through his greedy mind and they were all ways of making him richer.

During the next few weeks he hatched a few moneymaking plans that would help him achieve his dreams. One of them involved little Gordo and his journey into space.

February... March... April... May... June... July

Gordo entered into his training with enthusiasm. It was tough to keep going day after day but he enjoyed it. Five days a week, and sometimes six, Rachel would collect him from his cage and take him into the buildings. She was constantly with him, encouraging him and helping him.

Most days Jamie was there too, cycling as fast as he could from school. The last lesson would drag and he would count the minutes until the final bell went and he could rush out to his bike. Rachel had given him the job of looking after Gordo's cage for which he was paid a small amount.

He saved up his wages diligently. Each night when he got home he would kneel down on the floor in his bedroom and lift up a loose floorboard. He would pull out a small bag, tuck his earnings inside and then hide the bag again. He was not saving for anything in particular; maybe someday he would need it.

When the summer holidays came , Jamie was free all the time and he would get to the Space Centre early. These were his favourite times because he could help Rachel throughout the day and spend lots of time with Gordo.

When Jamie and Gordo were alone they were continually

chatting in his monkey language. In the company of others, Gordo could still talk to Jamie. No one else would understand and Jamie would talk to him in English as if talking to any animal. Over the days their friendship grew and no one realized they could communicate. Their secret remained safe.

Every night after training, Gordo was returned to his outdoor cage which he found very comfortable, especially after Rachel and Jamie had it made even bigger by extending it a little further along the wall. He was never ill and therefore never missed a single day of training, and some of the team of scientists who saw him every day started calling him 'Little Old Reliable.' They had worked with other monkeys on the Monkeynaut Training Program but they found Gordo to be the best they had ever trained. It was all going very well.

Rachel worked closely with Ray, who was a technical engineer. It was Ray's job to create an environment in the nose cone that was suitable for Gordo, and for this he had a team of four people who worked under his instructions. The nose cone needed to be specifically tailored to the requirements of a little squirrel monkey. Ray thoroughly enjoyed his work. He considered the capsule his work of art and was always looking for ways to improve it.

It was of primary importance that it was functional; everything needed to be in the right place and able its job efficiently. The nose cone was incredibly complex with seven miles of wiring and 10,000 parts which needed to be working perfectly. The most important functions were air supply, back-up systems and of course insulation against the extremes of temperature that would bear down upon the capsule. This was all highly scientific but Ray had a sense of beauty too; he always kept an eye for pleasing designs. If he thought a curve would be more attractive than a straight edge he would include it if possible. If a green panel would add some colour in the right place he would have it painted and he would take great care choosing which green.

Ray would always treat Gordo kindly. He would talk to

him all the time, although he had no idea that Gordo could understand any more than the intonation of his voice. Now and again he would be surprised, however, at the way Gordo seemed to do the right things and get into the right places at the right time. Gordo noticed this and had to be careful to act as if he did not understand.

Occasionally, once every few weeks, Jamie would hide Gordo in the bag on his back and smuggle him out for the day. The little monkey would stay completely still as they cycled past the security checkpoint. Jamie found it easy because he was well known at the Space Centre; he was there most days. To start with they would ask to see his official pass issued by Rachel and sometimes check his bag. However, as time went on, the guards did not even bother to stop him and he just cycled around the barrier with a friendly wave.

As soon as they were out of sight, Gordo would pop his head out of the bag, or climb out and ride on top of the bag.

One time, he took Gordo to his house in City Point, an eight mile ride on his bicycle. When his grandmother entered his bedroom she was astonished to see a monkey swinging from the curtain rail.

"This is Gordo…" began Jamie.

"Get that animal down from there!" she screeched at him, "It'll be breaking everything! It should be in the trees, not in houses… or going up into space! Get it out of my house!"

She turned and slammed the door. Gordo leapt down onto the bed, got into Jamie's bag and they left immediately to have a picnic by the sea. Gordo had his first swim in the Atlantic Ocean.

On another occasion they climbed up the Cape Canaveral Lighthouse. It was situated a little way inland and had been moved brick by brick some years earlier when the crumbling coastline threatened to destroy it. Now it stood proudly amongst the launch pads looking very much like a rocket itself.

Jamie knew the keeper and he was very happy to take them up. The view from the lantern room at the top was stunning. Gordo looked wide-eyed at the view. He jumped off Jamie's shoulder onto the window ledge and started climbing around the glass windows, peering out in all directions.

"Ha! Look at him!" the lighthouse keeper had remarked to Jamie, "That monkey knows how to climb. I hope he's gonna be strapped in well in that spaceship!"

They also spent some time outside on the two circular balconies. Gordo was fearless, treating the railings like the branches of a tree as he climbed down from the higher balcony to the lower and then back up again.

The months passed and in the spring, fresh new leaves sprouted on Gordo's laburnum tree home. Soon it hung with yellow flowers like small waterfalls of colour. Then the hot Florida summer brought thunderstorms and rising temperatures. 20°C rose to over 30°C.

Gordo loved this humid subtropical climate. When he was sitting in his tree in the cage he would sometimes close his eyes and imagine he was in a rainforest in South America. He would have loved to be there but he was committed to the space flight and wanted to make it a success, so he was happy to wait. He enjoyed the company of human beings. Rachel was always bright and cheerful and had a way of making his training fun.

Gordo was of great interest to the press. Space Travel was developing year by year and a monkey going into space made a good story. His picture began to appear in newspapers and magazines, and his fame grew until most people in the USA knew about him. Gradually the story of the little squirrel monkey, and his preparations for space flight, spread to other countries until Gordo was known throughout the world.

Monday 21st July   1.23 a.m.

Gordo was sleeping in his nest in the laburnum tree. The night was still. Occasionally, the hoot of an owl would echo in the warm air and the purr of a car's engine would pass by, fading gently into the night stillness. But Gordo heard none of these things as he slept deeply and dreamt that he was swinging through the trees in a jungle in South America with the sun shining brightly through the canopy of leaves above his head. He was enjoying moving from branch to branch, in and out of the sunshine, when a noise jolted him out of his dreams. He blinked as he woke into the Florida night where the full moon was shedding a pale silver light around him.

For a moment there was silence, and then, behind him, over the wall and further along, something scraped on the bricks.

He lifted his head and peeped over the edge of his nest.

Then he heard a soft thud near the shed in the corner of the garden. In the moonlight he saw a dark figure crouching low and then straightening up. A torch clicked on creating an oval of light on the grass.

The figure moved slowly, cautiously. The torchlight zigzagged on the ground. The gentle sound of soft shoes on the grass – creeping... creeping... closer and closer – moving around the cage and to the door. He heard the cage door being pushed gently and then the click of metal cutters as the padlock was severed and fell to the ground with a thud. Each sound was clear in the still air of the night.

From above, he saw the dark figure enter his cage. He stayed completely still, not wanting to be seen, but the beam of torchlight was gradually moving around the cage. First it shone below and then higher, searching out every area. It was only a matter of time before the light would pick out his nest.

Suddenly, there was a clatter from the shed in the corner of the garden. A low groan was followed by the click of the latch being lifted. The first torch clicked off while a new beam of light shone out through a crack in the shed door. The door opened with a creak. A man emerged into the moonlight rubbing his head but it was too dark for Gordo to see his face.

Then a rake fell out through the shed door and hit the man on the back of his head with a whack. The man ducked his head down sharply and spun around, raising his arms quickly in defence. He realised that he was not being attacked and kicked the rake in annoyance.

The torchlight fell upon the ground as he moved stealthily around the cage and to the door. When the man reached the open cage door there was a sharp intake of breath and then the torch inside the cage clicked on, lighting up the face of the second intruder.

"You!" the first intruder exclaimed with a loud whisper, "What are you doing here, Jeff?"

"Be quiet," whispered Jeff, who was now shining his torch in the other one's face. It was Frank in his cowboy hat. "Do you want to get us both caught?"

"What were you doing in that shed?" enquired Frank.

"I was waiting until the moon went behind a cloud, but then I fell asleep. You said that the best time to do a robbery was at the full moon so that you can see… and tonight's the full moon."

"I know that," whispered Frank, "That's why I'm here, you idiot."

"The trouble is, Frank," Jeff continued, "the trouble is that with the moon, other people can see us…"

Frank jerked in shock. "Who?" he exclaimed, looking around. When he saw that there was no one there his tone turned to sarcasm. "Who?" He looked around again, this time in mock alarm. "There's no one here, is there?"

"Not now, but we *could* be seen… we're *easy* to see."

Frank waved an arm towards the shed, and whispered accusingly, "It doesn't matter if we're seen because, thanks to you, we can be heard! All that noise you made in there is enough to wake up half of Orlando!"

Jeff shook his head and rubbed it again. "I don't know how it happened… those brooms and things just fell. But at least it woke me up."

"But, what are you doing here anyway?"

"I'm here for the monkey, of course," whispered Jeff rubbing his head again, "Remember I said about my wife's birthday, well her birthday's next week…"

"You're crazy!" whispered Frank, "You break in here,

Cape Canaveral, to steal a monkey for your wife! It's ridiculous…"

"No!" whispered Jeff loudly, "I'm not giving her the monkey! I'm gonna sell the monkey to get the money to buy a present for her. I'm broke!" Frank sighed. "Listen, I know it's stupid Frank, but… well… I just want to give her something really special on her thirtieth. You know… to show my love for her. But… hang on a minute," whispered Jeff, looking thoughtful, "If I'm crazy, then what are you! Why are you here?"

"For the monkey, of course!"

"Why don't you drive back to Naples to steal a few monkeys then?"

"'Cos I'm broke too! I can't even afford the gas. But I know where to sell this one again somewhere else and get more than $1800 this time. I know this guy… he'd probably pay $2000… maybe more."

"That reminds me," whispered Jeff angrily, "Where's my half. You never paid me! You locked me in that truck and you never paid me!"

"You didn't want to do it!" Frank's voice was agitated. "I had to take the monkey in myself."

"You still owe me," Jeff was still whispering, but it was a shouting whisper, "I've done a lot for you and I want my money!"

Jeff suddenly produced a gun from his pocket and pointed it at Frank's chest. Frank immediately jerked a gun out of his pocket and aimed it straight at Jeff's head and then pushed the barrel against his forehead. For a moment they were both completely still, then Frank whispered.

"You wouldn't shoot me, you're too weak!"

"I would!" replied Jeff, "I want my money – you owe me $900 plus the cost of the petrol… and loads of oil."

"How can I pay you if I'm broke?"

Jeff pushed the gun into Frank's chest.

Frank smiled. "If you shoot me, you idiot, you'll never

get it, will you? You hadn't thought of that had you?"

"But I'd be rid of you and I'd get the monkey!" whispered Jeff.

Frank leant towards Jeff and moved his gun closer to his head. "Bang!" whispered Frank.

Jeff jumped back.

"See," said Frank, "You're afraid and you can't do it. But I could shoot you!"

Jeff thought for a moment and realized that Frank was right.

"Listen, Frank, we should be working together," he whispered. He lowered his gun. "This is stupid. We shouldn't be standing in here arguing. We both want the monkey."

"OK then," Frank said calmly. He glanced around, looking for the monkey, and then continued. "We take the monkey and sell it, and split the money, agreed?"

"OK, but I..."

"Who's there?" shouted a guard's voice from the darkness towards the buildings.

Frank and Jeff switched off their torches.

"Run for it," whispered Frank.

They slipped out through the cage door and ran. A beam of light, brighter than both of their torch lights, picked them up as they were scrabbling over the wall. Frank lifted his gun and pulled the trigger; the sharp crack echoed in the night air. The bullet thudded into a tree near the guard, who instantly shot back and then shot again.

"Argh!" cried Jeff, as they jumped off the wall on the other side.

The circle of torchlight danced on the wall and for a moment picked out Jeff's head, which quickly dipped out of sight. Frank and Jeff were gone.

Gordo relaxed and looked down at the open cage door. He could escape if he wanted to but it did not cross his mind; he was happy here with his new friend Jamie and he was enjoying the daily training.

The guard hesitated for a moment, wondering what to do. It was Carl Greeber, a man of fifty-nine, just a year away from retirement and dressed in his blue guard's uniform and cap. He was average height and slightly overweight.

He ran to the cage and closed the gate. Then he moved quickly to the wall, still holding his gun, and cautiously peeped over. There was no one there. Blowing air through his cheeks in relief, he walked back to the cage, entered and then leant back on the door to close it. He held the gun up and looked at it; his hand was shaking. It was only the second time he had fired a gun in action. He slipped it back into its holster and lifted a walkie-talkie to his mouth.

"Greeber calling central security, over," he said, and released the switch.

The walkie-talkie hissed. He waited and then pressed the switch again.

"Greeber calling central security... come in central security, over."

The walkie-talkie hissed again and a voice snapped, "Central security. What do you want, Greeber? It'd better be important... Over."

"This is no joke," said Greeber quickly, "I just disturbed two men trying, I assume, to steal Gordo! Over."

"What? Over," exclaimed central security.

"Look. Are you half asleep? Two men. They shinned over the east wall... and I hit one of them. Over."

"How? Over."

"He shot at me! So I shot back and heard him cry out. Never knew I was such a good shot. Get 'round there quick. You might catch 'em. Over."

"Did they get the monkey? Over."

"Dunno. Get going! And call the cops. Over and out."

Greeber slipped the walkie-talkie back into its holster and shone his torch around.

"Now, Gordo, are you still here?" he said, as the beam of light cut through the darkness.

Gordo looked out of his nest and down at Greeber. He blinked as the light shone on his black and white face.

"You good little fella," he said looking up at Gordo, "Didn't even try to escape. Probably too frightened. Miss Chandler will be so pleased you're still here."

He picked up the severed padlock and stepped out of the cage. He took his belt off and used it to secure the cage door and then walked away along the path.

CHAPTER 6

Monday 21st July   8.50 a.m.

Rachel entered the Space Station Centre, opening one of the pair of glass doors and letting it swing to behind her. She shook the rain off her umbrella, then closed it and placed it in a rack. A long hallway stretched away in front of her and on her right was a reception desk with the porter sitting behind it, a cheerful-looking young man with a navy blue uniform.

"Morning, Danny," said Rachel, walking up to the desk.

"Morning, Rachel," Danny replied, "Have you heard about the break-in?"

"No. What happened?" Rachel sounded concerned.

"Last night. They were after Gordo…" he began.

"What!?" Rachel exclaimed.

"Don't worry," he said, holding up a hand, "They didn't get him. But it seems they were after him. They…"

He turned when he heard Greeber walking down the

corridor towards them.

"Ah, here's Greeber," Danny said, "He's the one who saw them. And he shot one of them. He'll tell you all about it."

Greeber strode towards them with his keys jangling on his belt and holding his rain-wet cap in his hand. His friendly face was topped with grey, thinning hair.

"Hello, Miss Chandler," said Greeber.

"What happened, Greeber?" she asked.

"There were two of them. It was the torchlight that alerted me. I was just on my rounds, in the east building when I saw the light... just caught my eye through the window... and I knew something was up, miss."

"And you shot one of them?"

"Well, yes," replied Greeber, patting the gun in his holster, "They were escaping over the wall and they shot at me... so I shot back. One of them cried out so I must have hit him... they still escaped."

"Have the police been told?" asked Rachel.

"Yup," nodded Greeber, "They've come and gone. They took the bullet they fired... it was embedded in a tree trunk. They're checking the hospitals for a man with a gun wound."

"And how's Gordo?" Rachel enquired.

"Oh, he's fine, miss," Greeber smiled. "He was watching everything from up in his tree. He saw it all!"

"Are you sure they were after Gordo?" asked Rachel.

"Well, the padlock was cut, and they were in there... actually in the cage when I disturbed them," Greeber shook his head, "That's pretty conclusive. A minute later and they'd've had him out of there."

Rachel shook her head. "That's terrible. Thank you, Greeber, for acting so quickly. But why... why would they want Gordo?" She thought for a moment. "To sell him?"

"Yep," Danny joined in from behind his desk, "Gordo's a world-wide celebrity now, isn't he? Everyone knows about Gordo."

Rachel nodded. "I suppose they do... yes, he is famous... with all the paper reports. And TV."

RENO EVENING GAZETTE

A Newspaper for the Home

Information and enjoyment for every member of the family

EIGHTY-SECOND YEAR—NO. 223   PHONE FA 3-3161   RENO, NEVADA, SATURDAY, JULY 19, 1958   PHONE FA 3-3161   18 PAGES   10 CENTS

WEATHER
Variable Cloudiness
Little Temperature Change
Minimum 34   Noontime 43

MONKEY WILL GO INTO SPACE

Check Sent to California

Nevadans Miffed When No Meeting Precedes Move

BY WALT MACKENZIE

Nevada's $200,000 contribution to the 1960 Winter Olympic Games at Squaw Valley will be used to build an athlete's center in Olympic Village, it was learned today.

The check covering Nevada's contribution has been issued to the California Olympic Commission, although there has been no public discussion on how the money is to be spent.

As a matter of fact, Nevada Olympic Commission Chairman G. J. Quilici has announced that the commission's first official meeting will be held Dec. 20.

However, the commission already has authorized payment of the $200,000 to the California Olympic group on a state controller's check issued Dec. 2.

TELLS OF PROJECT

Charles R. Blyth, chairman of the California Olympic Commission, said in Burlingame this morning the money would go to build an athlete's center.

Blyth, said he hadn't yet received the check but admitted he was aware that the check had been issued. "This is fine, wonderful, we certainly can use it," it is likely that Quilici, who once again will make a formal

UN Windup Near
DEADLOCKS ON SPACE, ALGERIA

UNITED NATIONS, N.Y., July 19.—The U.N. General Assembly neared the final hours of its 1958 session today, unable to agree decisively on the controversial issue of the future of Algeria.

The eastmost deadlock over occupied space also remained as the Russian assembly sought to wind up a lockianer week ago,

YAQUINA BAY, OREGON: Coast guardsmen call this type of work "routine patrolling," but it's not recommended for the average yachtsman. This 52-foot patrol boat heads into heavy seas off coast of Washington during a patrol. Picture illustrates hazards faced by coast guard when it goes on a risky rescue mission. (UPI Telephoto)

COPS CATCH THREE KIDNAPERS
In Washington Last Night

GORDO IS THE STAR AT CAPE CANAVERAL

By Fred L. Hopperstone

WASHINGTON, July 19. (AP) — A little squirrel monkey, called Gordo, will ride a rocket to the very fringes of space later this year, blazing a trail for man to follow.

The launch is scheduled for December 13th from Cape Canaveral, when it is hoped Gordo will survive a meteor-like ascent to about 300 miles above the Earth.

The workers at the Space Station Centre have nicknamed Gordo, Little Old Reddo, because he trains so well. M. Max McMurphy, Director of Space Travel, is leading the team, and the able Miss Rachel Chandler is Gordo's personal trainer.

"Gordo seems to love his training," said Miss Chandler. "He's certainly a fine little monkey."

If the mission is successful, it is virtually certain that a manned rocket will soon follow, bringing the dream of sending a man to the Moon, ever closer.

So, while Gordo is being prepared for his historic trip into space in a Jupiter IRBM AM-13 rocket, America holds her breath in hopeful anticipation. This plucky little monkey, with a unique patch of golden hair on top of his head, has captured the hearts and the imagination of the nation - and indeed the whole world.

Gordo - the monkey with the golden head, in training for rocket ride

State Lottery Plan Up Again

SACRAMENTO, (P). — The chairman of the state board of equalization said Friday the governor's

George R. Reilly said Friday he will ask Assemblyman Allen Prince (R-Sabono) to push the plan before the legislature in January.

Republican leaders haven't got far in the east

"I'll tell you what," laughed Greeber, "You're getting quite a reputation too, miss."

"I hope not, Greeber!" said Rachel frowning.

"It's true," added Danny, "They say that the way you look after that monkey is something to see… you and young Jamie. Something special. They say you have a way with monkeys. After all, you can get him to do anything, can't you?"

"He's a good monkey… that's all," said Rachel dismissively, "But I must go and see him now. Thanks again Greeber for what you did."

"You're welcome, miss. Oh… and I had to put a new padlock on the cage door. Here's a key."

"Thanks," she said, taking the key and slipping it into her pocket. She took a step and then turned back.

"Oh, Greeber," she said, "We'll have to get someone to be on regular night-time guard duty… to guard Gordo that is. Would you do it?"

"For a beautiful girl like you… I'd do anything, miss."

"Oh, thanks Greeber," she smiled and blushed, "I'll put the idea forward. If they agree could you start tonight?"

"Sure, miss. I'm doing night shifts at the moment anyway."

"Great," she said as she turned and walked down the corridor.

The main door opened and Ray entered.

"Morning, Danny…" he said, taking off his fedora hat and shaking the rain off it, "Morning, Greeber."

Then he saw Rachel.

"Hey, Rach, wait for me," he called out and jogged after her.

As they walked together to Gordo's cage she told him about the break-in.

"He'll have to be guarded through the night," said Ray.

"It's all arranged," she smiled, "Well… virtually. I've just got to get old Mr. McGrumpy to agree."

"You mean McMurphy?" Ray laughed, "Oh he'll agree. Why not? I'll try to speak to him as well… if I can book one of his precious appointments. He always seems so busy, and yet, what does he do?"

"Nothing," stated Rachel, "As far as I can see. Nothing of any use anyway. Just sits in his office and gives orders about things that are being done already! Or complains."

Ray nodded, "I agree. I think he just likes being important. And when I see him I'll tell you what you called him!"

Rachel laughed, "Don't you dare."

They left the building and walked through the rain and down the path to Gordo's cage. Many plants in the garden were now in flower and it looked beautiful with the rain pattering gentle on them.

"Gordo?" called Rachel looking up into his tree with an anxious face.

Gordo chirruped, "Hello," and climbed down.

Rachel unlocked the cage door, went in and the door swung back behind her. Gordo leapt onto Rachel's shoulder and she stroked him affectionately on the head.

"It's strange to think, Rach…" Ray commented, smiling at her, "That he knows who broke in! He saw them. If only he could tell us."

Rachel nodded and smiled. "Thankfully, Greeber did a good job and scared them off."

Gordo chirruped and snuggled up to her.

"Anyway," she said, "We'd better get to work."

"Yup, you're right," he said, opening the cage door for her, "I've nearly finished designing his bed for the nose cone, so can I have him for an hour today? I need him to test out the prototype."

"Fine. When?" she asked.

"Oh, later on this morning… let's say eleven… is that OK?"

"Yes, that fits in fine," she agreed.

They walked together up the path, into the building and then along a corridor. Ray turned left and Rachel, with Gordo on her shoulder, turned right.

"See you later," said Ray over his shoulder, "At eleven."

"OK," replied Rachel.

4.05 p.m.

The lift doors opened on the fifth floor of the International Space Centre and Rachel stepped out and looked along the corridor to her right. Jamie stepped out after her with Gordo on his shoulder.

"Right, Jamie," she said quietly to him, "Let's go and meet the great man."

She walked a few paces and paused at a half open door. She pushed the door open and entered. Jean Smith stopped typing and looked up from her desk. Her face brightened into a welcoming smile as soon as she saw them.

"Rachel!" she said, "How nice to see you. And you, young man."

"How are you, Jean?" asked Rachel.

"I'm fine, thanks. What brings you here?"

Rachel smiled back. "I've come to see the boss," she said.

"You'll be lucky!" Jean exclaimed, "Even with an appointment he usually cancels, but without an appointment... no chance."

"I know," said Rachel, moving closer and then sitting down, "But this is important... very important."

Jamie sat down next to her.

Jean gave a resigned shrug of her shoulders. "Important or not... doesn't matter. He only meets the people he wants to meet."

"I know what he's like," Rachel persisted, "But I've got to see him."

"Yes, we've got to see him," Jamie joined in.

"You see it's about Gordo here," Rachel continued, lifting her hand to scratch Gordo under his chin. He chirruped in pleasure. "Did you know that two men broke in and tried to steal him last night?"

"Yes," Jean nodded, "I heard about that."

She looked affectionately at Gordo who was climbing down from Jamie's shoulder to settle on his lap. He peeped over the edge of the desk at Jean.

"He's so sweet, isn't he? Look at those beautiful eyes!"

Jamie stroked Gordo on his back. Rachel pulled something out of his pocket.

"I wanted to show you this," said Rachel and put a round cloth badge on Jean's desk, "It's Gordo badge - for his space suit. Ray made it. What do you think?"

Jean smiled. "It looks great! MASA - oh I see - like NASA - but what does MASA stand for?"

"Monkeynaut Aeronautics and Space Administration," replied Rachel, with a chuckle, "It will go on Gordo's spacesuit. It's a bit of fun really. But we thought he ought to have a badge!"

"So he should," stated Jean, "it's perfect."

"Did you hear about the break-in?" asked Rachel.

"Yes... everyone's talking about it. But why do you want to see Mr. High and Mighty?'"

Rachel smiled. She knew that Jean was having a difficult time working as McMurphy's secretary.

"Gordo needs to be guarded through the night, so I'm going to ask... um... Mr. High and Mighty himself."

"I admire your optimism... and your courage," Jean remarked, "Most people get their heads bitten off as soon as they go in there."

"Can you get us in?" Jamie asked hopefully.

Jean thought for a few seconds. "We'll find a way... in fact..." she smiled, "I've got an idea."

In his office next door, Max McMurphy was gazing out of his window through the rain of the pale afternoon. He had taken his glasses off, swivelled his office chair around and stretched his legs out straight in front of him, crossing them at the ankles. The luxurious leather chair was like a good friend to him and he sank down comfortably into a relaxed slump. He then entered into a long daydream about the game of golf he was going to play tomorrow. He arranged it under the guise of an important business meeting and Jean Smith had booked it into his diary. Now he was imagining himself playing the best game of his life. Every ball was hit sweetly and he was the envy of his opponent who was gradually growing more and more cross. But the ease of the golf and the comfort of the chair had begun to lull him to sleep. His head tilted back, his mouth opened and he began to snore.

Just as he was shaping up for the winning putt, a sharp

noise distracted him and the ball trickled into a bunker. He flung his putter onto the green in anger. Then the noise came again.

He awoke with a jerk and a snorting sound, to realize that it was the buzzer on his desk. He sat up and turned his chair around until it faced the desk once more. He reached out with his wiry hand and pressed the button.

"Yes," he said gruffly.

"Miss Chandler to see you, sir," replied Jean Smith, "I'll show her in."

McMurphy quickly pressed the button, "No," he snapped, "I'm too busy."

He released the button and listened. No answer. He pressed again.

"Jean? Are you there?" he snapped.

There was silence.

"Jean!?"

There was a knock on his door. McMurphy quickly picked up a pen and looked down at some papers on his desk.

"Yes?!" he shouted, snatching his glasses off the desk and putting them on.

The door opened and Rachel and Jamie entered. He glanced up and then looked down again, pretending to read.

"Thank you so much for seeing me," she said.

No reply.

"Thank you so much for seeing me," Rachel repeated slightly louder.

"Can't you see I'm busy!" he growled without looking up. "Have you an appointment?"

"Yes… no… not exactly."

She sat down in the chair in front of his desk and Jamie sat next to her with Gordo in his arms.

"Then why…" he began slowly with astonishment, "Why are you here? You have to have an appointment…" He looked up crossly and then glowered at Jamie. "Children aren't allowed here… who are you?"

Before Jamie could answer, he noticed Gordo and his hard expression softened. "Ah… and is this the monkey with the golden head. The monkey that's going up in a few months?"

"It is," Rachel replied, "And his name's Gordo."

"And you are?"

"Rachel… Rachel Chandler."

"Oh, yes. Oh, yes. And you look after him and train him don't you?"

Rachel nodded.

"Well, Miss Chandler, what can I do for you?"

Rachel wondered about his sudden change of attitude towards her.

"It's about the attempted theft last night…"

He frowned. "Hmmm… oh yes, of course, last night, yes, the attempted theft. A terrible thing. Terrible. But, thank goodness…no harm done."

"True, but Gordo here…" She stroked his head as he sat on Jamie's lap. "Gordo obviously needs protection. He needs a guard on duty through the night."

"I agree," stated McMurphy.

His money-making plans for Gordo flashed into his mind. He could almost feel the money and see a very healthy bank statement in front of his greedy eyes. The monkey must be protected.

"Yes, absolutely," he agreed.

"And Greeber could do it," said Rachel brightly, hardly believing how smoothly this was going, "Greeber would be happy to do it."

"Greeber?" asked McMurphy.

"He's one of the guards."

"OK then," McMurphy smiled. He reached for the intercom button.

"Yes, sir?" said Jean's voice.

"Could you arrange for Greeber to see me as soon as possible?"

"Certainly, Mr. McMurphy. Anything else?"

"No, Jean, that's all."

"Thank you, sir," said Jean.

The intercom clicked off.

McMurphy smiled. "Leave it to me, Miss Chander."

"It's Chandler," corrected Rachel.

"Sorry… Miss… er… Chandler. I'll sort it all out, OK?"

Rachel stood up.

"Thank you very much," she said politely.

Jamie stood up too and Gordo climbed up his clothes to settle on his shoulder. McMurphy rose to his feet, walked around his desk and held out his hand to Rachel. She shook it.

"Well, that's excellent, Miss Chandler," he commented, looking down at her, "Good… good. I'm sure all will go well… especially with the care of the monkey in your good hands."

"Thank you," she said, "He's very easy to look after."

"Well… good bye then," he said as an artificial smile stretched his lips.

"Good bye," replied Rachel.

They left the room and Jamie closed the door behind him. In the corridor they stood still for a moment in puzzlement. Then she spoke quietly to Jamie.

"He's a strange man, Jamie. First he's so rude and then he's so friendly."

"Yeah," Jamie nodded, "What was that about?"

Rachel shrugged. "I don't trust him. But I've got to say he sorted this out very quickly."

Gordo whispered into Jamie's ear, "I don't like him."

They turned into Jean's office and she looked up from her desk and asked, "How did it go?"

"Perfect!" exclaimed Rachel, "No problems!"

"Well, that's a first. And you've still got your head on! Good for you, Rachel. Well done. You must have a certain charm that I lack!"

Rachel smiled, "I doubt that. But thanks for getting me in."

"Any time, Rachel. It's nice to see you... both of you. Or rather, I should say, all three of you. Pop up to see me any time you like."

"We will," said Rachel, "Bye!"

"Bye."

Jean smiled and then she looked at Gordo with a kind expression, "Look after that little fella. He's a real darling! Bye, Gordo."

Rachel and Jamie turned and left, with Gordo on Jamie's shoulder looking back at Jean. She smiled at him, waved with her fingers until the door closed behind them, and then she began typing again.

4.25 p.m.

Jamie took Gordo back to his cage, walking down the path through the rain, which had turned into a fine drizzle. Rachel went to her office to make a couple of phone calls, grabbing a mug of coffee on the way. She had a small room with a desk underneath a window and shelves along one wall. A row of about thirty books of various sizes showed her main interest; they were mostly about monkeys. Apart from this, the shelves were adorned with well-grown potted plants, a few of which displayed exotic flowers. Others hung down with leaf-laden tendrils. On the other side of the room, Rachel sat in a comfy chair.

At twenty-five, she was the youngest applicant for the job

that she had now held for just over a year. It was her fervent enthusiasm, coupled with her knowledge of monkeys, that impressed the panel of interviewers. They were surprised by her qualities because she was ahead of all the other applicants in spite of being younger. Her hard work paid off and they offered her the job.

She liked to keep her office simple and uncluttered. She used it to do paperwork and make phone calls but she also came here to enjoy moments of peace and quiet. She got up from her chair and put some gentle music on, and then returned to relax for a few more minutes.

One thing filled her thoughts; the attempted theft of Gordo. She wondered who the criminals were and whether they would be caught. Greeber had shot one of them, and the police were going to check the hospitals, so maybe that would lead to an arrest. Nothing more could be done. It shocked her that Gordo was now so well known that he needed protecting but it surprised her even more that McMurphy had been so helpful in arranging it. Why had his unwelcoming, rude response to her, suddenly changed into charming friendliness? She decided she would talk to Jean to see if she could throw any light on it.

She finished her coffee and got up. On her way out, she quickly watered the plants with a fine spray, touched one of the flowers tenderly with her fingers, and closed the door behind her.

Jamie had taken Gordo back to his cage. Now that they were alone, they were able to talk. Jamie sat down with his back against the tree and Gordo sat in front of him. The little monkey picked up a berry and popped it into his mouth. The tree sheltered them from the rain, apart from a few drops dripping off the leaves.

"What happened last night?" asked Jamie.

"I knew them," Gordo said, looking at Jamie, "It was the same men… the ones who caught me."

Jamie looked surprised. "The same men? Are you sure?"

"Yes… they're called Frank and Jeff."

"Did they say anything?"

"Yes. I heard them whispering together." Gordo fidgeted. Just the thought of the men made him feel nervous. "They were both trying to steal me separately... but the reason they were there together was something to do with the full moon. When they saw each other they started arguing…" He spotted another berry and scampered into the rain to get it. "I couldn't hear it all…" he continued, eating the berry, "They were arguing and they both had guns. They were going to steal me and sell me again…"

"They'd have had a job catching you! You're faster than a firecracker!"

Gordo returned to the shelter of the tree and Jamie reached out and scratched him affectionately under the chin.

"Listen," said Jamie, "I'll see what I can find out about it. But at least they were scared off, and we know you're safe at nights now… with Greeber here."

"Yes," Gordo agreed, "With Greeber around I feel safe."

"Good," said Jamie, "Rachel did well to sort that out… she's great, isn't she? She'd do anything for you, you know."

"I know."

Jamie stood up. "I've got to go… my grandmother will start worrying."

Gordo climbed up Jamie's trousers and shirt and then onto his shoulder. Jamie turned when they heard Rachel walking down the path towards them.

"What are you two chattering about?" she joked.

Jamie laughed, and joked back. "Gordo was just telling me all about the two thieves!"

"He really likes you, doesn't he?" said Rachel, who was by the cage now and looking in, "He always chats so much when you're around."

"I know," said Jamie, "Beautiful little sounds aren't they?"

"Yes… but they sound so expressive. As if they mean

something."

Jamie stared back. Did she suspect something?

"I know that their sounds mean things," she continued, "But perhaps they mean more than we think. Like a language that we can't understand... or not yet anyway. I'd like to research it someday."

It crossed Jamie's mind to tell her their secret. In fact, he would love to share it with someone and he knew she loved Gordo and could be trusted to keep the secret. He would have to ask Gordo first.

Gordo leapt off Jamie's shoulder and onto the tree, grasping a branch with one hand and swinging around and up. With stunning skill and a few quick movements he was on the highest branch and looking down at them, leaving a few branches bouncing up and down in his wake. Rachel laughed.

"You're a little show-off," she joked, "See you tomorrow."

Gordo replied with a row of cheeps which Jamie understood as, "I don't need to show off... I'm just good at climbing!"

Jamie chuckled as he walked out of the cage, locked it and then called out, "See you tomorrow, Gordo."

"Great!" said Gordo.

The cousins chatted as they walked up the path and into the building.

CHAPTER 7

Tuesday 5th August   10.25 a.m.

Elliot Smudge was a burley, balding cop. His police cap hid the wispy patch of hair which was stranded on the top of his head where the rest had receded. His face bore the evidence of years of worry etched in wrinkles onto his forehead and around his eyes. He was an obstinate man and the way he carried his tall frame gave him a look of confident superiority. He had become a policeman two days after his nineteenth birthday and had been one ever since. Now in his late fifties he was beginning to look forward to retirement.

He had lived alone since he had left his wife and daughter four years ago. His main interest and pastime was to go fishing and he would spend many hours on the riverbank.

At work, he was usually morose because he resented the fact that his expectations of promotion had not been fulfilled. This was a grudge that he had held onto with a grip as firm as his hold on his fishing rod when the float on the water twitched with the promise of a catch.

This morning, however, he was in a jovial mood and ready to tackle the task before him. With a positive attitude he strode up to the front door of 117, Sharnfore Road in Orlando. One step behind him was a policewoman, Ruth Anderton, who was just twenty-two but looked younger. She was freshly out of the Police Training Academy and this was her very first day in the job at the start of her probation year.

She was attractive and very slight, the complete contrast of Smudge, and she looked as though a light breeze would blow her away. Smudge had been given the task of helping and advising her in her first few months of work. They both wore their police caps with the silver badge on the front which matched the one on the left of their smart navy blue uniforms.

"Now," he said, looking down at her, "I'll show you how it's done."

He ignored the bell and knocked loudly on the door.

"These sort of people…" he said, "you know… criminal types, seem to sense who it is at the door and then they keep you waiting on purpose."

He only waited a few seconds before he impatiently knocked again, this time even louder than before.

"Perhaps," Ruth offered, "Perhaps, sir, it's because they're always in trouble and they're afraid who might be calling on them."

"Yeah, maybe," he replied.

He lifted his fist to knock a third time and would have knocked even louder but the door opened just as his fist hammered forwards. He lost balance and fell into a short dumpy woman, in her late twenties, who jumped back in shock. He overbalanced sideways into the door, bumping his head against it and his cap slipped forward and over his face. Regaining his balance, he stepped back quickly with his cap still covering his eyes. She glared and frowned at him.

"What are you doing?!" she exclaimed.

Smudge pushed his cap up so that he could see again.

"Eh hem... sorry, madam," he said, embarrassed, "Just... er... knocking, madam."

He regained his composure. Ruth was trying to stifle a giggle.

"Officer Smudge," he announced and he held out his ID. She nodded and asked, "What d'ya want?"

"Mrs. Marks?" he asked.

"Yup."

"Your husband... in, is he?" snapped Smudge.

"Why? What's he supposed to have done?" she asked.

She was Jeff's wife, Mary-Anne.

Smudge moved slightly closer and looked down on her with disdain. "Just need a few words with him, that's all."

She spoke with mock friendliness. "He's not in I'm afraid... officer."

"I know he is in, so don't give me that. Just a few words..."

"As I said," she interrupted, "he's not in. You'll have to come back another time, if that's not too much trouble... if it is, then don't bother."

A man's voice called out from inside the house, "Who is it, Mary-Anne?"

Mary-Anne smiled and shook her head. "He's a fool, bless him... but he hasn't done anything wrong."

Smudge looked stone-faced. "Let me be the judge of that."

Mary-Anne looked past Smudge to see if any of her neighbours were watching. "I suppose you'd better come in."

"That's better," said Smudge, now feeling in control and pleased with himself.

He felt he was giving an excellent demonstration to his

young apprentice of how to deal with criminals. His fall through the door was unfortunate but he had completely regained his composure. He pushed past Mary-Anne and into the house, followed by Ruth.

"Who's she?" Mary-Anne snapped.

Smudge did not reply but walked straight into the lounge where Jeff was slouched in a chair watching television. When he saw Smudge he jumped up with surprise. Smudge stepped towards the television and ran his finger lovingly along the top of it.

"Hmm! Well, look at that!" he exclaimed, "Colour TV. Now that's something that me and my Mrs. can't afford."

He reached down and turned it off.

"But you can," Smudge continued, "Now how does something like that happen, Jeff Marks? Here am I working hard in a proper job, and there's you… unemployed and enjoying luxuries like this! Come into some money, did you?"

"I saved, didn't I?" he said, then he turned to ask Mary-Anne, "Didn't I?"

"Every cent," she confirmed, "It was for my birthday. He loves me and looks after me, you know. Don't you look after your wife, officer? What've you got? Black and white?"

Smudge ignored the comment and stared at Jeff.

"Where were you on January 14th?" he snapped.

Jeff looked puzzled, "Ey? That's ages ago. January 14th?"

"That's right."

"Which year?"

Smudge looked daggers at him.

"This year, of course. Just answer the question."

"Now let me see," he began, pretending to search his memory, "At 10 o'clock I went to the shops. No… it was exactly 10.17. The shopkeeper will confirm this, of course. I bought a loaf of bread, some butter and 10 tons of potatoes. I remember it well because the bus driver charged me extra for the potatoes."

Mary-Anne laughed and Ruth again tried to stifle a snigger. Smudge glanced at her disapprovingly. He stepped closer to Jeff.

"And did you buy any bananas? Like a big box of 'em? And put them in the back of a stolen truck?"

Jeff nearly panicked. His eyes flicked away from Smudge and then back again.

"Bananas?" he looked puzzled. He decided to ignore the mention of a stolen truck. "No… why should I? I don't even like bananas. I hate them." He stared back at Smudge, and then turned to Mary-Anne. "Don't I, dear?"

"Hates 'em, he does," she agreed, "He never goes near a banana… never."

"Look, officer," began Jeff, "As much as I like talking to you, I have things to do. Have you really come here to ask me about bananas?"

Mary-Anne laughed and said, "No, no, Jeff. We must take the man seriously. There's someone going 'round stealing bananas and escaping in some stolen truck, and he must be stopped. The officers here are probably on the trail of the thief – a trail of banana skins!"

Smudge looked angry and said slowly, "Ha… ha… ha. What about the stolen truck then? Does that ring any bells?"

Jeff again pretended to search his memory and paced up and down, looking up to the ceiling. "No, I haven't stolen any trucks. I did shop-lift a bunch of bananas the other day. So I am guilty of that and you can arrest me for that if you like." He held out his arms ready for handcuffs. "But I am innocent of stealing some truck or any other crime you may dream up."

"OK, OK," Smudge said and paused. He was thinking what to say next. "Where were you in the early hours of Monday July… the…" He took out a notebook and checked the date. "July the 21st?"

"Early hours?" he asked. Smudge nodded. "How can I

remember? No, hang on, I can remember 'cos every night, at eleven o'clock, I go to sleep. Every night. Don't you? And I sleep right through the night, always. Don't I Mary-Anne?"

"It's true," she said, "He sleeps every night… and like a baby. I can confirm that absolutely. You couldn't wake him up with a fog horn!"

"Well," said Smudge, "If you're so innocent, you won't mind if we have a look around, will you?"

Jeff shrugged. "Have your look around and then get out… and go and catch some real criminals."

He reached down to switch the TV on again, collapsed down into his chair and stared at the screen. Smudge and Ruth Anderton left the room and had a quick look around and then Mary-Anne showed them out. They got into their car and Smudge drove off.

"That's how you interrogate, Miss Anderton," he said sounding pleased, "We now know that we have nothing on him and have to rule him out of our investigations for the moment. But we don't forget him… oh no… we keep him in mind in case something else comes up... some new evidence."

During the silence that followed, Smudge assumed that she was suitably impressed and that she had learnt her first lesson in the subtleties of police work in action. He stopped at a junction.

Ruth fidgeted.

"There was something, sir," she said.

"Good, good," he said smugly, "Ask me whatever you need to know."

"It's not questions, sir," she said, "It's things I noticed. When I was training they told me that the most important thing was to be observant. To stay aware. To observe everything; to listen and to look for clues."

"Very good, Miss Anderton. You're right, of course."

"Firstly, sir, there was the limp," she said.

"Oh… the limp?" he said slowly, as he pulled away from

the junction. He had not noticed any limp.

"Maybe... just maybe... he got shot in the leg..."

"Shot in the leg?" he looked surprised, "Why on earth would you think that?"

"Well," Ruth began, sounding very matter of fact now, and becoming more confident, "Well... there is the attempted theft of the monkey at Cape Canaveral where the guard shot one of thieves, and there's the truck with the blood and bananas. I can't help thinking that monkeys do eat bananas, so there may be a connection. Maybe our friend Jeff was involved in not just one of them, but both."

"I think..." began Smudge slowly. He felt very uncomfortable about being upstaged by this young female on her very first day of work. He had over 30 years experience and he was meant to be teaching her. This was not enjoyable. "I think you're stretching things a bit with that idea, don't you?"

"Well, no, sir," she replied, "I'm not saying it is the case, but just that it might be. There could be a link."

"Could be... might be," Smudge said with a tinge of sarcasm, "If I worked on 'could be' and 'might be' I'd... well, I'd have criminals running circles round me and laughing as they did it!" His mouth spread into a grin and then he laughed. Ruth ignored him.

"Also, there's other things, sir," she continued.

Smudge adjusted his collar and shifted uncomfortably. The smile faded from his face.

"I got the TV number, sir."

"What?"

"The TV number, sir," she repeated.

"I didn't see you write it down."

"It's here, sir," and she tapped her temple with her forefinger, "They taught me at training school to remember things like that. WTF 565 04. That's the number, sir. And if it's stolen it could be traced."

Smudge frowned. This was going from bad to worse.

How could she remember that number? She was putting him to shame.

"Also, sir," she carried on, "Did you notice that when you mentioned bananas he glanced away? Only for a split second, but he did. Did you notice, sir."

"Of course," Smudge lied.

"A sign of guilt, sir," she said, "Well… could be."

"Absolutely," Smudge agreed, "Well spotted."

"Also, there were strange things about that house, weren't there, sir?"

"There were," he agreed, not knowing what she was talking about, "What did you think?"

"Things out of place," she said, "Obviously the expensive TV. You picked that one up yourself, sir. But other things that were too expensive for people living in this area… and with Jeff Marks out of work as well. Lots of things. Like that clock in the kitchen; the bedroom furniture; that china set."

"I know what you mean," he said nodding again.

"And those pens!" she exclaimed, "He's a fool to leave them in view. Alright, they were up on a shelf… but not really hidden. If I was a criminal I'd put them completely out of sight."

"Pens?" asked Smudge finding it hard to hide his confusion.

He was so distracted that he almost ran into the back of the car in front but broke just in time.

"Yes, the pens," she continued with enthusiasm, "What does he want with high quality fine black ink pens like that? They're not cheap, sir. He's either an artist specialising in miniature pen and ink drawings… and there were no signs of that being true… or else he uses them for forgery. I learnt that at training college, sir. Pens like that in a suspect's house… well that's extremely suspicious, sir. Who knows what he forges? … documents perhaps… false IDs."

"Is that all, Miss Anderton?" Smudge asked, hoping her answer would be 'yes'.

"Not quite, sir," she said.

Smudge sighed.

"Well, sir, that old Divco truck was stolen in south Orlando, wasn't it?"

"Yes, in North Derment Avenue in Kissimmee," said Smudge, pleased to show some knowledge, "From someone's front drive."

"And he lives... our friend Jeff Marks... in Sharnfore Road," she continued, "What does that tell you?"

He wished she hadn't asked him. What was the answer? What was she talking about now? His mind went blank. He decided to avoid the question.

"Why's the traffic so busy today?" he mumbled.

"Stations, sir!" she announced, ignoring his comment, "Stations!"

"What?"

"There's a train station very close to where he lives... you know, Apopka... and there's one in Kissimmee. They must be forty miles apart, but by train, well, it's a nice easy journey. He steals a truck, and then off to Naples for a quick crime. The evidence begins to collect."

"But, Miss Anderton," Smudge regained his composure and assumed his superior attitude, "You can't arrest a man for living near a station."

"No, but we ought to check him out, don't you think, sir?"

"Yeah," said Smudge.

He knew he had been shown up; badly shown up. But his pride stopped him from following her ideas with any enthusiasm.

"I'll get the lads to find out what they can about him."

"But isn't it more important than that, sir? You know... with the blood in the back of the truck?"

"Yeah, maybe," he conceded.

Ruth looked enthusiastic. "Shall I ask them now, sir?" she asked, reaching out for the intercom.

"No, I'll do it," he snapped, "I'll do it when we get back to the station. I know there's blood... but it's most likely someone's just hit their head or something. No, we'll do it my way. Quietly and softly, and if he is involved we'll find out in due course. Investigation is a matter of working at it steadily and methodically, Miss Anderton. Gathering facts through research and interrogation and... and... er... observation. Moving on to analysis, elimination and conviction. It's like casting a net around the criminal until they have nowhere to run. Nowhere, Miss Anderton."

With these words the conversation ended. They finished the rest of their journey to the Orlando Police Headquarters in silence.

Friday 8th August   2.40 p.m.

Max McMurphy sat at his desk in his office reading some letters. He signed one and placed it on top of a neat pile to his right. He liked things in order and under his control. The desk was tidy and so was the spacious room which hung with the pungent smell of cigar smoke. He only smoked expensive cigars as a matter of principle; you had to be rich to afford them.

He stood up, tapped his forefinger twice on his cigar to shake the burnt tobacco into the ashtray and turned to look out of the window behind him. His office was on the fifth floor and there, spread out before him, was a panorama of his kingdom; the buildings of Cape Canaveral Air Force Station and in the distance, beyond the office buildings, was the launch pad where the Jupiter AM-13 rocket would carry little Gordo into space. To the left of that stood the distinctive landmark of the Cape Canaveral Lighthouse with its unique black and white paintwork.

As McMurphy glanced proudly across all this, a light shower was falling, catching the sunlight to create a rainbow. Oblivious to this beautiful scene, his eyes dropped to the car park below. He found he had to keep checking to make sure it was true; that very morning he had collected his new black and grey Rolls Royce Silver Wraith Parkwood Limo. It glimmered with luxury in the afternoon sunlight. He had achieved part of his dream.

The phone rang. He sat down and picked up the receiver.

"Max McMurphy here," he said.

"This is Brenda Haslett from Collins Worldwide Advertising Agency."

"Aaaah," purred McMurphy, "You've received my letter?"

"Yes, and we are extremely interested. This space monkey - when is it going up?"

"December 13th."

"And when would you have it?" asked Brenda Haslett.

"Well," McMurphy began, thinking it out as he spoke, "Well, let's see. The actual flight only lasts fifteen minutes… then after he lands…"

"Fifteen minutes!" Brenda interrupted, sounding shocked, "I thought you said it was going into space?"

"It is," replied McMurphy still sounding charming, "Rockets travel extremely fast, Miss Haslett. The monkey will be weightless in space for eight minutes."

"So when will you have it?" she asked again.

"Well... he'll need to be tested and so on, after the flight... and recover, of course. The 13th is a Saturday... so the following week? Does that sound alright? Say Tuesday or Wednesday?"

"Fine, and by that time it'll be even more famous!"

"Yes, that's right, Miss Haslett," McMurphy was smiling with glee, "The whole world has got its eyes on this one. If this is a success it opens the doors for men to go up next."

"There's one thing though. Will the monkey survive the trip?"

"It's looking good," McMurphy said, taking a puff on his cigar, "Very positive. All the signs are there that it will go well and yes, the monkey will survive."

"Excellent."

"So shall I contact you then?" asked McMurphy smiling.

"As soon as possible after the flight," Brenda said, sounding pleased, "I have about fifteen clients waiting. Big, big companies. He's been in the news so much already, but after the flight... well, he'll be a household name. And they love the golden fur on his head! The most wanted advertising tool. This could be massive. Are you ready to retire, Mr. McMurphy?" she joked.

"Maybe," he laughed, "I thought this could be big but it's exceeding my expectations. Thank you, Miss Haslett, I'll be in touch."

"Goodbye, Mr. McMurphy."

"Goodbye," he said and put the phone down.

The smile on his face grew into a beam. He gripped his fingers into a fist and let out a cry of anticipation for the money that would come his way. The cigar flew out of his hand and he quickly picked it up and placed it on the ash tray.

The intercom on his desk buzzed. He pushed the button and Jean Smith's voice spoke.

"Are you all right, Mr. McMurphy? I heard a shout."

"Yes," he replied calmly and just about managing to contain his excitement, "I'm fine thank you, Jean, just fine. Absolutely fine. Could you bring in a bottle of champagne and if you'd like to join me, bring two glasses."

"Well, thank you, Mr. McMurphy sir, but what are we celebrating?"

"Something has just turned out well - very well indeed. But never you mind about that, just bring the champagne."

He took his finger off the button and leant back in his chair, nudging his glasses up his nose. He pushed a foot against his desk and his chair spun around a complete circle. With a big smile still on his face he closed his eyes and gleefully thought of all the money coming his way.

Monday 11th August   9.30 a.m.

In the main office of Orlando Police Headquarters there were sixteen desks and about half of them were being used. The room was buzzing with conversations and activity, with people moving back and forth on various tasks. Smudge sat casually at his desk which was somewhere between being organized and chaotic. There was a great untidy pile of papers on his right that needed his attention, but at least they were stacked together. In front of him was a fishing magazine, which he was leafing through with interest. A blue wisp of smoke rose from his cigarette as he crushed it into the ashtray amongst a dozen other butts.

He leant back in his chair and in a moment he had drifted off on a daydream where he was fishing on his favourite riverbank.

A voice close by made him look up suddenly from his desk.

"Stolen, sir."

It was Ruth Anderton. His face tensed. She was becoming a thorn in his side.

"What is?"

"The TV," she replied brightly.

He looked puzzled.

"You know," she continued, "Marks' TV… the colour one… remember?"

"Yes, yes," he said impatiently, "Well that's no surprise.

Right then, Miss Anderton… you are about to witness your first arrest. We'll pick him up later today. Later, mind you… there's no need to rush. Now what happens at an arrest is this…"

"But, sir," she interrupted, still sounding bright, "Is that wise? At the moment he's a homicide suspect. We mustn't arrest him for a petty crime like stealing a TV, or accepting stolen goods… because we want him for the bigger crime… so surely we ought to wait, build up the evidence, watch him, find out what he's really up to."

For a moment they looked at each other. He knew that she was right, of course, but losing face to her made him cringe inside. He wanted to stay in control.

"Well done, well done," he acknowledged, "Yes, you're learning well. We'll hold back on this one for the moment."

She nodded.

"Now," he said decisively, "We've got a busy day. Only minor crimes, yes, but they need attention."

He peeled some of the papers from the top of his pile and read them.

"Let's see now… there's a burglary in East Dyman Avenue, Winter Park… a complaint about domestic noise in Eatonville… and a tip-off about thirty-three stolen kettles… it says here that one's turned up – lady bought it from a door-to-door salesman. These things need dealing with but I've got a few things to do first… be back here in ten minutes and we'll get to work."

Miss Anderton gave a pointed look at the open fishing magazine on his desk and looked at her watch.

"I'll be back in ten minutes exactly."

She hurried off through the busy scene and he watched her go. As soon as she had left the room, he started leafing through the fishing magazine again. After a while, he reached down to his case, pulling out an envelope he had received in the post that morning. Today was his birthday and he knew who this card was from; he had recognized the handwriting immediately. He placed it in front of him, on top of the magazine, looked around the room and tried to gather his strength.

Through his life he had dealt with many difficult situations. He had faced hardened criminals, even murderers on several occasions. He had witnessed violence and clamped the handcuffs on the wrists of a variety of lawbreakers. But somehow, this was the most difficult situation of all and now he felt he could not face it. He sighed despondently, picked up the envelope and dropped it into the bin.

Guilt swept through him like a wave over a sand castle, destroying his attempt to turn his back on his daughter who he had not met for almost four years. He was surprised by the power of his rising emotion. He reached down into the bin, lifted out the envelope and opened it quickly before he had time to change his mind.

The picture on the card was a country scene with a river winding into the distance. It was a beautiful sunny day. A man was fishing on the bank, his line tight with a catch as he leant back to pull it in. He opened the card and read the message:

To Dad

Happy Birthday
and Happy Fishing!

From Emma,
your loving daughter xx

1438917

At the bottom of the page was a phone number: 1438917. He had not seen her or spoken to her since he left the family home in 1954. Emma had been 18 at the time and he had walked out following several miserable years of arguments with his wife and daughter. The good times, the early years when Emma was younger, seemed lost and gone forever. In those days he called her 'my little angel', but after this everything had gone wrong. Now she wanted to speak to him, to meet him, to start again. This annoyed Smudge. He felt guilty for leaving and cross with her for all the arguments. For these reasons, he dug his heels in and ignored all her attempts to get in touch with him.

"Sir."

Smudge jumped. Ruth was standing in front of his desk. She glanced down at the card.

"Your birthday, sir?" she smiled.

"None of your business," he snapped back.

He slipped the card back into the envelope and put it on the pile of papers. Ruth was now staring at the fishing magazine.

"Ready for work, Miss Anderton?" he asked.

Tuesday 19th August   10.55 a.m.

Max McMurphy lifted his cup and took a sip of coffee. With a push of his foot he swivelled his luxury chair so that he was facing away from his desk and could see out of the window. He gazed out at the view and could not resist dropping his eyes to look smugly at his new Rolls Royce. A few crumbs of biscuit rested on his black suit which he brushed off casually and then turned his mind to the consideration of his plans.

The scheme involving Gordo was turning out to be much bigger than he thought at first. The advertising world was lucrative and if all went well he could rake in a fortune. He wanted to make absolutely sure that everything did go smoothly.

His mind reached into the future and traced his scheme through to the end. On the way, there were people who might oppose him and he thought of ways to overcome these hurdles. He considered carefully the most important part of the plan; he had to make sure he could get the monkey after the flight. He pondered this for a while and tried to think of anyone who might get in his way.

His mind kept returning to the young lady who was in charge of the monkey's training and looking after him. She might agree that he could take the monkey as a pet but if she resisted this, his plans could fall apart. He felt determined that one young lady was not going to ruin it all.

He had to do something about her. What he needed was

a threat that would scare her into doing what he wanted. He could threaten to sack her and he could bribe her by offering her money but this was not guaranteed to succeed. There was too much at stake to risk it.

He looked up at the clouds and at that moment the idea came to him, a flash of inspiration and he knew what to do. The idea was simple and easy for him to arrange. It made him smile and then chuckle.

He swivelled his chair around so that he was facing his desk and pulled out a notebook from his inside suit pocket. He pushed up his glasses and then flicked through the pages until he found the number he wanted. Reaching out for the phone he picked up the receiver and dialed 9 for an outside line followed by the number.

A man answered in a sharp, unfriendly voice. "Hi."

"Ron?" asked McMurphy.

"Yeah, who is it?" asked Ron.

"It's Ricky here," said McMurphy.

"Oh, Ricky," Ron said, his voice transformed into exaggerated friendliness, "How are you, buddy?"

"OK, thanks. I've got a job for you…"

"Yeah…?" said Ron, "I'm a busy man you know… plenty of work and no time to spare."

"But it's something small and quick, and good money too," stated McMurphy, "I'll pay you well for this one."

Ron sighed. "You know I'm always ready to oblige. Always ready to help a friend out in times of need. But listen, buddy, I've got a lot on…"

"Ron!" McMurphy interrupted, raising his voice, "Do we always have to go through this?"

"What?" Ron asked in mock surprise.

"This old bargaining routine. Just tell me your price?"

Ron laughed. "OK, buddy. What's the job?"

"It's a piece of cake. Simple break in. Private house, probably no alarm. One young girl lives there. Interested?"

"Depends," Ron said, "I might be if you make it worth

my while. My time is precious."

"A thousand... plus you keep whatever you can steal. Also, break a few things while you're there. Especially if they're expensive things as I want to hurt her financially. But don't overdo it - be discreet. Also I need info. Anything about her that might be... well... usefully used against her, if you see what I mean."

"Not just theft but bribery and blackmail as well, eh?" said Ron, "That's nasty stuff. One thousand? You've got to be kidding! I've got to risk my neck hunting through drawers. Three thousand and I'll do it."

"Two," said McMurphy quickly.

"Two and a half."

"Two thousand, two hundred and fifty, and that's it."

"Done!" said Ron, "Two thousand, two hundred and fifty dollars exactly. Sold to the man with the Rolls Royce!"

McMurphy gasped in shock and sat up in his chair. "How did you know that?"

"I know who you are, Mr. Maximus Patrick John McMurphy," stated Ron, "You were born on February the twelfth 1903 – and what a sad day for the world that was! And I know all about you... and everything you get up to. All the games you play to make yourself wealthy. I know where you live and where you work."

McMurphy opened his mouth to speak but he was so stunned he did not know what to say.

Ron continued. "It's just my own little insurance against you in case you get silly ideas and don't pay. Everyone needs insurance. If ever you try a quick one on me... well... now you know what will happen. So... the agreement is two thousand, two hundred and fifty... half before and half on completion. Meet at the usual place, at 7 tonight... bring the address and the money... and check if there's an alarm. If there is that's an extra three hundred."

McMurphy was fuming. "You didn't say that just now."

"Well, now I have," stated Ron, "Take it or leave it."

"OK," agreed McMurphy, "But no more extras. When will you do it?"

"Some time next week."

"And if it goes wrong…" said McMurphy slowly, "You don't know me… OK?"

"Of course, buddy," said Ron with surprise, "All the usual rules apply… that's how I work. You can trust me. But nothing will go wrong. I'll see you tonight then, Mr. McMurphy?"

"Sure."

McMurphy replaced the receiver, shook his head in frustration and then thumped his fists on the arms of the chair in anger. For a moment, he was still, breathing deeply and trying to relax. He was powerless to do anything about Ron, but after this job he would sever all connections with him by not dealing with him again. The problem would go away.

He reached out and pushed the intercom button.

"Yes, sir?" asked Jean.

"Coffee!" he snapped.

Thursday 21st August   8.15 a.m.

The morning rose softly, bringing bright, summer sunshine to warm the white sands of Cocoa Beach. The waters of the Indian River Lagoon were calm today. Little waves lightly lapped at the beach's edge with a gentle rhythm which would soothe any anxious mind as surely as it was smoothing the sand. On the mainland, the city of Rockledge was stirring, rested and refreshed from the night, and now poised for the activities of a new day. Belstone Lane, where

Rachel lived, was a short road with houses running all along it on both sides as it curved gracefully east to west.

Rachel's front door opened and she stepped out into the bright morning. As she pulled the door closed behind her, she felt the warmth of the sun on her skin and paused to look around. It was a beautiful day with a clear, blue sky above. She breathed in the fresh air deeply and then leisurely exhaled.

She smiled; life was wonderful. Her work with Gordo was always enjoyable, she loved the house she lived in and she had some good friends.

Then a thought entered her mind and momentarily dampened her high spirits; she was in debt and finding it hard to pay the bills. She was paid well but before getting her present job she had borrowed money to finance her expensive trip to South America to study squirrel monkeys. After this, circumstances had worked against her and now she was struggling.

The singing of a bird cut through her heavy thoughts and made her look up. As she listened to the cheerful birdsong, she felt uplifted and her money problems seemed less important again. With another smile, they melted away into the summer day and her burden was gone. She walked to her car feeling happy again.

She reversed out and headed off to Cape Canaveral, passing a white, parked truck with 'Henley Plumbing - Family Business' written on the sides and back.

A few minutes passed.

The truck moved slowly along the road and parked by her house. A workman, with Henley Plumbing written on the back of his white overalls, stepped out. He carried a bag of tools as he cut across the garden and walked casually around to the back of the house.

8.35 p.m.

"It's curious, miss," said the policeman.

Rachel was sitting opposite him at the table in her kitchen, her eyes red with crying and a tissue in her hand. Jamie was there too, leaning against the worktop. The policeman who faced her took a sip of coffee.

"Very curious…" he continued, "To go through your private papers. One would expect everything of value to go, which it has… but private papers!" He shook his head. "And all the damage done! The electrics will take some sorting out… the fuse box smashed and every wire cut or pulled out! This is more than just a simple burglary. Thieves just take what they want and get out as quickly as possible but this one spent time systematically vandalising your home, miss. Do you have any enemies, miss?"

"No," Rachel replied, looking surprised by the question.

"Are you sure?"

"Yes," Rachel nodded.

The policeman took a last gulp of coffee, tipping his mug back to drain it all and then putting it down on the table with a bump. He stood up and eyed Rachel intently. He turned to address Jamie.

"And you, young man," he said, "Any ideas on this?"

Jamie brushed his black hair out of his eyes. "No… 'coz who'd dislike Rachel? Everybody likes her."

The policeman turned back to Rachel.

"Maybe you'll think of something," he said, "Someone

has got it in for you and if you can think who it might be then let me know, won't you?"

Rachel nodded again and stood up as well.

"I think we've done all we can here," the policeman said, and then turned his head to call through the doorway, "You finished in there?"

A voice said, "Yes."

"I'm sorry about this, Miss Chandler," he said kindly, "It's not fun. You've lost a lot today and it'll cost to sort it out. But you can claim it on insurance."

Rachel shook her head and sighed.

"No, I'm afraid not... my payments have lapsed."

The policeman shook his head again. "Now that is a shame. Have you got some friends to help you out?"

"Yes," said Rachel, "I think so."

"We want to catch whoever did this. So, think hard and let me know... I'm Officer Gillet, OK?"

"OK, officer," said Rachel.

The policeman's boots rapped on the kitchen floor as he left the room, calling to the other policeman, "Let's go."

The door closed behind them and Jamie walked around the house to see the damage. Rachel sat down again. She slumped forwards over the table, her head resting on her arms. For a few minutes she stayed there, occasionally shaking as the emotion welled up and tears flowed. When she stood up her face was tear-stained but expressionless. She made herself another cup of coffee and sat down again to reflect calmly upon the break-in to her house.

Jamie came back into the kitchen and sat beside her. They sat for a while in silence, Rachel sipping her coffee. She was the sort of person who bounced back from difficulties. Her cheerful countenance and positive outlook gave her strength; she would not let this get her down and she would deal with it in a practical way.

Rachel looked up at her cousin.

"I guess you'd better go," she said.

"No, not yet," Jamie replied, "I can't leave you like this. I'll help you tidy up."

Rachel smiled at him. With Jamie's support she felt calm and strong now. "Thank you so much. Shall we start in the lounge?"

"Yep… let's go."

September… October… November

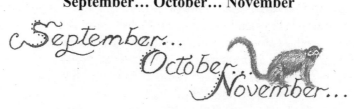

The next few months passed by and the launch date of the rocket grew closer. The burglary of Rachel's house made life extremely difficult for her financially. She had borrowed money to repair all the damage and now the repayments drained her wages every month. There was a hole in the roof of the house which leaked every time it rained and the water would seep through, dripping from her bedroom ceiling. She moved her bed to the other side of the room and would listen to the rain splashing into a bucket as she drifted off to sleep.

She decided that the only solution was to put her house on the market. In the meantime, until a buyer could be found, she managed by being very economical.

In spite of these difficulties, Rachel retained her bright, happy character most of the time. She refused to let it effect her work and her care for Gordo. When she arrived at work each morning, she left her problems behind and enjoyed her days with the little monkey.

Gordo continued to enjoy his training too. He experienced simulated weightlessness, practiced wearing his space suit for long periods and spent many hours in the nose cone of the space ship. The scientists looked after him very

well. He was the reason for the whole trip; the purpose was to see how a monkey could cope with the stresses and strains of space travel.

Rachel treated him with the greatest respect and care. She would usually bring him a treat to eat when she collected him from his cage every morning. She made sure he had everything he needed. After the attempted night-time theft of Gordo, Greeber was posted outside his cage every night. He was pleased to take on the duty.

Jamie would visit Gordo on most days. When the summer holidays ended and he was back to school, he would cycle to the Cape Canaveral Space Centre as quickly as he could, straight after the final bell. During weekends he would get there early on Saturday and Sunday and enjoy both full days with his little friend. There would always be times when they were alone and could chat without the fear of being heard.

With all the care and attention, Gordo felt happy and safe. But in spite of this he still yearned for the free life which was natural to him. He longed to spend his days in a jungle. He knew that in due course, if all went well, he would enjoy swinging freely through the trees once again. Jamie had promised that he would make sure this happened after the space flight and Gordo trusted him completely.

Thursday 6th November   1.26 pm.

It was a hot humid day on the coast of east Florida with the temperature rising to 30°C. The grounds of Larshley Beach Hotel & Golf Club were now quiet as people ate lunch or sipped cool drinks indoors. In the restaurant Jo and George had just finished a meal and were drinking coffee. On the table beside George, lay his car keys and a copy of the Florida Post newspaper. He picked it up and started reading. When he was several pages in, something caught his attention.

"Hey, look at this," he said to Jo, passing the paper across to her.

She reached over, took the paper and smiled.

"A monkey, just like the ones living in the trees here…"

She scanned the article.

"It says it's going into space… it's called Gordo and nick-named Little Old Reliable… it will be the first monkey into real space… launch scheduled for December."

She studied the picture again.

"That's why it's holding onto that model rocket. Oh, look at that sweet face…"

"Maybe," said George thoughtfully, "It could be the one stolen from here…"

Jo looked back to the article and read it quickly.

"No, it says it was captured in Brazil."

Jo put the paper down on the table.

"I wonder what happened to the poor little monkey from here."

George shook his head, "I guess we'll never know."

After the meal they sat in the lounge and George finished reading the paper. Half an hour later, they left, pausing under the trees to look up at the colony of monkeys. George put the paper into a bin and they walked to their car.

The squirrel monkeys were high in the branches of the palm trees, quietly enjoying the hot weather. A young monkey, called Jojja, had been watching Jo and George, and saw them throw the newspaper away. The monkeys took pleasure in looking at human newspapers; they could not read them but enjoyed the pictures. However, it was usually a page that had blown on the wind, or if they were lucky several pages that they had to put together, so a complete newspaper like this one was quite a find.

The young monkeys would play games with the papers, showing off as if they were finding amazing news stories and then pretending to read them aloud to the others. This was why Jojja had her eyes fixed on the paper as it lay in the bin.

Since Gogo had been captured, the monkeys had been far more cautious in their forays down to the ground and the younger monkeys were banned altogether. But this was tempting. This was too tempting. Making sure the others did not see, Jojja eased her way down the tree. With a sudden burst of speed she was down, scampering to the bin, grabbing the paper and running up the tree again with her trophy.

All the other monkeys looked down at her, some with disapproving comments and others, mainly the youngest ones, with excitement when they saw the newspaper.

"Behave!" commanded the ancient Jabe, his white whiskers shaking with anger, "I've told you... I've ordered all of you young ones not go down there. Why did you do it?"

Jojja looked frightened and glanced up nervously at the old monkey. She was lost for words and in the end just held up the paper as her answer.

"A paper..." Jabe growled, "I've seen hundreds in my day, complete copies that is, with all the pages, and I tell you... it's not worth looking at them. Full of rubbish nowadays, they are. When I was younger there were some decent photos... not any more!"

Jojja looked up timidly. Jabe looked down with an expression of utter disdain and then loudly shouted at her.

"Rubbish!"

"Rubbish," agreed Yulla. She was sitting beside him and she placed a hand on his arm. "Calm down..."

"I am calm!" he snapped back.

"It's not good for your health to get so cross..." she continued and then looked down at Jojja with disdain. "Mind you... the behaviour of the younger generation tests my patience too."

Jabe growled.

Another monkey, called Hab Dab had grabbed the paper and torn it out of Jojja's little hands. He opened it and began leafing through, 'reading' pretend stories as he turned the pages.

Then he gasped in shock.

"Look at this!" he exclaimed.

In a moment all the monkeys were bunched around the paper and trying to see.

"It's Gogo!" said Hab Dab, "It's him! It's definitely him. He's sitting on a rocket!"

"What's a rocket?" asked one.

"If only we could read it," another commented, "What does it mean?"

"It means he's still alive," Hab Dab replied, and then added thoughtfully "But why is his photo in a newspaper?"

They passed the paper around as they chatted about it and tried to work out what it was about.

Friday 21st November   8.45 p.m.

In the lounge of the small house in Sharnfore Avenue in Orlando, Jeff sat with his wife Mary-Anne as the heavy rain rapped on the window pane. He had sunk deep into his armchair and drifted off to sleep, his head tilting to one side. Mary-Anne was watching TV from her armchair and sipping a mug of tea when the phone rang. She got up, walked into the hall and picked up the receiver.

"Hello," she said.

"Hello Mary-Anne, it's Frank here. Can I speak to Jeff?"

"He's out," snapped Mary-Anne.

Jeff had woken up at the sound of Mary-Anne talking.

"Who's that?" he called out.

"No he's not," said Frank, "I heard him!"

"He doesn't want to speak to you," she said crossly, "Not after all that stupid business with the monkey and him getting shot in the leg. And the cops visited us about it. He's only just walking again."

"Ask him," Frank persisted, "Ask him if he wants to speak to me. He's a grown man isn't he...?"

Jeff got up and limped into the hall. He grabbed the phone from Mary-Anne and snapped into the receiver.

"Frank, I told you that I don't want to have anything more to do with you."

Mary-Anne nodded in agreement.

"You tell him, Jeff," she said.

She went upstairs and pretended to go into the bathroom. She closed the bathroom door and then tip-toed into their bedroom and picked up the phone.

"Listen," Frank spoke quickly and with urgency, "It's a really good one this time and it's worth a lot... a lot of money. This isn't peanuts this time. Big money. It'll set you up nice for a while. You..."

"But," began Jeff, speaking quietly so that Mary-Anne would not overhear. He glanced up the stairs and lowered his voice even more. "It always goes wrong with you... always!"

"What?" asked Frank, "I can't hear you."

"I said..." said Jeff speaking slightly louder, "It always goes wrong with you."

"Not this time. I tell you, this is a good one. You remember that monkey?"

"How could I forget, Frank? I've got a bad leg to remind me."

"And I've got a bullet hole in my hat," Frank added

crossly.

"Is that all?" asked Jeff, "My leg hurts every day… every day! How would you like a bullet through your leg?!"

"More important is - did you go to the hospital?"

"No – Mary-Anne looked after it."

"Good," Frank sighed with relief, "They might have traced you…"

"Is that all you can think about! I'm limping now and…"

"Anyway," interrupted Frank. "It's going into space - the monkey that is. 'Gordo' it's called. You must've seen it in the papers. And it's golden head… we picked the right one there… that makes it even more special! And I know a man… a rich man… he buys cars like you buy sweets. He doesn't know what to do with his money, Jeff. Well… he wants it."

"What? The monkey?" asked Jeff.

"Yes. He wants the monkey that's going into space. Come to think of it… it'd be better still to get it for him after it's been into space. He'd pay more… definitely. Anyway… he's loaded. He's got cars and boats and planes and art and everything. He thinks this would outdo all his friends. And he'll pay good money. It's all arranged, more or less."

"What do you mean 'more or less'," Jeff said, sounding sceptical.

"Look, he wants it, OK. All we have to do is get it. Interested?"

"I don't know, Frank, Mary-Anne said I mustn't even see you again and…"

"Forget Mary-Anne," Frank sounded desperate.

"What?!" Jeff sounded cross, "Forget my wife!?"

"Don't be soppy. You're a grown man now, Jeff. This is your decision and its big money this time. Big money. Mary-Anne… well, she'll love you even more when you buy a new house and give her clothes and things. This one's big… it's the big one. It'll make everything else you've ever done seem… well… pathetic. Honestly. You can be in on this one, Jeff. I'm doing you a real favour an' you'll thank me for the rest of your life. I'll pay you what I owe you, but that'll seem like peanuts when this one happens."

"You'll pay me what you owe me, Frank?" asked Jeff, "Before this job?"

"Yes. I'll pay you before the job... I promise."

There was a pause whilst Jeff thought about it. He certainly needed the money, in fact, he was desperate. He glanced up the stairs again.

"What about the cops?" he asked, "They called on me, you know."

"Did they arrest you then?"

"No," Jeff replied.

Frank snapped abruptly, "Well then, what's the problem?"

"It makes me nervous, that's what."

"Don't worry. Listen, what about this job? Will you do it?"

Jeff sighed and thought about it again, "I'll need to think about it, Frank."

"No time. Decide now or I get someone else. And they'll get all that money."

There was a pause. Frank waited.

"OK then, I'll do it."

"That's great, Jeff. It'll work... honestly," said Frank sounding relieved. "It's the best decision you've ever made."

"When do we break in?" asked Jeff.

"It's a little more complicated than that. We'll have to meet to plan it out, especially if we steal it after it's gone into space. Can we meet, say... tomorrow?"

"Next week, else Mary-Anne will be suspicious," said Jeff.

"Monday then, six-thirty at Murray's. I'll buy you a meal and tell you all about it."

"And pay me what you owe me?"

"Of course."

Upstairs, Mary-Anne put down the phone. She crept

quietly to the bathroom door, opened it and closed it loudly, and then descended the stairs.

"Bye then, Frank," said Jeff, and then, hearing Mary-Anne coming down, he added crossly, "And I don't want to hear from you again. Is that clear?" He slammed the phone down in mock anger.

"We won't be hearing from him again!" Jeff said to Mary-Anne.

She sat down in front of the TV again, thinking about what to do.

Tuesday 25th November   2.45 a.m.

Orlando was bathed in pale moonlight. A gentle breeze moved the warm air through the streets and rippled the surfaces of the hundreds of small lakes that dotted the great city. The roads were empty as the city slept.

South Amber Street was deserted. An ambulance moved onto it, turning left off Turforle Avenue. The engine echoed in the quietness of the night as it proceeded towards Orlando Hospital. It turned into the hospital grounds and drew up outside the Accident Department. The driver got out, glanced at his watch, and walked into the building. It was a typical hospital with all the usual sights and smells. A corridor with a shiny floor ran away from him and displayed department signs at every turning.

"OK, Ed?" enquired the young nurse at reception.

"Yep," he replied as he walked towards her desk.

She shook her head. "Another false alarm?"

"Not really," replied Ed, "He didn't need to come in though. Quiet tonight, isn't it?"

"Yeah… too quiet for me," she smiled, "I get bored you know. Nights like this are murder. I need to be busy."

She looked along the corridor where a lady sat with her bandaged arm resting on her lap.

"Still," she continued, turning back and resting her head in her hands with her elbows on the counter. She smiled at Ed. "I'm not bored any more with you around."

He beamed at her.

"Coffee, Donna?" he asked.

"Please," she replied.

"Right," he said, "Have you signed me in?"

She nodded.

"Thanks. I'll be back in a minute."

He walked down the corridor and disappeared into a room. Donna looked down at some papers. The entrance door opened and Jeff rushed in. He was carrying a bag over his shoulder and walked along the corridor.

Donna looked up.

"Can I help you, sir?" she enquired.

"No, I'm fine," said Jeff politely, carrying on walking, "Just visiting."

"At this time of night," she said, sounding surprised, "Who?" she asked.

"My uncle… he's not well, not well at all. He's on… er… Stewart Ward," he said, "Sounds like a person… Stewart Ward… doesn't it?"

He laughed as he walked past her.

"Name of the patient, sir?" she called out.

He was now past the desk and along the corridor. He called back over his shoulder, "It's alright. I know the way… second floor. But thanks."

Ed came out of the room carrying two mugs of coffee and saw Jeff turn at the end of the corridor.

He carefully carried the mugs of coffee to the reception

desk.

"Who was that?" he asked Donna.

"Just a visitor. But they shouldn't come this way, you know. What's wrong with the front entrance?"

"Yeah," agreed Ed, putting the mugs down, "Too lazy to walk 'round."

She nodded, "They treat this as a short cut."

Jeff climbed some stairs to the first floor, his feet echoing on the hard steps. At the top he looked right and left down the long corridors that stretched away from him. On the right there was someone walking towards him, so he decided to turn left where the corridor was empty. As he walked, he glanced through the glass windows on the doors. He was looking for something. He stopped by a door and took a closer look. He opened the door slowly.

"Can I help you?" said a voice.

"Um… Stewart Ward?" Jeff replied looking around the door at a white-coated lady who was taking a bottle down from a shelf. She shook her head and frowned.

"No, next floor up."

"Thanks," said Jeff and closed the door.

He walked quickly on along the corridor, stopping at another door and looking through the window. He passed into the room and glanced around. There was no one there. On the opposite wall was a row of hooks with various garments hanging on them. He moved swiftly over to them, lifted two white doctor's gowns off the hooks and checked to make sure they had identity badges on them. He moved his hand to remove a badge and then changed his mind, rolling both gowns into a bundle and stuffing them into his bag. He opened the door to leave and came face to face with a middle-aged doctor.

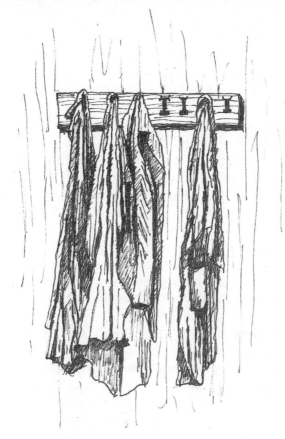

"Sorry," she said.

"No, I'm sorry," said Jeff, smiling nervously.

She looked at him carefully. "What are you doing?" she asked.

"Collection for the lab," he said, his mind reeling with panic.

She was blocking his way out.

"Rush... rush... rush," he said, "They suddenly demand... and it has to be done. I've got to get something over to the lab in a hurry."

He patted his bag, and immediately regretted it. Who would carry something to a lab in a tatty old bag?

Jeff felt the palms of his hands damp. She paused and looked at him intently. She knew this was wrong but she was afraid. She did not want a confrontation. Then she had a brainwave.

"Have you seen Dr. Chine?" she asked, knowing there was no such doctor.

"No, at least not… um… recently… sorry," he smiled uneasily, "Look… I've got to go."

He pushed past her and strode away down the corridor. The doctor went straight into the room, and over to the phone.

"Something's not right here," she thought.

She picked up the phone and dialed 1… 2… 3.

"Is that Security?" she asked.

Jeff hurried swiftly along the corridor, down the stairs and towards the main entrance. He was panicking. She must have noticed his nervousness. She was definitely suspicious. He started running. Two long corridors and he was out of breath with his heart thumping in his chest. He had to get out.

He noticed the reception nurse on the phone. She looked up, and straight at him, as he skidded to a halt. He immediately knew that she was being told about him, complete with description. He turned back on himself and ran.

A sign at the end of the corridor pointed a direction - 'Way out - East Entrance.' Would it be open at this time of night? He decided to chance it and ran at full pelt. He turned a corner and saw the way out ahead.

"Hey, you!" shouted a voice from behind, "Stop!"

He reached the exit door just as a uniformed guard appeared through a door just behind him.

"Stop!" cried the man as Jeff pushed the door open.

The guard lunged at Jeff and caught hold of his sleeve. Jeff twisted and pulled away, his jacket ripping as he broke free. He slipped out through the door and ran into the night.

CHAPTER 9

Tuesday 25th November   5.17 p.m.

The launch of the spaceship Jupiter IRBM AM-13 was now just over two weeks away. There was a growing confidence in the team of people involved because the project was going so smoothly. Nevertheless, as the date of the launch approached, they were working long hours to get everything organized and make sure that nothing was overlooked or neglected. They felt sure that Gordo would do well because he had cooperated perfectly throughout his months of training and successfully passed all tests.

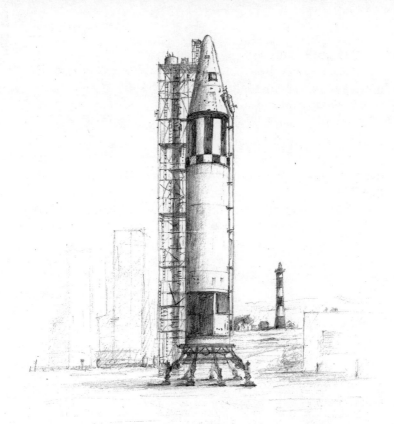

It had been a hard day for the team working on the Jupiter project. Rachel was sitting in the canteen with a cup of coffee. Ray had bought it for her and was facing her on the other side of the table. Jamie was with them too.

"You look tired," Ray said, smiling.

Rachel smiled back.

"It's been a long day," she said, "I feel exhausted. I had to come in early today. It's early to bed for me tonight! I just need to sit for a moment and relax."

Ray sipped his coffee and studied Rachel's face.

"Something's on your mind," he said, "What is it?"

"Money problems," she said with a sigh, "Jamie knows all about it."

Ray looked concerned.

"Since the burglary?" he asked.

"Yes. It was fine before that... well, just about. But now... I can't pay the bills so I'm having to sell my house."

Ray shook his head in sympathy.

"I would lend you some money," he offered, "If I could... but I've got none to lend!"

"I've saved some money," Jamie piped up, "I save everything you pay me for all the jobs I do. You can have that."

"That's kind of you both," she said. She gave her head a little shake as if to shake away the problem. "But don't you worry, Ray... I've borrowed some already. And, Jamie, I wouldn't dream of taking money from you. I'll get through it."

"I'm sure things will improve, Rachel," Ray said positively.

"Thanks," she nodded.

"Let me know if I can help in any way," he added.

"That's kind of you," Rachel replied, "I will. I know I can manage until Christmas and I just want to concentrate on Gordo until his flight's over."

"He's doing well, isn't he?" asked Ray.

"Very well," Rachel agreed taking a sip of her coffee, "Actually, he's amazing."

Ray looked absentmindedly around the canteen where there were a few people eating and drinking. He was wondering about Rachel, Jamie and Gordo.

"I know what you mean," Ray said, "About Gordo being amazing. He seems to be able to do everything, and get the hang of it so quickly. It's uncanny. I've never seen anything like it. But you're with him more than anyone, Rachel... and you, Jamie. Well... what's the secret? How does Little Old Reliable do it?"

He looked at Rachel quizzically and then at Jamie. He suspected that they were hiding something about their success and he was intrigued to find out what it was. Rachel liked Ray very much but there was nothing to tell. Jamie still wanted to share the secret with someone and was tempted to tell them both.

"It's… well…" he began, hesitating. He could not tell them; he had promised to Gordo. Rachel and Ray stared at him with interest until he continued. "It's… it's just that we get on so well. We have this understanding… you see, Gordo…"

"Rachel," called someone through the canteen door, "We've finished. Gordo's ready for you now."

"OK. Thanks, Mitch," she turned to Ray, "We'd better go."

Ray looked disappointed and looked at Jamie. "We can finish our conversation another time. OK?"

Jamie opened his mouth but before he could answer, Rachel spoke.

"Yep, OK. Perhaps tonight?" she asked hopefully, "After work perhaps. We could all meet here…"

"After work's no good for me," said Ray, "Sorry… I'm busy."

"Oh well," she said, "Never mind. Another time, maybe."

She stood up, pushed her chair under the table and leant on the back of it.

"Thanks for the coffee," she said to Ray, "See you tomorrow."

"Yeah. See you."

She turned and walked out through the tables and chairs followed by Jamie.

Rachel and Jamie took Gordo back to his cage, closed the door and locked it. A light shower fell dampening the path to the building. They were just standing by the pond and waving goodbye to Gordo, when they heard someone walking down the path behind them. They thought it would be Greeber arriving for his guard duty. Rachel looked up and was surprised to see the tall figure of Max McMurphy striding toward them. He was rarely seen out of his office so they wondered why he was here.

Max McMurphy was in no doubt as to why he was here.

"Hello, young lady," he said, ignoring Jamie and putting on a smile, "How are you Miss Chandley?"

He held out his hand.

"Chandler," said Rachel correcting him and shaking his hand, "How are you, Mr. McMurphy?"

"Fine," he smiled, "Just fine. It's wonderful, isn't it? A monkey going into space and all's going well! And I've heard you're doing a fine job with the little monkey."

"I try my best," Rachel replied, "He's very easy to work with, you know."

"Well, that's good," he remarked, stepping towards the cage and looking into it, "And I've heard about it. People say that it is such a good monkey - they even call it 'Little Old Reliable'!"

"They do," said Rachel, "But his real name is Gordo."

"Nevertheless," he said looking at her affectionately, "Your reputation is growing too. They say that you can get the monkey... um... Gordo... to do anything."

"As I said, I try my best."

"Where is Gordo?" he said, peering through his glasses, which were now dotted with rain, and looking for him, "They are wonderful creatures, don't you think?"

Rachel smiled and nodded. "He is wonderful, yes," she said with enthusiasm, "He's up there in the tree, in his nest - look."

McMurphy followed Rachel's finger, glanced up and spotted Gordo watching him.

"Oh yes, I see. He's looking down at me. Amazing little creature! And that golden fur on his head... that's pretty unusual isn't it?"

"I think it's unique," replied Rachel, "I've never seen it before."

"Ha," McMurphy laughed, "That is really something!

But have you thought what will happen to it after the flight?"

Jamie was suddenly on tender hooks. He hoped Rachel would say that Gordo would be set free. He opened his mouth to speak but Rachel spoke first.

"Yes, I'm glad to say I have, Mr. McMurphy. We'll set him free, of course. Somewhere where he can enjoy the rest of his life. I can't wait to see him climbing the trees. He'll deserve it, don't you think?"

"I'm sure he will, my dear," McMurphy looked down at the ground. His expression was thoughtful and concerned. "But do you think it would be wise?"

He looked up, pushed his dark-rimmed glasses higher on his nose with one finger, wiped some rain off one of the lenses and stared straight at her to see her reaction.

"But of course," Rachel replied, surprised by the question, "Why not? It would be the wisest thing to do… and the kindest."

McMurphy frowned. This is exactly what he had feared but he was prepared. He wanted the monkey and if she got in his way he had his plans already set. He had made sure her finances were in a bad way and now he could use money to force her under his will. He could sack her, or even bribe her if necessary. He would be ruthless.

"But…" he began, "I'm not so sure. Not sure at all. It's been locked up here for so long that it would never survive in the wild," he said decisively, "It's too… domesticated. It's used to humans now. It needs to stay in captivity… yes, being looked after as a pet. I'll have a nice big cage made for him in my garden - bigger than this one - and I'll give it the best food. It'll live like a lord! But, this monkey let loose in the wild! No, no, no. Think about it, young lady."

"I have," she answered with a decisive ring in her voice which showed her determination.

"Well then," he smiled at her, "Surely you must agree with me."

Rachel shook her head. "No. I don't. Not at all. You're

wrong about this. I know monkeys and how they react to situations. They…"

"Listen," he interrupted in mock kindness. He touched her on the arm and she pulled away. "Listen. I know how you feel, and it's nice that you feel that way. It's… kind… and considerate. I admire you for that. But, it's out of the question I'm afraid, my dear."

"But Gordo belongs in the jungle."

Jamie could resist no longer and he blurted out, "Yes! In the jungle! He must go to the j…"

McMurphy interrupted and turned on him with an angry scowl. His voice was as cutting as a brisk north wind. "You stay out of it," he growled, "It's none of your business."

"It is my business!" piped up Jamie.

"Shut up, boy!" snapped McMurphy, "What are you doing here anyway. Get off the premises… now!"

"I work here," retorted Jamie.

Rachel felt panic arising in her. She wanted to defend Jamie. She loved little Gordo and felt responsible for him too. She knew that to be back in the jungle was what he needed. But this man was powerful, the top man at Cape Canaveral. She felt she had to convince him. She tried to stay calm.

"He would be OK," she continued, "I know monkeys. I spent some months in Brazil studying them… actually in the jungle with them. He will be fine, I know that. I know he would settle quickly in a jungle. And besides, he deserves to go back to his freedom."

"I've made up my mind," McMurphy snapped, his voice becoming harder and more like a teacher telling off a pupil, "My mind is settled on this one."

"You can change your mind, Mr. McMurphy, and do the kindest thing for Gordo."

He shook his head. "I actually think… I am sure… that what I am proposing is the kindest thing for him."

"But… but…" Rachel began.

"No 'buts'. I didn't come here to argue with you," he

said, raising his voice and holding his hand up to signal a halt to her opposition to him, "And I'm not going to argue…"

"Well I am!" exclaimed Rachel.

Tears welled up in her eyes.

"Stop now," McMurphy snapped, "I strongly recommend, that if you value your job, you don't argue with me."

"But...."

"I said no 'buts'!" He spoke sharply and coldly now, his eyes narrowing and glaring at her with hate. He was not going to let this young woman spoil his plans. "After the trip I want him brought to me." The frown on his brow deepened as he spoke. "My wife and I will give him a good home. We'll look after him. We'll feed him well and have a large cage for him, like the one he lives in now. I've decided and that's that!"

"I will never bring him to you!" Rachel shouted. She had lost all respect for this man and even though he was her boss she was not going to be bullied by him. "Never! After the trip I'll set him free! It's the right thing to do!"

Jamie was full of admiration for Rachel's courage.

"We are headstrong, aren't we?" McMurphy sneered, "But you'll do no such thing. I have given you your orders!"

"I don't follow wrong orders!"

"Then, if you step beyond what I say, you step beyond Cape Canaveral." McMurphy's face was turning red with anger. "Your foolishness has just lost you your job!"

"Then the flight will be cancelled," said Rachel, pleased to be able to counter attack against this bully. Jamie nodded. "Gordo will only work with me. He only does things for me, and Jamie here! You ask the others - they'll all tell you."

"OK... OK." McMurphy realized that she was right and tried to calm down. "If the monkey is not brought to me after the flight then you lose your job, understand?"

Rachel did not answer and for a moment they stared at each other. Then he spoke again.

"I get the feeling that I've made my point!" he said firmly.

He turned and strode up the path and into the building. He would have to resort to the measures he had already prepared for; as soon as the flight was over he would sack her or bribe her, or he may have to use both. Then he would own the monkey, and the fortune from advertising that would flow into his bank account would be legally his.

He was also concerned about the boy and he would have to work out a way of dealing with him as well.

Rachel unlocked the cage and went back in. Gordo pulled himself out of his nest, climbed down the tree and into her arms.

"Why does he want you as a pet?"

She looked into his round eyes and smiled.

"He's up to something," she said, "He's got a plan of some sort."

"You're right," Jamie agreed, walking into the cage behind her, "He's devious. I'm sure there's more to this than he's telling us."

He stroked the little monkey.

"I promise you, Gordo," he stated, "He's not having you as a pet."

Thursday 27th November   1.15 p.m.

The main office of Orlando Police Headquarters was busy and noisy. Smudge sat at his desk looking glum. The neatly stacked pile of papers on his right had grown slightly taller. In front of him was a crime report which he was studying and to his left a new fishing magazine which he had bought on his way to the office. He pushed the report to one side in favour of the fishing magazine. A blue wisp of smoke rose from his cigarette as he crushed it into the ashtray.

The phone on his desk rang. Smudge sighed and then picked it up.

"Yes?" he snapped.

"Smudge?" asked a male voice.

"Yes?"

"Any news on that stolen Divco truck?"

Smudge sat up as he recognized the voice of his superior officer, Sergeant Tilson. "Stolen truck, sir?"

"Yes, Smudge, wake up!" snapped Sergeant Tilson, "The one with the blood in the back. Remember?"

"Yes, sir. Of course, sir." Smudge grimaced, "I have a lead I think, but nothing definite yet."

"It could be a homicide, Smudge. Serious stuff. I want this sorted and out of my hair. I've just had another phone call from Fred Huggett in Special Investigations. Next time he phones I want to give him something… like some solid facts for example… not just 'I've got a lead, I think.' Understand?"

"Yes, sir," Smudge said.

"So get onto it and let me know, OK?"

"Yes, sir," said Smudge again. He was not enjoying this phone call and was keen to put the phone down.

"Oh, and Smudge. One more thing. Make sure you have that new girl… er… what's her name?"

Smudge cringed and just about managed to say her name, "Anderton, sir."

"That's the one… Officer Anderton. Make sure you have her working with you on this one. Sounds like you could use some help and she's got the makings of a good cop."

"Yes, sir."

Smudge quickly put the phone down. He reluctantly put the fishing magazine in a drawer and closed it so that he would not be tempted. Then he reached out, slid the pile of papers towards him and started leafing through them. He was looking for the report on Jeff Marks. He had hated the phone call but at least it had lifted him out of his lethargy.

As he looked through the papers, an envelope slipped out from the pile. It was the birthday card he had received from his daughter four months ago and he had not looked at it since. He had put it out of his mind and then forgotten about it, but as his eyes rested on the writing on the envelope, the same intense emotion arose in him. He pulled the card out of the envelope, opened it and read it again.

The phone number jumped off the page.

He decided he would try to contact her now and his hand reached out for the phone. Then he hesitated and excuses started flooding in. She was bound to be out at this time; she would be cross with him for not contacting her sooner and that would lead to an argument; anyway, he did not really love her now… it had been too long; he needed to get on with his work.

He decided that it was not the right time but he would probably phone tomorrow. He put the card back into its envelope and slipped it into the drawer with his fishing magazine.

Friday 28th November   5.20 p.m.

Smudge knocked loudly on the front door of the house of Jeff and Mary-Anne Marks. Just behind him was his assistant, Ruth Anderton. He had seriously considered not taking her with him but knew that his boss, Sergeant Tilson, was likely to find out, so he reluctantly told her to come. She was so clever and sharp during their last visit that she was upstaging him and for a veteran of police work, this was very embarrassing. He was meant to be in charge and he constantly felt uncomfortable with her.

He felt tired and was in a bad mood. This was his last job of the day and he just wanted to get home and put his feet up. After he had rested, he would go fishing for a couple of hours. He knocked again and looked at the windows, first the ground floor and then above. Then he put his ear to the door and listened.

"They're out, Miss Anderton… out," Smudge snapped and brushed past her.

"But, sir…" she said as he strode down the path and into their patrol car.

Ruth shook her head and followed down the path, suddenly looking around at a bedroom window. She just saw someone jerk back out of view. She got into the passenger seat as Smudge started the engine and drove off.

"They were in there, sir," stated Ruth, "Or at least one of them."

"And if they were?" he asked her crossly, "What then? Break the door down? He's probably nothing to do with it. We have no facts, Miss Anderton."

Ruth knew that there was no point arguing with him so she sat in silence and spent the time thinking about the case. Smudge dropped her off at a bus stop and drove home.

CHAPTER 10

Monday 1st December   2.17 p.m.

A fierce storm blew off the Atlantic Ocean sweeping cold rain across the open land of the Cape Canaveral launch pads. It was a flat, open space, dotted here and there with trees which were swaying and shaking in the wind. Leaves, twigs and other bits of debris were sweeping through the air and tumbling across the ground. In the distance, a solitary rocket pointed skyward, stately and immovable, rooted on its launch pad in the wild, swirling scene of the storm.

The whole area was about 25 square miles.[1] Banana River ran along its western coast with a causeway linking it to a larger body of land where three main buildings stood; the International Space Station Centre, the Headquarters,

---

[1] See the 'Cape Canaveral' map at the beginning of the book.

and the Operations Centre and Checkout. This strip of land was in turn connected to the mainland by a bridge running across Indian River. The road across the bridge, the SR 405, led to the great city of Orlando. Driving along it towards Cape Canaveral, though the torrential rainstorm, was an 18 year old Ford Pickup truck.

Time had taken its toll on the truck, reducing it to a dilapidated state. It looked as though it had escaped from the breaker's yard and was about to fall apart. It was dented in several places and possessed a slight tilt of a few degrees from the horizontal. The body work was extremely rusty and it seemed to be a miracle that it was moving at all, especially through such wild weather.

The man behind the wheel was Frank Leemas, wearing his cowboy hat. He had carefully mended the hole where the bullet passed through the rim, stitching a patch of similar material over it. Sitting beside him in the passenger seat was Jeff Marks.

The rain was heavy but somehow, despite the truck being such a wreck, the wipers were sweeping it off both sides of the split windscreen.

"Slow down, Frank," said Jeff, "And put the lights on like everyone else."

It was early afternoon but due the storm and the driving rain the light was poor. Frank clicked a switch but only one headlight and one red rear light came on.

"You're still driving too fast!" complained Jeff.

"Stop worrying!" snapped Frank, glancing sideways and scowling at Jeff, "You're always fussing."

The truck jerked to the left and a car blared its horn as it flashed past in the other direction.

"Watch the road!" exclaimed Jeff, gripping the sides of his seat, "That was close. That was really close!"

"It was skilful driving," retorted Frank.

"Slow down!" Jeff shouted, "I don't want to end up drowning in the river."

They passed onto the bridge with Frank continuing at the same pace. The truck rattled across and when they were back on land Frank pulled up at the side of the road.

"Not far now," said Frank, peering through the windscreen, "Got the ID cards?"

Jeff nodded. "Here," he said, triumphantly pulling two ID cards out of his pocket.

"Who did them?" asked Frank.

"Me... I did," said Jeff.

"Oh no," sighed Frank, "Why are you always doing things on the cheap? If they're anything like those number plates you made!"

"But what about my delivery note," stated Jeff, "That fooled 'em."

"True," Frank agreed, nodding, "That was not exactly a masterpiece but just about good enough. OK then, Jeff, let's have a look."

He reached over and snatched the cards from Jeff.

"Hey... these aren't bad," he exclaimed holding them up and looking very surprised, "You did these?" he asked.

"Yep," smiled Jeff, "Piece of cake. I pinched them from a hospital. Just walked in and got them. They needed slight adjustments but I used my special pens... new names... new photos... and hey presto... there we are."

"I've seen better," said Frank, "But I've seen worse. They should do the trick if they don't look too closely."

"Also," added Jeff, reaching into his bag, which was by his feet on the floor, "These!"

He pulled out the two white doctor's jackets. "We'll really look the part in these."

"What part?" asked Frank.

"Scientists, of course. They need to think we are scientists, don't they?"

"Yeah, suppose so," Frank nodded, "OK, then."

They both slipped on the white jackets and dropped their ID cards into the pockets. Frank tried to start the engine. After several attempts it spluttered into life. It pulled away with a judder and they rattled on through the rain.

A drip of water fell from the ceiling onto the brim of Frank's hat. Then another fell, followed by another. The drips turned into a trickle. Frank chuckled.

"I'm sure glad I've got this ol' hat of mine!"

"There it is," said Jeff.

"Now," began Frank, "Don't rush to show him the IDs… keep him waiting in the rain and he probably won't look too closely. This weather is playing right into our hands."

They were approaching a checkpoint where a barrier blocked the road. It was the same one they had passed through many months ago with Gogo in the back.

"I've just had a thought, Frank," said Jeff, "What if it's the same guard, Frank, the same one who let us through last time we came here."

"It won't be," Frank reassured him, "And if it is, that's almost a year ago. He'd never remember, would he?"

Jeff quickly combed his hair in a different direction to his normal style but it hardly changed the way he looked at all. Frank took his hat off and leaking rain water spattered on his head.

They drew up in front of the barrier and eased to a halt. The guard came out of the hut.

"Oh no!" said Jeff, "It *is* the same one."

Frank wound down the window.

"Terrible day!" he exclaimed.

Rain was driving into the guard's face and he turned his face away from it.

"Terrible, sir," he replied, chewing on some gum, "Can I see your ID, please?"

"Oh, yes," Frank answered, "Hang on."

He pretended to search his pockets. The guard waited and held his hand out impatiently. He wanted to get back into the shelter of the hut as soon as possible.

"Sorry," said Frank, "They're a nuisance, aren't they? These cards, I mean."

He pulled his out of his pocket and held it up for the guard to see. He glanced at it and nodded.

"Have you got yours, Jack?" Frank said to Jeff.

Jeff started looking for his, which he really had lost.

The guard looked at the pickup.

"Holy Moly! This old banger has seen better days!" he remarked.

"Yeah," Frank agreed, "It still goes OK though."

Then the guard noticed the leak where a steady trickle of water was landing on Frank's head.

"Got a leak?" he asked looking at the roof from outside, "There's a hole there!"

He pointed with his finger.

"You want to get that mended, you do," he remarked. Then he had an idea. "I know…"

He smiled, took his chewing gum out of his mouth and pushed it into the hole.

Jeff found his ID card and passed it over to Frank, who held it out for the guard to look at.

The guard took it and studied it. Rain splattered on his hand and on the card. He hesitated, and then nodded.

"Thanks," he said, handing the card back. Then he stooped down and nodded to Jeff. "Thank you, sir."

"Thanks," said Jeff.

"How's that leak?" the guard asked.

The trickle had eased and had changed to a steady rhythm of drips.

Frank smiled, "Much better… thanks."

"You want to get rid of this old scrap heap before it falls apart."

Frank wound up the window and pulled away.

"Just as I thought," said Frank, "No problems."

He picked up his hat and put it back on.

"What do we do now?" asked Jeff.

"We snoop around a bit. You know, we need to make plans. We need to work things out. We need to watch and find out what we can. We have half the plan… now for the rest."

They drove past buildings on their right. First the Headquarters, and then the Operations Centre and Checkout, and finally the International Space Station Centre. They began to cross Banana River by the causeway.

"Frank," said Jeff, "The cops called on me again yesterday."

"What?!" Frank jerked in shock and turned to face Jeff. The pickup swerved into the wall of the causeway. There was a thud, and then a grinding sound as the pickup scraped against the wall.

"Get control!" screamed Jeff in a panic.

Something rattled and fell off as Frank pulled the pickup away from the wall and regained control.

"Sorry, but… the cops! Why didn't you tell me before?"

"It was nothing," said Jeff, relaxing again after the bump, "I didn't even answer the door! I could see them from above… the same balding Big Daddy with his young chick. They're just guessing."

Frank was cross. "How do you know that?"

"From the last time, you know, when they called on me a few months ago."

"So what did they ask you when they spoke to you then?"

"They were just fishing around. They asked me about that day when we caught that monkey and the day we tried to steal it again. They knew the dates. And they asked about the stolen truck."

"Jeff," Frank said looking alarmed, "Don't you realize? If they are linking those two things… this is serious. If they've come back… then they're suspicious. What did you tell them?"

"Nothing, Frank, honest. I denied everything."

"We'll have to lie low."

"What do you mean?" asked Jeff.

"Listen," Frank sounded earnest, "We are about to do the biggest job we've ever done. In fact… this is *the* big one. After this I retire. I'll go somewhere abroad where I can't be found. So, I'm not going to have *you* spoil it. We lie low, stay out of the way, go into hiding somewhere."

"Where?" Jeff did not like the sound of it. "And anyway, won't it be more suspicious if I suddenly disappear?"

Frank thought for a moment. The pickup trundled off the causeway.

"I need time to work it out," he said eventually, "I'll think of something."

"But, Frank," said Jeff, twisting around to look back along the road, "Don't we need to look around back there. That's where the monkey is kept."

"I've got a better idea," said Frank smiling, "A much better idea. Look there."

He pointed ahead.

"What?" asked Jeff, peering through the rain.

"That!" snapped Frank, "Look… that lighthouse."

"What about it?"

"It's perfect, isn't it?" Frank looked at Jeff and then back at the road. "The perfect lookout."

"Hmm, maybe, but won't there be someone in there?"

"I doubt it… not in the day," Frank stated. Then he added sarcastically, "They turn lighthouses on at night, remember?"

"That doesn't mean… well, there still could be someone there," said Jeff.

They arrived at the foot of the tall building, which towered above them like a rocket. It was the Cape Canaveral Lighthouse and was painted in six sections of black and white horizontal stripes. It stood more than 150 feet tall.

Frank pulled off the road and bumped onto the grass.

There was a small building close to the lighthouse and he parked beside it. He turned off the engine and pulled the hand brake but there was a crack as the cable broke.

"What a wreck!" complained Frank.

"Leave it in gear," said Jeff.

Frank pushed it into gear. The rain was still torrential and the strong wind rocked the old pickup.

"See," said Frank, "No cars… no one else here."

"That means it's locked, Frank."

Frank dropped his hand into his trouser pocket and pulled out a small, metal box.

"Always be prepared, Jeff," he smiled, "I've been practising. With this I can get into anywhere. Come on, let's go."

The two men stepped out of the truck and into the stormy weather. Rain lashed into them and their white doctor's jackets flapped in the strong wind. Frank threw his hat back into the truck, grabbed a bag and slammed the door.

They cowered from the elements and dipped their heads as they ran to the lighthouse entrance. Frank tried the handle of the double-doors.

"Locked," he shouted.

There were some outside steps curling around the lighthouse wall.

"Up!" commanded Frank. They clung on to the rail as they climbed the twenty-one metal steps and reached another door. By this time they were soaking, with their faces glistening and their hair flattened by the rain.

"Go on then, Mr. Fancyfingers, get us in," shouted Jeff, huddling against the door, "But make it quick."

Frank struggled to get his lock-picking box out of his pocket because his hand was sticking to the wet material. He tried using two hands, and jumping up and down to

shake it loose. Eventually, the box jerked out and he began working on the lock.

"Hurry up!" shouted Jeff.

After five minutes Frank had not succeeded and after ten, Jeff was getting more and more agitated.

"I thought you said you'd been practising…" he shouted.

Rain was dripping down Jeff's face and into his mouth as he shouted, "I'm soaking wet, Frank. We've tried… let's go!"

"No," Frank snapped, "Wait, I'm almost in…" He turned to face him and smiled. "Sweet success," he announced proudly, and opened the door.

They slipped inside.

Suddenly they were out of the blast. It was quiet and still. They looked up at the metal spiral stairs. Water dripped off the two men and splattered onto the floor. Jeff put his finger to his lips.

"Shh," he whispered, "There still might be someone here… either down there…" He pointed below. "That's where the keeper lives… or up there where the light is." He pointed up.

"Doubt it," replied Frank, "It's all locked up, isn't it? But I suppose we'd better take care."

They took off their wet doctor's jackets and put them into Frank's bag.

"Right then," whispered Frank, and he pointed up the steps, "Let's go."

Frank led the way and they began to climb. After about a hundred steps they paused to rest by one of the porthole windows. They sat down, breathing heavily.

"How much further?" whispered Jeff.

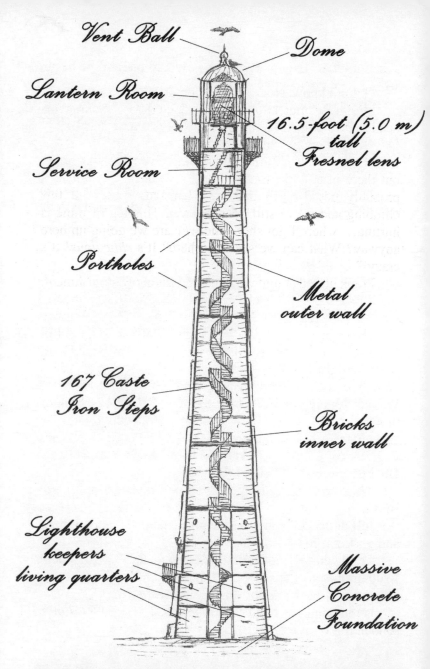

Vent Ball

Dome

Lantern Room

16.5-foot (5.0 m) tall Fresnel lens

Service Room

Portholes

Metal outer wall

167 Caste Iron Steps

Bricks inner wall

Lighthouse keepers living quarters

Massive Concrete Foundation

CAPE CANAVERAL LIGHTHOUSE
46 metres (151 feet) tall

"I don't know. Not much, I hope. It's getting narrower."

"Can't be much further," whispered Jeff shaking his head as he slumped on the steps, "This is crazy."

"It's not crazy," snapped Frank, "Not at all."

"Look," began Jeff, "I'm soaking wet after standing out there in a storm for half an hour waiting for you. I'll probably get ill. I'm tired... exhausted... after all this climbing and we're still not there yet. This leg of mine is hurting... where I got shot. And *why* are we going up here anyway? What can we see from here? It's *ridiculous!* It's crazy!"

Frank glared at him with an expression of astonishment.

"It's not crazy, it's clever," Frank began, "From the top we can see everything. We can plan. Think of the monkey and the money. Think... think... think. Your pockets full of money. Money under your mattress. Money in the bank. A decent car... no... more than that... a flashy sports number... a Corvette perhaps... open top... red and white. Would that suit you? Would that keep you happy? Think of that!"

Jeff reluctantly nodded his head and sighed. "Yeah, you're right I suppose. Yeah, I must remember the money. OK then."

"Also," whispered Frank, "It's nice and warm in here, isn't it?"

Jeff nodded. Then he suddenly remembered something and glared at Frank.

"And what about the money you owe me?" he snapped, "You promised."

Frank smiled. "Aren't I a man of my word?"

He slipped his hand into his pocket and pulled out a sodden roll of notes.

"Hey," said Jeff with surprise, "I'm sorry I doubted you."
Jeff took the roll of money.

"They're wet," he grumbled.

"They'll dry," said Frank, "Then they'll be as good as new."

Jeff began to put the money into his pocket and then pulled it out again.

He unrolled the notes carefully so as not to tear the wet ones. Then he began counting them.

"Can't you trust me?"

Jeff ignored him and carried on counting.

"880 dollars," announced Jeff, "That's 20 dollars short."

"Are you sure," said Frank looking surprised.

"I've just counted it haven't I?"

"OK, OK," Frank sighed, "So I owe you 20 dollars."

"And the petrol money. Don't forget that."

"OK," Frank nodded, "And the petrol money."

"And the money for all that oil we had to put in. Don't forget that either."

"Come on. Let's go," said Frank.

They started climbing again. Jeff was struggling with his bad leg and after about 40 more steps he was relieved when they reached the lantern room at the top. Frank was in front and stopped to listen. Then he cautiously poked his head up to look around.

"No one," he announced triumphantly, "Just as I thought."

They ignored the doors leading out onto the balconies and stepped up into the lantern room. The walls were made of panes of glass running from the ceiling to the floor, and in the centre was the massive light, standing more than twice as tall as them. It was like a beehive-shaped jewel and could send out a beam that could be seen far out at sea, up to 22 nautical miles away.

Jeff ran his hand along the light. "This would make a great bedside reading lamp, Frank."

Frank chuckled. "We ought to change our plans and steal this instead. How about it? It would be our best crime ever... our crowning glory."

"I'd give it to Mary-Anne for Christmas."

"Don't be stupid, Jeff. Think of the paper you'd need to wrap it up!"

They walked around the light until they were looking towards the buildings they had passed earlier. The rain lashed noisily against the glass behind them.

"The view's amazing," said Jeff.

They gazed out at the scene. They were both still out of breath after the climb and as they stood they gradually recovered. Jeff turned to Frank and leant back against the glass.

"It's a shame about the lousy rain though."

"Yeah, just our luck," grumbled Frank, "But we can still see everything from up here."

Jeff was gazing back across Banana River with his eyes slightly screwed up. "But we can't see much over there where they keep the monkey."

Frank reached out and took some binoculars from a shelf.

"But you can through these," he announced smugly.

He raised some binoculars to his eyes and rolled his finger across the wheel on the top to adjust the focus.

"Holy Mackerel! These are powerful," he exclaimed, "I can actually see into the offices."

"Can I look?" asked Jeff.

"Get yer own," said Frank, "There's more pairs on that shelf."

Jeff picked up another pair and gazed through them.

They watched the buildings and observed the movements of the people who worked there. They paid particular attention to the guards. As they watched they discussed their plans.

They were totally unaware that below them, someone was silently creeping up the steps. The person stopped just below the lantern room, sat down and listened.

3.25 p.m.

The rain was rapping on the window of Jean Smith's office as she picked up the phone and dialled.

A lady's voice answered. "Patrick Air Force Base."

"Good afternoon," said Jean, "Can I speak to Officer Charlie Scott, please?"

"I'll put you through, madam."

There was a pause.

"Officer Scott here," said a man's voice.

"Hi, Charlie," she said, "This is Jean here."

"Oh, hi! Aunt Jean," Charlie said with delight, "How good to hear from you. How are you and the family?"

"Oh, we're all fine, thanks," Jean answered, "I'm at work so I have to be quick… I'm calling to ask for a favour. It's a big one, but very important…" Then she added, "Of course, if you can't do it I'll understand."

"Aunt Jean!" Charlie exclaimed, "Of course I'll do it for you!"

"Don't say that… you don't know what it is yet and I don't want you getting into trouble."

Charlie laughed. "I don't mind getting into trouble for you. This sounds exciting… just what I like. So, tell me… I'm all ears!"

Jean took a deep breath. "I need a jet," she said, her words sounding very matter of fact.

"We've got plenty of those!" laughed Charlie, thinking it was a joke, "But, why, Aunt Jean… you taking up flying?"

Jean chuckled at the thought and then continued earnestly. "Charlie, I *really do* need a jet… seriously. It's not for a few days yet… and I need a pilot too, preferably you. Is it remotely possible do you think?"

Charlie's light-hearted tone changed into a more sober one. "You're serious, aren't you?"

"Definitely," stated Jean, "It's important… very important. Else I wouldn't ask. It's to do with a guy in a high-up position who's involved in crime. I'll tell you all about it, but is the jet possible?"

"As it happens," Charlie said thoughtfully, "Now that I'm an officer, I think I could possibly do it. I could count it as a training run I suppose 'cos I'm due for one. I'd need to know where and when… and of course why. Tell me more about this high-up criminal guy."

"OK."

"I'm all ears, Aunt Jean," Charlie was relishing the task. "Tell me the details."

4.20 p.m.

Frank and Jeff spent almost an hour studying the buildings through the binoculars and talking about their plans. Frank put his binoculars on the shelf where he had found them and turned to Jeff.

"So that's decided then?" he asked.

"I don't like it, Frank." Jeff shook his head, lowered his binoculars and looked at Frank. "I'm sure there must be another way."

"There isn't," Frank raised his voice slightly, "We've been through all that, haven't we?"

"Yeah, I suppose so." Jeff sounded uncertain. "Look, if I can think of a better plan then we'll change it OK?"

"No," Frank snapped, "We stick with this. It'll work, I know it will. Besides, we've got to make arrangements, and quick. So… is it OK? Are you in or not?"

Jeff still looked doubtful. "What if something goes wrong?"

"Nothing will go wrong. It's easy money, that's what it is."

"Not that easy," groaned Jeff.

"Well, if you drop out I'll just get someone else. That's no problem. Guys would line up for this one. I just thought that I'd offer it to you first. We go back a long way, Jeff."

Jeff turned and gazed blankly out of the window.

"Listen Jeff. Think of the money. The red and white

Corvette. Think. Imagine it… driving that up the high street in some distant place!"

"OK," Jeff nodded slowly, "OK. I'll do it."

Just below them, the person who had been listening to every word with great interest started silently descending the winding stairs.

Frank rubbed his hands together. "Well, that's excellent! Exciting!" He beamed as he walked around the light. "We'll soon be rich men, Jeff. Very rich."

"Yeah," agreed Jeff, "For the first time in my life. I just wish it was all over now."

Frank looked down on Jeff and clapped his hands around the tops of his arms. "It will be over soon… and then we'll be laughing all the way to a holiday in Bermuda… or a Mediterranean Cruise… or a weekend in Paris… or…"

"Let's go, Frank. Now we've decided I want to get out of here."

"Yeah," Frank nodded, "We've got work to do."

He moved towards the steps. "And don't forget to leave those binoculars where you found them."

Jeff placed them back on the shelf and then followed Frank, who led the way as they started down the steps.

"You know the first thing I've got to do," said Frank, "is buy a new hat."

The eavesdropper was now well below them.

Tuesday 2nd December   6.17 p.m.

Rachel and Jamie sat in the canteen enjoying a drink and a cake.

"I've something to tell you," said Jamie.

"Yes, what is it?" Rachel asked with concerned interest.

"It's alright," he said, "You'll like it. Gordo has agreed…"

"What?" Rachel quizzed, "What do you mean?"

"Gordo…" he began, "Gordo and I… we can speak to each other."

"Of course you can," she said, "So can I. I speak to him all the time."

"No, no… listen. It's more than that… much more. Much, *much* more. It's a monkey language."

Rachel nodded. "Monkey language, yes. Monkeys have a whole variety of sounds meaning different things. Chirrups and cackles, and all those funny little peep-like noises. They definitely have over 30 different sounds…"

"No!" Jamie interrupted, "More than that. All those sounds that Gordo makes… it's a real language with sentences. He's actually speaking."

"Speaking?" she quizzed.

"Of course," replied Jamie, "We chat about things all the time."

Rachel looked puzzled. "But… what do you mean?" she asked.

"I mean talking! It's just like us talking. It's the same. It's proper talking. Real talking."

"As I said," Rachel continued, "I speak to him all the time… and it's great isn't it? It sometimes almost seems as if he's understanding."

"But that's what I'm saying! He *is* understanding." Jamie stated, "and he talks back to me and I understand *him*."

Rachel smiled. "Jamie - listen to me. I want to believe you, of course. You're always honest. But having a conversation with a monkey… you've got this one completely wrong. Gordo makes lots of different noises that mean things - that's true. But don't imagine, because you're so fond of him, that it's any more than that. Thay have 30 different sounds, as I said. That's a language… yes. Let's just leave it at that."

"No," Jamie insisted, "let me prove it to you. Let's go and see Gordo now and I'll show you."

Rachel shrugged. "OK, if you like. It's not that I don't trust you… but you have got it wrong, that's all."

She looked at him intently.

"This is a joke, isn't it? You're playing a joke on me."

"Can we go now?" asked Jamie.

"Sure," Rachel nodded.

Jamie led the way out of the canteen. He was walking quickly ahead, keen for Rachel to know the truth, and in a couple of minutes they were walking down the path, around the pond, and then entering Gordo's cage.

"Hi Gordo!" said Jamie.

Gordo was in his tree and he immediately climbed down and jumped on Jamie's shoulder and gave his ear a little tug.

"Have you told her?" he asked Jamie.

"Yes," Jamie replied in Gordo's language, "but she doesn't believe me. But we can easily prove it..."

"Easy," agreed Gordo, "Tell me to do things and then she'll see."

Rachel was listening and smiling, now quite certain that Jamie *was* playing a joke on her, and that he'd been practicing sounding like a monkey.

"Run around Rachel three times," instructed Jamie in English.

Gordo jumped off Jamie's shoulder and scampered around Rachel three times.

Rachel looked surprised.

"So he understands English now as well, does he?" she laughed, "It's a clever trick, but you've trained him to do that."

"Yes, he can understand English - but he can't speak it," Jamie confirmed, "OK, then. You tell him to do something."

"Climb up the tree and hang upside down from the top," she said.

Gordo did it and Rachel's jaw dropped in shock. She gave him another instruction, then another, and Gordo performed them exactly as she said.

Rachel looked stunned.

"OK then," she said slowly, gathering herself in spite of the shock.

She could feel excitement growing inside her. This might be true.

She took a pen and paper from her bag and wrote something down.

"Ask him, in his language," she began, "to do this."

Jamie took the paper and asked Gordo. Gordo immediately picked a leaf from a bush and gave it to Rachel.

Her legs felt so weak that she sat down and leant against the fence. It began to make sense but it was still such a ridiculous thing to believe.

"But how!? How did you learn his language?"

"I don't know," Jamie shrugged. "All I know is that when I first met Gordo I just found I could speak to him in his language… just like that. And he could speak to me… and I could understand him."

"It's amazing," she concluded.

Her mind was flashing back now and remembering how Gordo seemed to understand his training so well.

"It's crazy that he can understand English too?"

"Yes," Jamie confirmed, "The colony he lived with learnt it."

"And how did that happen?" she asked, "How could they even hear English in a jungle in Brazil?"

"He's not from there," Jamie explained calmly, "He was caught by some crooks – in Florida I think."

"How do you know that?" she asked.

"Gordo told me."

Smiled and shook her head.

"That's crazy!" she exclaimed, "The whole thing's crazy! A monkey talking and you talking to a monkey! It's crazy!"

"Crazy but true," stated Jamie.

Rachel nodded slowly.

"It does explain a few things," she said, "Yes, that's why he does things so well."

It took her a moment as she began to get used to this revelation.

"Why didn't you tell me about this?" she asked.

"I promised," he replied, "to Gordo. Monkeys don't like telling humans…"

She beamed at Jamie.

"I'm really sorry I didn't believe you," she said, "This is going to take some getting used to."

6.38 p.m.

Rachel, Jamie and Gordo were having their first three way conversation. Jamie should have left for home by now but this was too important. He was acting as interpreter so that Rachel could understand Gordo. They were discussing Max McMurphy and trying to work out why he was so interested in Gordo.

"I will set you free," Rachel said to Gordo, "And I'll lose my job if that's what it takes… but I don't care. You are far more important, Gordo."

"I just hope you can do it, Rachel," Gordo replied from Jamie's shoulder, "McMurphy wants me as a pet. Why?"

Jamie translated it into English for Rachel.

"I'll find a way to stop him," she said, sounding confident, "He can't bully me. I've already got some ideas and started working on a plan. The other way to do it… is to set you free before the trip."

"That's kind of you," Gordo said. He jumped from Jamie's shoulder to hers and gave her hair a gentle tug of affection. "Very kind. But, no. I have agreed to go, I've trained for months, and I'm ready. I'm actually looking forward to it. And so many people have been good to me. I couldn't let them all down. Also you're both keen that I go, aren't you?"

"Well, yes…" said Jamie, "But not if McMurphy gets you…"

Gordo jumped off Rachel's shoulder and onto a branch and turned to look directly at her.

"You said you've got some ideas," Gordo said, "Tell me about your plan. OK?"

Jamie translated.

"OK, but not now," agreed Rachel, "It's not very clear yet. I'm going to work on it tonight. Anyway, Jamie's got to go now. Tomorrow we'll have more time so we'll be able to discuss it properly then… all of us. I promise you we'll find a way."

Gordo had got to know Rachel well and he knew that she was a person who meant what she said; if she said she would do something she would do her utmost to see it through. This kept his spirits up and gave him a strong sense of hope that all would be well.

Rachel smiled. "I never thought I'd be talking to a monkey!"

Jamie hurried out through the gate and Rachel followed. Gordo leapt off the tree and onto the side of the cage. With lightening skill he took his favourite route, up the side, along the top and then dropping down into the highest branches. He watched them move up the path and then disappear into the building.

Gordo swung down into his nest at an angle to avoid hitting the waterproof canvas roof and settled down comfortably. He was glad that they had shared their secret with Rachel, in fact it was a relief to be able to communicate with her. He heard the soothing sound of a few drops of rain patter on the canvas as he closed his eyes and began to doze.

Wednesday 3rd December   11.45 a.m.

The launch was ten days away. The Jupiter AM-13 rocket had been transported from the hangar where it was built and was now in position on launch pad LC26B. It stood in stately silence, patiently awaiting the moment when the engines would burst into life.

Surrounding the rocket was a gantry where engineers and scientists could work on any part of the rocket that needed attention. Rachel was standing on this, just outside the nose cone. The view was a stunning panorama of the Cape Canaveral Space Centre bathed in morning sunshine. Gordo sat on her shoulder as they surveyed the scene below them; launch pads and small buildings dotted the green expanse and the occasional rocket reflected star points of bright light off shiny metal parts. To the west was Banana River, then Indian River and beyond that the sunlit Florida mainland. To the east, the great Atlantic Ocean, blue and vast, stretched away to meet the clear sky at the curved horizon. Not far to the northeast was the lighthouse with its distinctive black and white stripes.

Gordo jumped from her shoulder onto a railing which he gripped with his hands and feet. One slip and he would be plummeting to the ground, over eighteen metres below, but for Gordo it was like climbing on the upper branches of a very tall tree. Rachel watched as he ran around the railings and disappeared behind the rocket. After completely circling it, he surprised her by jumping onto her shoulder from behind.

"Hey, Gordo," she laughed, "Stop playing tricks on me!"

They were just about to open the door of the small entrance into the nose cone when they heard someone call out from behind them. A warm breeze blew Rachel's auburn hair across her face and she brushed it back with her hand.

"Hello there!"

They both looked to see a slim, brown-haired lady in her mid-thirties stepping out of the lift and clipping across the metal floor towards them. It was Jane Larkin, the manager of the space project. Rachel met with her once a month to keep her up to date with Gordo's progress. On their first meeting Rachel had found Jane to be friendly and efficient and they got on well. As their meetings progressed Rachel began to know her better and noticed a harsh, ambitious side to her. Jane Larkin hid this beneath a calm, friendly personality but really she was more concerned about being seen to be doing a good job than the actual quality of the job she was doing. She would twist the truth a little for her own benefit.

"Morning, Rachel," she said warmly, as she approached them, "How's it going?"

"Very well," replied Rachel, "No problems."

Jane stopped in front of them and looked at Gordo, sitting on Rachel's shoulder.

"He looks well," she remarked, "Is he ready for the trip?"

"Oh yes," Rachel nodded and smiled, "Definitely."

"I've had excellent reports about you and your work with Little Old Reliable here," stated Jane.

She reached out to stroke Gordo on the head but Gordo

recoiled.

"Excellent reports," she continued with a smile, "You're doing well, Rachel. You're both doing well… yes, very well."

"He's worked hard," Rachel acknowledged, "I wanted to make sure he had completed all the preparations and training in good time. He could go up today and he'd be fine."

"Excellent," Jane approved.

She waved a hand towards the capsule door.

"Can I take a look?" she asked.

"Of course," Rachel replied and pulled open the thick capsule door.

Jane placed a hand on either side of the door and leant forwards to put her head in.

"This looks great!" she commented, "Really cosy. Nice colour scheme too!"

"Oh, that's Ray," said Rachel from behind her, "He's done a good job… he's got an artistic eye."

Jane pushed back from the capsule.

"I would like to suggest something," she said, "From what I have heard, the way this monkey has taken to the training has been exceptional and I think there is every chance that this trip will be a great success. In fact, with you looking after him, I'm completely confident about it."

Rachel smiled, "Thank you."

"All being well, we will be the first team to successfully send a monkey into outer space, real space, and by that I mean that the monkey survives the trip and lives on. And I've been thinking about this… thinking about the future… and I have a suggestion. But I wanted your thoughts on it… in fact I'd like your approval."

Rachel and Gordo waited in anticipation.

"I'm sure you'll agree. I've thought about this for some time and my mind is made up. I may have some opposition from other places but I would like to know that I can count on you."

Jane paused and looked away, gazing across the expanse of land below and to the Atlantic Ocean. She looked back at Rachel and into her eyes and then spoke earnestly.

"I need your full support on this one."

Rachel and Gordo were on tenterhooks now.

"What is it, Jane?" asked Rachel.

"I want to keep this monkey on for another trip… a second trip. The next one goes up in May next year and I want Gordo on it. What do you think?"

She stopped to wait for Rachel's reaction. Gordo straightened his back in shock and Rachel's face showed dismay. Jane looked surprised but then relaxed and smiled at Rachel.

"A bit of a bolt from the blue? Yes, I know… but hopefully it's good news."

She looked at Rachel enquiringly who stared back.

"No, I don't agree at all," Rachel stated calmly.

Rachel felt she was just coming to terms with the problem of Max McMurphy and his selfish schemes for Gordo and now she had to deal with this woman's plans. She had quickly worked out what was probably behind this woman's suggestion.

"No," continued Rachel, "I don't agree. And besides animals are only meant to make one space flight. That is what happens and you know it. It's not fair on Gordo. To send him up a second time could be dangerous; we just don't know the effects yet."

For a moment Jane's expression seemed to soften and she looked at little Gordo. She smiled and Rachel thought that she had won the argument.

"I see what you're saying, Rachel," Jane began, but then her expression hardened again, "But, no, I cannot agree. The use of animals in space… well, it's a new science… we are learning more about it all the time… why can't a monkey make two trips? There's no scientific reason why not. It's only an animal, anyway. Nothing is set in stone and this little fella, well, he's so good… we'd find it hard to find another like him. Anyway, he'd enjoy another trip."

She reached out again to stroke him on the head. This time Gordo struck out and before she had time to move her hand away he had bitten her on the finger. She jumped back.

"Owww!" she exclaimed.

"There," said Rachel, "He doesn't want to."

"Don't be silly," Jane gripped her bleeding finger tightly with the other hand, "He can't understand… he's an animal! Look!" She held her bleeding finger out to show Rachel. "You're treating him like a human, and that's not right!"

"Animals should be treated fairly," said Rachel, "They…"

"I came here with a positive plan…" Jane interrupted firmly, "Hoping that you'd see sense. Some hope! I've asked you to be reasonable about this… to look at it sensibly, and consider it. Why don't you think about it, say overnight, and we'll speak again tomorrow?"

"No!" snapped Rachel, "I'll feel the same tomorrow and always. And another thing… Mr. McMurphy won't agree. He wants to keep him as a pet."

"Does he?" she looked surprised. She pulled a tissue from her sleeve and dabbed her bleeding finger. "I'll have to sort that out. He'll see the sense of what I'm saying. Anyway, I've already arranged to see him later today about this… I wanted to tell him that you agreed. You will find, Miss Chandler, that Gordo will stay on for a second flight with or without you! In the meantime, if you want to challenge my decision you can follow the official line and put it down in writing."

Rachel sighed, "And then you'll do nothing."

Jane turned to walk away, and then glanced back. "I will not change my mind."

"And I won't change mine," Rachel retorted.

Jane turned again and hurriedly walked away, got into the lift and pushed the button for the ground level. Then she called out, "Keep that monkey under control!"

The doors closed and she was gone.

"Well done, little monkey!" said Rachel with a smile as they watched the lift descending.

"She deserved it," Gordo said.

Of course Rachel could not understand, but got the gist. She nodded.

"But I wonder why she's so set on a second trip for you?" asked Rachel thoughtfully, "I wonder… she's an ambitious woman, and I think she wants it to seem like it's her success so that she can get promoted."

Gordo moved around the back of her neck and onto the other shoulder. "Oh, Rachel! Why does everyone want me for all the wrong reasons?"

"This is ridiculous," Rachel sighed, "First McMurphy and now this woman! I hope you don't think all humans are like them. There are lots of good people too."

"Yes, like you and Ray," said Gordo snuggling up under her chin.

Rachel wished she could understand Gordo's chatterings.

"Come on, Gordo, we've got work to do."

Gordo jumped off her shoulder and onto the nose cone. He swung down and through the door and Rachel followed him in.

Friday 5th December   6.15 p.m.

Mary-Anne was just sitting down in front of the television when she heard a loud knock on the door. As she got up, another knock echoed along the hall. She walked down the hall and as she reached out for the door handle the knocking hammered again, this time louder than before.

"OK, OK," she called out, "I'm here."

She opened the door to see Officer Smudge holding out his Police ID for her. Standing beside him was Ruth Anderton.

"You!" she exclaimed, "Well, he's not here!"

"Listen, Mrs. Marks," Smudge growled, looking down on her, "We just need to talk to him. Like before… remember?"

"He's not here."

"Just a little talk and we'll be gone. Now where's the harm in that."

Mary-Anne's face grew stern and she barked at him, "There's a lot of harm in what you've done… frightening him like that."

"Come now, Mrs. Marks…" Smudge began.

"Don't talk to me like that," she shouted, "Last time you came here he was upset for days. He's sensitive. He doesn't like being accused of things he hasn't done. Would you?"

Smudge felt the anger rising in him. He opened his mouth to shout back when Ruth came to his rescue.

"Mrs. Marks," she said calmly, "We just need to talk to him, that's all."

"But you can't!" she exclaimed angrily, "He's not here! How many times do I have to tell you?"

Ruth smiled, "You did say that last time… and he was here then, wasn't he?"

"Yes, but he's not now," she stated, "Honest."

She glared at the officers and they stared back. She realized they would not go away until she had let them in.

"OK then… OK… come in and see for yourselves," she snapped. She stepped back and let them in. They walked through into the lounge followed by Mary-Anne.

"He left a few days ago," she said, sitting down on one of the soft armchairs and staring out of the window.

Smudge sat down on the other armchair and looked at her.

"And, no…" she continued, "I don't know where he's gone. Packed a bag and left me. Said he needed a break." Then she added, bitterly, "After all I've done for him…"

"Have you got a photo of him we could take?" asked Smudge.

"I wish I had," she replied sadly, "But, no. No photos."

"I can't believe that!" Smudge shook his head.

"Well you'll have to…"

"It's a real shame, Mrs. Marks. You know it really would be better if you cooperated."

"I've let you in and I'm doing my best," she said, glaring at him.

Smudge looked at her suspiciously, and then continued.

"And he gave no indication of where he was going?"

Mary-Anne shook her head.

"None at all?" he persisted.

"None," she confirmed.

"Any relations or friends he might have gone to stay with?"

Mary-Anne was still staring out of the window as she spoke. Ruth slipped out of the room unnoticed by her or Smudge.

"Jeff? No," Mary-Anne replied. "The only relations he keeps in touch with are in Tampa. I really don't think he would have gone there."

"Address please," he ordered, taking his notebook out of his chest pocket.

Mary-Anne, now looking tearful, looked up at the ceiling.

"Um… um… yes, I know," she began, "Rorbridge Road… no… Redbridge Road, Tampa. They're called Streever."

Smudge wrote it down.

"What about a house number?"

"Sorry… I can't remember."

"And is Streever with two Es… or is it E, A?"

"Double E."

"Phone?" asked Smudge.

"No phone," she replied.

"And you're sure about that as well, are you?"

"Absolutely," she said emphatically.

Smudge looked thoughtful. Then he got an idea.

"What about your address book?"

She hesitated and then said, "I'll just get it."

Without getting up she reached out and opened a drawer.

"I usually keep it in here," she said as her hands foraged around amongst some papers, "Oh!" she exclaimed, "It's gone, unless I put it somewhere else... but I can't think where."

Smudge shook his head. "See if you can find it, Mrs. Marks. It would be most helpful."

Mary-Anne looked thoughtful. "It was definitely here. Definitely. I know... he must've taken it. Oh, I wish he hadn't gone!"

She turned to face Smudge. Her lower lip quivered and her eyes began to fill with tears. She lowered her head and began to cry.

"Well... um... um..." Smudge stammered.

Her crying had surprised him and he was unsure how to proceed. For a moment he said nothing. She dabbed her eyes with her sleeve. Smudge looked thoughtful.

"Mrs. Marks," he said, "Don't worry... we'll find him. I assure you, we'll do our very best."

"Thank you," she said sniffing.

"And..." continued Smudge, "If he turns up, you let us know straight away. Just phone the station."

"I will. What were your names again?"

"I'm Officer Smudge, and this is..." he nodded towards Miss Anderton who was standing in the doorway, "This is Miss Anderton... er... Officer Anderton."

Mary-Anne nodded.

"Oh, well," said Smudge, "I think that's probably all...

for the moment anyway."

Mary-Anne stood up and wiped her cheek with her sleeve again. "I'll show you out then."

They walked to the front door and the two police officers stepped out into lightly falling rain.

"Let me know if you find him, won't you?" she said.

"Of course," said Smudge.

They walked to the patrol car in the failing light.

"Well," said Smudge, "That's that… at least for the moment. She wasn't telling us everything… but she did seem sincerely upset. I even felt sorry for her. And we don't even have a photo of him to circulate."

"Haven't we?" asked Ruth smiling.

She reached into her pocket and pulled out a photograph of Jeff and Mary-Anne Marks.

Tuesday 9th December   8.19 p.m.

Jamie had just finished dinner and was sitting in the lounge. Bertha sat on the other side of the room.

"Gran?" Jamie asked politely, "It's alright to go to the launch on Saturday, is it?"

"What time is it?" asked Bertha.

"Three-fifty," replied Jamie, "In the morning."

Bertha tilted her head back slightly and snorted with laughter.

"At that time of night?!" she exclaimed, "Of course you can't!"

"But, Gran…" Jamie objected, "There's no school the day after so I can lie in…"

"Jamie! Stop now!" she snapped at him, "Don't even think about it! Life is not for lounging around in bed. You can't go… and that's that!" He opened his mouth to speak but she glared at him with such threatening intensity that he only managed 'but..." before she drowned him out. "You spend far, far too much time with that stupid monkey anyway! If it doesn't make it back alive… that'll be the best thing that could happen. I'll have a little celebration!"

Jamie felt the anger rise in him. The thought of any harm coming to Gordo filled him with alarm. For a moment their eyes were locked together in mutual dislike, until Jamie turned away, marched out of the room and up the stairs. He went to his bedroom, determined to find a way to be there on the night of the launch. Zorro was curled up on his bed and looked up as he came in.

Jamie flopped down, with his knees on the floor and his chest on the bed, and stroked the soft fur of his cat.

"I can't take this much longer, Zorro," he said, "What shall I do?"

Zorro purred loudly and Jamie put his ear to the grey cat's body and listened to the comforting sound. In a couple of minutes he had calmed down and began to think about his problem.

He had to be there. He had a vital part to play in the plot to free Gordo. How could he escape from his grandmother on that important night? He needed to find a way and he decided to talk it over with his friend, Doug, who was always bubbling with ideas. Between them, he was sure, they would work out a plan.

CHAPTER 12

Wednesday 10th December   8.15 a.m.

Jean Smith, McMurphy's secretary, usually got to work at 8.30 to prepare for the arrival of her boss. He came to work at about 9.00 and would immediately demand a black coffee. He would snap at her and treat her more like a personal slave than a secretary. Even if he was in a good mood he would still boss her around impolitely and expect her to cater for his slightest whim. He seemed insensitive to her feelings and never showed her any thanks. Before he got the job, Jean Smith enjoyed her work but from his very first day that had changed. His arrogant, selfish ways had cast a dark shadow across her life in the office.

On this particular morning, she walked through the main doors of the building a quarter of an hour early at 8.15.

"Morning, Jean," called out the porter from the reception desk.

"Good morning, Danny."

"You're a keen worker this morning," he said cheerfully, as he ticked her name and jotted down 8.15, "Or is the old dog working you hard."

"He always works me hard, Danny," she replied as she paused to talk, "To tell the truth I would give anything to have Mr. Harwood back, and I thought he was difficult at the time! To work for him would be like heaven compared to this."

"Yep," Danny shook his head, "He only speaks to me if he wants something done."

"It's a bit like the song," she smiled, took a deep breath, stuck a dramatic pose as if on stage, and began to sing the popular blues song of the time, "I've almost lost my mind…"

"You've got a great voice there, Jean," Danny said, "You're in the wrong profession."

Jean laughed, "Listen, Danny," she said, stepping closer to the desk and lowering her voice, "Could you do me a favour?"

"For you, anything," he replied, "But I'll expect your autograph in return."

Jean chuckled. "It's a deal," she said, "When McMurphy arrives can you let me know?"

"Sure, no problem, Jean. I'll ring through."

"Thanks, Danny," she said, "You're a real pal. I'll sign the autograph when the job is done."

Danny smiled.

Jean lowered her voice to a whisper, "And… there's something else. Can you switch off his safe alarm?"

Danny's expression changed. His mouth dropped open as he stared at her in surprise.

"Jean? What are you asking me to do?"

"I'm not stealing anything… you know me. It's just something I have to find out."

"What?" he whispered, sounding alarmed "What do you have to find out?"

"It's… it's… listen, Danny… I haven't got much time. Can I explain it to you later. Sorry to jump this on you but it's important. You've known me for years. Can you trust me on this one?"

"Of course, Jean," he whispered immediately, "Of course."

"I'll ring through when I want you to turn it back on…"

A voice behind them made them both jump.

"Private conference, is it?"

Jean jerked her head around. Charles Spratt looked down on her. She smiled at him.

"Turn what back on?" he asked, staring at Jean and smiling.

There was an embarrassed pause.

Jean's eyes flicked nervously down, "Um… the um…"

Danny came to her rescue and butted in. "We're testing some of the electrics. Nothing sinister, Mr. Spratt," said Danny cheerfully, "I'll sign you in."

"Thanks," he said, looking at them intently, "But if you go 'round whispering about ordinary things, people are bound to get suspicious. Still… if it's only to do with the electrics…" he said with a tinge of disbelief in his voice, "Well… I must get to work. Make sure you don't get up to any mischief, you two. Have a good day."

Charles Spratt turned and strode briskly away down the corridor.

"Phew…" sighed Jean, "Thanks, Danny."

"He was suspicious," stated Danny, "But… he doesn't know what he's suspecting… neither do I!"

"Danny, I must go," she looked directly at him, "You'll do what I said?"

"Sure," he confirmed, nodding. Then he smiled at her. "But don't forget the autograph."

"I won't," she said moving away, "And I'll tell you all about it later… and… thanks."

"Hang on," called out Danny, "You might need these."

He jangled the keys of her department in the air. Every evening the last person out of each department left their keys with the night porter and the first person in the morning collected them from Danny.

Jean turned and he threw the keys to her. She missed the catch and they jingled onto the floor. She was nervous already.

"Thanks, Danny."

She picked up the keys and slipped them into her pocket.

She looked at her watch and noted the time and the position of the second hand, and then walked along a corridor to the lift and pushed the button. She heard the lift moving and waited for it to arrive, tapping impatiently on the wall.

"Come on," she thought.

It arrived and she rode up to the fifth floor. As she walked to her office, she thought about her plan. An opportunity had come her way to pay McMurphy back for the last eleven months of his arrogant, bad-mannered attitude towards her. When the offer had been made she had hesitated and asked if she could have a day to consider it before making a decision. She found that the more she thought about it the more attractive it seemed and so the next day she phoned to say that she had decided to go for it.

There was a great risk involved but she was prepared to take it. After all, he deserved it. She would be helping justice. Within her was something she could not ignore: a strong sense of right and wrong. She was determined that McMurphy should not get away with what he was doing.

She accepted the offer three days ago and since then it had been constantly on her mind; there was fear, of course, the fear of being caught, but also the excitement of the challenge; there was a sense of being dishonest, but the stronger feeling of playing her part in bringing justice to bear. The three days had dragged, and now, at last, the time had come.

"This is it," she thought as she fumbled with the keys.

Her hands were shaking as she unlocked the door to her office and entered.

She felt gripped by nerves and took several breaths, blowing out the air to try to calm herself. She hung her handbag on the back of her chair and checked her watch. It had taken her 1 minute 25 seconds to walk from the entrance hall, take the lift and reach her office.

She checked the time: 8.26.

She was behind schedule. She quickly left her office and moved down the corridor to the next door. The brass plate announced 'Mr. Max J. P. McMurphy' almost as if he was there watching her. She glanced along the corridor nervously. A deep breath, and then she unlocked the door and entered. She closed it quietly and locked it again.

"What am I doing?" she thought.

She leant back onto the door for a moment, gripping the door handle with her hands behind her and gathering her strength. She knew she had to see it through and she had to work quickly.

She went straight to a painting on the wall. Pulling one

side of the painting, it clicked and opened like a window, revealing the safe behind it. The red light was off.

"Good old Danny!" she thought.

She turned the dial carefully. Clockwise to the 2, back to the 7, forwards again to the 3, and back to the 9. The dial clicked gently and the door opened. She took out a pile of folders and papers, placed them on his desk and sat down. Her hands were trembling as she quickly leafed through the papers scanning for anything suspicious. She knew he was making money in illegal ways and all she needed was some evidence.

It did not take her long to find what she was after. At the bottom of the pile was a folder without any label on the cover. She opened it and studied the first sheet of paper which was a letter. She continued leafing through but leaving the letter sticking out from the rest. This continued until she had worked through the whole file and selected eleven sheets. She started working her way through these, jotting down a few details in a notebook. She had dealt with nine of them when she heard the phone ring in her office. For a moment she froze. She glanced at her watch; there was time and it might be Danny.

She stood up, unlocked the door and ran out of the office and into hers. She thoughtlessly put the keys down on her desk and snatched the phone receiver up.

"Jean?"

"Yes," she replied.

"He's here," said Danny, "On his way up now."

"Thanks," she said, jerking the phone down.

He was early.

"Why is he early today?!" she thought.

She rushed out of the room. She had less than 1 minute 25 seconds and almost bumped into a lady walking down the corridor.

"Morning, Jean," said Katie French, who worked in an office close by, "You're in a rush! Are you alright?"

"Fine," replied Jean, trying to appear calm, "Overworked as usual."

"It's the name of the game, isn't it?" said Katie, stopping to chat, "What's he got you doing now?"

"Sorry, Katie, I've got to rush. Something I've got to have on his desk before he gets in."

"They ask too much, don't they?" said Katie.

Jean walked past her. "Sorry, got to go."

"See you later, then," said Katie, looking snubbed.

Jean dashed back into McMurphy's office and closed the door. She had forgotten the keys. No time now to go back.

"Don't panic! Don't panic!" she thought.

She ran over to the desk, knocking into the corner of it but ignoring the pain. She imagined him in the lift now and glanced at her watch. 35 seconds to go. She looked at the last two sheets of paper, made a few quick notes and pushed them back into their places in the file.

Footsteps in the corridor.

Her heart missed a beat. She grabbed the whole pile of folder and papers, fumbling clumsily with them and thrusting them into the safe. The couple of sheets fluttered off the top and onto the floor.

She heard him right outside the door and panic took over. She reached for the fallen papers, whipped them up and shoved them into the safe. Her hands were shaking.

"Jean?" she heard McMurphy call.

She closed the safe door and twisted the lock. Her breath shallowed to nothing.

The door handle turned.

She pushed the painting back and it clicked into place.

McMurphy entered.

"Jean!" he said gruffly, "What are you doing in here?"

For a second, which seemed like eternity, she stared at him. Her mind was blank. Numbing fear gripped her face. Then she heard herself speak.

"Just checking everything is nice and tidy for you, sir."

How did she sound so calm?

"Hmm… where's my coffee?"

"It'll be with you…" she said brightly. Her mouth was dry and she swallowed. "It'll be with you in a jiffy, sir,"

As she walked towards the door her legs felt hollow.

McMurphy moved towards his desk and then stopped.

"What's this?" he said, stooping to pick up her notebook.

Jean seized up inside. It felt as if she had been hit in the stomach. Fear shuddered through her body like a wave of nausea. How could she have been so careless?

"Oh, that." Again she was amazed how calm she sounded. "That's my notebook."

He held it in one hand and looked at it. She knew he was going to open it.

"It's… well… private, sir," she blurted out.

"I didn't know you had secrets, Jean." He looked at her intently. "You look nervous. Afraid I might look inside?"

"Yes, sir."

Using his thumbs he opened the notebook, but he kept his eyes fixed on her.

"Sir, please…" she pleaded, restraining her panic. She took one step towards him and held out her hand. Surely he would notice her damp palm. "As I said, sir, it's private."

"And am I interested in your private life?" he questioned, "Don't worry, I'm not," he said scornfully, and snapped the little book closed, "Coffee is what interests me right now."

He held out the notebook to her. She reached out quickly and grasped it. She felt as if she had been given the most precious thing in the world and she gripped it tightly. She tried to control her emotions.

"I'll get your coffee, sir."

She left the room, closing the door and pausing to let out a long sigh of relief. She was still shaking. Back in her room she put on the kettle. She picked up the phone, dialled and waited.

"Danny?"

Her voice was trembling.

"Yes. Are you alright?"

"Yes, just about," she said softly, "Can you turn it back on, please?"

"Right," said Danny.

There was a pause.

"It's on. Did it go OK… whatever *it* was?"

"Yup," Jean said, "Very well, thanks… in the end. I'll tell you later."

She put the phone down and glanced out of the window. A bright winter sun bathed the buildings of the Space Centre. Everything looked as it should at the beginning of a normal day. This comforted her. She relaxed and smiled. She had done it.

She opened her notebook at the back page, dialled 9 for an outside line followed by 4361272. She tapped her notebook with her fingers in time to the ringing tone. The phone was picked up at the other end.

"I've got it," she said.

10.24 a.m.

McMurphy leant back in his luxury swivel chair and smiled. His plans were going well. In a few days he would have the monkey and then he would be able to make the arrangements which would bring a series of large payments to him. In his mind's eye, he saw the envelopes lying in his mail box and imagined himself picking them out and opening them. Then he saw himself in the bank, paying in the cheques and observing the cashier, unable to contain a slight lifting of the eyebrows at the large amounts. His mind wandered on through a variety of scenes; he was buying a yacht, gambling large amounts on one throw in the casino, giving luxury gifts to his admiring friends.

A knock on his door jolted him out of his dreams.

"Come in," he called.

He knew it was Jean by her knock and because it was time for his coffee.

Jean came in carrying a cup of coffee and some biscuits on a tray. She placed it carefully on his desk.

"I've been thinking, Jean," he began, looking down at the tray. "About this morning…"

"Yes, sir?" she asked.

"You weren't snooping around, were you?" He looked up to face her and she felt the challenge of the accusation. "Looking at things that you're not meant to… like cleaners do…"

"I'm not a cleaner, sir," she stated defiantly, avoiding the question.

He stared back. "Curiosity killed the cat. You weren't being a curious cat were you?"

She looked back, making sure that her expression

portrayed complete bewilderment. Was he threatening her?

"Why did you drop that notebook?" he snapped.

"Why does anyone drop anything?" she said, "I was tidying up… that's all. Why would I snoop around, sir? I'm your secretary… I know about all your work anyway, sir."

"A notebook is for notes, Jean," he snapped, "I don't know if I trust you…"

Jean laughed. "But, sir… what are you talking about? Have you something to hide?"

"You obviously have!" he growled, "I wish I'd looked in that notebook now. What's in it that's so secret that you don't want me to know?"

She felt tears rising, and so she let them come. Her mouth quivered.

"None of your business!" she blurted out and turned away, "My private life is private!"

She rushed out of the room and back into her office.

McMurphy stood up and walked over to close the door. As he walked back he looked around. Had he left anything in view that he did not want anyone else to see? He reached out for the picture and pulled it out; the red light was on. By the time he sat down again he had decided that his suspicions were unfounded. But he would keep an eye on her just in case.

He sat down again. His plans were going well but he was still concerned about Rachel and the boy. He knew they would oppose him in some way and this was the only spanner in the works. He had to do something about them.

He pushed the floor with his foot and the chair turned to face the window. He glanced down to to look at his Rolls Royce, looking spendid in the bright morning sun.

He turned his mind to reflect on his plans and thought about Rachel first. He recalled the scheme already in place to deal with her. The threat of losing her job, coupled with a financial bribe should do it, especially after he had made sure that her finances were under pressure. He knew the burglary had left her struggling. He was so confident that this would work that he turned his mind to the boy.

He had often seen him arriving and leaving on his bike, looking scruffy in his old clothes and with his scraggly, black hair. Apart from this, he knew only a few other facts about him. The boy was Rachel's nephew and she gave him small jobs to do; he cleaned out the monkey's cage, fed it and carried it here and there. This shabby-looking youth probably liked the monkey – all children like animals – which meant that he could endanger his plans. He had to do something about him too.

He jabbed the floor with his foot and the chair swivelled

back to face his desk. He pulled out a black notebook from his inside suit pocket and touched his glasses with a finger to push them up. A sigh breathed out through his nose as he opened the little book.

He had decided not to deal with Ron again. However, this had to be done quickly and he would make sure that this would be the last time. He found the number he was looking for and dialled.

"Yeah?" asked Ron, "Who's that?"

"Ricky," said McMurphy, "I've got a job for you."

12.35 p.m.

Jamie and Doug sat on a wall and gazed over the sun-bathed, noisy playground as they talked.

"I've got to be there," said Jamie.

"Of course," Doug agreed, "I don't see the problem... just go."

"It's not that easy. She'll try to stop me. She'll call the police and report me as missing... I don't want anything to get in the way of this. It's really important."

"Yeah, I know," Doug nodded, "You love that monkey don't you. I love my dog. So... you've got to go without her knowing."

"OK," nodded Jamie, "But, how do I do that?"

"You need a cunning plan... a really good plan so that when you're gone she doesn't even know you're not at home," stated Doug, "And then have back up plans in case she finds out. This needs careful planning. Firstly..."

Doug paused to think.

"Yes?" asked Jamie.

"Listen. I want to come too. This sounds exciting!"

"It may be exciting," nodded Jamie, "But it's not just a game… this is real."

Doug looked serious. "I know. Can I come?"

Jamie smiled and nodded.

Doug looked up to the sky. "Oh no! I've just remembered… I've got a tennis match on Saturday and I can't miss that. Club tournament under 14 singles final… at eleven thirty. So I can't come all the way… but I'd like to be part of the great escape. Just to help you get there."

"OK," agreed Jamie.

"Right then…" Doug was brimming with enthusiasm. "We need pencil and paper… and we'll make detailed plans, with times and everything. A watertight plan that can't fail. What shall we call it? It's got to have a code name."

"Operation Jupiter?" asked Jamie.

"Yes," Doug confirmed, "Operation Jupiter it is."

2.15 p.m.

Officer Elliot Smudge and Ruth Anderton were driving across the bridge that spanned the Indian River. As always, he was driving and they had taken the SR 405 eastwards out of Orlando and were heading towards Cape Canaveral. It was a clear day with bright sunlight sparkling on the flowing water of the river. A flock of ring-billed gulls soared off the bridge as the police car crossed. They circled once and then descended again.

"This may be the evidence that we've been waiting for,"

Smudge said.

"Yes, sir," Ruth agreed, "If it is Marks… if the guard confirms that it was him… then it's an amazing coincidence. Too much of a coincidence to ignore, sir. And there are all those other clues connecting him to the crimes. And there's the blood in the back of the truck. Do you think he's a murderer, sir?"

Smudge lifted his eyebrows. "I've met murderers… arrested them…" he replied proudly, "and Marks, yes, I think he could kill someone. He's got that deceitful look about him."

Ruth shook her head. "I don't know, sir. I don't think he's tough enough. It's in the eyes… he's got kind eyes."

Smudge did not respond. He hoped she was wrong so that he could be right about something and make a point. She had outwitted him in everything so far and he had been forced by her to accept that Jeff Marks was probably involved. The indications that linked Jeff Marks with the stolen truck and the attempted theft of the squirrel monkey were adding up. The fact that it was Miss Anderton who had discovered most of them, as well as having the intelligence of mind to work out how they fitted together, made Smudge uptight with irritation. However, as he was the officer in charge of the investigation, he knew that he would get the credit and he would certainly try to make it seem that he played the major part.

"The evidence is building, Miss Anderton," he said smugly, "Remember what I taught you… steady investigation… methodical investigation. First of all we gather facts through research and interrogation and… and, of course, observation. It's like fishing, Miss Anderton… fishing."

Miss Anderton looked quizzical, "Fishing, sir?" she asked.

"Yes, fishing, Miss Anderton. Sitting on the riverbank with everything set up, the line thrown out and the float bobbing on the water. Beautiful. And then observing for signs of crime… the slightest movement, like signs of guiltiness or other clues. Then comes the analysis, sifting through the facts we've gathered, eliminating the red herrings and retaining the… er… the er… the good fish, so to speak, which are the real criminals, the bad people, the ones we want to catch. And then the catch itself, the hook goes in… that's the handcuffs… and dragging them fighting to the station! The thrill of hauling them in, Miss Anderton."

He looked at her. She had never seen him look so alive.

"Finally, the crowning glory…" he continued, "Conviction… stuffing the fish and having it on your shelf at home… that's when it gets written down and the criminal goes to prison."

Ruth was staring at him with surprise. Smudge's enthusiasm had made him seem like a different person as he spoke. She was used to him being glum and grumpy most of the time but here he had shown a completely different side to his character.

For Smudge, his description had made an image flash into his mind. It was the picture on the birthday card that his daughter had sent to him, with the fisherman on the bank of a river, pulling in a catch. He still had not contacted her and he quickly forced the image and the feeling of guilt out of his mind, and focussed on the road in front.

He slowed down as they approached the checkpoint which controlled traffic going in and out of the Cape Canaveral International Space Centre. The barrier was lowered and they pulled up before it, swinging over to park at the side of the road. The guard came out of his hut to meet them and walked towards the car. Smudge and Ruth got out and into the bright sunlight.

"You from Orlando?" the guard called to them.

"Yup," answered Smudge, "I spoke to you this morning."

"Oh, yes. Come in then," the guard invited, nodding his head towards the hut.

"Thanks," said Smudge.

When they were in the hut the guard made them all mugs of coffee and they sat down around a small table. In the centre of the table lay a photograph of Jeff and Mary-Anne Marks. Smudge took the original photograph out of his pocket and placed it next to the other one.

"I'm Officer Smudge," he said, "And this is Officer Anderton."

"Howdy," said the guard.

"So," began Smudge, "You think you saw this man?"

"Yup," the guard replied, "I'm pretty sure that's him. When I saw that photo earlier today I thought, 'I've seen him before.' I thought, 'Where have I seen him?' Then I remembered I saw him last week."

"Tell us what happened," said Smudge.

"Well," the guard began, looking up at the corner of the room and to gather his thoughts, "He was here. I saw him. It was last week… Thursday or Friday, I think. It was that stormy day… heavy rain…"

Ruth butted in, "That was Friday, the fifth."

The guard thought again, "Yes, you're right, it was Friday. They were in an old pickup truck… really old, you know, falling apart. I thought to myself at the time, 'That heap of rust is falling apart.'"

"What make of truck?" asked Smudge.

"Ford," answered the guard, and he laughed, "Except Henry Ford would turn in his grave if he'd seen the state of that thing! It was leaking inside as well. When I saw it I thought to myself…"

Ruth leant forwards and interrupted, "You said 'they'… how many were there?"

"Two," he replied, pointing at the photograph, "this one was the passenger. They had passes, you know, IDs." He paused for a moment and then looked at Smudge, "What have they done?"

Smudge was just taking a sip of his coffee. He put the

mug down. "We're investigating a homicide case. He's a suspect. Anything else you remember?"

The guard looked thoughtful and then answered slowly, "No… I don't think so."

"Are you sure that is him?" asked Ruth.

"Yup, 'cos I looked at him. I always check that the faces match the IDs, and his did. Oh, and they had white coats on. I noticed because I thought at the time, "Why are they in their coats already?" You see, most scientists slip them on in the buildings. At the time it seemed… well, a bit unusual."

Ruth looked at Smudge, "Another connection!" she exclaimed.

Smudge was puzzled, "What?" he said.

"Orlando Medical Centre," she said, looking at him as if he should know what she meant, "Didn't you hear about it? A week ago… two white jackets plus identity cards stolen. Now that's a little thing… a minor crime… but the hospital manager was very concerned because the last thing they wanted was some madman wandering around pretending to be a doctor. That's why it received such attention from us. And, of course, our friend Jeff Marks lives in Orlando."

"I see," said Smudge nodding, but feeling uncomfortable. Once again this young novice was outwitting him.

"And they've got a description of the thief," she continued, "From several people, sir."

"Good. Well done, Miss Anderton," he said rising from the chair, "And thank you for all your help, Mr.… um…"

"Greentram," said the guard, "Gudge Greentram."

"Thanks for your help," Smudge said, turning for the door.

Ruth followed him out and then she paused in the doorway and turned back to the guard, "Just a couple of other things, Mr. Greentram. Did they keep you waiting?"

"Yes they did. Looking for their IDs. Why?"

Ruth smiled. "Well, wouldn't you keep a guard standing in the pouring rain if you didn't want your false ID cards to be studied too closely?"

"Hmm... yeah, I suppose I would."

Smudge looked around to see why she was not right behind him.

"Also, I was just wondering," she went on, "You didn't happen to recognize them, did you? I mean from some time before."

"It's funny you should say that," he answered, "I didn't say anything because it's a very vague sort of memory. But when I saw them I thought to myself 'I've seen them before.' I don't know where or when, but, yes, I think so."

Ruth smiled again, "Thanks for your help," she said as she turned and walked quickly to catch up with Smudge.

They got into the patrol car. Smudge swung the car around, bumping over the grassy verge, and they headed back to Orlando.

Thursday 11th December   8.15 p.m

Rachel and Ray were sitting opposite each other in a restaurant. The lighting was dim. A candle flickered and glinted on the silver cutlery which rested on a white tablecloth.

The flight was tomorrow night; over a year of dedicated work would produce a fifteen minute journey into space and back. Rachel and Ray had completed everything they needed to do today and had decided to relax over a good meal. Earlier in the day, Rachel had talked to Gordo and Jamie, and together they had decided to let Ray into their secret. He was honest, loved Gordo and might be willing to help with their plan to free Gordo after the trip.

Now, as she sat opposite him, waiting for their food to arrive, she wondered how to begin. She turned and gazed out of the window and thought about it.

"Rachel?" he asked. She turned to face him. "I'd like to know what's going on... I've overheard things... and um... well I don't know..." Ray paused, watching her reaction. Her resigned smile prompted him to continue. "And you've been looking under strain. I'd like to help you... really I would... what's wrong?"

Relief swept through Rachel's mind. She felt ready to tell him everything.

"You know about my money problems already... but there's more, and it's all to do with Gordo. There's something important you need to know about him. He can speak... not in English... in his own monkey language."

Ray looked stunned and then laughed.

"Rachel," he began, "monkeys can't talk - everyone knows that. Well, they can with their different sounds. Is that what you mean?"

"No," she stated, "Gordo can speak a full language just like ours... as complicated as ours... with a complete vocabulary."

Ray smiled again in disbelief.

Rachel continued, "You know I've been saying to you for ages that I think there's something more to monkeys' communication... more than everyone thinks. I was right all along. It's so exciting!"

"Why are you saying this, Rachel? Tell me why you're saying this."

"There's no reason," she replied, "but just to let you know the truth... because you're a nice guy and we can trust you not to tell anyone else."

"We? Who's *'we'*?

"Jamie and me," she answered, "and Gordo of course."

"You're not serious... are you?"

"Absolutely, yes! Monkeys have a language, and Jamie can speak it. He can talk to Gordo and Gordo can talk to him. I didn't believe it at first either. They had to prove it to me. But when I heard it happening... well I couldn't deny it. It *is* true, Ray."

"Wow!" he exclaimed, slightly too loudly and glanced quickly around to see several people looking straight at him. He turned back to Rachel and spoke in a near whisper. "That's… incredible… unbelievable."

"It seems unbelievable – that's what I thought when Jamie told me. But now I've heard them together, I know that it's true. Look... I know I can't expect you to believe without seeing it... I didn't. But we can show you later."

Ray stared at her. "I've heard some strange things. But this is the strangest ever!"

"And," continued Rachel, "Gordo can understand English!"

Ray was staring at her and trying to take this all in.

"So when I talk to him he can understand me?" he asked.

"Yes. But there's more to tell you," she continued, "And I do need your help…"

"I already offered…"

"You did, I know," she acknowledged, "But I don't think you realise… it is difficult and very dangerous…"

"OK," he said, "Try me."

Friday 12th December   11.27 a.m.

Elliot Smudge knocked on the office door of his superior officer.

"Come in!"

Smudge entered.

"Ah, Smudge," said Sergeant Tilson, looking up from his desk, "Sit down."

"Thank you, sir."

Smudge walked to the chair and sat down. It was only a few steps but it felt like a mile. He knew that this was trouble.

"Now…" Sergeant Tilson began, scratching his head, "What are we going to do with you?"

Smudge pretended to look puzzled.

"Sir?" he queried.

"You must know what I'm talking about. No?" he asked. Then his voice became stern as he snapped, "The Marks' case… does that ring any bells in that thick skull of yours?"

Smudge nodded. "Yes, sir. Of course, sir. I'm working on it."

"But not well enough, Smudge. Not… well… enough!"

He smacked his hand down on his desk making Smudge jump.

"I want it sorted out soon. It's dragging on much too long. Huggett is breathing fire down my neck about the percentage of unsolved cases we are carrying… it's the worst in the county and you are affecting the statistics. He wants results and so do I. I spoke to the Anderton girl and found out more from her in five minutes than from you in a month of Sundays! Marks is up to something. We have the blood in the stolen truck… human blood… the bullet from a .45 Colt when he tried to steal the wretched monkey again, and… in fact, loads of leads to follow. And what's happened now? He's disappeared!"

Smudge fidgeted uncomfortably. "My theory is, sir, that he's hiding 'coz he knows we're onto him…sir."

"Exactly," Sergeant Tilson sighed, and then added with heavy sarcasm, "Well done, well done. When you could have arrested him, you didn't… and now that we want to, we can't. Why not? 'Coz you've scared him off."

Sergeant Tilson waved his hand with a gesture of despair.

"One week, Smudge, that's what I'm giving you. One week to resolve this business one way or the other."

"Yes, sir," Smudge nodded with a smile, but inside he was seething.

"If you haven't solved it by then, you're off the case. I might even give it to Anderton to tackle by herself. Understand?"

"Yes, sir."

"Good. Now, get out and get to work."

Smudge got up and walked to the door, like a dog with its tail between its legs.

Sergeant Tilson growled loudly at him, "And do whatever you need to do to crack this one... OK?"

"OK, sir," Smudge responded and closed the door behind him.

6.15 p.m.

Jamie and Doug had planned Operation Jupiter in detail. They had written it all in a notebook and then made a duplicate of it so that they had one each. Today they would put it into action.

Before arriving home, Jamie had lingered down the road for ten minutes so that his late entrance would annoy his grandmother. This was to get her in a suitably bad mood. It was stage two of the plan; he had already made his shoes muddy using the hose in the garden and some earth – stage one.

He parked his bike in the shed and went inside. Then he left his pair of filthy shoes lying untidily in the middle of the hall with a few thick smudges of mud on the wooden floor. Stages three and four completed.

He could not help a discreet smile as he walked into the lounge and flopped in front of the TV. Zorro jumped onto his lap, purring with delight. Now it was just a question of waiting.

It wasn't long before she walked into the hall and saw the shoes. Jamie was listening from the lounge and heard her shriek with horror. A second later she burst back into the lounge. Zorro leapt off his lap.

"What do you think you're doing?!" she snapped, "I haven't brought you up to be a slovenly good-for-nothing! Your parents would be horrified! Those shoes cost good money, you ungrateful child! You'd better clean them until they're shining like new... and while you're at it clean the mud off the floor too!"

He knew from experience that she was half way towards completely losing her temper, which is what he wanted. All it needed now was just three words, exactly the right three words; the three magic words. That should be enough to ignite her disapproval into anger. It would be like lighting the touch paper of a firework. He had done it before.

He took a deep breath and then shouted back, "No I won't!"

She glared at him.

"Do as I say," she hissed, "And then go to bed!"

The plan was going well, but to make absolutely sure, he to decided throw in one more phrase.

"Why should I?!" he shouted.

The effect was like throwing paraffin onto a fire. She was out of control.

"You will!" she screeched, "And you'll go to bed without supper... and... in the morning I'll expect an apology."

Jamie had achieved stage five – a blazing row. Looking extremely disgruntled, he cleaned his shoes and the floor, and then stomped up the stairs with Zorro running behind him. His bedroom was a converted attic and at the top of a further set of stairs. When he was half way up these, the sleek, grey cat flashed past him and into his bedroom, jumping onto his bed. Jamie followed, closed the door and chuckled. He sat on his bed and stroked Zorro affectionately.

"Stages one to six completed, Zorro," he said, "Now we wait."

He took out his notebook, opened it and crossed them off:

* Make shoes very muddy.
* Arrive home late.
* Leave shoes on hall floor.
* Put lots of mud on floor.
* Have gigantic row with the dragon!
* Get sent to bed early.

It was just after seven and he knew his grandmother usually went to bed between ten and half past ten. She always looked in on him and this time he would pretend to be asleep. When she had gone to bed, he would leave a note for his grandmother to find in the morning; he had written it already. It would tell her that he was so upset that he had gone to stay with a friend for a few days.

However, the real plan was to take all the money he had saved from working at Cape Canaveral, which was hidden under the loose floorboard. Then he would creep down, leave by the back door and he would be off on his bike to meet Doug.

In the morning she would find the note and start phoning his friends. She would start with his best friend, Doug, who lived on a farm. Doug would make sure he answered the phone and would politely reassure her that Jamie was there.

But now it was all going wrong; there was a spanner in the works. He had waited for over three hours, reading and working on a model to pass the time, and she still had not come up to bed. The only thing that ever delayed her was when she fell asleep in front of the T.V.

At quarter to eleven Jamie was getting anxious and wondering what to do because he had to leave. He decided to chance it. If she was asleep he could sneak past the lounge without waking her. He opened his bedroom door a crack to peep out. All clear. He started creeping down. Just as he reached the foot of his stairs and was about to take the next flight to the ground floor, he heard her.

She was moving around downstairs, and walking across the wooden hall floor to the foot of the stairs. He turned and sped up the stairs as quietly as he could back into his room, hoping that she had not heard him. He closed the door gently, slipped into his bed and huddled under the blankets.

He listened as she climbed the stairs and went into the bathroom on the floor below. She came out a few minutes later and mounted the steps to his room. Jamie heard his door open as she looked in to check he was asleep.

"Jamie?" she asked quietly.

She almost sounded kind. He lay still, pretending to be asleep. The door closed, and he heard her descending again. The hall light clicked off and the house was plunged into darkness. Jamie managed to restrain his urge to leap out of bed and run down the stairs and out. He waited five minutes and then made his move.

He reached under his bed and pulled out the note for his grandmother which he had written earlier. He crept to the door, placed the note on the floor where she would find it, and turned the handle. He was about to pull it open when something happened that made him jump with shock. The key rattled in the lock.

Then he heard her voice through the door. It was almost a whisper and loaded with mock kindness.

"Jamie," she said quietly, "Sleep well. You're not going anywhere tonight. I will see you in the morning. You need to apologize to me... remember?"

Jamie froze. He did not answer. The key was withdrawn from the lock and he heard her footsteps move down the steps and back into her room. He waited a minute. Very slowly he turned the door handle and pulled to check. It was locked.

He closed his eyes and gripped his hands in frustration. She must have guessed his plans and crept up to his room. Now he was trapped here as securely as a prisoner in a cell. He stepped back to his bed and fell onto it in despair. This was the worst thing that could happen and he had no choice but to give up. His quest was over. Doug would be waiting for him now and expecting him to arrive any minute. The plan to free Gordo would fail without him and he had let down Rachel and Ray as well.

He felt Zorro jump onto the bed and brush up against him, purring. Jamie felt so upset that he pushed him away and Zorro almost slipped off the bed, just holding on with his claws and then pulling himself up and looking at Jamie, wide-eyed. Straight away, Jamie reached out to stroke him.

"Sorry, Zorro," he said, "I didn't mean it."

Zorro relaxed. Jamie knew that this beautiful grey cat with the silky-soft fur was a wonderful friend in times like these. He sat up on the bed, pulled his pillow up behind him, leant back and closed his eyes. Zorro's loud purring soothed his agitation as the cat stepped gently onto his lap and curled into a ball.

Jamie's mind turned over what had happened. His grandmother had outwitted him. He had been sure that Operation Jupiter would work and he had never expected her to be one step ahead. His head dropped forwards and he fell asleep.

11.05 p.m.

Gordo was excited. Tonight the Jupiter AM-13 would take off to carry him on his 2000 mile journey into space and back. There was also another thing that was constantly in the back of his mind. It slipped into his dreams and was at the centre of his hopes for the future; he would soon be living freely in the jungle.

The night was dark and cloudy as he huddled in his canvas nest in the tree. This had been his home now for almost a year and he had grown very fond of it. He decided he should be enjoying this last hour here. The tree swayed gently in a slight breeze, lulling him towards slumber like a beckoning finger. He drifted off into a light sleep.

11.19 p.m.

The little town where Rachel lived was held in the velvet hush of night. Only a solitary owl defied the silence with the soft-edged sound of its hooting. In a tree somewhere, it watched over its kingdom. Suddenly, it took to the air, gliding soundlessly past Rachel's house to land in a tree close by.

Rachel switched off her bathroom light. She walked down the hall past her bedroom, glancing in and snatching a torch off a small chest of drawers. At the top of the stairs she put on her coat and descended quickly.

She was not late, but she knew she must be efficient so that nothing went wrong. The plans had been thoroughly worked out and she hoped they would be successful. Gordo's freedom depended on it.

Hanging over the banister post at the foot of the stairs was a rucksack. It was packed with everything she would need and the torch was the last item. She tucked it into a pocket on the side, swung the bag into the air and slipped her arms through the shoulder straps. A quick glance at her watch told her she was nicely on time. Everything was prepared.

At the front door she paused and leant back for a moment against the wall, resting on the bag on her back. She closed her eyes and sighed at the task that lay ahead. She was frightened and tried to gather her strength together. By herself she doubted that she had the courage to see it through but she knew she would have Jamie with her. This was a comforting thought. Her fear subsided and although she knew it would return later, she felt ready.

She opened the door and stepped out. The air was fresh and she breathed in deeply. The rich sound of the owl's hooting made her look up into a tree in her front garden and she saw its silhouetted shape. She smiled. It was the first time she had seen it in her garden and she thought playfully that maybe it had come to wish her good luck. She walked to the car and got in.

The engine sparked into life, drowning the owl's dulcet tones. She reversed out and drove off. The car's noise faded into the silence and the owl hooted loudly, as if reclaiming his place as the lord of his night-time kingdom.

11.28 p.m.

Jamie awoke with Zorro jumping off him and onto the floor. He wondered how long he had been asleep and glanced at his watch. Nearly half past eleven. He shook his head and sighed heavily with despair; all the careful planning, all the notes that he had made with Doug, all the discussions, were now useless.

He watched Zorro twist his head around to lick his back

and then trot to the window, jumping up to sit on the sill. Jamie felt refreshed by the short sleep and as he stared at Zorro an idea appeared in his mind; he knew what he had to do.

He remembered something that happened three years earlier which proved that it was possible to escape – for a cat.

Zorro had been dozing in Jamie's room with the door closed. Half an hour later, Jamie had been surprised to see him in the garden, so he rushed up and found that his window was open just enough for a cat to squeeze through. He looked out onto the sloping roof and marvelled at Zorro's climbing skills. Since then Zorro often sat on the window sill wanting to be let out but Jamie never let him go; it looked far too dangerous.

Jamie slid off the bed and felt his legs go weak as he thought about what he would have to do. He would escape through the window and Zorro would show him how. He imagined himself climbing on the roof and a cold sweat broke out on his brow; he hated heights.

With a shaking hand, he grabbed his Operation Jupiter notebook and slipped it into his pocket. He turned out the light, picked up his bike lamp and switched it on. Then he heard a sound at the window. This was followed by a sharper one and a crack appeared running across a corner of the glass. He rushed to the sash window, lifted it so that it slid open and looked down into the dark.

As expected, it was Doug who was looking up and just throwing another stone. It hit the window frame, bounced down the sloping roof and almost hit Doug as it landed.

"Jamie!" called up Doug.

Jamie shone his torch into his friend's face who blinked and held up a hand.

"Shhh…" Jamie ordered, and then speaking softly but mouthing the words slowly, "She's locked me in, but I'm coming out now…"

"How?"

"Following Zorro… if he can do it, so can I. Wait there."

"OK."

Jamie could hardly believe he was saying it. By putting on such a confident air, he was trying to convince himself. He would do this for Gordo.

Zorro was sitting on the sill inside the window.

"Do you want to go out, Zorro?" he asked.

Zorro looked at him and lifted up his nose to be stroked. Jamie ran his hand down Zorro's head and scratched him under the chin. Then he opened the window.

"There you are Zorro," he said softly, "Show me how you did it."

Zorro held up his nose again for another stroke.

"No, Zorro… go out now… go on."

He lifted Zorro out but the cat just settled down on the sill outside.

"Zorro! Go! Go!"

When Zorro did not move, he gave him a gentle push but still he stayed. Jamie picked him up and dropped him onto the roof.

"Please, Zorro, please!"

Instead of climbing down, Zorro walked up, towards the top of the roof. Jamie began to climb out and then paused, glancing back into his room and remembering something. He jumped back in and moved quickly towards his bed, crouching down to lift up a loose floorboard. His hand reached in, grasped the small bag containing his savings. It was a mixture of notes and coins and it chinked as he pulled it out. He knew how much was there: six dollars forty-eight cents, and to him it seemed like a fortune. He slipped the bag into his pocket.

A nudge with his foot pushed the floorboard back into place and he moved quietly back to the window. He scrambled out, stepping cautiously onto the roof and pausing, gripping the window frame with one hand and the bike lamp with the other. Very slowly, he straightened his body and tried to find his balance. Then he remembered something; he must close the window to hide his escape. He shone the lamp on it and slowly pulled it down.

A split second glance down was a mistake and enough to ignite his fear. His half-bent legs began to shake. He felt as fragile as a butterfly. He wondered how he would get out of this, because he was frozen with dread, unable to move up the roof or back in through the window.

A fine drizzle touched his face, cool and refreshing in the night air and he tried to concentrate on it to clear his mind. But he could not help thinking that the rain was dampening the tiles and making them slippery, so he shone his lamp up the roof. Moss dotted the roof where the tiles joined, and large patches of green algae looked slimy in the damp. As he looked up, the gradient seemed impossibly steep.

"I can't do this," he whispered to himself.

He thought of Gordo, and somehow, with a great effort, he started climbing slowly. After two cautious steps, his foot slipped and he fell forwards. He was still holding the lamp in one hand and it whacked onto the tiles with a sharp rap, while the other hand landed flat and supported his weight. He started climbing again but this time using his feet and both hands, with one holding the lamp which tapped each time he moved.

He looked up to see Zorro walking casually along the apex of the roof. He shone the lamp at him. The cat glanced down, two discs of bright light, and then sat down.

Jamie panicked and scrabbled upwards, his shoes slipping and sliding dangerously and his hand stinging as it scraped on the rough surface of the tiles. At the top, he peered over. It was terrifying and Jamie was tempted to go back and slip into the safety of his room.

He closed his eyes, swallowed and considered turning back. Then he decided.

With his fingers over the top of the roof he pulled himself up with one arm and lay there for a moment, an arm and a leg hanging down each side and his body, face down, stretched along the apex. His heart was racing.

He lifted his head to see Zorro walking away from him on the apex of the roof. Then the cat turned, moving down the sloping roof over the other side. Jamie peered over to watch Zorro. The roof dropped away into the darkness but he could just see the grey shape of his cat balanced on the edge with his feet on the gutter. Jamie shone the lamp at him; Zorro was poised and ready to jump, and the next second, he leapt into the shadows.

Jamie turned, so that his legs were going down first. He began to descend slowly, like a crab but backwards. One foot slipped on some moss and he lost his grip. Panic took over as he felt himself sliding. He tried desperately to stop his fall, flailing his arms wildly and grasping at the tiles but he was out of control.

As he slid downwards, he rolled onto his back and his feet thudded hard into the gutter. He felt it give way but the impact had halted his fall for a moment. In a flash he saw Zorro's round eyes staring at him from a tree and he knew that he had one chance. He pushed down with his legs and leapt.

He landed on the nearest branch with a heavy thump

and dropped the lamp which thudded onto the ground below. The air had been knocked out of him but he was alive and that was all that mattered. For a while, he lay there on the branch, clinging on with both hands. He knew this tree and had climbed it many times, although his fear of heights had kept him in the lower branches. He had found Zorro's secret escape route.

He felt a paw on his back. Zorro climbed onto him and nuzzled up to the back of his head.

"Thank you, Zorro," Jamie whispered, "but next time, pick an easier route, please. Now... to get down."

"You OK?" asked Doug from below.

"Yeah," replied Jamie, "I'm coming down."

Climbing down was not easy. Out of fear, he did not look down, but fixed his attention on his hands and it worked. In a few seconds he was jumping down onto the grass with Zorro just behind him. Doug was holding the lamp.

"That..." he began, smiling and shaking his head, "was some escape. I told you it would be exciting."

A noise above made them look up to see a length of guttering falling from the roof, directly above them. Jamie pulled Doug away just in time; the guttering embedded itself in the grass in between Jamie and Zorro.

"Phew!" Doug whispered, "Thanks."

"Where's your bike?" Jamie asked.

"I left it round the back and climbed over the wall. I'll get it and meet you in the road."

"OK."

Doug passed the lamp to Jamie and then rushed off into the bushes. Jamie hurried across the garden to the shed where he kept his bike. Zorro followed. A rustle in the dark trees behind made him stop and gaze into the shadows. He shone the lamp towards the sound and he saw two eyes staring back at him.

A movement made him step back only to see a tabby cat jumping down from a tree and then slipping away silently into the night. He relaxed and glanced back at the house. All was well.

He lifted Zorro onto a branch.

"Stay here, Zorro," he whispered and scratched him on his head.

He put his hand on the shed door-handle when suddenly a light went on behind him. He heard a window opening and then his grandmother's voice hit him like a slap on the head.

"What are you doing?!" she yelled.

Without looking around, he pulled the door open. He slid the lamp onto the fixture on the front of his bike, grabbed it by the handles and started to wheel it out. It caught on something; the pedal was tangled in the spokes of his grandmother's bike. This was odd. He had parked his bike ready for his getaway. He shook it in a panic and both bikes rattled and slipped towards him, locked together. He knew she would be down the stairs by now, heading for the back door; he could see her in his mind and feel her fury.

He must calm down. He looked at the bikes and saw the answer. He reached down, felt the pedal and eased it out of the spokes. His grandmother's bike crashed into the wall and his was free. He pushed the door open with his front wheel, and saw his grandmother. She was storming down the path.

Jamie jumped onto his bike and swerved onto the grass. She stepped off the path at once and dodged across to grab him, catching him by his jacket.

"Get off!" he yelled.

He jerked his jacket and it slipped out of her grasp. He stood up on the pedal making his back wheel spin on the grass. He tried again and it gripped. He was away.

"Where are you going?!" she cried, "Jamie?! Come back!"

Without looking around Jamie shouted his reply.

"I'm staying with a friend…"

He was speeding away now and as he passed the house he heard her shouting after him. At the end of the drive he was about to turn right when an idea struck him and he skidded to a halt. He paused for a moment, glancing around and hearing her footsteps running past the house. He made sure that she could see him before turning left onto the road.

"Don't worry about me, Gran!" he shouted, "I'll be back in a few days."

Her voice rising in pitch to an ear-piercing screech. "Where are you going?!"

"I'm staying with Doug!" he yelled.

"Where does he live?!"

He was almost out of earshot now and without turning his head, he made up, "Yashgolast terbi…"

Her voice sounded distant now as she shouted, "What?!"

He sped down a slope and away into the darkness, leaving her standing there engulfed by helplessness and frustration. She stared after him for a moment, shook her head and growled in anger, and then walked back to the house.

11.40 p.m.

As Rachel drove, she tried to stay calm but the excitement of the launch and the apprehension of the daring plan to free Gordo kept rising in her. It was like trying to hold a balloon under water. After leaving her house she had realized she had left her compass on the kitchen table; she had turned the car and gone back for it.

Now she was on the SR 405 again and crossing Indian River. She pulled the car to a halt by the check-point barrier and wound down the window. Gudge Greentram, the guard, came out and greeted her with a friendly smile.

"The big night, Miss Chandler," he stated as he approached the car, "Good luck!"

"Thanks, Gudge," she replied.

"Will the launch be on time?" he asked.

"Should be," she nodded, "Everything's gone smoothly so far. Will you be watching it?"

"Of course," he replied, "I'm on duty here but I might just climb up on the roof."

Rachel looked at the roof of his hut. "Good idea. Anyway… must get going."

She wound up the window as he lifted the barrier and then she pulled away. She switched on the wipers and they brushed away the drizzle from the windscreen. A few minutes later she had parked her car and was walking up the pathway to the Cape Canaveral International Space Centre building.

11.42 p.m.

Jamie and Doug had met up in the road and cycled off together as fast as they could. Their legs were burning. They had been cycling flat out now for five minutes and pushing hard. They knew that the delayed departure would make Jamie late and the only thing they could do was to try to make up time by cycling as fast as they could. They had stopped once for Jamie to switch on his rear light, although it was hardly necessary; there was no traffic at this time of night. Their front lights lit up the road ahead.

They struggled up a slope and freewheeled down the other side, letting their bikes accelerate without peddling.

When they were on level road again their pace slowed; they were tired and settled into a steady speed, riding side by side. Now they were able to talk about how Operation Jupiter was going.

"What an escape!" stated Doug, "I told you it would work..."

"Yeah," agreed Jamie, "But up on the roof..." he shook his head, "that was scary!"

"The old bat couldn't stop you," Doug said with glee.

"But I'll be late," sighed Jamie, "They'll be wondering where I am."

"Yeah, but not too late. It'll be alright."

"I hope so," Jamie said, "Hey, Doug... you don't have to come any further."

"I know... but I'm enjoying the ride. I'll leave you in a minute."

A sharp bend caught them by surprise. Jamie was in front and he skidded and slowed just in time, and so did Doug, but as they did they heard something falling off Jamie's bike. It was small and metal, which pinged on the hard road and hit Doug on the leg. Jamie looked around, just as his bike jerked and then juddered. The back wheel had lost one of the nuts and began wobbling and shaking. A second later, the chain jammed and the bike stopped abruptly. Jamie's world turned upside-down as he tumbled over the handlebars, over a grassy verge and plunged into a hedge. His head glanced off the trunk of a tree and he landed on his back with a thump. Doug's bike crashed into Jamie's and he fell off onto the road.

In the aftermath of the crash everything was still. Jamie felt winded and gasped for air. His head hurt and his cheek was grazed. The darkness crowded around him in indistinct, eerie shapes.

"Doug... you alright?"

"Yes, I think so."

Jamie's breath returned and he sat up. He felt dazed and

shaken and checked his limbs, moving them one by one. Nothing broken. Then he felt his cheek with his hand; it was tender and moist with blood. He stood up and his head thumped. He leant back on the tree and sighed. Doug stepped off the road and onto the grass verge, shaking his head in dismay.

"Why did this have to happen now?" he said.

"Why today?" asked Jamie.

Jamie growled in frustration through clenched teeth – it sounded loud in the silence. His bike was lying on the road with Doug's beside it. The lights were still on, Jamie's sending a beam across the road and Doug's pointing straight up. The rear ones glowed red in the dark.

"Let's check the bikes," said Doug.

One glance dampened their hope of continuing; a closer look extinguished it completely. Jamie's wheel was badly buckled and completely off the frame of the bike, attached only by the chain.

"This is very odd," he said. He took his lamp off and shone it on the bike. "Look! Both wheel nuts are gone."

Doug gasped with shock. "You mean... someone did this! But who?"

Jamie's memory flashed back and he saw his pedal entangled with his aunt's wheel. Someone had been there, removed one nut and loosened the other. Whoever did it wanted to stop him making this journey tonight and they had achieved their aim.

Jamie's notebook for Mission Jupiter had fallen out of his pocket as he crashed and was lying there on the road, splattered with mud. He picked it up and opened it, shining his lamp on the pages.

"This is useless now," he thought.

Doug had his lamp in his hand now and was inspecting the damage done to his bike. He had a flat tire, the frame was bent and the front wheel would not turn. Both bikes were wrecked. They dragged them off the road.

Once again, disappointment overcame Jamie and he slumped down on the grassy verge in deep despair. Doug sat down beside him.

"We can't give up," he said, trying to be positive, "This is bad… very bad… but Operation Jupiter must go ahead."

Jamie did not reply.

CHAPTER 14

Saturday 13th December   12.15 a.m.

Gordo awoke to the sound of the light drizzle on the canvas roof above him. He enjoyed rain and he held his hand out to feel it on his palm. After a minute, he swung out of his nest and up the tree. The water was refreshing and he rubbed his hands vigorously over the fur of his body, arms, legs and tail.

When he had finished washing he looked around his cage. He had lived here now for eleven months. It had been a happy time with Jamie, Rachel and Ray. They had looked after him with the greatest care in every way. Rachel and Gordo had spent most days together, and Jamie had been there almost every day after school and at weekends. For Jamie, the summer school holidays had been the best ever;

he spent many full days at the space centre doing odd jobs and spending time with Gordo.

Gordo would be sad to leave but he knew that his natural home was the jungle. Deep within him was a yearning to live in a rain forest in South America. This was his dream but first there was his trip into space and the difficulties of the people who wanted him after the flight. Jamie had promised that he would get him to the jungle, and Rachel had shown that she was just as keen and had the same determination to do it. They had promised…

His thoughts were interrupted by a door opening, followed by the sudden appearance of a beam of torchlight and footsteps. Gordo recoiled, slipping down a branch and then dodging down into his nest.

"Where's Greeber?" he thought.

He had seen him earlier, sitting in his chair by the wall. But where was he now?

"Who's there?" said Greeber's voice from the darkness.

The footsteps stopped and the torch created a great oval of light on the ground. Gordo heard Greeber draw his gun from its holster.

"It's me," said Rachel.

Gordo relaxed.

"Oh, miss," said Greeber, stepping onto the path and into the torchlight. He switched on his own torch. "I'd forgotten you were coming."

"Greeber!" exclaimed Rachel, "How could you forget? It's the big night."

"I'd only forgotten… sort of in the moment, miss," Greeber replied, "When I'm here night after night and nothing happens at all… for months on end… well… all nights seem the same."

"Well, this is your last night, Greeber," she said cheerfully, "In fact, your last few minutes. You've done a great job."

"Thank you, miss."

"I don't think you need that," said Rachel, nodding at the gun which he was absentmindedly pointing at her feet.

"Sorry, miss."

Greeber slipped the gun back into its holster. His torchlight caught her face making her blink. Her skin glinted in the drizzle.

"Are you watching the launch, Greeber?"

"I don't know, miss," he said, "I haven't been invited."

"Well I hereby officially invite you," announced Rachel.

"Oh, thank you, miss," he said gratefully, "Thank you."

"I'll tell you the best place, Greeber…"

"Yes, miss?" said Greeber sounding interested.

"The lighthouse. Have you been up there?"

"No, miss."

"The view is great, and it's close to our launch pad – 26B. It's worth a try, don't you think?"

He nodded.

"Good. I'll tell the keeper to expect you then."

"Thank you, miss."

"Anyway," she continued, "You're off duty now. You can go, if you wish."

"I'll see you into the building first, miss, if you don't mind."

"Thank you, Greeber," Rachel said, "I'll only be a minute."

Rachel turned and walked toward the cage.

"Gordo?" she called out, shining her torch up into the tree.

"Hi, Rachel," he replied, swinging quickly down the tree.

Rachel entered the cage and Gordo leapt onto her shoulder.

The moment had finally arrived; she was collecting him to take him to the launch pad.

She whispered to him gently, knowing that he would be nervous and could understand her words.

"You'll be fine," she comforted, "You've practiced so many times. You're in tip top shape."

"Where's Jamie?" he asked.

He jumped off her shoulder and onto a branch so that he could face her. He looked around anxiously and gestured with his hands. She guessed what he was asking.

"Jamie should be here by now," she whispered so that Greeber could not hear, "I'm sure he'll be here soon." She looked at him intently. "I hope you're clear about our plan. I'll go over it and you nod if you know the answer."

Gordo nodded.

"Which lever?" Rachel asked.

He nodded again.

"Third from the right," she stated, "But it's clearly marked and the setting dials are above. And the angle?"

He nodded and held up four fingers.

"Good... four degrees," Rachel confirmed. "How long?"

Gordo paused and then held up three fingers on one hand and one on the other.

"Well done!" she praised, "3.1 seconds... set it on the dial, OK?"

Gordo nodded again.

"Good," she said, "Then you flick the lever and belt in tight!"

Gordo swung under the branch and then up again, arriving back where he started and smiling at her. She patted him on the head.

"You're ready."

She swept him up into her arms and walked out of the cage and along the path to where Greeber was waiting. The drizzle was easing now and the moon was trying to break through the clouds.

"Thanks for waiting, Greeber," she said.

"It's a pleasure, miss," he replied. He reached out and stroked Gordo on the head, "How are you, little fella? Ready for the big adventure."

"He's ready," said Rachel.

They walked to the building, Greeber opened the door and they went in.

A minute later Rachel and Gordo emerged from a door on the other side of the building. Gordo looked at Rachel with a worried expression and gave her hair a little tug. She knew what he meant.

"It's strange," she said, "Very strange that he's not here. What's happened to him?"

She stopped walking for a moment and wondered what to do.

"We have to carry on without him. Perhaps he's gone straight to the rocket."

They weaved their way between the buildings and along paths lit by occasional lamps. The drizzle stopped and a crescent moon shone momentarily through a gap in the clouds and bathed everything in pale light. Through the trees, gentle moonbeams cast shadows across the grey paths.

They came to a road, stopped and waited for a couple of minutes. The darkness deepened as clouds drifted across the moon and they were pleased to hear the sound of a vehicle approaching. It appeared around a corner, the headlights piercing the night. It was a small mini-bus and Rachel waved it to a halt. She climbed in and sat in the front seat with Gordo on her shoulder.

After a few minutes ride, they entered the dark, open expanse of Launch Complex LC26, and there in front of them was the launch pad with the tall Jupiter rocket looming ahead. The clouds parted as if preparing for the path of the rocket, and the moon again shed its pale light. Now they could see the rocket more clearly, towering high towards the night sky. Within a few minutes several other vehicles arrived and a team of over fifty people were gathered at the foot of the Jupiter AM-13.

12.45 a.m.

Jamie sat on the verge of the road with his head lowered in thought. He had tried so hard and still failed. The crash had been the final straw that battered him into submission, and now he felt exhausted from cycling with such energy. This was the end of his quest to save Gordo and he would have to give up.

Doug had been lucky because the crash had left him with only one injury which was a graze on the back of his arm just below his elbow. He was sitting beside Jamie, thinking about how Operation Jupiter could go ahead. Their bike lamps lay between them; they had turned them off to preserve the batteries leaving the darkness lying thickly all around them. Doug's voice was clear in the silent, night air.

"You can't give up now," he said.

"Why not?" groaned Jamie, "Everything's gone wrong."

"I know," agreed Doug, "But what about Operation Jupiter? Secret agents don't just give up... they find a way."

"But..." began Jamie, sighing out the words, "It's impossible now."

"Secret agents find a way..." Doug repeated firmly, "We must try."

Jamie shrugged despondently.

"Every path has its puddle," stated Doug.

Jamie frowned. "What?!" he asked.

"It's an old English proverb," said Doug, "Don't you remember? Egg told us. It means that if you meet a problem, something which stops you doing what you are trying to do, you shouldn't give up. You find ways of overcoming the problem..."

Jamie thought he had learnt nothing from Egg but he had

to admit these few words were encouraging. He tried to pull his thoughts together. An image of Gordo's face flashed into his mind and his determination rose again. He lifted his head and nodded slowly.

"You're right," he said, "We must try... somehow."

He picked up the lamp and made himself stand up and look around. He turned the lamp on and shone it to his right, where the road ran away into the darkness and then to his left, where it rose up the slope. He longed to hear a car approaching but the night was silent apart from the chirping of a cricket from a field beyond a low hedge across the road. Beside him lay his bike, always a companion to him and his means to freedom, but now as useless as a pile of rust. The buckled wheel lay forlorn on the grass verge.

"What shall we do then?" asked Jamie. "I can't get there now and you are meant to be playing the tennis final tomorrow. We're stuck here."

Doug looked thoughtful as Jamie continued.

"I'm too late to go to Cape Canaveral, so I must go straight to Patrick Air Force Base..."

"OK," nodded Doug, "Maybe a car will come by and we can wave it down and get a lift and...?"

"And..." interrupted Jamie, "If no cars come by, then what?"

There was silence for a minute until Jamie spoke again.

"We have to get... our own car," he said slowly.

"How?" said Doug, looking interested.

"Oh, I don't know. It's just a silly idea. And anyway, we can't drive."

Doug shook his head. "I can drive... a bit. I've driven around the farm."

"That's it!" Jamie exclaimed, pointing his lamp across the road at a field, "Do you think that could be a farm?"

He crossed the road and shone his lamp over a low hedge.

"Broccoli!" he announced, "It *has* to be a farm! And on

the farm there could be a car!"

Doug took up this idea immediately. If they could find a car, they would have to start it somehow, and then take it. It would be stealing, but in this desperate situation, it felt more like borrowing it for a very important reason. Those things could be faced later.

"Which way?" Doug asked.

Jamie looked up and down the road, shining his lamp.

"Let's go right," he said.

Doug switched on his lamp and they started running beside the hedge, looking for a gate, praying for a farmhouse with a car parked beside it.

After a while they found what they were looking for. They slipped through a gate, crossed a field and entered a farm yard.

12.55 a.m.

It was a spectacular moment when the lights were turned on. The whole area was flooded with the powerful beams of the spotlights. The rocket itself was dotted with lights, as pretty as those on any Christmas tree. Above the towering structure, the gap in the clouds had widened to expose the watchful moon resting in the star-speckled darkness of the sky. Rachel paused for a moment to gaze upwards in awe.

"Look at that, Gordo," she said, "Isn't that amazing?"

"Amazing," he agreed, "And scary!"

They entered the lift.

"Are you alright?" she said to Gordo who had been far more quiet than usual.

"Yes, I'm fine really," he replied in her ear, and nodded so that she could understand.

"Good," she said as the lift doors closed, "The sooner we get you settled into the nose cone the better."

She pushed the button and with a jerk they began their ascent.

Gordo tensed as he felt butterflies in his stomach. The launch was close now and he would soon be strapped into the capsule. There was no turning back.

Rachel felt his tension and stroked him with her hand. She felt tense as well. In different ways, they were both about to embark on the most dangerous challenges they had ever faced. Gordo was about to be launched into space in a rocket with awesome power, and at the same time, Rachel would be putting into action the plan to free Gordo after the flight. The plan was daring and risky, and she was terrified.

1.04 a.m.

Jamie was looking through the dusty window of a wooden garage and shining his lamp around. It was the second farmyard building they had tried. He smiled when the beam of light revealed a wonderful sight; a Chevrolet Pickup. It was waiting for them.

The window frame was old and rotting, so Jamie pushed it firmly and a gap appeared. Doug found a stick, jammed it into the gap and levered it open to the sound of splitting wood. It fell inwards and the glass smashed. They both grimaced, hoping it would not awaken anyone in the farmhouse a few buildings away.

Jamie climbed through first, followed by Doug, and they jumped down lightly onto the floor, their sneakers crunching on the broken glass. Guided by their lamps, they crept towards the pickup. Doug tried the door and it opened.

"Can you drive this?" whispered Jamie.

"I think so," replied Doug, getting in and holding the wheel, "But I've no idea how to start it without the keys... are there any keys hanging up anywhere?"

Doug jumped out and they both shone their lamps around the garage. Doug's beam landed on an open-topped John Deere 820 tractor, painted green and yellow.

"Now that..." he began, "I can start. They don't have keys. And I've driven a tractor quite a few times."

They abandoned the pickup and crept towards the tractor. Then Jamie turned back. He had remembered what the heroes always did in films; they disabled the car that might pursue them. He looked around for something sharp enough to puncture a tire and spotted some tools on a shelf. He grabbed chisel and a hammer. One blow to each of the front tires was enough; the air hissed out and the car dropped.

He re-joined Doug, who whispered to him, "Open the garage doors."

Jamie tried. "They're locked," he said, "We'll have to

smash our way out."

He had also seen this done in films and it always worked. They climbed up into the seat of the tractor, managing to sit side by side in the single seat.

Jamie felt like a criminal and a sharp jab of guilt pricked his conscience.

"I feel sorry for the farmer," he said, "We're stealing his tractor."

"No," replied Doug, "We're borrowing it… for something extremely important. Alright, without his permission, but I'm sure he'd agree if he knew. It's just we haven't got the time to ask him. Let's leave a note for him."

"No time… I have another idea."

Jamie slipped his hand into his pocket and pulled out his bag of money. He knew there were over six dollars in it and he threw it onto the ground beside the tractor for the farmer to find.

Blood was trickling down from the graze on his cheek so he wiped it with his sleeve. His head was still aching from the crash.

"Start her up then," he said to Doug.

Doug looked at the levers and controls in front of him and thought for a moment, remembering the correct sequence. Starting a tractor with a two cylinder diesel engine was far more complicated than starting a car. He had to do this right. He shone the lamp over the controls and tried to remember accurately.

First he had to start the little pony motor. He turned the mixture screw half a turn, pulled the choke out and then pushed the starter. The little motor spun but did not start. He turned the mixture screw further and then tried again and then again. On the fourth attempt it did not even spin.

Jamie sighed.

Doug waited a moment, pushed the starter again and immediately it sprang into life. He thrust a lever forwards to engage the main engine and after a few splutters it began to chug loudly and puff out dark smoke from the tall exhaust pipe on the bonnet. They both grimaced at the engine noise – surely they would be heard. They had to get going quickly.

Doug flicked a switch on and the headlights, which were mounted on the wheel arches either side of him, cast two yellow circles on the doors in front. He slipped down in his seat and stretched his foot to push the clutch pedal, gripped the long lever rising up from the floor on his right and pushed it into gear. He lifted the clutch pedal much too quickly and the tractor lunged forwards with a jerk and accelerated.

They were both thrown back into the seat. Jamie dropped his lamp and nearly fell off. Doug gripped the steering wheel tightly as the great machine smashed through the wooden, double doors. They ducked as bits of wood flew all around them and when they bobbed up to look, they were careering down a slope and across the farmyard towards a barn. In a panic, Doug yanked the wheel, turning to the right, and the tractor tipped out of control, two wheels lifting off the ground. He turned the steering wheel back and the tractor bumped down, the huge back tire bouncing like a ball.

It was like riding a wild horse with a will of its own.

They knew they would hit the barn at an angle and they tensed for the crash. The impact turned the tractor and it ran along the side of the barn, scraping and grinding as it went. A few planks of wood were ripped off and clattered onto the ground. When it reached the end of the barn, the tractor had lost some of its shiny green paint and gained a large dent.

Doug still clung onto the steering wheel as he steered across some grass and onto a path which led out of the farmyard. As they passed the farmhouse, they saw an upstairs light turn on. Slipping down on the seat, Doug tried the brake and then pulled a lever sticking up in front of the steering wheel which slowed down the running speed of the engine. He was gaining control.

At the gate he managed to stop the tractor, by taking it out of gear and pushing the foot brake. Jamie jumped down and dashed to open the gate.

"Hey!" shouted a voice behind him.

Jamie ran back and scrambled up to join Doug in the seat. They heard the sound of feet pounding down the path after them at a fast run.

"Quick!" Jamie panicked, "Go!"

"Stop!" shouted the farmer who was only a few meters away now.

Doug forced it into gear with a loud grating sound and they lurched forwards and onto the road. The chasing man had caught up now and with a lunge, grasped the back of the tractor. Jamie turned and hit the farmer's hand as hard as he could. With a cry, the man let go.

They were on the road now and Doug turned the wheel to the right but it was too late. The tractor mounted the grass verge on the other side of the road.

"Stop!" shouted the farmer as he ran beside the huge back wheel, "Stop!"

"We're only borrowing it!" shouted Jamie, "Just for tonight!"

"Stop then!" screamed the angry farmer.

The great machine was now heading in the right direction but with two wheels on the grass. It was tilted over dangerously and flattening a hedge with its huge rear wheel. Doug steered right and the tractor dropped off the verge, and swung right across the road. The pursuing man had to drop back to avoid being run over. After a few zigzags, they were heading up the slope in the centre of the road and leaving the farmer behind. He stopped running, his chest heaving as he gulped for air. His eyes stared despairingly after the young thieves.

After a moment, he turned and started running back to his house to get his car keys. He would give chase in his car.

The slope levelled off and the boys could see that the road ahead was deserted. Doug tried changing up a gear, and then another, until he had moved through all six and was trundling and bouncing along at thirty-five miles an hour.

"We did it!" Jamie smiled, "Well done."

"Piece of cake," said Doug.

1.25 a.m.

The preparations needed to be thorough. Everything had to be checked, double-checked and then checked a third time to make absolutely sure everything was working. The extreme complexity of the rocket meant the task of inspecting it took time and it was the responsibility of the team of scientists and engineers that nothing would be overlooked. No human errors should jeopardize the success of the flight. They were sure that 'Little Old Reliable' would not let them down because they had seen him in training and knew how well he had done.

Once in the nose cone, Rachel helped Gordo into his little space suit and placed his leather-lined plastic helmet on his head. Then she put him onto his moulded rubber bed. She connected him to various instruments on the ends of long wires; a thermometer under his armpit, a microphone, a heartbeat sensor, and other instruments to follow his breathing patterns.

They were worried about Jamie. They knew he would not miss this unless something had prevented him being there but there was nothing they could do. They had to carry on.

Rachel went through the plan with Gordo and he nodded to show that he understood. When she had finished and it was time for her to go, she felt tears welling up. The wires connected to him were long enough for him to climb off his bed and into her arms. He clung onto her hair and laid his head on her shoulder.

"Listen," Rachel said, "We'll meet soon, I'm sure." She glanced at her watch and made an effort to stop crying. "Yes… in about... well, under three hours."

Gordo dropped back onto his bed. He looked up at her and smiled to reassure her. She pushed him gently back onto his bed and then clicked the safety harness into position.

"Now," she said, "One last time, undo it."

Gordo pushed with all his might, using both hands and the harness clicked free.

"Now do it up again."

He positioned it correctly and then 'click.' It was locked in position. She stroked him gently on the head.

"Gordo," she said, smiling, "Thanks for doing this. You're very brave."

He smiled. She glanced around and then started to move away.

"I'd better go," she said.

Gordo grabbed the sleeve of her jumper and pulled her back. He grabbed her finger and squeezed twice and then shook it. Rachel understood the gesture and his look. He was telling her, "Good luck."

Rachel climbed out of the nose cone leaving the door open because she knew Ray would check Gordo before the launch. The little monkey lay back on his bed and closed his eyes.

2.15 a.m.

Jamie and Doug had driven the tractor as fast as they could down the main road which ran south along Indian River. They then crossed the river on the 404 which took them straight to Patrick Air Force Base.

"There's the jet!" shouted Jamie, "on the runway!"

"We can still get there," shouted Doug, "Hold on!"

He turned the great machine off the road and smashed through a hedge and a fence and headed onto the runway.

Rachel was climbing into the jet through the door in the fuselage floor when she saw the tractor.

"Jamie!" she shouted.

The tractor bounced towards the jet and when it was close enough Jamie jumped down and sprinted towards her.

"Good luck!" cried Doug.

Rachel hauled her cousin in.

"Jamie!" Rachel exclaimed, hugging her cousin, "Jamie... it's great you're here! But... holy buckets! What were you doing on a tractor?!"

Jamie beamed.

"It was Gran... she locked my door, but I escaped through the window. Then, we... we cycled away, but we crashed... because... um... because, well, I don't know why... but I *had* to get here, so we sort of borrowed a tractor... and Doug drove - and here I am."

"Wow!" Rachel exclaimed, "That's some story... I'd like to hear it in more detail, but later. Right now, we have a very important job to do."

They strapped in for take-off, Rachel in the trainee pilot's seat and Jamie in the room in the back. He was exhausted.

A moment later, the engines roared and the jet began to taxi along the runway. Through the window Rachel caught a glimpse of the tall, lean figure of Max McMurphy running out of the airport buildings towards an awaiting jet. This concerned her. She knew that the jet he was running towards was carrier based and she also knew that out in the Atlantic Ocean was the aircraft carrier that would be already waiting to retrieve the nose cone when it splashed down. This must be where he was going but she knew he was meant to be at Cape Canaveral. It was always the case with space missions that the director, the manager and the controller of operations stayed on site at the Control Desk where they could oversee the mission. This was part of their job.

'What was he doing,' Rachel thought, *'jumping on a jet and heading out to meet the nose cone as it splashed down?'*

She shook her head in disbelief.

'Why is he flying out there? It can't be about Gordo, can it? Well... if it is, he won't get Gordo with me around!'

3.06 a.m.

Rachel was enjoying riding in the cockpit of the jet, a Lockheed T-33A Shooting Star, a two-seater training jet, as it sped eastwards over the Atlantic, cruising at 460 miles per hour. She was in the training seat directly behind the pilot. Jamie was in the room in the fuselage behind the cockpit, sitting with his back against the side, fast asleep.

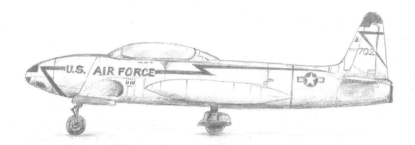

They had left Cape Canaveral miles behind. Rachel got to her feet, crouching beneath the glass cockpit roof and leaning on the back of the pilot's chair.

"Hi," said the pilot, lifting up one side of his headphones and turning back, "You OK?"

"Fine, thanks," she said.

"And young Jamie?"

"He's fine," she replied, "he's asleep."

The pilot was Charlie Scott, Jean Smith's nephew. He was in his mid-twenties, smartly dressed in his American Air Force officer's uniform and with a crew cut.

Rachel looked at all the dials, lit up around her.

"This is amazing, Charlie," she commented, "I don't know how you understand it all!"

"Oh, it's not so difficult," he replied, "Just a few years training and there you go."

She smiled and leant past him to point at one of the dials. "What's that one then?" she asked.

"Vertical speed."

"And that one?"

"Altitude."

She pointed to a switch. "And that?"

"Undercarriage selectors."

She smiled again. "Hmm…full marks."

She looked past him and through the front window where she could see white swirling clouds rushing by, lit up by the headlights of the jet. She felt they were descending and she glanced around the instrument panel for the altitude gauge - 700 feet and falling. Their speed was dropping too.

She looked at Charlie. He seemed perfectly at home. The cockpit was his kingdom and he was the king. He was in complete control. It made her feel safe but she knew it was just the calm before the storm. She was committed now to her dangerous plan, the most challenging thing she had ever done.

"Thanks for this, Charlie," she said, "You're wonderful!

But how did you arrange it?"

"Booking this old tin can out for a training flight was fairly straightforward... now that I'm an officer. I just had to bend a few rules."

"Some tin can!" exclaimed Rachel, "A four hundred miles an hour tin can!"

"All the young pilots go for the new jets every time, if they can. This T-33 is perfect for us... it dawdles along at a good speed doesn't it?" he added with a smile.

"A very good speed," Rachel smiled, "I'm very thankful, Charlie."

"It's a real pleasure."

Rachel glanced at her watch. A shudder of anticipation swept through her and her stomach fluttered.

"How long?" she asked.

"Eight minutes," said Charlie, "You'd better get ready."

"What if I go down in the wrong place?"

"Look, I told you, I can drop you on a dime," he said, smiling with confidence.

"I know."

"I just wanted to hear you say it again, Charlie. I believe you."

"The wind is increasing and I think the rain might get heavier," said Charlie, "But you might be lucky and miss it."

"Wish us luck then," smiled Rachel.

"Good luck," he said seriously, "I hope you know what you're doing. You need to get ready now."

Rachel squeezed past her chair and out of the pilot's cabin and into the small room behind. Jamie awoke.

"How long before we're there?" he asked.

He uncoupled his safety belt. The graze on his cheek looked red but had stopped bleeding.

"Are you alright?" said Rachel firmly, "That bump on your head looks nasty. And you're exhausted."

"Not anymore," stated Jamie, struggling to get up.

"I've rested and I feel much better. I'm ready."

As he stood up he felt dizzy but he did not let on. He was determined to go and tried to look confident. Rachel eyed him with suspicion but she knew she could not argue with him. They put on their fur-lined waterproof jackets and zipped them up. Then they slipped parachutes onto their backs, threading their arms through the shoulder straps and pushing together three metal clips at the front, giving each of them a pull to check they were secure.

They both put on life jackets.

"Pull that string," instructed Rachel.

The jackets hissed and inflated.

Rachel stepped back into the cockpit and sat down and Jamie followed her and leant on the back of the seat. Rain pattered heavily on the window and roof. They looked downwards over the sea. It was not far below, a vast deep expanse of black water, looking turbulent and dangerous in the dark. Jamie closed his eyes but made himself open them again. His terror of heights made him feel weak; his face was ashen.

Suddenly Rachel felt her fear deepen too; she was afraid of the sea, afraid of Max McMurphy, afraid of Jane Larkin.

Jamie reached over and took her hand and squeezed it. "We're doing this for Gordo."

Rachel closed her eyes and took a deep breath.

"We're ready," she said to Charlie.

"Good," he replied, "When the red light starts flashing you have two minutes. When the green light goes on then jump. OK?"

"OK," she confirmed.

As Jamie moved back into the room, the red light started flashing and his legs felt weak and shaky. Rachel followed, taking another deep breath. She blew out the air and then slid back the door. The effect was like switching on a force ten gale. She held tightly to the door frame and

Jamie's hand, and looked down and out, squinting her eyes against the rush of air. Cold rain hammered into her, stinging and freezing her skin. Over to her right she saw it; the dark shape of a fishing trawler bobbing on the fierce waves and with several lights flickering in the fierce weather. She watched as the jet banked and lined up to fly over the boat.

The jet slowed. Less than a minute.

"I'll go first!" she shouted to Jamie.

She pulled her woollen hat down over her forehead and got ready to jump.

"The weather's getting worse," announced Charlie over the intercom, "You don't have to do this..."

"We're going," shouted Rachel.

The red light stopped flashing and the green light went on.

"Now!" shouted Charlie.

Suddenly there was fear in her throat, and she hesitated.

"Now!" shouted Charlie again, this time louder.

Jamie nudged her and she jumped into the void. Jamie closed his eyes and followed. The parachutes unfurled and they were descending through the cold wind and rain. The black sea rushed up to meet them. Her delay meant that they were off target; they would miss the boat. Just before she splashed down in front of the fishing trawler, she saw some men in yellow water-proof jackets waving and throwing a rope towards her. She hit the freezing water. The combination of the impact and the shock of the icy water was too much for her. She passed out.

Jamie landed close to her. His head was spinning. The effort of getting to the jet in time and the blow to his head had left him weak. He bobbed on the surface in semi-consciousness, the black water numbing his legs.

3.22 a.m.

Gordo was strapped into his bed and everything was ready for the launch; half an hour to go. Ray entered the nose cone to check everything for the last time.

"Hi, Gordo," he said.

"Hi, Ray," Gordo chirruped in reply.

"So you can speak, little fella!"

Gordo nodded.

This was their first meeting since Rachel had revealed the secret of the monkey's speech to Ray and he shook his head and smiled. He wished he could speak the monkey language too and it crossed his mind that he would have to learn it.

He carefully checked everything in the nose cone. Then he made sure Gordo was comfortable on his bed, before moving around the capsule again to give it another thorough inspection. Gordo watched him and was pleased that he was so meticulous with his preparations. Once Ray had completed everything and felt sure that he had covered every possible switch and moving part, he shifted across to the door. He turned and smiled at Gordo.

"Good luck, little fella!" he said, reaching back and stroking him on his head, "We'll see you soon. You look great in your space suit!"

Gordo smiled at him and made some little friendly sounds. Ray stepped out. The door closed with a clunk and Gordo was alone.

3.52 a.m.

Gordo was extremely nervous. The seconds ticked by. He knew that it would only be a few minutes before he would be three hundred miles above the Earth and weightless, looking down on the great planet. It was a mind-boggling thought which was terrifying and exciting. He saw the countdown on a screen on the instrument panel.

32... 31... 30... 29...

There was a camera on the other side of the capsule facing straight at him. A watching eye. He knew how to disable it at the necessary time. Rachel had made sure that the wire was just within reach. A sharp pull should do it.

17... 16... 15... 14...

It was all part of the plan. The plan for his freedom.

10... 9...

He gripped the sides of his bed.

7... 6...

He held his breath.

3... 2... 1

The roar of the rocket was ear-splitting. It was the loudest noise Gordo had ever heard. Everything began to shake as the energy gathered, waiting to be released.

Clouds of smoke swirled around the dazzling white and yellow blast as the rocket began to lift away from the gantry. It rose with extraordinary acceleration, forcing up and away from the Earth. Gordo was pinned back onto his bed, sinking into the soft rubber as if invisible hands were pushing him down heavily. The rocket forged its way upwards with raw power.

CHAPTER 15

Saturday 13th December   3.55 a.m.

The people in Cape Canaveral Lighthouse at the time of the launch had enjoyed an excellent sighting of the lift-off. The view extended for miles and launch pad 26-B was close enough to give the enthusiastic gathering a perfect view of the spectacular event. Some stood on the two circular balconies outside and others packed the lantern room which housed the great light, the Fresnel Lens. Shipping had been warned that the lens would be switched off for the short time of launch.

After two and a half minutes the first section of the rocket finished and fell away, followed by the second and then the third, each of them only blasting for a few seconds. From the lighthouse these could only just be seen as faint flairs of light in the black sky, but it still produced 'oos' and 'aahs' from the eager observers.

Among those inside, Greeber was one of the fortunate spectators. There were also two police officers in plain clothes - Smudge and Ruth Anderton.

"That was amazing!" said Ruth after they had gazed up into the clear night sky until the flame of the rocket could no longer be seen.

"Trouble is," said Smudge sulkily, "How does this help us to find Jeff Marks?"

Ruth stared through the window across the night scene of the Canaveral launch pads. The other spectators were all filing out now and entering the stairwell. In a moment they were all gone. Smudge yawned.

"Being here may help us, sir," Ruth sounded optimistic, "I think we're in the right place. The clues have led us here."

Smudge leant back against the light in the centre of the room and sighed. He could feel it coming. This would be another lesson in police work from this young woman, young enough to be his daughter, who was showing up his incompetence. She was good – he knew this – she was very good. She was observant and intelligent. Most annoying of all was the way she was always cheerful and keen.

He found himself tensing as she began to speak again.

"Think of what we know already, sir. We know he's up to something illegal. We have a whole load of information now, which tell us certain things. He stole Divco truck from Kissimmee and the monkey from Naples. He sold the monkey to the space station posing as a nonexistent company. He tried to steal the monkey back again, with an accomplice… probably to sell it somewhere else. So we know there are two of them. That's why he stole the two white coats and IDs from Orlando Hospital… and they recognized him from the photo. Then he came here, with his partner in crime. It seems like they've been through the checkpoint barrier illegally on two occasions, and once was so long ago that the guard only just remembers, but that fits the timing of everything as well. That's way back in January when they first stole the monkey in Naples and brought it here. And there's the blood in the truck, human blood. He may have killed for this… we don't know… but it's possible, which makes this all high priority."

Smudge sighed, remembering how Sergeant Tilson had

reprimanded him. Ruth continued.

"The bullet in the tree could be important… from when he tried to steal the monkey for a second time. From that we know the gun he carries, or his accomplice… it's a .45 Colt. Find the gun and we can see if the bullet is a match. But the question still remains… why did he come back here again?"

She paused to listen to the sound of someone climbing the stairs.

"That's probably the lighthouse keeper," barked Smudge, "He needs to light up again. Come on. Let's go.

"Just a minute, sir. About this case… the monkey is the common factor and the monkey is now up there." She pointed upwards into the deep darkness.

She paused to think and gazed out again. The footsteps were louder now.

"But… this monkey…" she continued, "Is famous. Perhaps, the most famous monkey ever. That makes it rare and… valuable." She paused to think. "That's it, sir! Must be. He wants the monkey to sell it, but not just for peanuts. That monkey could be worth a lot of money if sold to the right person and…"

"OK, OK," Smudge interrupted. He had to nod in agreement. It all made sense. "So, when the monkey comes down then we have work to do."

"And that is soon. We must…"

Smudge held up his hand and interrupted. He wanted to stay in control.

"So…" he said decisively. All he wanted was to get home now and have some sleep. "So we return here tomorrow, make some inquiries and keep an eye on things."

"But, sir, the monkey splashes down just after 4 tonight."

"What?" exclaimed Smudge, "It's only just gone up!"

Ruth looked at him earnestly. "He's only up there for fifteen minutes, sir. We need to act now. So, we'd better go and introduce ourselves to Mission Control. That's the building there, sir."

She pointed to the three buildings; the Headquarters, the

Operations Centre and the Checkout. She turned and walked quickly to the top of the stairs.

"Come on, sir," she called back to Smudge.

Smudge reluctantly resigned himself to working through the night and dragged his lethargic body after her. Just then Ray appeared at the top of the stairs.

"Are you two the cops?" he said, breathing heavily after the long climb.

They nodded.

"Look," he began, "I've got a lot to tell you…"

"Really?" queried Smudge, "And who are you?"

"Sorry…" he smiled, "I'm Ray Furley. Technical Engineer. I designed the nose cone. But we need to be quick."

Smudge looked surprised, "Why?"

Ruth was already reading into the situation.

"Nice to meet you, Ray," she said, "Can you take us to Mission Control?"

"Of course," he replied.

She nodded. "Excellent. And you can tell us what you know as we go."

3.56 a.m.

The rocket powered upwards through the night-shadow of the Earth and suddenly burst into the sunlight. Gordo looked out of his tiny window and blinked in the dazzling brightness. Ray had positioned his bed to give him an excellent view. He looked away from the sun and into the inky blackness of space, studded with multitudes of stars and then lowered his eyes to the Earth. The shadowed part was star-speckled with cities, clearly defined by thousands of night-time lights, and the rest, bright with daylight, was blue and white, with greens and browns smeared across the land.

Gordo's breathing had slowed down during the lift off, but now, as the engines cut and the speed of the rocket became stable at 18,000 miles per hour, his breathing returned to normal. To Gordo, with the Earth so far below, it seemed as though the spaceship was hardly moving.

His arms floated up in weightlessness. He straightened his legs and they felt light. For a few moments he let his limbs float and enjoyed the sensation.

The rocket was now a quarter of its original size after dropping the first three stages. It glided as silently as an owl on the wing, briefly caught in orbit, held from speeding out into space by the gravitational pull of the Earth. Gordo gazed out of the window and then scanned the instruments to check all was as it should be. He decided to enjoy this time - eight minutes of weightlessness, suspended above the Earth.

To see such a breath-taking view was a special treat. He could see the shadow of night curving across the Earth. The horizon was lit with a bow of blue. The great planet was still and peaceful, a vibrant, bright ball resting in the vast, black expanse of space. He stared in amazement and awe. Was this really happening?

4.01 a.m.

Over three hundred miles below, in the Mission Control Room in Cape Canaveral, thirty-seven people sat watching their glowing computer screens. Every aspect of the trip was being monitored and analysed carefully. The room buzzed with movement and conversation but it fell quiet when Colonel Newton spoke.

"Little Old Reliable's fine," he announced, "Time to bring him down. We'll fire RCS steering thrusters and begin descent in…" He paused with his eyes fixed on the screen in front of him. "… in one minute exactly."

The buzz in the room resumed, this time much quieter, so that when Colonel Newton spoke again everyone could hear.

"Thirty seconds and counting."

Everyone stopped talking and the silent atmosphere hung with anticipation.

"T minus ten seconds… nine… eight… seven… six… five… four… three… two… one… ignite thrusters!"

4.03 a.m.

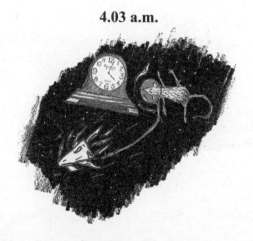

Gordo jumped when the steering thrusters suddenly burst into life. The rocket turned towards Earth at an angle. The spaceship roared and gathered speed, accelerating and forcing Gordo back into his bed. A few seconds later re-entry had begun. Gordo sank further into his bed and still the rocket accelerated. Gradually, the pressure on his small body increased and he struggled to breathe. Through the window he could see the nose cone glowing with heat, first red, then orange and then white as it re-entered the Earth's atmosphere. 1,000 miles per hour, 2,000… 3,000 and still it accelerated. It hit an incredible 10,000 miles an hour and was still gaining speed. The pressure was now forty times the Earth's gravity. Flames and sparks flew by the window. It was like riding in a fireball.

Gordo closed his eyes and tried to breathe but his lungs were being crushed by the huge pressure. It was too much for him. He desperately needed air and started becoming dizzy and faint. His head was swooning. It would be so easy to let go, to drift away as if going to sleep.

Then the memory of Jamie and Rachel flashed into his mind. They would want him to survive.

The speed began to reduce and he found he could breathe again. He gulped in the air and relaxed. Normal gravity was returning. He looked out of the window just as the descending nose cone passed out of the sunlight and into the darkness of Earth-night. Lights inside the nose cone came on.

Relief flooded through him. He had passed through the most dangerous parts of the flight.

Then he remembered the plan. He glanced at the clock.

"Oh no!" he thought.

He was a few seconds late. He had things to do which had to be timed exactly right and now he was behind schedule. He stayed calm and quickly he reached behind him, feeling with his fingers out of sight of the camera and found a wire. Then he doubted.

"What if it's the wrong wire!" he thought, "This place is full of wires."

He knew he had to act, so he tugged at the wire and it came loose.

4.04 a.m.

Colonel Newton stood up, looking anxious.

"We've lost visual contact," he announced, "The camera's gone."

"Probably just a shift in energy, sir," said a man next to him, "It'll be back in a few seconds."

A few seconds passed. Colonel Newton grunted in annoyance.

"It's not coming back," he said, "What a shame at this stage. What about the other links?"

"All fine…"

"Well that's something…" the colonel acknowledged.

"Yes, we're OK…" said someone else, "We've got the heartbeat microphone… breathing monitor… and temperature info is still coming in…"

Colonel Newton nodded. "Alright then," he said, "We can follow through those."

He turned to address a man with an identity badge pinned to his white coat stating, 'MEDICAL TEAM – Dr. Eric Low'

"How is Gordo?" the colonel asked.

"Heartbeat normal. Breathing normal. Temperature a little high but O.K, sir," replied the doctor.

"That's good," Colonel Newton looked relieved, "We almost lost him on re-entry."

4.05. a.m.

Gordo tried to unfasten his harness by pushing the red button on his chest. He had done it before and just about had the strength but now he found he could not push hard enough. He was late already and the seconds were ticking away. The assault on his body during the re-entry had taken its toll leaving him weakened.

He tried again and his arms shook with effort. Nothing. He almost panicked but gained control and paused to gather strength.

"Big effort," he thought, "Come on. Big effort."

He forced both hands on the red button. Click. The straps released.

He was still attached to the instrument wires but could move around, so he quickly took a step towards the controls. He found the correct dial straight away and turned it to set the measurements; four degrees for two point three seconds. He flicked the switch. There was a loud 'ssshhh' of the RCS steering thrusters and the nose cone turned slightly. He reached up to turn another switch off, moved back to his rubber bed and fastened the harness.

4.06 a.m.

In Mission Control the buzz of conversation was interrupted when a young man stood up and blurted out in surprise, "I can't believe it, sir, but the thrusters have just fired for a couple of seconds!"

Colonel Newton looked alarmed.

"But that's impossible," he said, "They only fire from here… or manually. No, that's impossible. Check the trajectory of descent."

"It's altered - by four degrees."

"Very strange," Colonel Newton commented, shaking his head, "Must be a malfunction. Let's pray they don't go off again,"

"Yes, sir, but there's something else… the radio transmitter is off."

Colonel Newton's jaw looked tense. "Electronic failure?" he asked.

"Probably… maybe connected with the thrusters malfunction."

Colonel Newton nodded. "OK… but it's not a major problem. We've got the co-ordinates, radar, and hopefully, the flashing light on the nose cone. We'll find him." He looked across the room at the young man and asked, "Parachutes?"

"Should open any second now."

Five seconds dragged through the expectant silence.

"Parachutes open," announced a voice from near the centre of the room.

A small cheer arose.

"Excellent, I think we'll be OK."

Once again, the Colonel looked extremely relieved.

"Sir?" said Dr. Eric Low, pointing at his screen, "Gordo's

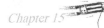

temperature reading is falling!"

"Oh, no," gasped Colonel Newton, "After doing so well. Are you sure?"

"Yes, no doubt. It's plummeting."

"At least he survived re-entry," said another voice.

Colonel Newton suddenly looked hopeful. "What about all the other readings? Heartbeat, breathing and the others?"

Dr. Low pressed a few keys and studied his screen, "All normal, sir."

"What does it mean then?" Colonel Newton asked urgently.

"It means he's fine," Dr. Low smiled, "Perhaps the sensor came loose. Yes, that must be it. He's probably wriggling around. But he's fine, sir. "

"Good, good."

Colonel Newton relaxed, shook his head and smiled. "Little Old Reliable! I knew he'd do it."

4.07 a.m.

Gordo was straining his eyes through the tiny window in the nose cone as he peered below. He was looking out for a fishing trawler, but with the darkness and the rain splattering on the glass, he could not see anything. The parachutes were carrying the nose cone gently down and after the tremendous speeds over the last quarter of an hour it felt like falling in slow motion.

Suddenly he heard a hiss which made him jump and look around. Then he realized it was the air bags inflating; they would keep the nose cone afloat on the water. The swelling surface of the black Atlantic Ocean suddenly appeared through the darkness. Gordo closed his eyes.

4.08 a.m.

The Mission Control Room was silent as everyone there held their breath in anticipation and hope.

"We have splashdown!" announced Colonel Newton.

A huge explosion of cheering and clapping broke the silence.

4.08 a.m.

Gordo felt the impact as the nose cone hit the water. It sank a few feet before the air bags lifted it to the surface again and it bobbed out like a cork. It rocked there, rising and falling on the heaving waves.

He unfastened his harness with a click and pushed himself off his bed. He was still connected to various sensors and his spacesuit was making him hot, so he took it off, pulling off the sensors at the same time. Then reached underneath the bed. His hand grasped a small belt that was just the right size for a little monkey. It had a collection of tools in carefully designed pockets; there were two screw drivers, a pen, a penknife, a telescope, a compass, an adjustable spanner and a pair of cutters. Ray had made it for him just in case he might need these things. He put it around his waist and fastened it.

He looked out through the window. Rain was driving into the thick glass with a muffled splattering. He saw the white air bags supporting the capsule. Waves splashed and washed over them leaving them shiny in the light of the nose cone.

Gordo jumped in surprise when a bright light flashed, lighting up the air bags and the waves all around. Then he remembered; this was the flashing light that would help locate the nose cone. He wanted to be found but by the right people and Rachel, Jamie and Ray had considered this. It would be best to turn the light off.

He took the pair of cutters from his belt and reached up. He studied a cluster of wires, pulled out a green one and cut it. The light stopped flashing.

He looked out of the window again. Beyond the air bags, the swelling surface of the sea stretched away into the dark night. He suddenly felt thrilled and relieved. It had been a success.

4.09 a.m.

"Well done, team!" announced Colonel Newton.

He pulled out a box of bottles of champagne from under the desk and placed them on a table behind him. Three waitresses entered with trays of food, placed them down and two left to get some more. The other one took out a bottle of champagne and started preparing to pop the cork.

"Just one last thing," he said, "We need to tell McMurphy on the carrier about the new splashdown co-ordinates, and especially now that the radio transmitter is not beeping. Habens… a job for you, and then we're done."

"Yes, sir," said Habens, and he turned to do it.

"You have done a magnificent job," he continued, "I feel proud to have led this successful operation. And now… to celebrate. The party begins in fifteen seconds!"

Laughter.

"Ten seconds and counting… nine… eight… seven… six… five… four… three… two… one…"

There was a moment's silence as the waitress strained to push the cork upwards with her thumbs. It popped off and shot into the ceiling and she quickly poured the first glass. The party had begun.

4.10 a.m.

G ordo had travelled 1,500 miles into space and back in the last fifteen minutes and it had left him feeling shaky and weak in the legs. He looked out of the window. By the light of the capsule, he could see waves splashing against the nose cone as it rose up and down on the swell of the ocean. Heavy rain was lashing against the little window and bouncing off the air balloons to be whipped away by the wind.

He wondered what had happened to Rachel, and whether Jamie had arrived to join in with the plan. He was expecting to see a fishing trawler appear out of the darkness with Rachel and Jamie on board. However, he had been late to adjust the descent of the nose cone, so maybe the trawler was waiting in the wrong place. He took out his telescope from a pocket on his belt, extended it, lifted it to one eye and looked through. In the darkness and the pouring rain he could not see far. He hoped that he would see the trawler soon, not only for his rescue, but also for their sake. He wanted to know that their plans had gone well and that they were safe.

4.15 a.m. aboard the fishing trawler, the Golden Gem

The Golden Gem was riding the ocean swell comfortably. It was a sturdy boat, painted dark green and built to withstand the roughest conditions out at sea. Two masts supported the intricate system of ropes and pulleys which was used to drop the fishing nets and then haul in the catch. With a cabin at each end and rooms beneath the deck, the trawler could carry a crew of twenty men. Tonight, the fishing equipment was not in use because the Golden Gem had a different task.

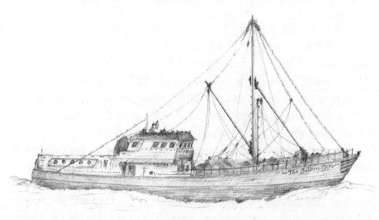

The boat ploughed through the ocean surface as the surging waves rose and fell. Foam and spray cascaded onto the decks only to run away as the boat tilted. Everything was drenched as the cold rain lashed through the darkness, rattling loudly on the windows of the cabins. The rugged fishermen on board enjoyed the wild weather and the rolling of the boat. They carried on with their sailing duties as usual.

The captain was at the wheel with the bo'sun standing beside him.

"We're in the right area now," he said loudly, to be heard above the sounds of the fierce weather, "But it's like searching for a needle in a haystack."

The bo'sun was using both hands to move a huge spotlight, which was fixed to the floor on a pedestal and could swivel through 360°. A long beam of light shone through the window and lit up the surface of the water, picking out the sweeping rain in the beam. He had just come in and his bushy beard was glistening with rain.

"What shall we do now?"

"Keep looking," said the captain, "We're in the right place but it's a circle at least five miles across. If we could get a radar fix on it, we could find it."

The bo'sun spread his rugged hands. "But we don't know what it is…"

"Yeah… the girl could tell us if she was conscious. Maybe the boy if he was well enough. Check the radar again," instructed the captain.

The bo'sun turned to look at the screen.

"Something massive, probably a cargo ship, and a small boat, probably fishing."

"OK," the captain nodded, "We'll keep looking."

He grabbed the spotlight with one hand and swept it around in a complete circle.

"Nothing," he observed, "There's nothing yet. Until the young lady comes 'round, and the boy has recovered… then they can tell us what we're looking for. But we'll continue searching anyway," he said, turning and lifting the lid to the voice pipe and speaking to the engine room below, "Maintain course."

"Aye, aye, Captain," came a muffled answer.

4.15 a.m. aboard the Air Craft Carrier 'Coral Reef'

The Coral Reef was a massive ship. Above the streamlined island superstructure, she was mostly deck, marked out with white dotted lines to create a landing and take-off runway. Half way along and on the side, the mast rose high from the top of the bridge. Opposite it and overhanging the sea, a platform extended out beyond the deck to form a helipad. This colossal ship was swaying slowly on the ocean as she cut powerfully through the waves. Lights shone from the tower onto the decks.

Max McMurphy was down below lying on his bed in his small, luxury quarters when he heard the hum of the massive engines grow louder. He left his room to rush up on deck. Above his head a light threw a pool of yellow around him as he looked through the pouring rain into the darkness. He

wiped his glasses and then tried to shield them with his hand.

The great ship was slowly turning.

The steep steps up to the bridge were well lit and McMurphy climbed them, gripping the wet rails tightly against the force of the wind. A young man in naval uniform stepped forwards as he was about to step off the stairway.

"What's happening," McMurphy demanded. The rain splattered into his glasses and face, and ran down his forehead. "Why's the ship turning?"

"No civilians up here, sir," said the young man, blocking McMurphy's way.

"I'm Max McMurphy," he said gruffly.

"Who?"

"Max McMurphy… Mr. McMurphy to you. I'm in charge of this whole shebang! Now let me up!"

An officer heard the fuss and approached them.

"Let him up, Jefferies," he commanded.

"Yes, sir," Jefferies said, stepping aside and saluting.

"Thank you, officer," McMurphy said, glaring at the young man.

He entered the bridge.

"What's happening?" he snapped at the captain.

"We've got precise co-ordinates for the capsule, sir," said the captain, "Just received them from Mission Control."

"Good," McMurphy acknowledged.

"But… there's a snag," said the captain, "It's come down further away than we expected I'm afraid."

"How far from here?"

"'Bout ten miles sou' sou' east, sir… just over."

"Ten miles?" McMurphy sounded shocked, "Why?"

"They don't know, sir. Some technical error I think."

"Can't you go any faster?" McMurphy asked irritably.

"Also," continued the captain, "The capsule's radio transmitter's not working. So we're relying on the co-ordinates… and our radar of course."

McMurphy grunted in disapproval and then snapped

again, "Can't you go any faster?"

"As soon as she's turned we'll rev her up, sir. It's only 11° but it'll still take a few minutes to turn and get going. Then she'll be cutting through those waves beautifully. Like a knife through butter, sir."

"Good… good," said McMurphy, "Pull out all the stops to get there as soon as possible, OK captain?"

"Yes, sir."

McMurphy left the bridge and hesitated at the top of the ladder. He turned to face Jefferies, the young sailor, who immediately stood to attention. McMurphy stepped towards him until their faces were a few inches apart.

"Now you know my face, don't you?" barked McMurphy.

"Yes, sir," replied the sailor, staring straight ahead at McMurphy.

"Well, don't you forget it. Understand?"

"Yes, sir," said Jefferies.

At that moment, the wind caught McMurphy's glasses and whipped them off his nose. Jefferies snatched at them but only managed to knock them upwards and they flew on the wind towards the sea.

"No!" cried McMurphy, scowling as he watched them go. He turned back to Jefferies, glowering, "Thank you very much!"

He descended the steep stairway and squinted across the wide surface of the decks. Lights reflected on the shiny wet boards and the sound of the sea filled the night air. There were several jets on one side and a helicopter sitting on the helipad opposite. He walked across and looked over the side and into the darkness. It was too dark to see much, even less now without his glasses, and McMurphy shuddered as the cold rain hit his face. If he had not been so caught up in his plans he might have enjoyed the thrill of being on this great ship as it ploughed through the Atlantic Ocean, but now, as he looked down at the black, murky water, he thought greedily

about the monkey and the money that it would bring in.

He turned and walked back across the deck to go below and put on his spare glasses. He was pleased to hear the engines surge. The carrier straightened and gathered speed.

4.15 a.m. aboard a small fishing boat, the Las Varas

The Las Varas was smaller than the Golden Gem and was being battered harshly by the waves. Although it did have a legal seaworthy certificate, the boat was over thirty years old now and the effect of many trips was inevitably taking its toll. The little boat was seriously in need of repair which was evident in the creaking and groaning sounds of the wooden structure. It possessed one mast, rising above a small wooden cabin which housed the wheel. The mighty ocean rose and fell with relentless energy and made no allowances for the poor condition of the little vessel.

At the wheel in the small cabin was the captain, a rugged swede called Henrik Blomqvist. He was tall and broad, built like a sturdy oak and looked perfectly at home as his boat swayed and creaked on the ocean swell. As a fisherman, he was used to these conditions but the same could not be said for the two passengers. They had hired the boat on the agreement that they would also be the crew. They were decidedly unhappy with the lurching motion of the small fishing boat and were huddled below and feeling sea sick. The room had a short stairway at each end that led to the deck above.

"This is turning out to be another stupid plan of yours, Frank," said Jeff, looking as pale as a sheet, "I should never have agreed."

"You won't be saying that when we've got the monkey and then the money," Frank retorted, "We knew it would be tough, so stop grumbling!"

Jeff groaned and held his stomach as the boat lurched.

"This is terrible!" he said, "I've never felt so ill in my life!"

"I feel ill too," snapped Frank, "But you don't hear me grumbling."

The boat swayed and a mug slid along the surface of the table and bumped against the ridge on its edge. Some tea splashed out and landed on Jeff's foot.

"I'm going to be sick," sighed Jeff.

"Well don't be sick in here," Frank said sharply.

Jeff suddenly got up, rushed to climb the steps, flung open the door and stumbled out with his hand over his mouth. The wind and rain blew in through the open door and Frank jumped up and slammed it closed. A minute later Jeff came back in and sat down again.

"Well at least I feel a bit better now," he announced.

Frank sat down at the table. For a moment they sat without talking, surrounded by the wild sounds of the wind and the sea and the creaking timbers of the boat.

"This boat sounds in a bad way," said Jeff, "Is it safe?"

"Of course… I told you…"

He stopped abruptly because he heard something – something that shocked them both. They heard the sound of someone coming up the steps from below. They looked at each other in astonishment. The fisherman was at the wheel, so who was it? There was no one else on the boat.

The footsteps grew louder.

They both stared open-mouthed at the door as it swung open.

"Mary-Anne!" exclaimed Jeff standing up, "What are you…? How did you…?"

He shook his head in a gesture of utter bewilderment.

"I just thought I'd join you for the trip," said Mary-Anne calmly.

"But… but…" stammered Frank as his jaw dropped open in complete surprise. He rose to his feet.

"I had to come…" she began, sounding very matter of fact, "I had to come to make sure you two get at least one job right! I've never known such a pair of losers in my whole life! Everything you two do, goes wrong! I've come to introduce some intelligence into your little attempts to make money. I'm gonna make sure this one succeeds."

They stared at her.

Then she ordered, "Sit down."

Jeff obeyed but Frank remained standing. She sat down opposite Jeff.

She gave Frank a cutting stare and then continued. "I have written down the new co-ordinates for the whereabouts of the monkey."

She handed Jeff a piece of paper.

"What do you mean?" asked Frank, looking down at her with a puzzled frown, "New co-ordinates?"

"I picked up the transmission from Mission Control to the Coral Reef. You two Joe Blows would have waited in the wrong place all week! Now, Jeff, take that piece of paper to the Captain. Tell him to head for that location."

Jeff was still dazed by the shock appearance of Mary-Anne and looked absent-minded as he stood up and took the piece of paper.

"Don't drop it," Marie-Anne snapped, "You look like a complete zombie... as if you've seen a ghost. It's me... your wife! I've come to help you. Now, get on and do the job I've given you."

Jeff resembled a schoolboy obeying orders as he climbed the steps at the other end of the room and opened the door. Momentarily the roar of the ocean waves filled the room and some rain gusted in on the wind. Jeff closed the door and the sound dulled. There was a moment of silence.

"Frank," said Mary-Anne looking at him intently, "I can tell you... now that Jeff is out of the way."

"What?" Frank looked even more surprised than before. Once again he stared at her. "What is it?" he asked.

"I came," she hesitated, "I came to tell you something... Jeff has his own plans, and they don't include you."

Frank looked puzzled. "What?!" he exclaimed.

"Once this is over, he's gonna get rid of you and take all the money."

Frank looked completely stunned. He sank onto a chair opposite Mary-Anne.

"Are you sure?" he asked.

"Yeah, it's true. He told me all about it. Thought I'd be pleased, coz he knows I don't like you. He's gonna kill you, Frank! But I can't let him do it. He'd get caught and then it'd be Death Row for him."

"I never..." he began, "I never even guessed."

"You must have suspected ... surely?"

They heard the engines grow louder.

"He'll be back in a minute," she said.

Frank was lost in thought, gazing at the table top. He was trying to remember if Jeff had done anything that might have suggested his secret plan. There seemed to be nothing.

"Frank," she said sharply to get his attention, "It's a great plan of yours to sell the monkey to Freddie Stober…"

"But I'm not…" he replied, still in a daze with shock.

"Larry Smoon?"

Frank nodded and then frowned. "How did you know that?"

"I thought you'd go for the top… someone with big, big money…"

"Of course… but tell me about…"

He stopped because he heard Jeff coming back.

"I must talk to you," she whispered. She looked around and up the steps at the door where Jeff had left. "I must talk to you alone… we've got to sort this out…"

They could hear Jeff about to enter now.

"Quick!" she blurted out as she grabbed him by the hand and dragged him towards the steps at the other end of the room.

She pulled him up the steps, opened the door and they slipped out into the cold rain which was pouring over the deck. They faced each other and Mary-Anne smiled at him through the deluge. Frank looked confused but then his expression changed. He was beginning to doubt Mary-Anne. Anger rose in him.

He stepped backwards.

"You're lying!" he shouted above the storm, "What are you up to?!"

"No," she replied, "It's all true, Frank!"

Suddenly an expression of terror crossed her face.

"Look out!" she shouted, "Behind you! Look… there!" and she pointed over his shoulder, "Out to sea! Look!"

He spun around. Mary-Anne placed both her hands on his back and pushed with all her might. Frank was thrown forwards and towards the edge of the boat with the gale behind him. He hit the railings hard and toppled over. He began to fall towards the sea but swung an arm back and grabbed onto the railings. He clung on for his life and started climbing back. Mary-Anne ran towards him.

"No!" he screamed.

Mary-Anne put her hands through the railings and pushed him so hard that one of his hands slipped off. He frantically lashed out and grabbed on again with both hands. Stretching through the railings with one hand, he grabbed Mary-Anne's coat and pulled her. They were now close together with the railing between them. Their eyes met; Mary-Anne's were filled with menacing hate and Frank's consumed with panic.

He opened his mouth to shout at her but the boat lurched and his hands slipped free. He fell, turning in the air and crashing head first into the freezing ocean. There was a splash and then he was gone.

At this moment Jeff came out of the cabin. Mary-Anne turned to Jeff looking distressed.

"What's the matter?" he shouted.

"It's Frank!" she wailed, "He fell over! I tried to save him, but he was too heavy!"

"Where?!" cried Jeff.

Mary-Anne pointed. "There!"

Jeff grabbed a life-saving ring hanging nearby and flung it overboard into the dark. He ran to collect another, flung it over as well and then stared down into the black water scanning for him. He was gone.

"Frank! Frank!" shouted Mary-Anne.

Jeff looked at her, rain whipping into his face. "Let's turn the boat…" he shouted and then looked overboard again.

"In this storm?!" Mary-Anne shouted back, "There's no point… he'll be washed away… we'll never find him now."

She pulled Jeff after her as she struggled against the wind and rain to the door. She opened it and dragged him in, letting the wind slam the door behind them, and then moving down the steps into the room.

"Jeff… what shall we do?" pleaded Mary-Anne.

Jeff shook his head in despair. "There's nothing we can

do... nothing at all. He can't survive in this."

Mary-Anne flopped down in a chair looking very upset. Rain dripped down her face from her drenched hair. Jeff pulled up a chair beside her, sat down and put his arm around her.

"What happened?" he asked.

There was a long pause.

"I pushed him," she said quietly. She leant towards him and rested her head against his chest. "But he tried to push me over first. He attacked me, Jeff. I didn't mean to push him over... it was self-defence."

"But why?" asked Jeff, "Why did he attack you?"

"Said he didn't want me in on his plans. For goodness sake I'm here to help you. He was an inconsiderate, selfish fool... but I didn't mean to push him over. I was protecting myself. Oh, it's so horrible!"

Again there was a long pause. Jeff was thinking things over.

"What happens now?" he asked.

Mary-Anne lifted her head and looked up at him.

"We carry on of course," she said, dabbing her eyes. It was only rain water but it looked like tears. "We just... we just carry on with the plan."

"OK... OK," he said slowly, trying to calm himself down after the shock, "But we must think things through... properly. Frank's gone... " Jeff said shaking his head. An involuntary shudder shook his shoulders. "But he could survive..."

Mary-Anne shook her head. "No way, I'm afraid."

Jeff thought for a moment.

"You're right. He can't swim... and in this storm... there's no hope."

4.30 a.m. aboard the Air Craft Carrier, the Coral Reef

Max McMurphy was on deck and sheltering from the driving rain beside the tower. Dark shadows contrasted with the shining deck where the lights reflected upon the wet surface. He heard the distinctive sound of a helicopter blade starting to rotate and he turned to see it on the lift pad at the other side of the carrier. He was meant to be on that helicopter. Anger rose in him and he started running across the deck.

"Hey!" he shouted, with rain driving into his face, "What's going on?!"

The helicopter's engine noise built up and it began to lift, tilting forwards, turning gracefully into the wind and then rising in the air. McMurphy caught a glimpse of a face at the window and scowled in anger; it was Jane Larkin.

The helicopter headed off over the sea. He gripped his hands in fury as he stood still for a few seconds trying to restrain his anger.

"What's she up to?"

The thought hung in his mind. He tried to work things out and started walking back to the tower. He descended the steep steps, with rain dripping from his clothes, and went below deck to his room. He changed and then took a bottle of whisky out of a cupboard and poured some into a glass. He sat down and took a gulp.

He deliberated upon the meaning of what he had just seen. After a while he decided that Jane Larkin must be after the glory and the fame. She wanted to be the first person there when Gordo emerged from the nose cone. She wanted to be in the limelight. Perhaps she had arranged to photograph and film it herself and those would go on television, in newspapers and magazines. She was after the fame.

"Well…" he thought, "She can have all that if she wants, no problem." He downed the rest of the whisky. "But… I'll have the monkey."

4.35 a.m. aboard the Las Varas

Jeff and Mary-Anne were sitting in silence. Jeff was coming to terms with the loss of Frank.

"But why did you go out?" Jeff asked.

"Oh, because… Oh, Jeff," she said, and leant her head on his chest. She had to make a good show of this. "I can't bear to think of it. Frank gone! If we hadn't gone out there he'd still be alive now. And all because he felt sick…"

Jeff believed her.

"What shall we do, then?" he asked.

Mary-Anne lifted her head off his chest and sighed.

"Nothing," she replied, "There's nothing we can do. His body might be washed up on a coast somewhere in some months, or years. But that's unlikely, right out here. He's gone, disappeared. And who cares? No one. He was good for nothing."

"Yeah, but Frank… dead!?"

"Accidents happen," she stated, now very matter of fact, "Especially at sea."

Jeff nodded and shrugged. "Yeah, I suppose so."

"What about getting the monkey?" she asked.

"There is a problem with that. He arranged to sell the monkey to some rich criminal. Now we don't even know who that is, do we? The whole plan is finished." He shook his head in despair.

"I know," she replied.

"Know what?" Jeff asked with surprise.

"I know the person… the person who wants to buy the monkey. I think things through, not like you. He told me when we were talking in here… so the plan's not finished. If we can get there before the Coral Reef and get the monkey then this little project can still be a success."

Jeff shook his head slowly. "I don't know," he said, "I can't believe what is happening. Frank… dead! I can't believe it! Everything is going crazy."

"Nothing will bring him back now," she said kindly, "Let's face it… he's gone. Now let's get on with the plan."

4.40 a.m. aboard the Golden Gem

The Golden Gem was now nine years old and throughout most of that time it had spent five days a week at sea. It could sail in this kind of weather comfortably. It was owned and captained by a good friend of Rachel's uncle, Edward Fontain. Such was their friendship that he had been happy to rent out his boat and the services of his crew. He loved the sea and after twenty years of experience he knew everything about navigating these waters. He was at the wheel, staring ahead through the window. Rain was splattering heavily on the roof and the windows of the bridge.

"She's woken up!" said one of the fishermen.

"Find out where she wants us to go," the captain said.

The door swung open and Rachel entered with her hood up.

"Hello Rachel…" he began.

"Hi, Ed," said Rachel. She pushed her hood back and beamed at him.

"You look as if you're feeling better now?"

"Yes," Rachel nodded, "Much better."

The door opened again and Jamie came in.

Rachel looked at him and then back at Ed. "This is my cousin Jamie," she said, "I told him not to come, but he's got this wild streak in him."

The captain laughed. "I know someone else with a wild streak!"

"Ed," she began, "It's great of you to do this."

"No problem," answered Ed, "Your uncle has helped me in the past… but you were going to tell me what it's all about…"

"It's about a monkey."

Ed laughed. "A monkey?! You're kidding! Out here…?" He waved a hand to indicate the ocean surrounding them. Then he remembered the work she did at Cape Canaveral. "Not the space monkey?"

"Yes," she said, "But I'll explain later. I need to know if there's a small vessel to the north-east somewhere. It's really important that we find it as soon as possible."

"We'll ask the navigator… follow me."

He opened a door and they filed down some steps and into the navigation room.

Jamie spotted the green radar screen with its circulating line. "Look, there!" he said pointing at a green dot being lit up every time the line swept around, "What's that? And that?"

"What are you looking for?" asked the navigator.

"The nose cone of a space ship," said Jamie, as if it was the most normal thing to look for.

"Aaah!" exclaimed Ed, then he continued, thinking it out as he spoke, "So the monkey went into space… earlier tonight. And now the capsule has landed… and it's floating in the sea. But why do you want to find it?"

"I'll tell you later…" Rachel said quickly.

"But there must be arrangements…" he said, "Official arrangements. Boats to retrieve the capsule. I don't understand. Is what we're doing official?"

Rachel sighed. "No, completely unofficial, but it's the right thing to do. Trust me. Listen, Ed, I'll explain in a minute when we're moving. We must get going! Navigator, what are these dots?" she asked pointing to them on the screen, "Are they boats?"

"That one is a small boat," he pointed to it on the screen, "Probably a fishing boat like this boat but smaller… and that one! That is big… very big. That's a massive ship. And they're both heading for that one, which is very small – it must be the nose cone."

"I know," said Jamie, "That big ship is the official one – the Coral Reef… an aircraft carrier. But that one there," he pointed to the nose cone, "That's our target. We must go there."

"Certainly, young man."

Ed pointed at the screen. "You said that was a small boat. But why is that heading straight for the nose cone as well?"

"Coincidence?" suggested the navigator, "It's probably fishing."

"Who'll reach the nose cone first?" asked Rachel.

"Hang on," the navigator replied thoughtfully, "I need to work this out."

He looked at a chart on the desk and jotted down some figures on some paper.

"OK," he said, "We'll arrive first, I think, if speeds stay the same. We'll be a good ten minutes before the Coral Reef. Which is good because I wouldn't like to argue with an aircraft carrier! We should get to it by five fifty-five."

"Excellent," Rachel sighed with relief, "Just enough time. Let's go then."

4.47 a.m. on the helicopter

"Can't this thing go any faster?" snapped Jane Larkin to the pilot of the helicopter.

He glanced down at the speedometer - seventy-eight miles per hour.

"No," he replied calmly, "We're at full throttle."

"Drop down further," she ordered, "We don't want to miss it. It should have a flashing light on the top."

The pilot descended until they were twenty feet above the ocean. Two spotlights, one facing down and forwards, the other down and behind them, glistened on the waves, but there was no sign of the nose cone.

"Sit back and relax, Miss Larkin," he said, "We have a circle of five miles to search. We might be lucky but this could take a little time."

4.50 a.m.

The dark night still enveloped everything as the storm began to weaken. The rain was dying out, leaving only the occasional drop flying on the wind which had eased but was still strong and fresh.

It was a race to Gordo's little space vehicle. The nose cone, stained black with burns from the re-entry, was the target as it bobbed innocently on the waves of the South Atlantic Ocean.

The massive bulk of the Coral Reef, now nine miles away from the nose cone, was cutting its way through the waves towards it. It could top thirty-three knots[2] but took

[2]The speed of boats is measured in knots. 1 knot is just over 1 mile per hour (1 knot = 1.151 mph). Therefore 33 knots is about 38 mph.

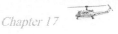

some time to reach that speed. It had just passed ten knots and could only accelerate a little more before needing to slow down for a good mile before reaching the capsule.

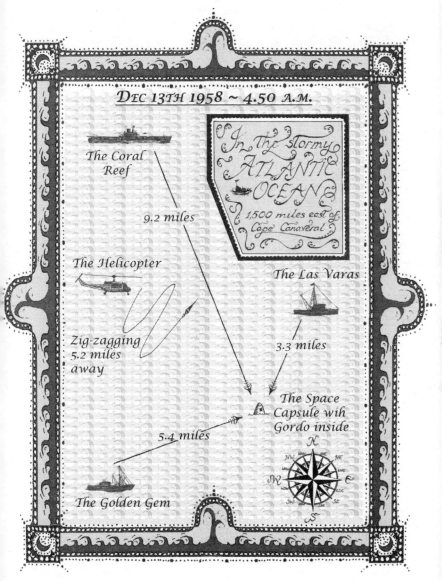

295

The small fishing boat, the Las Varas, was being tossed around on the choppy surface, with Mary-Anne and Jeff ready to steal little Gordo. With Frank out of the way, Mary-Anne was now the mind behind their plot and she was ruthless enough to kill. Due to poor navigation, the boat had been some miles to the north-east of the expected splash down area. Now that Henrik Blomqvist had the exact co-ordinates, he was heading south-south east towards the nose cone. Even with its old engines straining, it could only manage eight knots. Now that the storm had eased, the sails could have been used to help the Las Varas go faster but Henrik Blomqvist had refused to use them with such an inexperienced crew. They were now only three miles from the nose cone.

Rachel and Jamie were on board the Golden Gem willing it to go faster, but they could see that the crew of eight men, captained by Edward Fontain, were doing the best they could. They were five miles to the west-south west of the nose cone, with engines turning and sails billowing in the strong wind. They were making good pace.

The helicopter could travel much faster than any of the boats and the ambitious Jane Larkin was scanning waves below. Her face was tense; she was desperate to find the nose cone. The pilot had not received the new co-ordinates and Jane did not know that they were available yet, so the helicopter was methodically searching in the wrong place, the five mile, circular area. Without knowing it, they were nine miles west of the nose cone.

All of these were determined to be first to reach Gordo. It was just a question of who would get there first.

5.06 a.m. aboard the Las Varas

Dawn would not break for another hour. Aboard the Las Varas, Jeff was still feeling seasick and standing on the bridge. Henrik Blomqvist stood at the wheel, looking perfectly at home as his boat swayed and creaked on the ocean swell. He was as steady on his feet as if they were glued to the floor.

A few days earlier, Frank had contacted Henrik after making some enquiries in the criminal world. He soon found out that Henrik was well known in those circles as a man who hid his criminal activities behind the front of being an honest fisherman. He arranged to meet him to hire his boat. The negotiations had been difficult because Henrik had refused to hire his boat until he knew the exact purpose of the trip. Frank reluctantly explained everything about the monkey and the plan to steal it, whereupon Henrik had demanded a high fee to hire the boat as well as a cash bonus of 10% of the sale of the monkey.

The boat lurched and swayed on the rough sea. Jeff was pale and held a hand to his churning stomach as he clung with his other hand to the wall. His feet shuffled unsteadily with every movement of the boat.

"Where's Frank?" Henrik asked.

Jeff was scanning the water surface with a spotlight mounted beside the wheel.

"He's down below asleep on his bunk," replied Jeff, "He felt so sick... and so do I."

The door opened and Mary-Anne entered. Henrik stared at her in astonishment.

"Who are you?!" he demanded, "And what are you doing on my boat?"

Mary-Anne pushed the door closed behind her and

dampened the sound of the ocean.

"I'm with him," she said, nodding at Jeff.

"Who said?" Henrik barked.

"She's with us," confirmed Jeff, "But I didn't know she was coming."

Henrik looked back at Mary-Anne and stepped aggressively towards her.

"I have a way of dealing with stowaways," he growled, looking down at her with disdain, "Works every time. I throw them overboard!"

Mary-Anne stepped back, held up her hands and bumped into the door. The cabin shook and creaked with the impact. It was old and rotten, and badly in need of repair.

"I'm an extra pair of hands, OK?" she explained, "To help make a real success of this. Now what's wrong with that?"

"Everything!" Henrik snapped, "Because you're not meant to be here."

"Listen," she replied, "I know that… but we'll pay. We'll pay you well."

The mention of money took Henrik's interest. He looked down at the floor, shook his head and then looked up again.

"OK, then," he stated, "Frank agreed to 10% of the sale of the monkey… that's just gone up to 15%."

"OK," agreed Mary-Anne.

Henrik turned back to Jeff who was now holding the spotlight.

"You take the wheel," he said, "Just for a moment. I'll nip down and see Frank about the money."

"No," blurted out Jeff, "I've got to keep searching with this light. If we don't find the monkey then none of us get any money."

"He's right," Mary-Anne added, "Anyway, the money is no problem for Frank… none at all. He'll agree. He's feeling very ill. Apart from that, you may trust Captain Joe Blow here at the wheel," she nodded at Jeff, "But I don't."

5.09 a.m.

"Miss Larkin," said the pilot, "I've just heard from the Coral Reef," he said, "They gave me the exact location of the capsule."

He was turning the helicopter as he spoke.

"How long?" asked Jane.

"'Bout six minutes."

Jane smiled. "Good… get me there as fast as you can."

5.10 a.m.

Suddenly Jeff pointed, held the spotlight still and exclaimed, "That's it… over there… look!"

They peered through the darkness along the beam of light and sure enough, bobbing on the surface, was the nose cone, floating with the aid of its inflated bags.

"Get up close," said Mary-Anne.

Henrik put the engines in reverse and the boat turned. It took a few minutes to get it under control in the heaving waves but soon it was lined up beside the nose cone.

"Beautifully done," said Jeff, "You stay at the wheel and we'll go out and get the monkey."

They moved out into the blast of the wind where their hair was blowing and coats flapping. They looked over the edge at the nose cone, surrounded by its inflated white bags. It bumped against the side of the boat as it rose up and down on the waves.

"How do we get the monkey?" shouted Jeff.

Mary-Anne was tying a rope to the railings.

"Jump down there," she ordered, holding out the other end of the rope to him, which he did not take, "Tie this rope to it so that it doesn't drift away, and then get the monkey! Go!"

"I'm not going over there!" shouted Jeff, "It's too rough! Isn't there another way?"

Mary-Anne cupped Jeff's head in her hands, stared into his eyes and shouted, "There's no other way. Listen! We've come hundreds of miles for this! We've only got a few minutes before someone else gets here. Now get over there before I push you over."

Jeff just stared back. She forced the rope into his hands. He seemed frozen with fear and then she pushed him. She only meant to get him moving but with the strong wind and the slippery deck he lunged forwards and began to fall over the railings.

Mary-Anne grabbed at him but it was too late. With a cry of terror, he plummeted down, landed with a smack on his back on a wet air bag and began to slip off. He struggled frantically, trying to twist around as he flung his arms out but he kept slipping until he hit the water and disappeared.

"Jeff!" shouted Mary-Anne desperately, pulling at the rope.

Jeff's head re-appeared. He was gasping for breath but managed to pull on the rope and scramble up onto the air bag.

"I... I..." he cried, struggling to speak because the shock of the cold water had taken his breath away, "I... I... can't swim!"

Mary-Anne was staring at him.

"Tie the rope!" she screeched.

His hands were shaking as he fumbled with the rope but he managed to tie it to a plastic loop on the air bag.

"Now!" Mary-Anne screamed, sounding desperate, "Open the door and get the monkey!"

Jeff slipped down the air bag towards the door of the capsule. He grabbed the handle, which was set in a cavity in the door, and turned. Then he pulled the door upwards to open it and looked in. A second later he turned to Mary-Anne.

"It's empty!" he screamed up to Mary-Anne leaning over the side of the boat, "There's no monkey in there!"

"It's hiding, you idiot! Get in there and find it."

Jeff slipped in, feet first. As quick as a blink, Gordo jumped out of his hiding place, climbed up Jeff's clothes and onto his shoulder. With one leap he was out of the nose cone and slamming the door closed. He quickly took a screwdriver from his belt and forced into the cavity where the handle was located. It jammed.

Inside, Jeff grabbed the handle and let out an exasperated cry when he found it would not turn.

"Oh no!" screamed Mary-Anne and she kicked the railings in frustration. She looked over at Gordo. "Even a monkey can outwit him!"

At that moment she heard the sound of a boat's engine. She looked up and saw the shape of a boat looming towards her through the dark.

Gordo took his penknife out of his belt, opened the longest blade and sawed at the rope until he was through. The nose cone began to drift away with Jeff panicking as he tried to open the jammed door. The rest of the rope flopped down beside the boat with Gordo clinging on to it. His tail dipped in the water and then a wave washed right over him. He held on tightly and swiftly climbed up the rope and out of the water. In a moment he was up and onto the Las Veras, slipping the penknife back into its pocket on his belt.

He glanced around at the nose cone to see it drifting away with Jeff's terrified face staring wide-eyed out of the window. He turned back only to see Mary-Anne diving at him. He was too fast for her, scampering away as she crashed onto the slippery deck and skidded along. Gordo ran up the mast as she scrambled to her feet.

"Come here!" she called after him.

Gordo was already high up. The approaching vessel was almost level as she rushed to the bridge and burst in.

"Henrik!" she exclaimed, "Get going now! We've got the monkey – it's up the mast!"

Henrik pushed a lever forwards to full throttle and the engines surged. Mary-Anne hurried back to the mast and gazed up, looking for Gordo. He had gone.

The Golden Gem drew alongside with a gathering of people on the deck. The two boats scraped together.

"Gordo!" cried out Jamie, from the Golden Gem.

The little monkey was down on the deck now and got ready to jump across, crouching down low and gathering his energy. He sprung with all his might.

He felt a sharp pain. Mary-Anne had caught him by a leg and swung him back but the movement upset her balance and she tripped and fell backwards. Gordo landed on her face and bit her on the nose with his sharp little teeth.

"Aaahh!" she screamed in pain and let go of his leg.

He looked up to see that the Golden Gem had glided past; he had missed his chance.

5.17 a.m. in the Nose Cone

Jeff was still trying to get the door open. Through the window, he could see the screwdriver moving as he shook the handle. Suddenly, it slipped out and fell. He yanked the handle down and pushed the door open. The wind blasted in as he looked out in hope but his fears were confirmed; the capsule had drifted away from the Las Varas and in the dark he could only just pick out the lights of the boat, already some distance away.

He let the wind slam the door closed and slumped down with his hands over his face. He regretted ever becoming involved in this crime. Why did he let Frank persuade him? Everything had gone wrong now; Frank was dead and he was trapped in a tiny capsule floating on the Atlantic. It could not be worse.

His hands dropped from his face and he stared helplessly out of the window.

5.20 a.m. aboard the Las Varas

The Las Varas was gathering speed slowly. The old engine was straining at maximum revs which Henrik did not usually risk, but he wanted to get away. They had the monkey on board and that was what mattered.

He glanced along the deck, looking for Mary-Anne. A sound behind him made him turn, but he was too late. Jamie was already swinging a wooden plank which hit him on the back of the head and he crumpled to the floor, unconscious.

Jamie dropped the plank and looked at the controls. He fixed the wheel and pulled a lever. The speed dropped.

"Stop right there!" shouted Mary-Anne.

She was walking towards the cabin with a hand gun aimed through the window of the door and straight at Jamie. He ducked out of view, slipped through the other door and ran along the deck. Gordo was sitting on the side of the boat. The monkey jumped down and scampered to Jamie, climbing up his clothes and settling on his shoulder.

"The boat will turn and come back for us," Jamie told him.

Mary-Anne was creeping past the cabin and stepped forwards.

"Give me the monkey, now!" she commanded, shouting above the noise of the sea and wind.

She began edging along the boat towards them.

"Now!" screamed Mary-Anne.

The boat juddered, so she grasped the railing on the side of the deck but kept the gun pointing at Jamie.

"You heard me!" she yelled, "I want the monkey… and then you can go!"

Jamie stepped back. A shot thudded into the wooden planks under his feet.

"Stay where you are!" she screeched.

Jamie stood still. He had never been shot at before. He was shaking. Mary-Anne took a few more cautious steps on the swaying deck until she was a few paces away.

"Now," she began, "It's very simple. Your life or the monkey."

Jamie found himself saying, "My life then…"

"Don't be stupid," she scowled, "Then I kill you and get the monkey. Give me the monkey!" She took another step towards them. "Pass it here!"

"Start wriggling," Jamie said to Gordo, in his language, "Pretend to escape."

Mary-Anne frowned with puzzlement at Jamie's monkey noises. Gordo started struggling and screeching, and flaying his arms around as if desperate to get away. Jamie gave the impression of grappling to hold onto him. Mary-Anne stepped closer.

"Keep it still!" she snapped.

As the boat swayed back from a large wave, Jamie took his chance. He lunged at Mary-Anne and knocked her gun from her hand. It rattled onto the deck. Mary-Anne moved to get it, reaching down, but the gun slipped down an open hatch. She stepped down the hatch after it and slipped, clattering down some steep steps and into the kitchen area below. Jamie moved cautiously to the top of the stairs with Gordo still on his shoulder.

"Be careful," whispered Gordo.

Jamie looked down the steps. Mary-Anne had gone, so he began to climb cautiously down. A shot cracked, echoing around the kitchen and thudding into the stairs by Jamie's foot. He pushed up and out onto the deck again. A few seconds later the engines revved and rose to maximum and they felt the boat accelerating. Mary-Anne had gone into the engine room and thrown the throttle.

Jamie moved onto the bridge. He stepped over Henrik, who was still unconscious, pulled the lever and unlocked the wheel to turn the boat. Neither worked. Mary-Anne had been able to override the controls.

"Look!" exclaimed Gordo.

He was pointing at the Golden Gem as it followed them and tried to catch up.

"We'll just have to wait 'till they catch up," said Jamie.

"We'd better close the hatch," said Gordo jumping down and trying to lift it.

Jamie helped him and it swung over and slammed shut in the wind. Gordo took some wire from a pocket on his belt and gave it to Jamie who wrapped it around the catch until it was securely fixed. Then they huddled up in a sheltered corner and waited.

5.23 a.m. in the helicopter

"We should be there by now," said Jane Larkin.

"It's drifted - the capsule must've drifted," said the pilot,

"I'll drop down further."

They descended until they were just ten feet above the water with searchlights blazing across the waves. They dropped speed to thirty… and then twenty… and then they saw it.

"There!" shouted Jane in excitement.

The white air bags looked bright in the lights. They flew right over it, and then turned and hovered above. The pilot held the helicopter with expert control.

"Right," said Jane, "I'm going down."

She slid the door open and met the blast of the cold wind.

She strapped a small cage onto her back to put the monkey in and grabbed her camera from the seat beside her and hung it around her neck. Then she sat in the seat at the end of the winch and pushed herself out through the door. The winch let her down slowly and she landed gently on an air bag, stepped out of the seat and almost slipped off in the wind. She dropped onto her hands and knees and looked around for the door. Luckily she had landed right next to it, so she took a photograph and then reached out and grasped the door handle.

She lifted the handle and then hesitated; the monkey might jump out and fall into the sea. She opened it just a crack and peeped in through the opening. She was face to

face with Jeff.

Jane jerked her head back in utter astonishment. The door swung open and Jeff's head appeared.

"But… but…" Jane stammered, "Who are you?"

Jane was stunned. She was expecting to see a monkey but here was a man she had never seen before. She knew for an absolute certainty that Gordo would be in there. This was impossible.

"How did you get in here?" asked Jane, shouting above the sound of the waves and shaking her head in utter disbelief.

"I… er… er," Jeff realized this was very hard to explain. He could not explain without admitting the crime he was involved in. "Well… you see… I'm not meant to be here…"

"I know that!" Jane shouted.

"It's all a big mistake. I'm in here since… not long… it was a..." He stopped because he could not make up a reason that would make any sense.

"You're talking jibberish!" interrupted Jane, "We'll get you in the helicopter and you can explain later. Then I'll hear the truth." She looked past his shoulder. "Is the monkey in there as well?"

"No."

"Well where is it then?"

"I don't know," said Jeff gloomily, "It was in here, but it's gone."

"Where's it gone to?" Jane was shouting angrily now, "Tell me!"

"I can't remember, I told you!"

"If you don't tell me I'll leave you here, and you won't survive long."

"No! Don't leave me," he pleaded desperately.

"Tell me now then, otherwise, I promise you, I will leave you here. I have other things to do. Now where is the monkey?"

"It jumped onto the boat."

"What boat?" snapped Jane.

"The fishing boat."

Jane looked around, "What fishing boat?" she screamed.

"It's gone now."

"OK… OK."

Jane knew that the radar on the Coral Reef would pick it up. She prepared herself to be winched up, stepping into the seat and waving up to the pilot. A few moments later it was Jeff's turn. The winch, with the seat at the end, was lowered down. It swung around in the wind until Jeff caught hold of it, slipped into the seat and was hauled up. The pilot turned the hovering machine and then headed back towards the Coral Reef.

5.32 a.m. aboard the Coral Reef

Max McMurphy was still seething with anger because the helicopter had left without him. He had contacted the pilot on the radio just as Jane had dropped down to the nose cone. The pilot was watching from above, and described the extraordinary sight of a man's head looking out through the capsule door and talking to Jane.

"A man is in the capsule," the pilot said, "He's climbing out now."

"What?"

"A man."

"Did you say a man?" McMurphy could not believe his ears, "A man?"

"Yes, a man. Or that's the biggest monkey I've ever seen!" joked the pilot.

"But how could a man...?" McMurphy frowned thoughtfully.

This was a real puzzle; it was more than that. It was impossible. How could a man be in the nose cone that had just gone into space with only a monkey in it? And where was the monkey that he wanted so badly?

"Put Jane Larkin on as soon as she's up. I want to speak to her."

As soon as Jane was winched up the pilot passed the mouthpiece to her.

McMurphy barked at her, "What's going on?!"

"The monkey's gone," she said.

"How? Where is it? What happened?" stammered McMurphy.

All this was astonishing and impossible to understand.

"It's on a boat," she said, "Listen, I've got to help the man in now... he's just coming up. I'll talk to you when we get back."

She handed the mouthpiece back to the pilot.

"I've got to concentrate on keeping this thing still," he said to McMurphy.

"You know we've almost caught up with you now?" McMurphy said.

"Good, how far away are you?"

"Only about fifteen minutes,"

"We'll see you soon then," said the pilot and switched off.

McMurphy could not work it out, but the worst thing about it was that the monkey had gone and it seemed his plans were in tatters. However, he did know that the monkey was on a boat, so he set his mind to his next task. He had to find the boat.

5.46 a.m.

McMurphy stood on the deck of the Coral Reef and peered into the night through powerful binoculars. First he saw the helicopter's light and then he heard its distinctive sound. He picked it up with the binoculars and watched it approach. A few seconds later it burst out of the darkness that surrounded him and he quickly adjusted the focus to see it heading straight towards him. It flew over his head shaking the air all around him and then descending to the heliport. This time he had made sure he was close by; he was not going to be left behind when it lifted off again to search for the boat and Gordo.

His plan was still alive. The monkey was on a boat and it should be straightforward to find it. When he had been speaking to the helicopter pilot he had been in the navigation room where the radar showed two small boats in the area. The monkey would be on one of those boats; the only question was, which one. He would address that problem in due course but first he had to get into the helicopter and then control things from there.

The helicopter touched down gently. Immediately the door slid open and Jeff was pushed out. He landed on his feet and then fell and rolled, before scrambling up. McMurphy ran towards the helicopter. He had almost reached the open door when the helicopter's engine roared louder and it began to lift into the air.

"Stop!" shouted McMurphy, "Stop!"

He lunged towards the door and missed but caught hold of one of the wheels. He tried to climb up to the door but the helicopter lifted higher and the door slammed shut. The great machine hovered and turned. He hung on with all his might but the weight of his body was more than his arms could support. As the engine roared louder, ready to head off, he let go and dropped back onto the helipad with a bump, landing on his side. His glasses fell off and rattled across the deck.

A crowd of navy sailors had been watching in amazement and they dashed towards him. McMurphy lay on the deck and stared in anger at the departing helicopter.

"You alright, sir?" one exclaimed.

"Yeah," snarled McMurphy.

Jefferies was in the group and stepped forwards.

"Why did you do that?" he asked, then adding with a smirk, "Sir."

McMurphy scowled at him.

"You want to try getting in through the door, sir!" commented another.

They tried not to laugh but some of them could not contain a snigger. A couple of them helped him to his feet just as a gust of wind caught his glasses, causing them to slip across the deck. He rushed after them and after several attempts managed to catch them. One of the arms had broken off and he struggled to get them to stay on his nose. After some fumbling they settled at an angle.

He was not only embarrassed by what had happened, but he had hurt his ankle in the fall. Worst of all, in spite of being the director of Cape Canaveral, the person in the very highest position, the person supposed to be in control of this whole space project, he had not been able to get onto this helicopter. Suddenly the fury in him rose to the point where he lost all control and kicked the air, almost falling over.

He looked like a spoilt child. A ripple of laughter spread through the crowd of young sailors who were still gathered around him.

"Don't stand there gaping!" he shouted at them, "Get on with your jobs!"

5.51 a.m. aboard the Las Varas.

It was still dark. Most of the clouds had cleared now leaving black patches of star-sprinkled sky. Above the western horizon it had begun to lighten showing the first signs of the approaching dawn. The wind had dropped to a gentle breeze as the Golden Gem chased the Las Varas. The more powerful engines of the pursuing boat, together with the sails, gave it more speed and it had been gradually closing the gap until it was almost alongside. Jamie stood up with Gordo on his shoulder and got ready to jump across but a sharp noise behind them made him stop. It was the crack of a gun.

Mary-Anne had shot through the catch on the hatch, splitting the wire that Gordo had wound around it, and pushed it open. Her head popped up and she looked around. She saw Jamie and Gordo and aimed her gun at them.

"If you jump I shoot!" she shouted, "I told you. I want the monkey!"

Jamie stayed completely still and turned to face her. His heart thumped.

"OK," said Jamie quickly, "We're not jumping."

"Give me the monkey," Mary-Anne demanded, "Now!"

The Golden Gem had drawn level and was travelling at the same speed. Rachel and several fishermen were on the deck and looking across. Ed was getting ready to jump. Mary-Anne saw him and aimed.

"Get back!" she shouted, pulling the trigger.

The crack of the shot was followed by Ed's cry of pain as he fell to the deck. The other fishermen quickly dragged Ed's body behind the bridge cabin. Mary-Anne turned her attention back to Jamie and levelled her gun at him.

"The monkey," she said firmly, shaking the gun.

"OK," Jamie said, holding up his hand in submission. "Go on Gordo… she wins. You have to go to her."

Gordo resisted leaving him and Jamie had to prize the little monkey off as he clung onto his clothes. He dropped to the ground and huddled by Jamie's legs.

"The monkey will come to you if you call him by his name – Gordo," Jamie said.

Mary-Anne still had only the top part of her body above deck and her legs were on the steps running down to the kitchen. She moved up one more step and looked suspiciously at Jamie. She shook her gun at him.

"No tricks this time. I don't miss. Hands up!"

Jamie held his hands up.

Then Mary-Anne called gently. "Gordo… Gordo… come to Mary-Anne… I'll look after you now."

Gordo started moving straight towards her. Mary-Anne kept her eyes fixed on Jamie. He started to lower one hand.

"Don't you move. If you value your life, stay completely still."

Gordo was still walking towards Mary-Anne but he moved slightly to the left.

"Come here Gordo… there's a good monkey," she said, still keeping her steely gaze fixed on Jamie.

"Listen," said Jamie, "You don't need to do this."

"Shut up!" shouted Mary-Anne.

"We can work it out," continued Jamie, "Listen…"

"I'm not listening…" Mary-Anne snapped, "One more word and I'll sh…"

Her eye was caught by Gordo moving into a shadow. The little monkey's hand flicked forwards releasing his penknife which spun through the air. The blade flashed in the deck light and plunged into Mary-Anne's arm.

"Aaahh!" she screamed in pain and dropped the gun.

Rachel had been observing all this from behind the cabin on the Golden Gem. She rushed out and jumped across onto the deck of the Las Varas.

"It's over," she shouted, staring at Mary-Anne, her voice sounding full of authority, "No more! You have lost your little game!"

She moved towards her and kicked the gun away.

"No!" shouted Mary-Anne.

She moved down a step and swung the hatch behind her. It slammed shut.

Gordo ran to Jamie and climbed onto his shoulder and they jumped onto the Golden Gem. Rachel followed.

"You two live dangerously, don't you?" Rachel said.

"We don't mean to," said Jamie, smiling at her, "But so do you!"

"You need to warm up." She stroked Gordo on his head and then put her arm around her cousin. "Go inside and we'll get this boat going in the right direction!"

The fishermen were helping Ed to his feet. His arm hung loosely and a bloom of blood on his sleeve showed where the bullet had hit him. Rachel rushed to help him and noticed how pale he looked.

"It's not bad," said Ed.

Rachel looked at his arm. "We need to stop the bleeding. Come on... I'll sort you out."

The engines revved and the Golden Gem began to gather speed. As they descended the steps, Jamie spoke quietly to Gordo.

"You see, Gordo," he said, scratching him under his chin, "It's always worth having a plan up your sleeve!"

CHAPTER 18

5.59 a.m. aboard the Las Varas

Mary-Anne lay on the floor and sobbed. Her plans, which seemed to be so positive and likely to succeed, had gone terribly wrong. Henrik had been knocked out and she did not know how he was, and he was the only one who could navigate the boat. Frank was dead and Jeff, lost.

She had pulled Gordo's knife out of her arm and then bound the wound tightly to stop the bleeding, but it throbbed with a deep ache. She had hurt her knee when she fell down the steps and it was extremely painful when she tried to move. She knew that she could not lie there with the boat travelling out of control. She decided she would climb the steps up to the deck and see how Henrik was.

She was half way up when she heard the sound of a helicopter followed by an ear-shattering sound. It was the horn of a ship - a large ship. She scrambled up to the hatch and when her head rose above the level of the deck, the horn wailed again. It was the loudest noise she had ever heard and she put her hands over her ears to dull the blast. But worse than this, much worse, was the sight that met her eyes. Towering above the Las Varas as if it was a toy boat, was the massive hull of the Coral Reef.

The huge aircraft carrier was almost still now after slowing down over the last mile. There had been panic on the bridge when the Las Varas had been seen on the radar veering into their path. It was too late for the huge ship to turn; a collision was unavoidable.

Henrik Blomqvist groaned and stirred at the sound of the horn and opened his eyes to see the huge ship in front of him. The shock sparked him into action, and despite his aching head and weak legs, he managed to get to his feet. In a panic, he stepped to the wheel and grasped it, his energy quickly returning in the face of the crisis.

A second later there was a grinding crash as the Coral Reef smashed into the little fishing boat. The metal hull ripped into the wood, cutting a splintered gash through the Las Varas. For Mary-Anne and Henrik, it seemed as if the whole world was breaking up around them as bits of wood flew in all directions and they watched in horror as the side of the ship passed by. It stretched above like a high wall, so close that they could almost reach out and touch it. The massive impact split the fishing boat in two, the front half of which was mostly demolished and sank within a few seconds.

Water gushed into the other half. It began to tilt and Mary-Anne found herself sliding down the deck towards the waves. She frantically tried to grab onto something and with one flailing hand, she stopped her slide. Below her the water rose and she let out a terrified shriek. The boat was sinking fast.

She turned to climb up the sloping deck and saw Henrik

swinging past her on a rope. Desperately, she grabbed onto one of his legs and found herself being pulled upwards, away from the sinking boat, and bumping and scraping against the towering side of the Coral Reef. When they reached the top, they were hauled over the railings and onto the safety of the deck.

Henrik glanced down to see that his boat had gone, leaving a mass of debris rising and falling on the waves.

Above their heads a helicopter hovered. McMurphy rushed out and waited for it to land.

6.17 a.m. aboard the Coral Reef

Jack Jefferies descended the stairs to the laundry room where the sound of washing machines blended with the pulsating noise of the great ship's engines. On one side of the room, clothes were stacked neatly and in front of this, a long rail was hung with a row of clothes on hangers. Jefferies was greeted at the counter by a young man with a friendly smile.

"Hi, Jack," said the young man, and then he asked, "Collection?"

"Yeah, for Kennett," he replied, "Six complete uniforms, plus one new one for the new guy…"

"I wasn't told about that!" he complained, "I've got six here all ready for you." Still talking, he turned away to take them off the rail and placed them in a pile on the counter. "And one more?" he asked grumpily.

"Yup," nodded Jefferies.

"Why hasn't he got his own?"

Jefferies shrugged. "Arrived in plain clothes. Transferred

from Jacksonville and his luggage got lost during his flight."

"OK. No problem, I've got a few new ones over here. What size?"

"My height," stated Jefferies, "But a bit slimmer."

He returned with three new uniforms and placed them on the top of the others.

"I've given you three uniforms for him to try… but bring back the other two, OK?"

"Thanks," said Jefferies.

He forced his arm under the pile of clothes, held them against his chest and left.

6.24 a.m. aboard the Coral Reef

Officer Kennett was in his cabin at his desk. He was studying a letter handed to him by the new marine who had just arrived.

TRANSFER NOTICE

To Officer Neville Kennett,

Private Giles Turner transferring from Naval Air Station Jacksonville to USS Coral Reef Aircraft Carrier in effect from 13th December 1958.

Vice Admiral Charles R. Scott.

For the personal attention of Officer Neville Kennett.

Private Giles Turner transfering from:

NAVAL AIR STATION JACKSONVILLE

to:

USS CORAL REEF AIRCRAFT CARRIER

in effect from:

13 December 1958.

Charles R Scott

Vice Admiral Charles R Scott

He read it again and then scratched his head. This was very unusual. Why had he not been informed in advance? He had a full quota of men so why was he being sent another, especially with limited accommodation space? He needed to check that it was not a mistake.

He left his cabin and headed for the Ship's Radio

Room to contact Vice Admiral Scott by ship to shore radio communication. The radio operator soon connected him to Naval Air Station Jacksonville where he asked for the Vice Admiral. He was told that the Vice Admiral could not speak for another hour, so he left a message.

He was walking back to his cabin when a sailor approached him.

"Mr. McMurphy wants you to report to him, sir," the sailor said.

"Now?" asked Kennett.

"Immediately, sir."

Up on deck the helicopter had landed and Jane Larkin was getting out. McMurphy stepped forwards and was finally face to face with her.

"What's going on?!" he demanded.

"The monkey's on a fishing boat," she replied, "Let's hope it wasn't that one! But there's another one very close and it could be on there…"

"OK," McMurphy nodded, "But what have you been up to? Blatant insubordination which you won't get away with. I should have been on that helicopter not you, and you knew that. I will be writing an official report to demote you – a lesser job with a lower salary."

Jane stared at him in shock. She was proud of her position and desperate for promotion; demotion was a disgrace she could not bear.

McMurphy turned to Second Lieutenant Kennett who was waiting to speak to him.

"Get your men ready," ordered McMurphy, "I need them here in three minutes… full uniforms plus rifles. We're going on a helicopter ride."

6.52 a.m. aboard the Golden Gem

Rachel and Jamie relaxed in the warmth of the gully area of the fishing boat, each with a hot meal in front of them. Gordo was sitting on the table picking nuts and pieces of dried fruit off a saucer and popping them into his mouth. The boat was swaying on the ocean waves and occasionally the plates would begin to slide on the table top.

"We are on our way, at last!" said Rachel.

"To South America?" asked Gordo.

Rachel could not understand but picked up the gist of his question.

"Sorry, I haven't told you where we're going yet, have I?" Rachel smiled, "Venezuela. There's a massive rainforest there. You'll love it!"

He made a trill of delight and excitement, and launched into a climbing, swinging journey around the room. He arrived back on the table with a bump making the plates rattle. Rachel and Jamie laughed and stroked him affectionately.

"But what about us?" Jamie asked Rachel.

"Well, I thought we'd stay a bit. Not exactly in the forest, but close by in the Orinoco Delta. That's if you want to."

Jamie smiled as he thought how wonderful it sounded. Then his grandmother came to mind. What would he do about her? He would send her a message saying, 'Gone away for… for… some time (keep it vague). I'll be back… some time.'

"What about your job?" he asked Rachel.

"Oh, that," she said dismissively, "If McMurphy doesn't sack me…" she smiled, "Then… well, I haven't decided yet. I'll see. I certainly want a bit of a break and the freedom of the Orinoco Delta sounds attractive."

"Hang on," exclaimed Gordo, tilting his head to one side, "I can hear a helicopter!"

Jamie listened. The sound grew until they all heard it.

"I was fearing this," said Rachel calmly, "Gordo, you need to hide."

She looked around quickly.

"In here," said Jamie, reaching down and opening a cupboard door near the floor.

Gordo jumped down onto the floor, disappeared into the cupboard and Jamie closed it. Then Rachel and Jamie hurried up the stairs and onto the deck.

All the crew of the Golden Gem, except for the one at the wheel, were on the deck and she felt well supported by four strong fishermen and Ed, who had his arm in a sling. Ed had explained the whole story to the crew and they followed their captain's lead in supporting Rachel, Jamie and Gordo; they were determined that no harm should come to them.

The helicopter dropped to twenty feet above the boat and the door opened. A uniformed man looked out and shouted down at them above the engine noise.

"Second Lieutenant Neville Kennett from the US Navy Aircraft Carrier Coral Reef. Prepare to be boarded! Do not resist. We are armed!"

He descended on a winch with a rifle slung over his shoulder. He was followed by five other uniformed marines. Then another face appeared in the doorway wearing a suit and tie. It was the thin face of Max McMurphy. He descended onto the deck amidst the uniformed men and strode forwards.

"Who's in charge here!" he barked.

Rachel stepped forwards. "I am," she said from a few feet away, looking at him confidently straight in the eyes.

McMurphy looked stunned.

"You!" he said, looking surprised. Then he saw Jamie. "What are you doing here?"

Jamie stepped towards McMurphy. "What are you doing here?"

McMurphy glared back, angered by Jamie's lack of respect. He looked at Rachel and scowled at her. "I could've guessed you'd have your fingers in the pie. Give me the monkey."

"Excuse me, sir," she said with sarcasm, "Where are your manners? When I was a child I was taught to say 'please.'"

"You are in no position to joke, young lady."

"I'm not," said Rachel sharply.

His face was growing red with irritation.

"We will use force if necessary." He waved crossly at the marines standing alert behind him. "This is a matter of national importance and national security. Now, give me the monkey!"

"How do you know it's here?" asked Rachel, staying remarkably calm.

McMurphy knew he had to bluff. "I know. I've been told and I do know. Give it to me!"

He wanted his own way and quickly. He wondered why he was even having this conversation, and he turned to the marines.

"Search the boat, and you have my permission to search thoroughly."

"Yes, sir!" said Second Lieutenant Kennett.

"And by that I mean, turn over anything that might conceal a little monkey about the size of a squirrel... empty cupboards and drawers, prize open every possible secret compartment or hiding place. Understand?" he boomed.

"Yes, sir!" Kennett shouted again and the men began to walk toward the door. The fishermen moved quickly and blocked them.

"Don't make it difficult," shouted McMurphy, "Stand aside."

"No," shouted Ed, "I don't want your heavy-handed men barging around my boat!"

"I've warned you," boomed McMurphy, now red-faced with anger, "And that is all I'm officially expected to do! You are now resisting my command and so force is necessary!" He turned to the marines. "Use any force necessary to carry out the search!"

"Yes, sir," they shouted, and in a second they all had rifles in their hands and were aiming them at the fishermen.

"Shoot one in the leg," shouted McMurphy, "That'll make them move."

"Stop!" shouted Rachel, "You have forgotten something!"

McMurphy stepped towards her until he was looking down on her with disdain. He glared into her eyes with hate.

"Young lady…" he began. He was speaking softly but the severity in his voice was cutting. "I'm completely fed up with your interfering. I can arrest you. Mind you, I don't want to, but if you don't give me the monkey now, then you leave me with no choice…"

"Oil investments," Rachel interrupted calmly.

"What?" McMurphy asked, looking puzzled, "What did you say?"

"Oil investments," Rachel repeated, holding him with a steady stare, "A certain company called Stanley Energy in southern India? A certain employment agency in the Raye area? Certain funds going direct to a Swiss bank? A certain…"

"Stop!" blurted out McMurphy, looking at her in astonishment.

Kennett and his five marines still had their rifles raised and were waiting for an order. From where they were, they could not hear the conversation. McMurphy's eyes flashed with panic as he glanced at them.

"Shall we begin the search, sir?" asked Kennett.

"Er… no… er… not yet… not at the moment," he stammered, and then turning back to Rachel, "Who told you all this rubbish?"

"Rubbish, is it?" said Rachel still fixing her eyes on him, "It's not rubbish at all - it's true. I have all the details too. You have used people for your own greed, and just to put money in your own pocket!"

"You're making all this stuff up!" he retorted.

She felt her stomach tighten with fear as she realized the danger she was in. As she looked at his hard expression consumed with anger, she realized how ruthless he was. Everyone on the boat was in danger and it was her fault.

Jamie saw her hesitation and an idea flashed into his mind.

"She's making it up, is she?" he said to McMurphy.

"You stay out of it, boy," snapped McMurphy.

Jamie ignored him and turned to Rachel, "Tell him about your lawyers..."

Rachel stared back. What did he mean? Jamie willed her to understand.

"Your lawyers..." continued Jamie, "You know... George Long and Sons...they know..."

Suddenly Rachel understood and turned to face McMurphy.

"If I'm making it up how do I know those things? Tell my lawyers, George Long and Sons, that I'm making it up. They have all the evidence, and if anything happens to me, Gordo or anyone on this ship he will be on the phone to the police quicker than you would believe."

For a few seconds he stared at her, wide-eyed. He was used to being in control but now a feeling of helplessness took over. The world came tumbling in on him. He seemed to shrink physically and mentally. Jamie's bluff had worked; he had made up the lawyers. McMurphy looked around at the soldiers and the crew, and gathered himself together.

"Look... Rachel... I'm sure we can... er... sort this out," he stammered, and then he moved closer and said quietly to make sure that the others could not hear, "How much?"

"What?" said Rachel, astonished.

"How much do you want? Everyone has a price, what's yours?" he was pleading with her now, "Ten thousand...

twenty… thirty… you name it and you've got it." He knew he was completely cornered and that this was his last chance.

"You have lost this one," Rachel said quietly, "I know everything about you; the apartment in New York, and how you bought it; that flashy Rolls Royce that came from that crooked deal in Mexico. Need I go on? Now that I have really seen your true colours…" she paused and then continued her bluff, "The police investigation will be underway very soon."

The thought of a police investigation was embarrassing and painful. His head dropped.

"We need to talk this over…"

"Get off this boat!" Rachel shouted.

"But… " he began.

Jamie joined in. "Get off now. Go!"

Everyone on deck was stunned by what was happening. The roles had completely reversed. McMurphy had been the one completely in charge and now he was doing what he was told.

"We're going," he announced to Kennett.

"But, sir, what about the monkey?"

"That doesn't matter now," he said, looking ashen faced and with a blank expression, "We're leaving."

McMurphy went up first, looking sullen and worried, followed by Kennett and the marines, and soon the helicopter was speeding back to the Coral Reef. Rachel and Jamie immediately went below to fetch Gordo and then a little celebration broke out on the deck of the Golden Gem.

7.13 a.m. aboard the Coral Reef

Jane Larkin was feeling miserable because her plans were not working out. Finding a man in the nose cone was the strangest moment of all and she still could not fathom it out. Where had this man come from? No doubt it would all be explained in due course.

But now her misery had been doubled by McMurphy. After he had threatened her with the disgrace of losing her job for a lower one, her head was in a spin. She did not know what to do.

She walked along the corridor towards her cabin and passed the Recovery Room. There was a young marine standing guard outside the door and she thought he must be guarding the mystery man found in the nose cone. She wanted to interview him and find out how he had got there, but she felt too upset. She decided to go to her quarters for a few minutes first, think things over and try to calm down.

A minute earlier, two young marines had escorted Jeff to the Recovery Room. He was ushered into the room which was just big enough to contain four beds and some comfortable armchairs around a coffee table.

"Stay here," said one of the marines, "Someone will be along to interview you shortly."

The sailors left and closed the door behind them.

"Jeff?"

The voice came from someone sitting in one of the armchairs and facing the other way. He jumped at the sound of his name. The person got up and slowly turned to face him. When Jeff saw who it was, his breath caught in his chest and his jaw dropped in shock.

"F... F... Frank!" he stammered, "I thought you were dead! What happened?"

Frank was wrapped in a blanket and he smiled smugly.

"Here I am... alive and well. A miracle? No, I held onto one of those floating rings and then a helicopter fished me out." His smile dissolved into a scowl. "Did you celebrate my sudden, unfortunate death?"

Jeff shook his head quickly and beamed nervously at Frank.

"Of course not," he said, "But why…?"

"Because…" Frank interrupted, stabbing out the words with venom, "Because, with me out of the way you could take all the money. You were going to kill me, she said. Then she tried to kill me! That wife of yours is an evil monster."

"What are you saying?" asked Jeff, "She was distraught after you tried to kill her."

"Eh?!" Frank exclaimed, "What do you mean?"

"You tried to push her over…" he began.

"Is that what she said?" Frank snapped, "No… it's lies. Now listen to the truth… she pushed me in. She tried to kill me and now I'm back to haunt you!"

"Frank," began Jeff, "Don't try that one on me. I know the truth. I know what happened."

Frank scowled and shook his head in disbelief.

"She's lying through her teeth," he stated, standing up, "Maybe you are too. She has…"

The door opened and Mary-Anne was escorted into the room with crutches to take the weight off her injured knee. She had a bandage on her arm where Gordo had hit her with his penknife, and various scratches and bruises on her face and nose. Frank and Jeff sat down and tried to look relaxed in front of the sailor.

"Stay here," said the marine, "These people are also recovering after being rescued." He chuckled. "I don't know what's going on out there! Four of you in the space of an hour! There'll be someone along to interview you soon."

He left and closed the door after him. He reached into his pocket for some money and then went to get a drink from a machine along the corridor.

Jeff was staring in surprise at the state of Mary-Anne. "What happened to you?"

She was just about to answer when Frank turned to face her. Her astonished gaze fixed on him. Her mind was rushing. How was he alive!? The best thing to do was to stick to her story, after all Jeff had believed her.

"Frank!" she exclaimed, diving at him, "You tried to kill me!"

Jeff blocked her way and held her back, and she dropped one of her crutches. It clattered to the floor.

"How could you do that!" she carried on.

"You... you double-crossing liar," snarled Frank who was now on his feet as well, "You've twisted it all around!"

"You're the twister!" Mary-Anne exclaimed.

"Hang on!" said Jeff, "Listen! They don't even know that we know each other. If they hear us then they will know and they might work out what we we've been..."

The door opened and the marine on guard, who had just got back with his drink and heard the noise, poked his head around the door.

"What's happening?" he asked sternly.

"This lady," began Jeff, "This lady... just slipped and dropped one of her crutches."

Jeff picked it up and gave it to her. "Here you are. Are you alright?"

"I think so," said Mary-Anne, flexing her arm, "Yes... yes, thank you."

"Come and sit down," said Jeff charmingly.

They both helped her to a chair.

"It's alright now," Jeff said to the marine, "Thank you, but we're fine now."

The young marine was satisfied with the explanation and closed the door. Jeff sat down and glowered at Frank.

"You've got a lot to answer to, you have," he muttered at him.

"A lot," agreed Mary-Anne.

Frank gripped his hand into fists of rage. "Not as much as you!" he snapped at Mary-Anne.

Then he turned to Jeff. "You've got to believe me. She's the one making up a story."

"Frank," began Jeff, "Just stop it!"

"Oh, I see," said Frank slowly and thoughtfully, "You're

ganging up on me. It's your little conspiracy! Perhaps you planned it all along and now I've turned up to spoil your little plans."

There was a tense pause in the conversation. In the end Jeff broke the silence.

"We've got to get a story together before they come to talk to us... else we're all in trouble." He hesitated thoughtfully. "They've only rescued us - they don't know we were trying to steal that stupid monkey do they? How about if we say that I fell off..."

The door opened and Jane Larkin entered and closed the door behind her. She walked over to the soft chairs, sat down and looked around at the gathering. She had managed to compose herself.

"I'm Jane Larkin, the manager of this space mission."

"Space mission?" asked Frank, looking as if he'd never even heard of it, "What space mission?"

"The Jupiter AM-13 with the monkey? You must've read about it in the papers."

"Yes," said Frank thoughtfully, "I think I did read something..."

"I hope you're all feeling better?" she enquired.

They nodded.

"The water is freezing..." she continued, "But you look warm and dry now. So, you were picked up fairly close to each other and all within a short time."

She looked at them, from face to face and they looked blankly back at her. Jane raised her eyebrows in surprise.

"Don't you know each other?" she asked.

"No," replied Frank, acting as if taken aback by the suggestion.

"None of you?"

They looked at each other, shaking their heads and shrugging.

"OK... so... tell me your stories," she said turning to Jeff and looking at him with suspicion, "I'm especially interested in yours."

"Well… er…" began Jeff slowly, "Me first?"

"Yes," said Jane, looking quizzically at him.

"OK. Er… well… it was the storm…"

A loud knock on the door interrupted him.

"Come in," said Jane, standing up and walking towards the door.

The door opened and Smudge entered, followed by Ruth Anderton. They both looked smart in their police uniforms. The three criminals sank into their chairs in an attempt to hide.

"Officers Smudge and Anderton," announced Smudge.

Jane held out her hand. "Miss Jane Larkin, Space Project Manager."

She shook Miss Ruth's hand.

"Officers," she continued, "I'm glad you're here. I heard you were coming. But what's it all about?"

"A homicide, madam," Smudge replied as he shook her hand.

"A possible homicide," added Ruth.

Smudge continued, "So it is important. Important enough to fly us out here. But are we interrupting a meeting…" Ruth nudged him in the side with her elbow but Smudge ignored her and continued. "We'll talk to you, Miss Larkin, when you've finished." He turned to the door. "We'll take a look around until you're ready."

"Sir!?" persisted Ruth.

He turned to her and snapped, "What is it?"

"It's them, sir," she said, "Look!"

He suddenly noticed Jeff and Mary-Anne sitting on the comfy chairs.

"Holy Moly!" Smudge exclaimed.

He stepped towards them. The surprise melted from his face to be replaced by a wry smile.

"Well, what a surprise…" he said with heavy sarcasm, "A surprise and a pleasure, Mr. Marks… and Mrs. Marks.

We fly out here to try to find you, and here you are! We don't even have to look!"

Jane looked surprised. "You know these people?"

"Well, those two, yes."

"What have they done?"

Smudge lifted his shoulders. "Quite a few things… er…"

Ruth took over. "Stealing two highway vehicles and other goods, stealing a monkey, committing theft from a hospital, forgery of identity badges and other papers, breaking into Cape Canaveral Headquarters, breaking into Cape Canaveral Lighthouse, and they're under suspicion of a possible homicide."

Frank sat up. "Homicide?!"

"What?!" exclaimed Jeff and Mary-Anne together.

"Well… how interesting…" began Jane, ignoring them. "They stole a monkey! Are they after our monkey then?" she looked thoughtful, "They were all picked up separately and have just denied that they know each other. I think I'll leave you to sort it out."

Ruth smiled, "It's gonna take some unravelling, this one, isn't it, sir?"

"Hmm," Smudge was nodding, "It certainly is."

Then he addressed Jane. "Can we conduct the interrogation here?"

"You're welcome," Jane replied.

"But, sir," Ruth said, "Don't you think we should speak to each alone."

"Absolutely," Smudge agreed. Then he turned to the three prisoners and snapped at them, "I will hear the truth, and it had better be the same truth from each of you!"

Jane nodded. "And I want to know what they were up to… because we can't find the monkey now…" She pointed at Jeff. "We found that man in the capsule with the monkey gone!"

Smudge and Ruth looked astonished.

"In the capsule?" asked Ruth.

"Yes!" Jane confirmed, "He says the monkey's on a boat... so we are searching for boats in the area. We're hoping it wasn't the boat that sank."

"OK, then," Ruth began, "If we can have these three locked up somewhere individually then we can talk to them in turn."

"No problem," Jane said sharply, "I'll organize it. And there's also the man... said he's the captain of the boat we hit... the one that sank, that is. If he is who he says he is, he needs some more navigation practice. He collapsed when we got him on board and he's unconscious in the infirmary with a nasty bump on the back of his head. He might be involved too."

It was not long before six marines arrived with handcuffs. Jane gave them their orders.

The handcuffs were clipped on the unhappy trio and the marines left with their three prisoners, keeping them apart so that they could not communicate.

"Thank you," said Smudge.

"I'm sure you'd like a cup of tea perhaps..." asked Jane, "Or coffee?"

"Thank you, but I think we'd better..." began Ruth.

Smudge interrupted. "We accept, thank you. We'll drink them as we interview. It's good to know our suspects are safe... but as soon as we've done a brief interview with each of them, we need to fly them back to Orlando and file charges."

"But, sir," said Ruth, "Don't we need to stay here to find out what's going on... remember what Ray Furley said..."

"About Mr. McMurphy?" he asked, looking down at her as if she was a naughty dog snapping at his heels.

"Yes, sir."

"Did you believe all that nonsense? That young man struck me as someone with a chip on his shoulder... a big chip. Mr. McMurphy involved in crimes! I don't think so. No, we've got our criminals in handcuffs and the sooner we get them behind bars the better."

Ruth was shaking her head. He ignored her and turned back to Jane, who was looking curious about their conversation. "Do you think Mr. McMurphy is a criminal?"

"A criminal?" she asked with surprise, "Mr McMurphy? Of course not!"

"There you are," he announced triumphantly, "So… tea, interviews and then the flight. If you'd be kind enough to lead the way Miss Larkin."

Jane showed them to the restaurant area and gave them a cup of tea, but as she did she was thinking about McMurphy. Could he be involved in some sort of criminal activity?

She told Smudge and Ruth where to go for the first interview and then quickly climbed two sets of stairs. She emerged onto the deck to find McMurphy walking straight towards her. The last time they met he had given her a severe telling her off but straight away she noticed he looked different. His face was anxious and tense and he stared at the ground as he walked. He looked up, saw Jane and rushed up to her.

"Jane," he pleaded, "You must help me! Something terrible has happened."

"You're asking me for help?" she exclaimed, "But… but… why? You just demoted me."

"I know, but everything is different now. I didn't mean all that. I'll change it. Please, I need your help. Perhaps you can help, I don't know, but I'm desperate."

"What's happened?" asked Jane.

"It's that Rachel… and the monkey… and the boy… oh no, I can't believe it! I don't know what to do. Tell me what to do, Jane. I'm ruined!"

"I don't know what you're talking about," Jane shook her head, "What do you mean... ruined? Where are they… I mean Rachel and the monkey… and the boy?"

"They're on the fishing boat."

"You've found the monkey?!" she asked.

"Yes. I've just come back from the boat and Rachel's threatening me, sort of! She's found out things... certain things that I have done. Mistakes I have made, and now I'm in trouble... deep trouble!"

"Why?"

McMurphy shook his head in despair. "She's gonna let the cat out of the bag... to the police and everything... and keep the monkey."

"The monkey?" queried Jane, "Let her keep it then... you don't want it, do you?"

"Yes, I do," he sighed, "For advertising. For big time advertising... lots of money. But... can you help?"

Jane was stunned.

"How? I don't see what I can do."

For the first time Jane felt pity for this man who now seemed so weak and desperate for help.

"You can talk to her. Yes... that's it... you go in the helicopter and talk to her. Persuade her not to do anything. You're good at this sort of thing, I know you are. I'll pay you. I'll pay her. Whatever it takes. You can have thousands of dollars each. And promotion of course. Please, will you?" he pleaded.

Jane was tempted by the money. Also it seemed her job was secure and if she did this she would be promoted. Her plan of using the monkey for another trip faded away in the light of this new situation. The offer was too good not to accept.

"OK, I'll do what I can," she said.

Relief washed over his face like a wave smoothing the sand. Now there was some hope.

"Oh, thank you," he said, "Thank you so much. Can you go now?"

She nodded.

"Good. The pilot is still in the helicopter and he's ready to go. He's waiting for us now. I was actually coming to get you so I told him to keep the engine running."

A couple of minutes later Jane was wrapped up in her coat and climbing into the helicopter to join McMurphy, Second Lieutenant Kennett and the six marines under his command. The machine rose off the Coral Reef and headed out over the waves.

As they flew, Jane pondered recent events. It was only a few minutes ago that her life seemed to be falling apart; there was the inevitable demotion and the monkey disappearing. Now, all of a sudden, her job was not only secure but promotion was on offer, and they knew where the monkey was.

As the helicopter cut through the salty Atlantic air, with the dawn now paling the dark water, McMurphy explained in more detail what he wanted Jane to do.

7.42 a.m. aboard the Golden Gem

Rachel, Jamie, Gordo and the fishermen were below deck except for Ed Fontain who was at the wheel. He was the first to hear the sound of the approaching helicopter and he used the voice pipe to relay the message to the others. They all came up to the deck as the helicopter dropped to hover above the Golden Gem.

"What's this about, I wonder?" said Jamie.

"It can't be good," Rachel replied.

They all watched as the door slid open and one figure, wrapped up in a hooded coat stepped out and descended on the winch. It landed gently on the deck and turned towards them. The breeze caught the hood and blew it back to reveal Jane Larkin.

"Rachel," said Jane, "I've come to talk."

"I'm always ready to talk," said Rachel, "It's just that we may not see eye to eye. What do you want to talk about?"

"Can we go below, please? It would be easier to talk out of the wind."

"Yes, why not?" Rachel said and then she turned to the cabin where Ed had opened the door and was looking out. "Ed? Can you come with us?"

Ed stepped out and nodded at one of his crew. "Take over at the wheel please, Mitch."

Ed led the way down the narrow stairs and Rachel, Jamie and Jane followed.

Down below the four of them sat down around a table with a hot drink each.

"So?" asked Rachel.

"I'd rather speak alone," said Jane coldly, glancing at Ed, and then at Jamie.

"You're not in a position to demand or request. These are good friends and what you say to me you can say to them."

"Very well," she said reluctantly, "If you insist."

"I do," stated Rachel.

"I have come to persuade you to see sense. Let's put it plainly. Mr. McMurphy needs the monkey and... he needs you to agree that you will not... er... take things further."

"What things," snapped Rachel.

"Certain delicate matters which need to remain... er... not revealed. They need to remain hidden. So we want these two things from you; the monkey and your agreement."

"Why do you want Gordo?" Rachel asked calmly.

"Mr. McMurphy wants him for a pet... a special memento of this great event..."

Rachel shook her head. "No... there's more to it than that. But, whatever the reason, he can't have him."

Jane held up a hand. "Hang on! Hang on. Not so fast! I've only just started. Listen on. We want those two things. That's all. Now what do you want? That is the big question."

"Nothing," said Rachel smiling, "I have all I need."

"I can't believe that!" Jane exclaimed, "Everybody wants something, and everybody wants money... to buy things, pay off that mortgage, pay the bills, go on holiday... the holiday of a life time..."

"No," said Rachel firmly.

"To buy a new kitchen, a new car, a new house even. You know... have enough to live really well."

"No. You may, but I don't!"

Jane gazed at Rachel in amazement.

"What is wrong with you?" she asked, "Perhaps you don't realize how rich McMurphy is. He is loaded and could get you anything you want. You must want something!"

"No," said Rachel more firmly than before, "His money is dishonest money... I don't want a cent of that."

"Alright, then. Shall we start talking in figures. He told me what I can offer you."

Rachel sighed. "I don't think you understand," she said, "I'm not interested. Justice is more important than money."

"What?" Jane shook her head and put her face in her hands in frustration.

This was more difficult than she thought it would be. How could she persuade Rachel? It was becoming clear that this young lady was strong-minded and it made Jane feel weak. Rachel's last statement seemed to ring in her ears and repeat in her mind.

'Justice is more important than money.'

"Listen, Rachel," she began again, "Perhaps you need a moment to think about it… work out a figure. An amount that would make a real difference to your life…"

Rachel shook her head. "No," she stated.

Jane ignored her and turned to Jamie. "And you're included, of course. Your payment would go into a special account for when you're older…"

Jamie's response was instant. "Money for Gordo? No way!"

His firm response made Jane realize that it was impossible to change their minds. She gazed at them and shook her head in resignation.

"I can't persuade you, can I?" she asked.

They both shook their heads.

Jane shrugged. "OK then. I'll tell him I tried. It's your loss."

"It might be yours too," began Rachel, "The police will be investigating him and if you help him, as you are now… then you're assisting his crimes. You're involved. But why are you doing it? Is he bribing you?"

"No," she snapped, lying, "He… he's a desperate man. And anyway, I have to help him – he's my boss."

"You don't. He's my boss too and he's not controlling me."

"But…" began Jane, "but…"

She paused. Something that Rachel had said repeated slowly in her mind, word for word - 'Justice is more important than money.' It was as if a mirror was being held up to her, showing her who she was, who she had become, who she would be in the future. She had become greedy for success, and for money too. It touched her conscience like the sharp stab of a needle. She was lost in her own selfish ambitions and suddenly it felt like a burden.

She bowed her head and sighed. This was difficult. McMurphy's offer tempted her and helped her ambitions, but the things Rachel and Jamie had said had awoken her conscience; she felt guilty. She did not know what to do.

Then she thought of something; it was a way out that she had never entertained before. She could abandon all her scheming, all her ambition, all her selfish plans; she could abandon it all. Just the thought of it gave her a feeling of relief and the warm sense of freedom. She lifted her head and looked at Rachel.

"Rachel," she said slowly, "I think I agree with you. Does that sound ridiculous?"

There was a stunned silence.

"What do you mean?" Rachel asked.

"I just feel…" Jane said, "that you're right. I never thought I'd be saying this. I've always disliked McMurphy, but I didn't think he was making his money in criminal ways. Speaking to you has made everything clear. I'm not pursuing the agreement I came to get. I'm changing sides…"

"Changing sides?" Rachel questioned, not sure if she could believe what she had heard.

"Yes…" she shrugged, and then gave a little nod, "There it is. I've decided. I'm not helping McMurphy anymore and therefore I'm free to help you… if I can that is."

"In that case, perhaps you can answer some questions for us," Rachel began, "What happened to that other fishing boat? There was a lady on it with a gun who was trying to get Gordo too; very nearly managed it as well!"

"The lady…" said Jane, "that is interesting. I'll tell you what I know."

She related what had happened with Mary-Anne, Jeff and Frank and the arrival of the police officers. Then she told them what she knew of Max McMurphy and his money-making plan to use Gordo for advertising. She also mentioned her own scheme for Gordo to make another trip into space. She laughed at herself for being so ambitious. It all seemed so senseless now.

Ed smiled at her. "We all act like idiots sometimes," he said.

She stared at him, amazed at his kindness. Her world had become hard and loveless and now she was tasting something different and it felt good.

"So what happens now?" asked Ed, "And what will you do, Jane?"

"I have no idea," said Jane happily, "And that's a refreshing feeling."

"We'd better go up on deck," he said, "That helicopter has been hovering up there for ages!"

Jane nodded. "And we must tell McMurphy the news… he's not going to like it! But I'm not going back into that helicopter with him. You know he's got marines with him?"

"You can shout up to him, or use our megaphone…" said Ed.

The door burst open and everyone turned in shock. It was second Lieutenant Kennett with McMurphy right behind him, holding a hand gun.

"Arrest them," McMurphy ordered, "Those two," he added, pointing at Ed and Jane.

Kennett lifted his rifle and aimed it at them. "You two… out!" he shouted, "Now!"

"But…" began Ed.

Kennett fired into the wall behind Ed.

"We are serious!" snapped McMurphy, "The next bullets will make Rachel and the boy lame for the rest of their lives. Now move!"

Ed and Jane stood up and left, with Kennett behind them, and the door closed. McMurphy sat down opposite Rachel and Jamie. He lowered the gun slowly to the table in front of him, placing it down gently as if handling something very precious.

"OK," he began, "So… where do we stand?"

He paused with his steely eyes fixed on Rachel and then continued, his voice calm and calculated.

"I have taken control of this boat. I had to do this because you have decided to spoil my life. Now I'm going to spoil your life… both of your lives. I have been kind to you… I sent Jane to try to make you see sense, but you refused, and now she has turned against me… yes, I heard everything. She knows about my past and that is her downfall. Due to you, she will not live long enough to see the dawn. She will meet an accident… And you… you have refused money…"

Rachel interrupted. "I could reconsider the offer of money," she said.

"Oh, what a shame!" he sighed sarcastically, "Too late. If only you'd said that to Jane, then OK, I would have accepted. But now, how can I trust you? You're just saying it to get out of trouble."

He lifted his hand slowly and placed it gently over his gun.

"But, my lawyers," she said quickly, "If I die, they release all the information about you…"

"Ha! You're bluffing," he guessed, keeping his eyes on hers. A little movement, and a blink, told him he was right, and she felt her stomach flutter.

He picked up the gun and pointed it between her eyes.

She felt the numbing ache of fear take over her body. Her mouth was dry. She swallowed.

"This is your last chance," he said softly, almost in a whisper, "To say goodbye to the boy… and the world."

Rachel could feel the blood draining from her cheeks and a cold sweat broke out on her forehead. She stared at him in terror.

He pulled the trigger.

At the same moment, Jamie lifted up his side of the table with all his might, his hands pushing upwards as he stood up. The table tilted up, rapping into McMurphy's arm as the gun went off. The bullet thudded into the wall just above Rachel's head and the gun was knocked out of his hand. It clattered onto the floor.

McMurphy eyed the gun and dived for it at full length, pushing the table away and skidding on the floor. He grasped the gun, lifted it and aimed it at Rachel. He shot again. The bullet flashed through Rachel's hair and clunked into something metal behind her as she and Jamie both dodged away. They were now in the corner of the room and had nowhere to go. They were trapped.

"No! No!" Rachel cried, holding up her hands.

McMurphy took aim again.

"As I was saying…" he growled slowly, "say goodbye to the…"

Suddenly, Gordo appeared, leaping at McMurphy's head, knocking off his glasses and biting him on his chin. McMurphy was taken completely by surprise. With a cry of pain, he dropped the gun and used both hands to grab Gordo's head, prize his jaws open and fling him off. He crashed into some cans of food on a shelf which clattered onto the floor. Rachel rushed over, grabbed the gun and pointed it at McMurphy as he lay on the floor.

They heard the sound of feet running down the stairs.

"Are you alright, sir," someone called out.

The door opened and a marine entered, followed by another. They both held rifles. They looked at McMurphy lying on the floor with blood trickling from his chin and saw Rachel standing over him with the gun in her hand.

"What's going on, sir?" asked the first marine.

McMurphy scrambled to his feet and pointed at Rachel. "That woman tried to shoot me. Arrest her and lock her up," he ordered.

Rachel knew she was outnumbered and lowered the gun. The other marine moved towards her and then suddenly darted behind McMurphy, hooking his arm around his neck and holding a hand gun to his head, pushing the barrel into his cheek.

"What are you doing?!" McMurphy barked.

"Just sorting out a problem," the marine replied.

It was Ray looking very different; his beard was shaven, his hair short and dyed fair, and he wore black-rimmed glasses. He looked smart in a crisp new uniform. McMurphy had not recognised him and looked confused and angry.

"She's the problem," he snapped, glaring accusingly at Rachel, "Now, let me go!"

"Be quiet!" Ray ordered.

"What? Who do you think you're talking to…"

Ray jerked the gun, pushing it harder into McMurphy's skin.

"Ow!" he winced, "You won't get away with this!"

"I will," said Ray calmly and briskly, as if brushing aside an annoying fly.

The other marine was standing by the door and had lifted his rifle to aim it straight at Ray.

"Let him go," he ordered.

Ray tightened his grip around McMurphy and then spoke, his voice calm and determined as he looked intently at the marine.

"Drop your weapon," he ordered.

The marine hesitated and looked at McMurphy. Ray pushed the barrel harder into McMurphy's cheek, making him grimace in pain.

"Tell him," ordered Ray.

McMurphy scowled. Sweat broke out on his brow with the fear of being held at gunpoint.

"Do as he says," he sighed to the marine.

The marine pursed his lips in annoyance and dropped his rifle.

"That's better," Ray said, "I'm sure McMurphy wants to live a little longer, so it's best to do as you're told."

Gordo jumped down from the shelf and scampered on all fours to Jamie who lifted him up and onto his shoulder.

"Now…" began Ray, "All of the marines, and McMurphy, need to leave this boat." He thought for a moment. "McMurphy… you will order the marines back up into the helicopter."

McMurphy grunted a reluctant agreement.

The door swung open violently, banging against the wall. Kennett entered and stood beside the marine, with his rifle raised and aimed at Ray's head.

Rachel lifted her gun quickly and pointed it at Kennett.

It was a deadlock situation. For a few seconds, everyone was still. Kennett had his eyes fixed on Ray with steely intensity. He was trained for this type of situation and he had the confidence of knowing he was a top class marksman, so he took the initiative.

"So, Turner," he began, his voice cool and calm, "Private Giles Turner... if that's your name..." Kennett was working it out as he spoke. This was the marine who was mysteriously transferred to the Coral Reef a few hours ago. Anger rose in him as he realised he had been tricked, but he was trained to stay calm. "You're a phony..."

Ray nodded. "Sort of... but McMurphy here is the real phony..."

Kennett frowned with surprise and disbelief.

"Who are you?"

"To my friends I'm Ray... but to McMurphy here I'm a fly in the ointment..."

"Well, guess what? I'm in charge here. Let him go... now."

Nothing happened.

"I said, let him go," Kennett commanded, "You have one chance. I'll count to three and then I shoot... and I don't miss."

Ray stared back.

Rachel shifted on her feet. "Neither do I," she said.

Kennett did not flinch, keeping his gaze steady on Ray, but speaking to Rachel. "Shooting a naval officer is not recommended by the law young lady. You will be tried for murder. One..."

Ray shifted slightly to shield himself behind McMurphy. "Stop!" ordered Kennett.

Ray stopped immediately and snapped back, "I'll shoot

him first!"

He tightened his arm around McMurphy's neck and shook the gun against his cheek. McMurphy looked terrified.

"Before you count to three," said Ray, "I'll shoot him… and the world will be a better place without him."

Sweat ran from McMurphy's forehead. "No!" he blurted out, "No, no, no… please don't shoot…please don't…"

"Two…" said Kennett, his eyes still fixed on Ray, "You won't shoot because that would be murder… "

McMurphy suddenly yelled out at Kennett, his voice punching out in a stream of pure panic, "No! I order you not to shoot!"

At the same moment Gordo's hand swung forwards releasing the adjustable spanner he had taken from his belt. It spun through the air and hit Kennett on the forehead with a thud. He stepped back in surprise and looked down at Gordo who was scampering straight at him. He tried to grab the little monkey but Gordo passed through his legs, climbed up his back and bit him hard on his neck.

"Ahh," cried Kennett, dropping his rifle and reaching back for Gordo with both hands.

Gordo quickly climbed down his back and bit him on the leg. The marine kicked at Gordo but again he was too quick, dodging out of the way so that the kick hit Kennett's leg instead. Gordo darted quickly around him, grabbed one of the rifles that was lying on the floor and dragged it back to Jamie, and then went back for the other one. Kennett was holding the back of his neck where he could feel the blood oozing from the wound.

"This is not as it seems," said Ray calmly to Kennett, "And I know you are only doing your job… but McMurphy here is the one you should be arresting. He makes money illegally by…"

"Don't believe him…" blurted out McMurphy.

Ray gave the gun a sharp push into his cheek which was turning red now. He tensed in pain and stopped talking.

Kennett shifted on his feet and for a brief moment he looked puzzled, trying to work out who to trust. Then he made up his mind.

"I know who I believe," he stated, glaring at Ray, "You are impersonating a marine and holding Mr McMurphy at gunpoint. Put down your weapons before it's too late and someone gets hurt."

Ray pushed McMurphy's cheek with the barrel of the gun.

"Tell Second Lieutenant Kennett to take all his men off this ship and back into the helicopter. Tell him… order him."

McMurphy nodded. "OK, OK," he growled, and then looking at Kennett, "Do it. Do as he says."

Kennett obeyed and turned to the door.

"Wait," ordered Ray, "We all go together. Rachel, keep your gun on Kennett and shoot if he tries anything. Jamie too… use the rifle to cover Kennett."

Kennett opened the door and everyone filed out. Kennett was followed by Rachel and then Jamie with Gordo on his shoulder. Next came the marine, with McMurphy behind him. Ray was last, with his gun pushed into the back of McMurphy's neck.

Kennett led the way onto the deck and into the bright warm sun. The four marines were sitting with their rifles in their hands and keeping guard over the crew and Jane. They leapt up, immediately alert and ready for action. They raised their rifles and pointed them at the group.

"Relax," said Ray, "Put your guns down and no one will get hurt. Kennett… tell them."

"Put your guns down," ordered Kennett.

They looked shocked but responded to the order and placed their guns on the deck. Gordo jumped off Jamie's shoulder and dragged their rifles, two at a time, further down the deck.

Kennett continued. "We're leaving. Foster, you get winched up to the helicopter first. Then Williamson and everyone else."

Foster signalled to the helicopter hovering above and the winch descended.

"Before you go," said Ray, "Someone needs to go up and deal with any other weapons they may have. Who do you suggest Ed?"

Ed looked at his crew. "Jake, will you do it?"

"Of course," he replied moving over to catch the winch.

He was hauled up, disappeared into the helicopter, and threw out a mixture of guns which fell into the sea. Jake was lowered down and then, one by one, the marines were taken up. Kennett was the last to leave, who turned just before the winch lifted him and glared at Ray.

"You won't get away with this," he said intently.

"I will," stated Ray, "And send the winch down again for McMurphy. I can't wait to get rid of him."

Kennett slipped into the helicopter and sent the winch down again. Ray pushed McMurphy forwards and he rushed eagerly towards the seat, as if escaping from a dangerous animal.

"You're finished," Rachel said, "Finished, McMurphy. It's all over. Your wicked ways have caught up with you!"

McMurphy turned, his face pale with fear.

"Give me one chance," he pleaded, "Have pity on me, please. I'll give you lots of money. Thousands and…" He looked at Jane. "Jane, surely you will help me? Promotion and…"

Ed interrupted. "They have made up their minds, McMurphy," he shouted, "Can't you tell? The game is up. It's over!"

"One chance…" he implored, "Where is your compassion? Please…"

A sense of despair fell over him and he turned away. His only option was to leave, so he sat down in the seat of the winch, and with shaking hands, fastened himself in. Ray kept his rifle aimed at him as the rope was pulled and McMurphy was hauled upwards. In a minute he disappeared into the helicopter and the door slammed closed behind him. The helicopter tilted and headed off.

McMurphy fell back into a chair in the back of the helicopter. He felt exhausted. It seemed hopeless now, he would have to face the music and it would be horrible; he would be disgraced and lose everything. A prison sentence? Probably. He felt depressed and alone.

"Back to the Coral Reef, sir?" asked the pilot.

"Why not? But take your time."

He sighed as he realized that that might be the last time anyone would call him 'sir'.

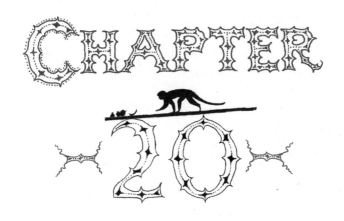

11.05 a.m. aboard the Golden Gem

The wind had dropped, leaving just a fresh salty breeze in the air and the sea was calm. The stormy rain clouds of the night had passed on. The bright sun shone from a clear sky and warmed the deck of the Golden Gem. All the crew were busy working on the boat and Rachel and Jamie sat side by side, cross-legged on the deck with Gordo sitting on one of Jamie's knees and looking out to sea. His long tail draped down onto the deck. The sun was warm on their faces and they were happy and relaxed.

"Thank goodness it's all over," Rachel said, stroking

Gordo affectionately on the head, "How do you feel after your trip into space?"

Gordo answered with a run of little cheeps and chirrups and Jamie translated.

"He said…" began Jamie, "That he can hardly believe it happened!" Gordo smiled. "Then he said it did teach him something. To see the Earth from right up there, like a ball, gave him a different view of things. It made him realize how all the arguments between people… and monkeys… are so small… so pathetic!"

Gordo added a few more cheeps.

"He says…" continued Jamie, "That he was greedy, and that's why he was caught."

"We've all learnt some lessons," agreed Rachel. "McMurphy was greedy. He got away with it for years… but now it's caught up with him…"

Gordo suddenly looked across the water and tilted his head to listen. His hearing was sharper than his human company. He climbed onto Jamie's shoulder and they both looked in the direction of the sound. Now Jamie could hear it too.

"It's a helicopter," said Gordo, pointing.

They could all see it now; a black silhouette, dropping out of the air against the bright blue sky. It crossed the sun as it descended to twenty feet above the water, then it turned and headed straight towards them. They watched it approach, until it was close enough to see the pilot.

"It's McMurphy!" exclaimed Gordo.

Through the front window they saw McMurphy's face, staring at them and mouthing angrily. The helicopter roared into top speed and bore down upon them. The crew rushed up onto the deck. Jane was with them.

"He doesn't know how to fly!" she shouted, "He can't fly!"

The helicopter juddered and lurched in the air as McMurphy struggled to keep control. It was on collision course for the boat.

"Abandon ship!" shouted Ed, "Into the water! Take the rings! Quick!"

There was a flurry of intense activity as life-saving rings were grabbed, thrown overboard, and people were jumping into the water. The helicopter was close now. In the rush, Gordo's tail got caught in the door as the rest of the crew came up from below.

"Gordo!" shouted Rachel, turning back as she was about to jump in, "Gordo!"

But there was no time left. The helicopter was about to hit.

"Jump!" Gordo screamed to Rachel.

Jamie turned and ran back across the deck towards Gordo. The little monkey pulled his tail free and scampered towards Jamie, who swept Gordo into his arms and then turned to see the helicopter a few feet away. McMurphy's crazed-looking face was staring at him, full of hate.

Jamie collapsed onto the deck. A moment later the helicopter was directly above. He lay flat, hoping the helicopter would pass over him, but it fell quickly with the loud throbbing sound of the rotor blades. Jamie looked up in terror to see one of the wheels just above him, so close that he could see the tread.

He scrambled to move, pulling Gordo with him, and then rolling sideways to escape. The wheel slammed onto the deck, right next to his head, only just missing him.

The engines surged again and the great machine lifted into the air. With a tremendous crunch the it ploughed into the mast and the rigging, ripping off the roof of the cabin and flattening the walls. The cabin burst into flames. Another surge of the engines and the helicopter rose, dragging bits of mast, rigging and the cabin door underneath it. It sped away, rising and then falling chaotically several times with bits falling off it into the sea. When it was almost out of sight, and most of the crew were back on deck, they saw it crash into the waves and explode in a bright orange and yellow fireball.

For a few seconds black smoke curled upwards from the floating wreck, and then it sank and everything was as still and calm as if nothing had happened at all.

2.07 p.m.

Smudge and Ruth Anderton had nodded off as the US Air Force jet had sped them back to Patrick Air Force Base at over 800 miles per hour. They had slept on the way out too, as well as during the car ride to Orlando Police Headquarters, which gave them just over five hours sleep for the night.

Mary-Anne, Frank and Jeff were handcuffed and strapped into their seats during the flight. When the jet landed, there was a van ready to take them to the police headquarters, while Smudge and Ruth had a more comfortable ride by car.

At the police headquarters, the three unhappy prisoners were questioned again, statements were taken and charges were issued. Blood samples were taken from each of them to see if their account was true; they had claimed that the blood in the back of the Divco truck belonged to Jeff. As homicide suspects they were locked up in cells until the blood tests were done.

Officer Smudge was sitting at his desk with an unopened folder in front of him. He stubbed out his cigarette and gazed blankly at the file, which was labelled 'STOLEN VEHICLES – Orlando Central Area.' He slipped his fishing magazine into the top drawer and was just going to open the file when a familiar voice called him.

"Sir!"

He swung around on his swivel chair.

"Yup," he replied as Ruth walked across the busy office towards him.

She stood in front of his desk and looked down at him.

"The blood, sir. I've had the lab report back."

"And…" he asked gruffly, looking up at her.

"It's his, sir, as they said. Jeff Marks. Their story holds up and there's no homicide."

"And everything else?" Smudge looked up.

"It all fits together like a jigsaw, sir," she declared, smiling at him.

He nodded slowly. "Good."

"And you heard about McMurphy?" she enquired.

"Yeah," Smudge growled, "Now there's a surprise for you."

"Not really, sir," she commented, "It's sad though…"

"Sad?" he asked.

"Yes, sir. He could have done so much with his life, a powerful man like that, but he blew it all just through greed…"

"It's called justice, Miss Anderton… justice. You'll see a lot of that in this job."

This case had been a burden on his mind for months and now that it was over a wonderful sense of relief ran through him. He sighed, blowing the air and making his cheeks puff out slightly.

"Have you seen the reports in the papers, sir?"

"No."

"The report is saying that the capsule sank... that's the official story. They don't want to show how wrong it all went."

Oakland Tribune

ESTABLISHED FEBRUARY 21, 1874

ASSOCIATED PRESS...WIREPHOTO...UNITED PRESS INTERNATIONAL...CHICAGO DAILY NEWS FOREIGN SERVICE

LAST EDITION

Missile Monkey Blazes Space Trail

Gordo Survives 1,500-Mile Ride In Jupiter Nose Cone but Perishes When South Atlantic Recovery Fails

By Edward D. Coffee

WASHINGTON, Dec. 13 - AP - Gordo, the tiny monkeynaut, rode a rocket in the early hours today to the very threshold of outer space, blazing a trail for man.

However, despite the success of the trip, he is missing and the popular little squirrel monkey, with a gold patch of fur on his head, is presumed to have given his life for science.

Gordo survived the meteorlike ascent to about 200 miles above the Earth. After the successful re-entry and descent of the nose cone it disappeared into the Atlantic Ocean down to a technical mishap. An aircraft carrier, the Coral Reef, was ready to recover Gordo but after hours of scouting the area had to abandon the search.

Second Lieutenant Neville Kennett, who led a group of marines in the search, said.

"My marines did a great job. We did everything humanly possible, but in the end had to accept that the nose cone, with Gordo inside, had sunk."

The nose cone, in which Gordo rode, splashed into the Atlantic about 100 miles from the launching point at Cape Canaveral, Fla. The reportedly proved method for recovering a cone before it sinks, failed this time.

13 MINUTES OF DATA

For about 13 minutes an automatic data transmitter, which was linked to microphones, thermometers and other equipment sent back data on how Gordo was taking the ascent. Scientists heralded it as a "realistic scientific data."

In general, Gordo showed only mild changes in his physical condition as the Jupiter rocket roared away from Earth and arched out beyond the atmosphere.

His heartbeat rose as the pull of gravity multiplied, but it soon returned to normal.

Colonel Newton, who was in charge of the launch from Mission Control, commented:

"It's wonderful to prove that life, even little monkey was weightless for about 8 minutes, living than any monkey in previous tests. It's just a great shame Gordo didn't survive."

8 MINUTES WEIGHTLESS

Museum Fire Hits Crated Monastery

A bay-alarm fire yesterday did what it feared to be irreparable damage to the priceless, centuries-old Monastery of Santa Maria de Ovila, whose thousands of stones have been stored in crates in San Francisco's Golden Gate Park.

The late William Randolph

Record Fall Dry Spell To Continue

Eastbay Water Consumption Sets December Mark

The Bay Area's driest autumn in 100 years of record keeping will continue into the latest five-day forecast of the Weather Bureau.

But the Weather Bureau said last night there is a 20 per cent possibility of rain tomorrow but only a fractional possibility of rain now moving between Hawaii and Kodiak, Alaska.

OVERCAST, COOL

This was expected to bring lower temperatures from a record Dec. 13 high of 74 degrees still slightly above average.

Strong winds, yesterday caused damage in Oakland and Berkeley. The wind and dry conditions resulted in an extension of burning permits in Oakland by Fire Marshal Raldwin.

In the Sierra Nevada foothills...

Soviets Renew Berlin Edict as NATO Meets

'ALL'S WELL,' ATLANTIC BALLOONISTS REPORT

SANTA CRUZ, Tenerife, Canary Islands, Dec. 13 - UPI—All was reported going well today aboard a balloon carrying three men and a woman on a history-making attempt to drift across the Atlantic Ocean to the Americas.

The flight of the "Small World" was the first recorded attempt to cross span the Atlantic in a free balloon. It was cast off from here yesterday.

The balloon was reported to have drifted 400 to 450 miles southwest of the Canary Islands by nightfall tonight.

A member of the flight's ground party here said the balloon-made radio emphatic hey (word reported).

"We've heard from the balloon. It radioed all was well aboard. It is somewhere over the Atlantic."

The balloonists hope to complete the 3,600-mile flight in three weeks. They have, however, taken along enough stores for three months.

Mao Ouster Report Bares China Unrest

Khrushchev Has Run Soviet Into Industrial Chaos

By VICTOR RIESEL

NEW YORK, Dec. 13 — I have no secrets. But I have certain facts. And today, under-cover men who are constantly talking to those from behind the Bolshevik curtain, are convinced that the Soviets into desperate trouble. There are experiment in economic and terrific suffering, new forced labor discipline...

Portland Bids for Oakland's Maestro

Piero Bellugi, conductor of the Oakland Symphony, has been offered a contract as conductor of the Portland Symphony Orchestra, it was disclosed last night.

Mrs. Paul Feidenheimer, president of the Oakland Symphony Association, said action are expected to be completed this weekend, according to Bellugi.

Bellugi was a guest con-

West Says Note Repeats Old Demands

Compiled from AP and UPI

PARIS, Dec. 13—Russia today renewed its ultimatum to the Western Allies to get out of Berlin here yesterday to coincide with the gathering of Secretary of State John Foster Dulles and other NATO foreign ministers in Paris for a conference on the crisis.

Authoritative Western sources said the note reported, in memorial, political language, to Soviet demands made last Thanksgiving Day that the United States, Britain and France withdraw from west Berlin and that the western sectors of the city be turned into a "demilitarized free zone."

A-TEST BAN REVIVED

A digest of the note called for a solution of the Berlin crisis by making West Berlin an unarmed free city. It also repeated old Soviet demands for suspension of nuclear tests, and a non-aggression pact between NATO and the communist East European nations of the Warsaw Pact.

While not detailing the contents of the note, the State Department said it was straightforward.

Even if the reports prove true, this would not necessarily allay the suspicions of the disciplined. new forced labor.

"The note is clearly directed at the Paris meeting of foreign ministers of the North Atlantic Treaty Organization."

This is Gordo, the highly intelligent squirrel monkeynaut, whose tragic death has left the nation in a state of sadness. His cute face, unique patch of golden fur on his head and pluky nature won him fans around the world.

Smudge shrugged.

"Still, it's probably better that way..." Ruth smiled, "Gordo can be set free without the press and half the world trying to catch him!"

Smudge smiled and nodded.

"So, that's it then?" he asked, "The case is over?"

"Yes, sir. McMurphy was the big-time lawbreaker. Frank Leemas and the Marks are just petty criminals... and pretty stupid ones at that! All the mistakes they made!"

This thought made Smudge tighten inside. It immediately reminded him of how she had picked up on all the things he had missed. She had even suspected McMurphy. At the same time he could not help admiring her, and he found himself complimenting her.

"Well done, Miss Anderton."

"Thank you, sir," she said.

"I'm afraid, sir, we won't be working together any more. They think I've gained enough experience to get me started and they've given me my own case to work on. I'm being sent to Sanford Police Department."

Relief returned and flooded through Smudge's burley frame. For the first time he really saw her face and realised how pretty she was.

"Good luck, Miss Anderton," he said, smiling at her.

He stood up and held out his hand. She shook it.

"Good bye, sir. See you at the trial."

She turned to go and then turned back.

"Oh... and sir?" she began, looking intently at Smudge, "You ought to ring her, you know. You're lucky to have such a wonderful daughter..." She shrugged her shoulders. "But it's up to you, of course..."

Smudge was taken completely by surprise. She smiled at him and walked out of the office leaving him open-mouthed. Her comment left him feeling cross but her charm had touched him too. He reached for the phone and dialled. As it rang he could feel his heart beating in his throat.

"Hello," said the voice the other end.
"Hello," said Smudge meekly, "My little angel?"
"Dad!"

Sunday 14th December   4.45 p.m.

The Golden Gem, now an extremely battered looking
fishing trawler, cruised smoothly up the Orinoco River in
Venezuela. On their journey they had passed the Windward
Islands of the Lesser Antilles, a scraggle of Caribbean
Islands, including Saint Lucia, Granada, Trinidad and
Tobago to the west, and Barbados to the East. It had taken
over thirty hours. During this time Gordo had enjoyed plenty
of exercise by darting skilfully around the boat with a display
of acrobatic moves. Soon he had created a circuit which took
him scampering and swinging around the boat, from the
prow to the other end and back again.

After being out on the rolling waves of the South Atlantic
Ocean, the river seemed like a haven. Trees lined the banks
and the rich sound of tropical animal life filled the hot humid
air, the loudest of which were monkeys and macaws.

The engine was in perfect condition in contrast with the demolished upper part of the boat, showing the shattered stump of wood which used to be the stately mast. Just behind it were the barely recognizable remains of the cabin, blackened by the fire. The wheel, now standing in proud isolation on the deck, had needed repair but once that had been done the Golden Gem had covered the 350 miles of ocean in good time. The boat had woven its way into the tropical Orinoco Delta where the great river divides into many branches as it approaches the sea.

Gordo was sitting on the mast stump and watching groups of squirrel monkeys climbing about in the trees. Just below him, on the deck and leaning against the mast, sat Jamie. Gordo called down to him in excitement.

"Look! This is what I've been dreaming of for months now. Living free in the trees!"

"And you'll be there soon," Jamie said.

"I'm free, Jamie," Gordo remarked, "At last – completely free."

Jamie smiled, "Which is how it should be."

"But I'll miss you. Will I see you again?"

"Of course." Jamie was so fond of this little monkey that he could not imagine that he would never see him again. "I promise you I'll come back to see you. I'll speak to Rachel about it."

The wounded boat moved through an intricate maze of thin channels and creeks where the river water ran across and around thousands of low islands. They passed through mangroves and palm forests and saw the native Warao people in their huts on stilts. This is where the fishing boat came to rest.

The Golden Gem had been running low on fuel and finally the engine gave its last splutter and drifted gently through a small village. The simple huts had roofs of dried grass and each one was connected to the others with raised walkways. Many of the native people started following the boat, running along the walkways and waving and smiling.

"What a beautiful place!" said Rachel.

"And beautiful people," added Jane, "Do you think we could stay here for a while?"

"Exactly my thoughts too," said Ed, "But where would we stay? It doesn't look like the sort of place with hotels."

The boat bumped against some stilts and came to a halt. Straight away some of the Warao people jumped onto the boat and a rope was tied to stop it drifting away. With big smiles they led the visitors, including all the crew, into their huts. Over the next few days they were treated like honoured guests. They fed them, gave them a hammock each to sleep in, took them on trips in their canoes and entertained them with wonderful violin music.

Within a few days, the Warao people had rowed Jamie, Rachel and Gordo across the delta waters in a canoe three times to visit the rain forest. On each occasion they met a different colony of squirrel monkeys and spent a few hours with them. Gordo picked the colony that he wanted to live with, and the following week he spent the day with them to see if they would like him. He had a wonderful time in the trees, climbing and chattering, and the other monkeys loved his golden head and picked some berries for him. They seemed to really accept him into the group and were very happy for him to join the colony.

The next day, a small boat chugged into the village; it was a trader making his monthly visit with variety of things for sale. He carried one can of fuel which he sold to the visitors and then returned two days later and filled up the tank of the Golden Gem.

One evening they were sitting on one of the walkways chatting and gazing at the sunset. Pink swept across the sky, transforming the low clouds in a mottled display of stunning beauty.

"This is the most wonderful holiday," said Jane, "I wish it could last forever!"

"I know what you mean," Rachel agreed, "But we will have to go back sometime. Now that we know Gordo can live here and join the group of squirrel monkeys, and we have refuelled the Golden Gem... we can go any time we like."

"In that case," said Ed, "Let's stay here for a couple days more and then go home."

They all liked this idea. However, the following two days were so enjoyable that they extended their stay even further. Jamie was very pleased because it meant he would have Gordo's company for a bit longer before the little monkey would join his new companions in the trees.

In the end, a week passed before they began preparing the boat for the long journey home.

Saturday 27th December 7.15 p.m.

The evening before they left was a time that Jamie had been dreading. When it came, there were dark clouds hanging above which released a heavy downpour of rain. Jamie was standing in the shelter of some trees with Rachel beside him and Gordo in his arms. It was almost unbearable. It was very nearly a year since he discovered he could speak with Gordo and since then they had been together nearly every day. Now they would have to part.

The colony of squirrel monkeys chattered in the branches above their heads and swung around like circus acrobats. They were excited about the new addition to their group. Gordo was looking forwards to his new home and companions as well, but like Jamie, he was also sad.

The three friends chatted for a while. Jamie translated for Rachel, although he kept forgetting because he was so upset. Then they started recalling things that had happened to them over the past year; looking back at some of the humorous things made them laugh and cheered them up. But when the light began to fade and they knew it was time to say goodbye, it was just as difficult as Jamie had imagined.

"Thank you so much," said Gordo.

He jumped from Jamie's arms onto a tree trunk, gripping the bark with his hands and feet, and then turning his head to face Jamie. Some large drops of rain were now dripping from the canopy of leaves above.

"It's been amazing!" he added.

"You've been amazing, Gordo," said Jamie, "You can tell your new friends that you were a monkeynaut! You'll be a celebrity!"

Gordo climbed onto a branch just above their heads.

"I've told them already," Gordo stated, "and they didn't really understand. Now I'll have time to explain it to them properly." Then he pointed up. "But to think I was right up there! So high!"

Rachel reached up to stroke Gordo on his head. "You've done very well."

Jamie translated and then added, "But I can't believe we're saying goodbye to you…"

Gordo looked down at Jamie. "You must come and visit me then. Ask Rachel."

Jamie turned to Rachel. "Can we?" he asked.

"Can we what?" she smiled, "You've forgotten again!"

"Sorry. He wants us to visit him. Can we?"

"Of course," nodded Rachel, "Perhaps we can do a yearly trip."

Jamie shrugged his shoulders. One visit each year seemed so little.

Gordo jumped off the branch and onto Jamie's shoulder and then slipped into his arms. The three of them had a final hug with little Gordo in the middle. Then Gordo was up on Jamie's shoulder again.

Rachel patted him on the back. "You must go now," she said, "Go and join you're your new friends. You'll have a great time here."

Gordo leapt onto the branch, swung up and began climbing.

"Bye!" he chirruped, "Bye!"

"Bye!" called Jamie and Rachel together.

Seeing Gordo moving up into the trees was the last straw for Jamie; he could not hold back the tears. Rachel put her arm around his shoulders as they walked away. She was crying too, so they comforted each other by sharing their sadness.

Sunday 28th December 8.20 a.m.

On a bright sunny morning, the Golden Gem set out through the channels of the Orinoco Delta. It was heading for the Carribean Sea and the seven day journey back to Florida. The Warao people had taken great delight in packing the boat with more than enough food and then crowded the walkways to wave them off. The visitors were sad to leave.

The voices of the Warao soon faded as the boat built up speed.

Jamie stood on the deck, leaning on the side of the boat, and watched the passing scene. He felt dull and exhausted after a sleepless night. He knew that to leave Gordo in the jungle with other monkeys was the right thing to do; the little monkey had craved to live there for so long, but saying goodbye to him had been so difficult that he had tossed and turned through the night as he kept thinking about it.

The boat moved on the calm waters though the trees. The sounds of the animals living in the rain forest echoed around them in the peaceful morning, but when Jamie heard the whooping of a monkey he dropped his head and started crying.

Rachel stepped beside him and put a comforting arm around his shoulders.

"It's what he wants," she said.

"I know," replied Jamie, "But I must come back to see him."

"Of course you must…" Rachel confirmed.

Jamie turned to look at her. "But more than once a year. It's much too long to wait."

"OK," she replied, "I'll see what I can do. And I'll come with you. And when we see him next I'll be able to speak to him, won't I? You said you'd teach me, remember?"

Jamie smiled. "I'd be happy to," he said. Then he added, sheepishly, "As long as I can live at your home…"

He had been plucking up courage to ask her.

"That's a wonderful idea," Rachel said with enthusiasm. "Can I live there too?"

Jamie spun around to see Gordo on the deck behind him.

"Gordo!" Jamie exclaimed.

The little monkey scampered across the deck, stopped just in front of Jamie, and looked up at him. "Gordo! But… but why are you here?"

"I missed you so much last night – I couldn't sleep," he replied, "It's great here, but you're my family now. And I missed my friends in my own colony too. They're my family as well… so I want to come back... I'd rather live with you and see my colony again."

Jamie laughed.

"Great!" he exclaimed with joy, "That's great!"

Gordo climbed up his clothes and onto his shoulder. His golden head glinted in the tropical sun.

"What did he say?" asked Rachel.

"He's missing us," Jamie replied, "He's decided he'd rather to live with us than the monkeys here!"

"That's wonderful!" Rachel said, beaming with delight, "But next time, Gordo," she joked, "can you make up your mind, please, before we travel hundreds of miles!"

10.40 a.m.

It was mid-morning when the boat passed out of the fresh water of the Orinoco River. Salt-scented air now filled their nostrils. The expanse of the open ocean lay in front of them, sparkling with sunlight, under a cloudless sky.

The Golden Gem pushed through the calm, shallow waters and out onto the swell of the ocean. A small school of dolphins joined the boat, leaping out of the water as they rode through the waves. Soon the coastline of Venezuela was falling away behind them. They were on their way back home.

Thursday 1st January 1959   2.15 p.m.

"I've been thinking…" said Mary-Anne, "Thinking about how your crimes always fail."

Jeff nodded. He was sitting opposite her in their lounge in Sharnfore Road in Orlando. Her plastered leg was stretched out in front of her, resting on a stool, as she watched the news on television. They had been granted bail until their trial came up in three weeks. Their relationship had changed dramatically since Mary-Anne had appeared on the fishing boat and involved herself with the attempt to steal Gordo. Jeff had heard the truth about her plan to kill Frank and was stunned by her guile and ruthlessness. He was still struggling to come to terms with the darker side of her nature which had come to the surface.

"It's always been the same with your crimes," she continued, "Why, I ask myself, do they always, always go wrong?"

Jeff glanced away from the television. "Well you didn't do any better, did you?"

She stared at him in fury. "I don't know how you can say that! By myself I'd have done it. Who was it who got fooled by a monkey?" she snarled, laughing mockingly at him, "Outwitted by a monkey! It was your fault that it all failed, not mine. Admit it!"

The phone rang which saved him from answering the question. He got up quickly, walked out of the room and picked up the receiver.

"Hello."

"Hello, Jeff. It's me… Frank."

"Hello, what do you want?" Jeff said lowering his voice so that Mary-Anne could not hear.

"I'm glad you answered and not that evil wife of yours. How are you?" Frank asked.

"Not good… not good at all," he said grumpily, and then lowering his voice, "Mary-Anne is terrible to live with now. I can't take much more of it!"

"Listen, Jeff. I've got an idea… a plan."

Jeff sighed again. "I'm not interested, Frank. I've had enough. Besides we've got the trial soon."

"Ha!" Frank laughed, "The trial is nothing. What have we done? Stolen a monkey. Stolen a clapped-out Divco truck and a pickup… both of which were complete wrecks and worth nothing. Tried, but failed twice, to steal the monkey again. What kind of crimes are those? We'll get a fine, OK? But that's all… and then we walk free."

"I know, I know," Jeff sounded cross, "But I've been thinking about something… I thought I might go straight now. You know, it could be my New Year's resolution."

Frank sounded shocked and disappointed. "Jeff! You'll never do it. Just hear me out, OK?"

"OK."

"The plan is this. We go somewhere where there's money but not many police. Another country. You can leave Mary-

Anne and start again. Like those outlaws... cowboys... you know, Butch Cassidy and the Sundance Kid. They went to Bolivia you know. They walked into a bank... poor, and walked out again... rich! Dead easy!"

"I don't want to go to Bolivia," Jeff snapped.

"No, you fool! Not Bolivia, but somewhere like that... as I said a place without loads of police snooping about."

"And where on earth is this heavenly place?" asked Jeff doubtfully.

"I'll do some research. That's all it needs. I've heard of places. Will you come?"

Jeff was silent for a moment. In the next few seconds Jeff made the first real decision he had made for some time. His little, selfish life seemed to flash before him. He had had enough of lies and deceit, of running away, of stealing. He wanted to trust and be trusted.

"You still there, Jeff?"

"Yeah," he replied, "But I've decided. I'm giving up crime."

Frank was astonished, "What?!" he exclaimed, "But you're my partner. And why would you give up?!"

"I'm fed up with it... with being frightened of being found out all the time," he said, "I'm fed up of being afraid all the time... afraid of who is knocking at my front door, afraid of just walking around in case I'm arrested, afraid of... everything! I don't want to be your crime partner or your friend. Good bye."

As he put the phone down he just heard Frank shouting down the phone, "Jeff, what are you saying..."

A moment later, before he had moved away, the phone rang. He reached out his hand for the receiver and then paused an inch away. He let it ring until it stopped.

He went back into the lounge.

"I heard you talking," Mary-Anne said, "It was Frank wasn't it?"

He ignored her question.

"After the trial I'm leaving here," he said. There was the strength of a firm decision in his voice.

Mary-Anne stared at him. Jeff had dropped a bombshell and she was stunned by it. Then she laughed. "You wouldn't dare leave me."

"I said what I said," Jeff replied calmly, "And I meant it."

"Yes, but..." Mary-Anne began. She was clearly shocked and there were tears in her eyes.

"You can come with me if you like..." Jeff continued, "You are my wife and you can come with me, but under my terms this time." He looked at her intently and his voice softened with kindness. "It's a chance. We sell up and go to start a new life somewhere else, a life with no crime. An honest life."

Mary-Anne was too shocked to answer.

He got up and went into the kitchen to put the kettle on, feeling better than he had for a long time. He had shed a burden and the freedom made him walk taller. The kettle whistled for attention. He made a cup of coffee, added a dash of milk and carried it into the back garden just as the sun came out.

The garden had been neglected for some time which had left the grass long and weeds overrunning the beds. He sat down on a garden chair and sipped his coffee. It tasted wonderful.

Friday 2nd January   4.25 p.m.

The day after the trip back from Venezuela, Rachel, Ray, Jamie and Gordo made a journey right across the great Florida peninsular to the west coast. Rachel and Ray took turns driving and as they travelled they talked about the recent events. Together they had risked their lives for Gordo's freedom and during the adventure they had forged a deep friendship.

As evening approached they were nearing their destination. The sunshine sloped through the car window caressing Rachel's cheek with warmth as she drove. The touch of the sun felt good and she felt happy with Ray beside her, Jamie in the back and Gordo jumping from person to person. He was excited about meeting his colony after so long.

They entered Naples. Ray consulted a map and they headed straight for the Larshley Beach Hotel & Golf Club. They parked in the grounds and looked around for the colony of monkeys. They were gathered in their usual cluster of trees and Jamie called out to them.

"Hello. I have brought Gordo to visit you."

"Gogo," said Gordo, "They know me as Gogo here."

All the monkeys looked down together; a row of black and white faces staring out of the trees in shock; they had never heard a human speak their language before.

"Gogo's alright!" Jamie exclaimed, "Here he is! I've been looking after him."

The monkeys gazed down and pointed, chattering to each other and not sure what to do.

"Should we trust the humans?" asked the young Jojja.

"Never trust humans," growled Jabe, "It's a rule we've

followed for years. How can he speak our language? It's suspicious, it is. Humans are dangerous…"

"But they know Gogo…" argued Hab Dab, "Look! He's on that one's shoulder."

"Don't talk to him!" Jabe snapped crossly.

Down below, the visitors looked up and listened to the monkeys' quick chattering.

One monkey called down, "Did you go into the sky?"

"Yes!" replied Gordo.

"Did you fly!" joined in Jojja, "We saw you in a paper."

Another added, "Are you a skymonkey?"

Jamie smiled, and called up to them, "He is… but actually they call him a monkeynaut!"

Ray turned to him, "What did they say?"

Jamie translated for him and Rachel.

Jamie looked up again. "Yes, he did go into the sky," he said, "We call it space."

On hearing this all the monkeys started jumping up and down and screeching with wild excitement. It was an extraordinary explosion of activity and noise. Jabe observed them from above, looking sulky and critical, and feeling he had lost control. Yulla sat beside him but she could not help joining in with the celebrations.

Gordo climbed the tree, swung up through the branches and following a route he used to use. The other monkeys surrounded him and bombarded him with questions.

After a while they calmed down and they all descended low in the trees, except for Jabe who looked down with disdain on the others. Jamie talked to the monkeys and they told him about George and Jo and how they had watched from above when they ran after the thieves and tried to save Gogo.

"They were here earlier," said Jojja, "I saw them. And I saw them go… some time ago now."

Jamie and Gordo had an attentive audience as together they described to the group of monkeys all the things that had happened to Gordo. They listened eagerly and asked questions.

"We need to go in there now," Jamie said to the monkeys, pointing towards the building, "We'll see you before we go."

The monkeys climbed up into the tops of the trees chattering away about the amazing news they had just heard. Gordo explained to them how he would stay with them for a few days and then go back to his new home with Rachel and Ray.

Rachel, Jamie and Ray went into the club. They crossed the thick pile carpet to the reception desk. Lizzie looked up.

"Can I help you?"

"Yes, we'd like to leave a message for George and Jo," answered Rachel.

"Oh, they were here earlier... you mean George and Jo Pinter?" she asked.

"Yes, at least I think so?"

"Well it's the only George and Jo we have as members, so it must be them."

"Good," said Rachel.

She borrowed a pen and paper and quickly wrote them a note. Then she placed it in an envelope and left it with Lizzie to pass on.

As they walked outside, the monkeys spotted them and called out with a collection of squeals and chatterings. Jamie ran to the car and came back with a bag full of bananas. The monkeys descended rapidly and flocked around to accept the gifts. They grabbed the bananas eagerly and rushed back up into the tree tops to enjoy them until only Gordo was left. He climbed onto Jamie's shoulder.

"How long do you want to stay, Gordo?" Jamie asked.

"A week?"

Jamie turned to Rachel. "Is it OK to collect Gordo in a week?"

"Yup," Rachel responded.

"See you in a week then Gordo," Jamie said, "Have

fun!"

Gordo took a banana, leapt onto a branch and was up the tree in a jiffy. The group of monkeys waved to them and called out with a chorus of good byes and thanks. The three friends waved back and then walked to the car.

Dusk was drawing as they drove out of the grounds and began their journey home.

Florida Supreme Court, Tallahassee
Monday 5th January   3.43pm

The court was waiting in silence. The jury would return soon with a verdict and a sense of expectation hung in the air. The judge, Chief Justice Millard J. Thorn, looked down and leafed through some papers and then lifted them upright with both hands. He tapped them on the desk to straighten them and then placed them down carefully.

The door opened and the jury filed back in. They all sat down except for one man who was the spokesman.

Chief Justice Thorn looked over his half-glasses and around the court. His eyes settled on the accused, who shifted uncomfortably in his chair.

"Will the accused please stand?" he said grimly.

Max McMurphy swallowed and then stood up. His forehead shone with sweat as he blinked nervously through his glasses and loosened his collar. He was flanked on either side by a policeman. A scar ran down across his cheek bone, an injury received when he ejected from the crashing helicopter.

The judge turned to the jury spokesman.

"Have you reached a unanimous verdict?" he asked.

McMurphy's heart thumped in his throat. He clasped his sweaty hands together.

"Yes, my lord," said the spokesman.

McMurphy closed his eyes. The evidence had been overwhelming but he was still hoping.

"Has the jury found the accused innocent or guilty?"

"Guilty on all counts, Your Honour."

McMurphy's legs turned to jelly. The spokesman sat down and the judge turned back to McMurphy.

"Maximus John Philip McMurphy…" he began gravely, "You have been found guilty as accused on all counts."

McMurphy swallowed again.

"The story of your life is a sad one. You have lied, stolen, cheated and been dishonest in many ways. You have acted with callous determination to pursue anything and everything that would increase your own material wealth while completely disregarding the wellbeing of others. You have acted unlawfully to men, women and children to become a rich man at their expense."

He paused and his words hung in the silence of the court room. McMurphy frowned and dropped his eyes to the floor, lifting them to stare at the judge again as soon as he continued.

"You are responsible for the misery and poverty of many people.

"The evidence against you has been confirmed… and without reasonable doubt… by the many witnesses who have spoken against you. The jury have heard the evidence and pronounced you guilty. Now your punishment needs to fit the seriousness of your crimes.

"Your investments, your properties and cars, in fact everything you own, will be sold. Then all this considerable wealth that you have amassed will be impounded by the State of Florida - every cent of it. Then 60% will be donated to the welfare state. The remaining 40% will be held in a trust fund to help anyone you have harmed through your crimes."

McMurphy's face twitched nervously. Everything he had worked for was gone. He was as poor as a homeless tramp. He had nothing. His legs gave way and he collapsed onto his chair.

"Stand up!" snapped the judge.

The policemen helped him to his feet.

"You will be taken from here to Florida State Prison where you will be imprisoned for seven years."

The judge brought down his hammer on the wooden block with a sharp rap. McMurphy jerked in shock. The sound felt like a gunshot to McMurphy and then echoed in his mind like a funeral bell. His arms were firmly pulled behind him and he felt the cold metal of handcuffs being fastened.

The full weight of his deeds fell upon him. In a flash he saw himself as a young man of nineteen. He felt the shame of the first time he deceived someone to make some money. If only he could return to that time, relive that moment, reverse that terrible decision and change his life. Now it was too late.

He was escorted out of the court, half walking and half dragged by the two policemen.

Watching from the back of the gallery were an elderly couple.

"He deserved it," sighed the old man, "But I can't help thinking that his life could have been so different."

He turned to the lady and saw a tear run down her face. He slipped his hand into hers.

"He's still our son," said the lady, "And I still love him."

"I know," he said, squeezing her hand, "So do I."

Tuesday 6th January 1.14 p.m.

George and Jo walked into the hallway of the Larshley Beach Hotel & Golf Club. After having lunch in the restaurant, they were passing the reception desk when Lizzie called out to them.

"There's a note for you, sir."

George stepped towards her.

"Oh, thanks, Lizzie," he said, "Who's it from?"

"Sorry, Mr. Pinter," she replied, "No idea. A young lady, a man and a boy… but I've never seen them before."

"Never mind… they'll say in the note. Thanks."

They left the building and walked down the path between the palm trees.

Jo looked at George. "Well, open it then."

They paused while George opened the note and read it aloud:

"I thought you might like to know that the monkey who was stolen from the Larshley Beach Hotel & Golf Club was Gordo who went into space. He survived and is alive and well. Thanks for trying to save him. Rachel and Jamie 4361272."

"The one we saw in the paper!" exclaimed Jo, "And who are Rachel and Jamie?"

George shrugged. "We'll have to phone them."

"As soon as we get home…" agreed Jo, "But how do they know we tried to save him?"

"Police?" suggested George.

"But you didn't give your name, did you?"

"That's true… so how could anyone know?"

"Lizzie…?" Jo said, "But no, she didn't know them."

"I don't understand it."

George scratched his head in puzzlement.

"And another thing…" he continued, "The papers said the monkey died. The capsule sank, remember?"

Jo looked at him directly. "Yes, but I prefer this version, don't you?"

"Well, yes," said George, "And anyway… why would anyone go to the trouble of leaving a note like this if it wasn't true?"

"They wouldn't," she shook her head, "No point. But the problem still remains… how did they know anything about us at all? I don't get it."

"Neither do I."

"I just can't get my head around this one, can you?"

"No, not at all…"

With the conversation continuing to go around in circles they walked down the path. Unknown to them, the monkeys, including Gordo, were watching, listening and chuckling from above until George and Jo were out of sight and their voices had faded into nothing.

The End

Gordo Needs YOUR Help!

Did you enjoy this book?

The more people who find and read Jasper's books, the more time Jasper has to write further exciting books and adventures for you!

How Can You Help?

If you enjoyed the book, then you can really help a LOT by following these two steps:

Step 1: Write a review here:
www.GordoMonkey.com/review

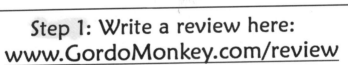

Step 2: Tell your friends about the book!

Do you have friends who like to read? Tell them about Gordo! You can also post to your friends about the book!

Bonus Sample Chapter:

CANDARA'S GIFT

Candara's Gift is the first book in The Kingdom of Gems Trilogy (also by Jasper Cooper)

This series of books is completely unrelated to Gordo and is set in a fantasy land called The Kingdom of Gems

The entire first chapter of Candara's Gift is here for your pleasure!

Enjoy...

The tall figure approached the woods with powerful strides. Just behind him, held on a metal chain which he shook every so often to keep it moving, was a great creature. As the darkly cloaked man and the creature moved, the plants nearby withered, their leaves falling to the dying grass, and flowers, so bright and beautiful the day before, drooped as if touched by invisible poisonous vapours.

Close by, and high up in an old oak tree, perched a snowy owl called Joog. He clutched a branch with his powerful talons as he slept soundly amongst the swishing leaves of the swaying tree. A powerful gale blew over the hills and through the valleys of the kingdom and ruffled his beautiful white feathers, but even this could not wake him tonight.

Joog was meant to be watching. He was always particularly vigilant during nighttime as it was his job to guard the kingdom, but tonight, however, he had slipped into a deep and absorbing slumber leaving the kingdom unprotected and open to intruders.

The wild wind whistled and sighed through the trees. It swept across the kingdom from the west, like a curtain drawn at the end of the day and now it persisted deep into the night, swirling across the whole kingdom with a groaning presence.

It seemed to herald the arrival of something unusual, bleak and unwelcome, something that forewarned of danger. In spite of this howling wind, however, Joog slept soundly and so did every creature in the Kingdom of Gems. Even the nocturnal animals were sleeping which was strange because during the dark hours of the night they were usually busy.

Then, as the dawn approached, the air seemed to grow weary of its swirling movements and the driving wind collapsed, like an exhausted wild animal that finally runs out of energy. But this was not a peaceful stilling, it was as if the air grew too heavy to be in motion any more, too thick to stir and its dreadful weight fell upon the land. This utter stillness that filled the kingdom, seeping into the very earth, was a brooding expectant atmosphere. The whole kingdom seemed to be wrapped in a weighty darkness, grave and intense, that awaited the arrival of something uninvited and unwanted.

Joog was still absorbed in a deep sleep.

Then a rustling sound, at first distant in the still air, but soon growing louder, broke the heavy silence. The shadowy figure, with the great creature following, was moving into the woodlands and striding steadily over the spongy leaf-strewn earth. Joog did not hear these approaching footsteps. He did not feel the strange sinister chill that had suddenly filled the air. He did not see the dark-cloaked figure far below him cross the border and enter the Kingdom. A Troubler had arrived.

It was growing lighter as the night began to soften into day, although the sun had not risen yet. The great creature looked in some ways like a massive crocodile but was in fact a Komodo Dragon. It had a rugged appearance and was covered with small smooth scales of dark green and brown. Its legs were short and looked exceptionally sturdy and strong and each leg had a five-toed foot with sharp claws. Its body was a muscular bulk and dragging behind it was a long tail which tapered to a point and rustled across the dried leaves. Its ferocious looking head was long and flat with a rounded snout. As it walked its body twisted to the rhythm of its steps. It gave every impression of being savage and vicious.

Around them as they moved, the oppressive heaviness hung in the air most strongly. The gentle early light, which normally wakes up the many colours of plants and flowers in the woods, was having no effect. Everything remained painted with the shadowy grey of night. They were well past Joog's old oak tree now and heading towards the town, leaving a path of dying plants and bushes behind them. The woods were so unnaturally quiet that their footsteps, rustling on the blanket of leaves and the shaking of the metal lead echoed amongst the trees and the Troubler's low mutterings could be heard some distance away... but there was no one awake to hear them.

The sinister looking duo followed a path, called Wellspring Walk, which led out of the woods. The path dropped south across the River Tazer where there was just enough room on the wooden East Bridge for the Komodo Dragon to cross. The path turned east again to follow the river towards the town of Candara. When they were in sight of Candara they left the path and walked into a small group of trees. It was just before dawn.

The Troubler tied the dragon to a tree by the metal lead and it immediately sank down to the ground to rest with a low groan that resounded in its massive leathery-scaled body. Its mouth dripped with bacteria-filled saliva that could infect anything that it bit, bringing a quick and certain death to the unfortunate victim. The Troubler sat down nearby on a moss-covered log to rest and look at the scene. As the sky began to grow lighter he looked through the trees to see the cottages and houses of Candara with the tall Spindley Tower rising above. On a hill beyond there was the palace, tall and pinnacled, overlooking the whole town. Suddenly the sun appeared above the horizon, at first just a star-point of light, growing to a glowing red disc. The dawn had arrived. At this moment Joog awoke.

He opened his large golden-yellow eyes and looked around. He wondered why he had slept through the night. Where was the happy dawn chorus that always filled the warm woodland air as the sun rose? Why was it so quiet? What had happened whilst he was sleeping? Had the other nocturnal animals been sleeping too? Had no one been watching? He felt an unusual chill in the air. And then he thought of something that instantly sent a wave of shock washing through him; perhaps a Troubler had entered the Kingdom. He realised that if this had happened he had to report to the King.

He stretched out his strong wings - he had one of the largest wingspans of all the birds in the Kingdom - and left his branch with a jump. He glided at first through the leaves of his oak tree home and then began to flap his wings to gather speed. He now felt the air rushing silently past his soft feathers - oh how he loved flying. He was a Snowy Owl and he made sure he kept his plumage of white and brown speckled feathers beautifully clean, bathing every day in one of the woodland ponds. But now, as he flew above the trees, his feathers were touched and tinted by the pink of the dawn sun.

Joog was the wisest and the most watchful owl in the whole Kingdom. He was in charge of an elite group of owls, selected for their special qualities of observation and reliability. It was their job to report to the King when they spotted anyone or anything entering the Kingdom at night because occasionally some kind of Troubler with a mind full of evil thoughts would enter the land. These brave and trustworthy owls were the Guardians of the Kingdom of Gems and each owl covered a length of the border. Joog was based in these woods, the Wellspring Woods, where the border zigzagged through and from his high lookout in his oak tree he could see for some miles around. In the past Joog had always spotted any strangers and reported it to the King so that guests could be welcomed and Troublers dealt with.

Joog followed the River Tazer and he flew as fast as he could because he knew that the situation might be very serious indeed. In fact this seemed to bring added strength to his outspread wings, but even though he was flying faster than he had ever flown before he kept watching the land below him - he was looking out for an intruder. He decided that before reporting to the King he would circle above the town and surrounding area to see if he could spot anything. He did not realise that he was passing directly over the Dark Troubler who was still sitting on the log, hidden even from Joog's sharp eyes by the rich green mass of leaves and branches above him.

The Troubler was obviously a wizard of some sort. This was clear from his long pointed hat and his dark cloak with his coat of arms set on the left. The cloak and hat of a real wizard are often covered with sparkling stars, but this wizard was different. He had stars on his hat and cloak, but they were black, blacker than the deep black of his cloak, blacker than the blackest black imaginable. They were so black that they looked like holes. His coat of arms was embroidered in gold and black, but it was unusual too; instead of representing light, wisdom and happiness this one was dark and threatening, with gloomy black symbols. There was a raven and a skull, as well as a compass and a crescent moon in the night.

The Dark Wizard Troubler was resting briefly and was eating some food he had taken from his bag that now lay on the withering grass beside him. The Komodo Dragon was lying flat, stretched out, tethered to a tree by the lead and half asleep as it rested after the long journey. Although the dawn air was warm their breath could be seen as on a frosty winter's day, because around them the Troubler's presence chilled the air. Everything near to him had lost its colour and like a black and white photograph showed only shades of grey.

As he ate he was hatching a plan. He clenched his teeth together, grimaced and closed his eyes as he tried to work it out. His hair and beard were black and long which made a strange contrast with his gaunt face of ghostly-grey skin. As he rested on the log he mumbled quietly to himself, his angular features twisting as he agonised over his plans. After a while the expressions on his face eased and relaxed as his plans became clearer. Then he chuckled and opened his eyes wide in glee; they were as black as coal. He nodded slowly as if he had made an important decision.

"Yes, Horrik," he said to the dragon with words as icy as a frozen pond in winter, "I have been working out a plan that will shake this kingdom to its very foundations. And then *I* will be king here."

Horrik stirred, lifted up her great head and spoke, opening her huge mouth to show two rows of serrated razor-sharp teeth, numbering about sixty in all. A long yellow forked tongue flicked out of her mouth dribbling with the poisonous saliva. Her large eyes were also black and her voice came in a deep and slow rumbling, "Will we rule here, Master?" she asked.

"*I* will rule here," the wizard's words hissed out in clouds of breath that momentarily hung in the air and then dispersed. "Through bringing the three gems into my possession... that will do it, but first... well... it is just the simple matter of dealing with the inhabitants who live here. And that..."

The wizard stopped speaking as something distracted him. A black mongrel dog, who had been watching him from under a nearby tree, jumped up and ran towards him. It was Jamaar, a young dog whose lifestyle was obvious from his matted and bedraggled fur and the strong unhealthy smell that accompanied him. He survived by scavenging for food and sleeping in woods at night. From time to time someone in the kingdom would take him in and give him a home, but it always failed and he would be thrown out in disgrace because he was so uncontrollable. He had become a stray not through bad luck but due to his own actions.

As he got close to the Dark Wizard he felt the chill of the air around the Troubler and he could see his breath in the cold air. Then he noticed the bland and colourless surroundings, but he was so hungry that he ignored the signs of danger. With one more step and a fast snap of his teeth he had grabbed the bag in his mouth and turned to run off with it. The wizard looked at him with surprise and suddenly moved extremely quickly, lunged and managed to grasp the strap of the bag. Horrik jumped up onto her short legs and stepped towards the dog, her chain lead tightening and digging into her scaly neck, her head straining forwards. The Dark Wizard and the dog stared at each other and for a moment it was a tug-of-war. Fear gripped Jamaar as he saw the wizard's icy black eyes and heard the rumbling roar of Horrik, still pulling at the end of her lead. Jamaar growled and pulled as hard as he could, but the wizard was strong… too strong.

"What are you doing?" the wizard shouted harshly as he pulled Jamaar along the ground making his front paws skid on the grass. When the poor dog was close enough the Dark Wizard kicked at him. Jamaar dodged and the heavy black boot whistled past his ear, but he clung on even harder. He was very hungry and now he that he was so close to the food that he could smell in the bag he clung on defiantly. But the wizard was much stronger than he expected.

"Get away you smelly creature!" the wizard snapped and he dragged Jamaar closer to him and pulling the strap of the bag upwards he lifted the dog's front paws off the ground. When he saw that the dog was still not letting go he scowled at it and swung his leg again at its head. This time the kick caught Jamaar on his nose and made him yelp and he let go and began to slink away, whimpering and crouching close to the ground.

"Get lost you ugly mongrel!" shouted the Dark Wizard, but then his expression suddenly changed; the angry scowl disappeared and a sly smile curled up the corners of his thin lips. His voice became soft, "Wait a minute! You could be of use to me, a strong young dog like you. Where do you live?" Then he turned to Horrik, "Easy now," he said to her and then pointing a finger at her, he snapped, "Down!" She relaxed and slumped down again until she was flat on the ground.

Jamaar stopped whimpering and stood still, frozen in fear of this stranger and the dragon, and still cowering close to the ground, he twisted his head around to listen.

"Where do you live?" asked the wizard again, his voice hissing with cunning and deceit.

"Anywhere I can," said Jamaar timidly, "I've got no home. I just wander around the kingdom."

"Would you like to move up in the world?" The Dark Wizard Troubler spoke with an inviting voice.

"What do you mean?" whimpered Jamaar still terrified of this black-eyed stranger.

"Well," the wizard began, "Live better. You're obviously hungry. You're thin. I could help you. But you'd have to help me in return. Think of it... food..." Jamaar felt the pain of hunger in his stomach and he licked his lips. "Food... that's what you need, isn't it? Well... no problem, I can give you plenty."

They were both standing still now with the bag between them on the grass and staring at each other. Horrik lay flat and listened.

"Interested?" said the wizard.

"I... I think so," answered Jamaar hesitantly and now pricking up his ears with interest, "But what do I have to do for you?"

"Well, we can do a deal," said the wizard calmly, "Come here." Jamaar approached cautiously and as the wizard reached out his hand Jamaar pulled back blinking and thinking he might be hit again. The wizard slowly stretched further and stroked him gently on the head, "You be my dog, obedient and faithful, and I will be your master and look after you well. Is it a deal?"

"Well, maybe," Jamaar responded, still afraid after being kicked on the nose, but feeling tempted by the offer of food, "Well… why not?" he growled, "Alright then, I'll give it a try… But I'd like to see the food first."

"Good, then come with me," said the Dark Wizard Troubler as he untied Horrik's lead from the tree and pulled at it to get the dragon onto her clawed feet, "Come on then, dog," he said to Jamaar over his shoulder.

Jamaar nodded towards Horrik, "What about that?" he said, "That thing will try to eat me."

"No," said the Dark Wizard, "She does what I say," and he turned to Horrik, "Don't you?" he spat out the words crossly.

The answer grumbled up slowly from the depths of her long body, as her forked tongue darted out of her mouth and back in again, "It smells," she said.

"Look who's talking," the Dark Wizard sneered, "The smelliest beast I've ever met." He looked at her with a malicious smile on his lips. Then he suddenly pulled at the chain with a sharp jerk and snapped crossly, "You do what I say, don't you?"

"Of course, Master," she growled, keeping her eye fixed on Jamaar with a stare that oozed hate.

"There you are!" said the wizard as if it was all settled, "So, for a better life, follow me." He slung the bag over his shoulder and strode away through the trees with Horrik on her lead glaring daggers at Jamaar. She felt consumed by jealousy and disgust for this young scraggy dog, this impostor who was receiving her masters attention. She was her master's pet and assistant and she did not want any competition especially from a youngster like this.

Jamaar hesitated and then decided. He hurried after his new master, passed Horrik, and trotted along beside the Dark Wizard Troubler. He had an extra bounce in his thin legs and the feeling that the good meal he so desperately needed would soon be tasting delicious on his tongue and filling his starving belly. As he followed he felt better and better; yes, at last he had found what he needed - a master to obey and follow - and although he was still afraid he felt that his new master had a special strength about him, a presence which he found terrifying and yet at the same time he was attracted to it. He also felt extremely pleased to have upstaged the malicious dragon; he knew the dragon hated him but already he had taken up a higher position; *he* was at his master's heels, whereas the dragon was behind *and* on a lead. When he thought of this he lifted his nose slightly higher with an air of superiority that made Horrik seethe with envy.

The Dark Wizard Troubler was now walking back onto the path which would take him towards Candara. His black wizard robe flowed out behind him. He stared at the ground as he walked with his breath hissing out in clouds; his thoughts intent upon the plan that was growing clearer in his mind. As he moved the icy atmosphere moved with him and filled the air with stifling heaviness and the flowers close by bowed and died. He glanced up to see Joog circling above the town and scanning the houses and streets below as if he was looking for something.

The Dark Wizard paused and stood still and so did Jamaar beside him and Horrik following. The wizard crouched as they all watched Joog circle once more and then turn and head towards the palace. The wizard's black eyes narrowed as he observed the speedy flight of the owl. Horrik turned her head towards him.

"Was it looking for *us,* master?" she asked.

"I expect so," said the wizard, "But it didn't see us. What's that tower for, dog?"

"People go up," replied Jamaar, "And animals. Birds land on it."

"But what's it used for?"

"It seems to be just a look-out," said Jamaar, "There's a

man who lives in it... in Spindley Tower. He lets everyone in and out."

The wizard turned his head away from the town, "The tower may be useful later, but we won't go into the town now. No need. When the time comes... at the right time... then we will act. I need to think."

"That owl," said Jamaar, "That owl lands on the tower sometimes and watches the town. It works for the King you know."

"And the king lives in that palace?"

"Yes," Jamaar nodded.

The wizard smiled, "He's got a surprise coming."

He stood up, gave the chain a tug to get Horrik moving and started walking back along the path with Jamaar padding along at his heels.

High above the town buildings Joog was enjoying the fresh morning air as he rose towards the palace that was silhouetted against the pink sunrise. From high in the air he could see the kingdom laid out before him like a richly coloured map; across the Flatsage Farmlands with its chequered fields was Blue Lake, reflecting the red sun in its still waters; and beyond that, the Snowpeak Mountains stood in stately stillness in the distance. Candara Palace itself looked beautiful too, dark against the bright rays of the rising sun and sitting proudly on the outskirts of Silvermay Forest.

Joog was always happy even in the most difficult situations. It was as if he was made of happiness; it was in his nature to be happy and he could not be otherwise. When flying he sometimes hooted with joy - it was so delightful to be airborne and this was how he felt today. He had certainly reached speeds today that had surprised him, and as he approached the palace he began to glide and then tilted his outstretched wings to reduce his speed. Most of the other owls, the Guardians, were heading for the palace as well and when they saw Joog they flew towards him. There were about thirty of various different kinds and sizes; there were Barn Owls, a couple of Sooty Owls with their massive eyes, Great Gray Owls, a couple of speckled Short-eared Owls, another Snowy Owl and even one tiny Elf Owl. They glided in gracefully from all directions, floating on the morning air, with their soft feathers making no sound as they headed faithfully for their leader.

Looking up Joog saw the King and Queen's bedroom window open as usual and he landed gracefully on the gold frame and turned to watch the others as they landed on the building wherever they could find a suitable ledge.

"You did the right thing," began Joog looking around at the group perched above and below him, "Mmm… exactly the right thing… to fly here, I mean. But tell me, what happened through the night?"

"I slept!" announced a large tawny owl and all the others nodded their agreement, and some others said, "So did I!"

"All through the night?" asked Joog.

"Yes!" chorused the owls.

"I thought so. So did I. Something very very strange happened last night. It must be a spell for something like this to happen. I think it is best…" he hesitated, considering carefully, "If you return to your areas for now and keep a good lookout for anything unusual. Ask around and see if anyone knows anything about it. Let me or the King know straight away any information that may throw light on this. Apart from that go back to your usual routine and I'll let you know if I need you. Alright?"

The owls hooted their agreement, spread their wings and with a flurry of silently flapping feathers flew off in various directions.

Joog jumped off the window frame and circled around as

he watched them go and then pulled his wings in closer to his body as he glided back through the open window. He landed not too gently on the end of the bed and the King awoke with a jerk. He sat up with his deep blue eyes still half-closed. His thinning hair was ruffled but long and tumbled down the back of his neck in silver curls. His face showed the character of a sensitive man who ruled his kingdom with fairness and dignity.

"Ahh!" the alarmed King blurted out, "Who's there?"

"It's me," said Joog calmly.

"Who's that?" the King said, beginning to feel more awake.

"It's me, Joog, it's me, Your Majesty."

"Oh Joog," the King said with affection, who was so surprised by Joog's sudden arrival that he did not know what to say, "Er…" he sat up, pulling his pillow up so that he could lean back against it. He looked puzzled. "What brings you here, Joog? And what time is it?" asked the King, whose eyes were now fully open and beginning to get used to the morning light.

"It's after dawn already. I'm sorry to disturb you like this, Your Majesty, but it is rather urgent… very urgent," Joog lowered his voice to almost a whisper as he had just noticed the Queen was still sleeping, "You see, there's something very strange happening and I can't say I understand it yet. I fear a Troubler may have entered the Kingdom! I feel it somehow - in the atmosphere. Everyone throughout the Kingdom has been asleep all through the night! And that includes all the Guardians! You yourself are always awake before dawn… and I slept too which has never happened before - never ever. What can it mean, Your Majesty? It must be a spell of some kind."

"Well it certainly is very strange, Joog. Did you see anything on your way here?" asked the King who was now wide-awake. His voice expressed his tender affection for Joog. Joog's eyes glowed a deep golden-yellow as he gazed back at the King.

"Well, it was so quiet... I suppose everyone must have been asleep and I didn't see anyone at all. I did spend some time looking around on my way but no... I didn't see anyone. I... well... I may have missed something. Of course a Troubler could have hidden... that's easy enough. Perhaps I should have looked more carefully but I thought I'd better get up here as quickly as possible to tell you about it all. Could a Troubler have arrived...?" Joog looked out of the window as he wondered about it. His eyes glowed brighter in the growing light.

"I think you'd better go and take another look," said the King, smiling at his friend, "Is that alright?"

"Yes, of course," replied Joog brightly.

"I'll tell you what," the King pushed his arms onto the bed to sit up more, "By the time you're back we'll have breakfast on the table for you. Your favourite cereal, Joog?"

"That would be great!" declared Joog, giving a hoot, "I'll have a good look from Spindley Tower first and then scout around the area."

"Be careful," said the King, earnestly, as Joog gave his feathers a shake. He raised his great wings, jumped off the end of the bed and flew towards the open window.

The King watched as Joog glided out. He got up and walked to the gold-framed window. The main town of the kingdom, Candara, certainly was still and the King gazed at it with affection as it lay below. At this height and distance it looked like a toy town with the many colours of the houses and cottages pale in the misty morning. It was built in the shape of a unicorn nestled at the foot of the Southern Downs to its south and with the River Tazer running through the centre of it. The tall Spindley Tower was easily the highest building and it stood out against the hazy background of the hills beyond.

He glanced to the east, across Silvermay Forest and towards Whitten. Then looking back he saw Joog glide gracefully through the hazy air and over the houses of Candara and thought how small and vulnerable he looked at this distance. Suddenly he felt deeply fond of Joog and hoped he would return safely. He watched as the owl, now just a tiny dot at that distance, landed on the top of Spindley Tower.

He turned to look affectionately at the Queen who was still in the land of slumber in the warm bed and decided to wake her.

... continue reading in Candara's Gift

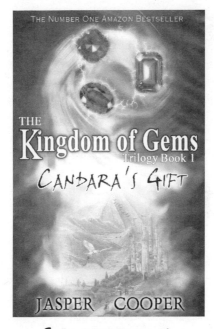

Get your copy at:
www.TheKingdomOfGems.com/BookOne

Author Message

Thank you for reading *Gordo*! I hope you enjoyed the adventure as much as I enjoyed creating this book.

I spent many months in my Creative Studio (a chalet in my garden) working on it, often with my wonderful cats, Oscar and Maple, sitting beside me!

I would definitely like to write more stories about Gordo in the future, so if you liked the book and would like to read more adventures about Gordo, please let me know!

In the meantime, there is a free, exciting, short story featuring Gordo waiting for you to enjoy! The details of how to get this story are on the inside back cover of the book.

To get in touch with me and follow what I'm up to with my writing, please make sure you follow me on Twitter or contact me. I always really love to hear from you! All the details are on the last page of the book!

Very Best Wishes,

Jasper Would Love to Hear From You!

 **Twitter**

One of the best ways to get in touch, see what Jasper is up to and get insider information about his latest books, is to follow him on twitter!

 **@Jasper_Cooper**
(twitter.com/Jasper_Cooper)

 **Other Contact**

If you don't have twitter, or you want to contact Jasper directly, you can see all the other ways of getting in touch on his website here:

www.GordoMonkey.com/contact

 **Blog**

Lastly, you can also follow what Jasper is up to or leave him comments at his blog here:

www.GordoMonkey.com/blog